THE Prophet's WIFE

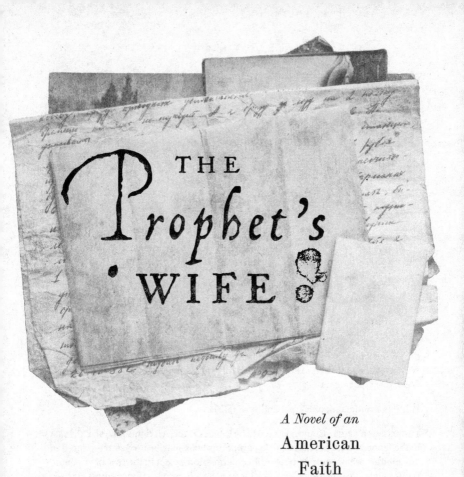

THE Prophet's WIFE

A Novel of an
American
Faith

Libbie Grant

WILLIAM MORROW
An Imprint of HarperCollins*Publishers*

P.S.™ is a trademark of HarperCollins Publishers.

HarperCollins books may be purchased for educational, business, or sales promotional use. For information, please email the Special Markets Department at SPsales@harpercollins.com.

FIRST EDITION

Designed by Diahann Sturge

Title page art © caesart / Shutterstock, Inc.

Library of Congress Cataloging-in-Publication Data has been applied for.

ISBN 978-0-06-307062-2

22 23 24 25 26 LSC 10 9 8 7 6 5 4 3 2 1

For Tim

Does the prophet see the future, or does he see a line of weakness, a fault or cleavage that he may shatter with words or decisions as a diamond-cutter shatters his gem with the blow of a knife?

—Frank Herbert, *Dune*

THE
Prophet's
WIFE

June 27, 1844
Nauvoo, Illinois

She sits at the long table, at its head, in the place of honor that belongs to Joseph by right. All her soberness is drawn about her like armor, her severity, the habitual silence, the habitual watching. She is calmer than she ought to be. She ought to feel something more, she knows, but after so long—almost twenty years—what more is left to feel?

The girls carry food from the kitchens. They lay it out on platters, the full length of the table. They've been frightened and disbelieving for days now; they can think of little else to do but cook. It might as well be a festival—buttered rolls and stewed greens, two roasted chickens, more besides. The food keeps coming. The table fills as if the girls expect to feed an army. Perhaps, Emma thinks, it will come to that, by and by.

Helen enters from the kitchen with a pie, still steaming from the oven. Emma looks at the pastry in its dish because she can't look at the girl. She never can look at any of them. Her eyes will not cooperate; they slide away like water from oil. Helen is the youngest. Sixteen now, or close to it.

"That's enough," Emma says. "Tell the other girls to stop, go and do something else, make yourselves useful."

A shy, frightened creature, Helen scurries away into the house, its long halls with many rooms, its great muted chambers of nothingness.

The very dimness of the room seems to have a sound, a subfusc hum as if the dark paneling along the walls were breathing out or moaning. She thinks she will weep, but she hasn't the leisure. She thinks she will scream.

Then comes a heavy tread of boots at the entrance, one man ordering the others away in a voice of authority. She turns toward the sound, darting, instinctive. A moment later the governor appears in the dining room and pauses, watching Emma.

She can see him taking her measure, deciding already what to do with her, how to handle her, whether he ought to dismiss her out of hand. This is a way all men have of looking at women. They never look at one another this way. It's an assessment they reserve for the feminine alone: eye the broadness of your hips and guess whether you can bear strong children; weigh the pleasantness of your features or your figure; stack you up against another woman for comparison's sake; determine whether they can rouse themselves for you, and if so for how many years. It used to upset her. Now she finds it foolish. She is forty years old and looks every day of it—looks older than her years, in fact, and by God, who would not be aged by everything she has seen and suffered? She had never been accounted a great beauty, but she had been thought passing pretty once, comely enough to catch the Prophet's eye before any other woman had managed it. Where does prettiness get you in the end? She stares back at the governor. It's she who sits at the head of the table, not Thomas Ford.

"You're Emma Smith," the governor says.

"I am."

"You are . . . a wife of Joseph's?"

"I am *the* wife of Joseph Smith Junior, wedded to him in God's sight and by law. By every law of the land."

"You Mormons think yourselves above the law, do you not?"

"Have you come here only to insult me?"

"No. Forgive me, madam."

He fixes his gaze on a roasted chicken as avidly as he ever fixed it on a woman. "Are you hungry?" Emma says.

"It was a long ride, to Carthage and back."

"You may eat."

Governor Ford sits at the opposite end of the table. He tears a leg from the chicken and makes short work of it, then two buttered rolls. He's a slight man—surprisingly small for one so angry and powerful. He has a pinched, delicate face, very white and fine above a high collar.

Emma calls for a girl, any girl. "Nancy. Melissa. Who is there?"

Melissa arrives, pink cheeks and flicking eyes.

"Water for Governor Ford," Emma says.

"Wine," Ford says.

She says again, "Water. Bring him a plate and a knife. A napkin, too."

"Shall I bring anything for you?" the girl asks meekly.

Emma shakes her head. She has no appetite. Likely she will never want to eat again.

When the girl has gone, Ford says, "I intend to speak to your church—your town. I've a message to deliver to your people, Mrs. Smith. A warning."

She waits.

Defensive in the face of one woman's silence, he explains, "It's necessary. I would tell your people what they may expect. It's just."

"How comforting," Emma says, "to hear that you are mindful of justice."

"After, I must return to Carthage. There are forms that must be followed, writs to sign, which I couldn't see to in the press of our arrival."

"You took my husband to Carthage four days ago. Had you really no time to see to your writs?"

"I'm afraid not. Your husband has attracted much attention from the public. There were crowds, protests—"

"Threats?"

He leans a little, one elbow on the tabletop, yielding physically to the question, which is as good as a confirmation.

"Riots," Emma says. She knows by now how these things proceed. "Who is protecting him? Tell me at least that Joseph is well."

"He was quite well when I left him at the Carthage jail. And his brother Hyrum was well, and the fourteen other men who were arrested with him."

"And will he be . . ." She falters, remembering the stream outside Harmony. She remembers the stones in the stream damming its flow, the pool of still water, the weight of her wet dress, heavy. And the men coming through the trees, shouting for Joseph to be taken away. "Will he be safe?"

"There's no need to fear. I can't think of many places safer than a jail cell. It keeps a man in, but it also keeps his enemies out. Joseph will be well, and the other men with him. I've brought letters for you, from your husband." He reaches into the breast of his coat, withdraws two letters, their seals already broken. He pushes them along the table as far as he can reach. "Once I've done my duties in Carthage, I shall return. Then, I must remain in Nauvoo until this business is settled."

This business. No more unusual than trading horses, to place a town under siege and take a woman's husband and send him off to jail.

"And your men?" Emma says.

"The whole militia will remain in Nauvoo."

"That isn't necessary, Governor."

"I'm afraid it is. I've a duty to the people of Illinois. It's my job to keep them safe."

"We are the people of Illinois."

"You Mormons?" He chuckles darkly. "You are not."

The plate and water arrive.

Ford helps himself to stewed greens and a great heap of potatoes. "You Mormons. What am I to think of you? What's anyone to think? You burned and looted your way through Missouri—"

"We were provoked. We acted in defense."

"Now here you are in my state. And this town grows by the month, God knows why."

She says nothing.

"These rumors we hear, that your men marry dozens of women, hundreds. That they take girls from good homes and corrupt them and damn their souls with adultery. It's little wonder my people are concerned."

"We do not abduct members for our church."

"Lilburn Boggs. What am I to make of him? The governor of Missouri, shot in the head, four times, Mrs. Smith, by order of your husband. By a would-be assassin."

"Joseph did not order the governor shot. He would never do such a thing; I would swear that before any judge in the land. And Porter Rockwell is my husband's guard, not his assassin."

"It's a miracle Boggs survived. You can see, can't you, why the people are frightened? They expect a show from me—a restoration of order. And so the militia will remain in Nauvoo until a judge has determined Joseph's fate. After that, we shall see."

He shovels up his food with the air of a man who thinks himself beyond reproach.

After a moment he puts down the knife and looks down the length of the table again. "You realize I must lodge here—in your home, I mean."

"I expected as much."

"You aren't troubled?"

"Have I any say in the matter?"

He smiles ruefully. "I'm afraid you have none."

"You wouldn't believe the burdens I've borne, Governor, and all because I've had no say."

"Aren't you angry?"

Now it's Emma who smiles, thinly, without amusement. Of course she is angry. She is full of outrage bordering on hate, but when, these past nineteen years, has she not felt this way? She will keep Nauvoo safe from Ford and his men if she must suffer a thousand insults, if she is cast down into the dust and humiliated. What has Joseph taught her, if not forbearance?

"You'll find my home comfortable enough," she says. "There is none better appointed in all of Nauvoo."

"None more populated," Ford says wryly. "All these young ladies I've seen flitting about—in the kitchen and peeking out the windows when I first arrived. They're Joseph's wives, are they not?"

She keeps her silence. At length the governor amends: "They consider themselves Joseph's wives. You may disagree."

"I must be civil to you, Governor, because of our unusual circumstances. But I will thank you not to provoke me, if you will be so kind."

"I meant no offense, madam. But you Mormons—you've become the subject of much speculation."

"What you call speculation, I call rumor. And I call gossip a sin."

"Even so, the rumors flourish. Not a person in Illinois, in all of America, hasn't wondered at your . . . peculiarities."

A silence falls between them. She has learned that she can draw truth out of men if she waits long enough, and watches.

"I admit I'm curious," he finally says.

"About what, Governor?"

"How it all started. This community, this church, whatever you consider yourselves to be. What made your husband so bold that he would defy the laws of the United States itself in pursuit of his own advancement?"

She sighs. Susceptible to the memory, she leans back in her chair as if pressed there by a great weight. It was half a lifetime ago. And it strikes her, in that moment, how much time has gone by, how many years she has done this. For what? For love, or something else—fear of God or devotion to Him, or simply because she had no other choice? She has asked herself this question a thousand times over and never found an answer.

The clock ticks. The house settles and whispers. Somewhere behind the walls the girls are moving, peering out the windows, hoping to see their Prophet coming home.

"If you truly wish to know," Emma says, surprising herself, "then I'll tell you. We've time to pass, I suppose, until my husband is returned."

I

Before the Foundation of the World

1825–1827

The beginning was unremarkable. Sometimes that's the way the biggest stories take you. You don't sense their unfolding, the subtle layering of cause and effect, the way one history rides upon a hundred others that have gone before. A November day, just before noon, cold but not yet snowing—even the cold was ordinary. Beyond the clearing where Hale House stood, the trees at the edge of the forest still bore scraps of golden leaves. Later, much later, when all of this was over (as over as it ever would be) she would look back on that morning and wonder why God had sent no sign. There should have been a wash of heavenly light, a golden halo hanging over Joseph's golden head. The earth shaking, rattling the hens in the yard until they tumbled off their feet. A clenching in her bowels, at least. If she'd had some sign to warn her, everything would have been different.

Emma tossed the last handful of feed to the chickens. The handle of her pail was grainy with rust and kernels of damp barley stuck to her fingers. She hung the pail on its peg and let herself out of the hen-yard, and went to her father, who stood beside the paling gate below a sign that read *Hale House, Rooms to Let, Inquire at Front Door*. Her father, Isaac, was tense with expectation—a hard set to his shoulders, squinting at the bend in the road.

"I've had a letter," Isaac said. "Some two days back. Your uncle William is coming, and he thinks to stay."

Now she understood her father's dark mood. Isaac Hale was a man of sense. He had no patience for the wild enthusiasms of a reckless man. Uncle William wasn't alone, though. The people of the countryside shared his fervency. It burned like brushfire from one village to the next, and the ground was still black and smoking when the next fit of zeal roared through.

"He's bringing men," Isaac said, "some pack of foolish strangers; I know not who."

"To board?"

Isaac nodded.

"Mother will be glad for the money," Emma said.

Hale House stood between the townships of Harmony and Great Bend, a convenient sanctuary for weary travelers. But winter had already come, even if the snows had not. There were few men on the road now, and little custom at Hale House.

"William and his friends," Emma said, "will they hunt in the hills?"

"God bless me if my brother William could hunt a haystack. No, my dear—they're coming to dig for treasure."

Emma folded her arms. Her father's words might count as blasphemy— she had never been certain of the finer points—but it was good to hear him invoke the Lord's name, even if it was in vain. He had confessed to Emma once, when she'd been a girl of sixteen, that he couldn't entirely credit the existence of God. What is God, anyway, he'd muttered that day, knee-deep in straw with a pitchfork in his hands, but the very embodiment of Man's worst desires? It had frightened her, to hear her father speak such dangerous thoughts aloud. In that moment, she had seen Isaac as a fragile thing, too honest and human. One day he must stand before the Creator and answer for his sins—the sin of doubt worst among them, perhaps unforgivable. Emma had fled the barn and run up to her room and fallen on her knees beside her bed, praying for Isaac's salvation. She had remained there nigh on two hours, weeping, begging the Lord for His mercy, until her knees had turned black and blue.

Standing beside her father with her arms wrapped around her body, Emma crossed her fingers: a charm against the Devil. Treasure-digging seemed exactly the sort of business that might attract Perdition.

"There comes a wagon," Isaac said, and spat.

A moment later, Emma heard it, too—the slide and clop of two horses trotting, their strides skewed out of unison, and the low, steady hiss of wagon wheels churning through mud. She followed her father's gaze down the gentle slope. A pair of tired bays appeared. The horses hauled a buckboard. A few men sat in its bed on a meager cushion of straw, hunched close together against the cold. The driver wasn't her uncle William, but Josiah Stowell, who lived not far off in a pretty white house with nine shuttered windows and pine trees in the yard. She frowned to see Mr. Stowell. His enthusiasm made Uncle William seem tame by comparison. But who didn't burn with religious fire in that time, that place? Pennsylvania, 1825, the countryside a conflagration.

Mr. Stowell pulled his team to a halt outside the gate. "Isaac Hale. The Lord bless you, my friend."

Isaac grunted.

"And Miss Emma," Stowell said, "beautiful as ever."

Emma frowned all the more. She wasn't beautiful, and well did she know it. Her face was as severe as her temper; she was too tall for a woman, though in a certain light, she might be called handsome.

"Look who I've brought to board," Josiah said. "Friends from New York, and your own dear brother William."

The men in the wagon made a slow unfolding, curling outward from their warm cores. Their breath hung thick and white in the air. The first to climb down was the youngest of the group. He was scarcely more than a boy, perhaps eighteen or nineteen years; he moved with easy strength and bouncing confidence—as if he believed, as all young men do, that he deserved a greater share of the world than the space his body took up, as if more and more were his natural due. The youth stepped up to Isaac, offering a hand to shake. There was something to him—a swagger, an accessory boldness—that intrigued Emma even while it vexed her. She had seen that kind of man before, oh, more times than she could count, in Harmony and elsewhere, even in her own home when young boarders had come to stay for deer season, or in the dark of winter to trap foxes in the hills. *Emma*, those men had said, *you are pretty enough to marry*, which she knew had been only flattery for their amusement. She had dealt with that sort of man—dealt with every last one of them until even the most persistent and the most dull-witted (the two traits often went hand in hand) had abandoned their courtship and moved on to catch softer brides. Men were all that way, between certain ages: convinced the world would fit neat as a plum in their hands.

The youth greeted Isaac, then turned to Emma. Her arms folded tighter around her body. He offered neither his hand nor his name. He only looked at her—a long stare, frankly assessing, like a man sizing up a mare in an auctioneer's corral. Then he broke into an insolent grin. He was handsome, Emma could grudgingly admit, and his smile, though far too bold, only made him pleasanter to look upon. She put paid to his brazenness in her accustomed way: drawing up to her full height and challenging him with a forbidding stare, the one she'd honed in the Harmony school, teaching the local farmers' whelps how to count and write their names. She was quietly pleased when the grin slid from the young man's face.

When everyone had descended from the wagon, Emma said, "Good morning, Uncle William," for it was certain her father wouldn't speak to William first. "Father told me you've come looking for treasure. Is it true?"

"True as the Gospel," William said. "A maid in New York told me where to find it. She's a proper young lady, this maid, a good Christian girl, not desirous of any personal gain."

"And she told you," Isaac began, but William finished: "She has a peep-stone, and gazed into it, and saw a great treasure buried in a hill a short way from here, just beyond the edge of your property, where it's naught but forest and no man can lay claim to whatever's in the earth—no man but what finds it, all as I told you in my letter. The maid swore the treasure is gold. Pure gold."

"How would a girl in New York know where my property begins and ends?"

Isaac had never set much store in the scryers and stone-peepers who peddled their services from one village to the next. Nor the fortune-tellers, nor the water witches with their forked sticks and unctuous smiles. At least, he set no more than the usual amount of store. Any sensible person gave cautious credence to the mysteries. The earth was a deep and fathomless place, and wise men remained open to possibility. There was an eight-pointed hex on the side of Stowell's wagon, crude and uneven, the lime-white paint flaking away. Emma crossed her fingers again, tighter this time, warding away evil.

"Surely, Isaac," Mr. Stowell said, "you've no objection to our renting a few rooms while we dig. We won't involve you in the business, if that's your wish."

"But you'll get no share in the gold," William added.

"For the rooms," Isaac said, "I leave it to my wife. And as for the treasure, I'll believe it when I see it." He turned his back on the visitors, stalking away up the yard.

Emma spoke in her father's absence. Someone had to. "Take the wagon to the shed, Mr. Stowell, and stable your horses in the long barn. There's new straw in the stalls. I saw to it myself this morning."

The visitors followed Stowell and his buckboard as it rumbled toward the hitching shed—all except the youth. He hung back, shifting from foot to foot, watching the others depart with the air of a boy about to get up to some mischief. When they were alone, he turned to Emma and grinned again. He was tall, broad-shouldered. The self-assurance that radiated from him almost made Emma blush.

"I'm Joseph," he said, as if confessing.

She realized her fingers were still crossed. Deliberately, she uncrossed them. "Miss Hale."

"May I not know your Christian name?"

"Are we such good friends that I ought to tell you?"

"We will be," he said, with a note of promise that startled her.

She deflected him. "Is there truly a peeper in New York?"

"Well, shore." His sudden rural twang fairly took Emma aback. "Don't you have peepers here in Pennsulvany?"

"I set little more store in peepers than my father does." Which was not strictly true. On all matters spiritual and Godly, Emma remained prudently open.

"What if I told you I could peep through stones? Would you believe me?"

In the distance, she could hear the front door of her home open and shut, her mother, Elizabeth, calling from the porch, welcoming the boarders to Hale House. She could hear the horses whickering as they were put away, the faint groan of the buckboard settling on its springs. The sky was heavy and dark, a plain November sky, ordinary.

"If you told me you could peep through stones," Emma said, "would you believe yourself?"

He bellowed with laughter, loud as a bull in a field. "Miss Hale," Joseph said as they started toward the house, "I think you and I will be very good friends indeed."

Once, before she'd chased all her suitors away, Emma had possessed a wild streak.

She was fourteen, fifteen years old. It's so long ago now that she can't recall her age. She remembers it was midsummer, and she pinched herself to stay awake until the house had fallen silent. She remembers stealing out to the long barn and bridling her favorite mare, and the way the dark had poured down the side of the barn—the barn and the trees, a slow descent from top to bottom, to the margin where she moved between a waking world and a world newly asleep. The interstice of dusk was violet, and crickets sang in the grass.

She could ride well with or without a saddle; saddling the horse would have cost more time. She jumped to the mare's back and kissed. The horse loped along the lane. She felt high above the earth, though her mare wasn't especially large. She recalls now how grand she felt, how great with possibility.

She found the revival tent by ear, following cries of wild delight, the Hallelujahs and Yes-Lords. She tied the mare to a snag and flowed through the darkness. Grass-heads whisked against her nightdress, pricking the backs of her hands. She went right up to the revival tent and stood in its opening as if she had every right to be there. No one noticed the girl watching from the doorway, though her nightdress made her bright against the darkness, bright as a vestal in her robes.

The interior of the tent was rank with the smell of bodies—sour sweat and a warmer, lower reek of arousal. She had found a meeting of the United Society of Believers in Christ's Second Appearing—the Shakers. She hadn't known what to expect, but when she realized she had found a Shaker meeting, she was caught momentarily by fear. She had heard stories of that sect. How they castrated their men in fits of zeal and copulated without shame, without regard for the bonds of marriage. They sacrificed children to their God, which wasn't the same God as the one the good people of Harmony knew, though He had the same name.

She wondered whether she would see a sacrifice that night. Or reckless adultery. She watched, breathless and transfixed, but the congregation only danced. Men on one side, women on the other, with palms upraised to the tent roof, up to God, they bent and stamped, the women's shoulders heaving and shivering under stiff collars. The lines marched one toward the other, and parted, and met again, and the poles of the tent rattled with the imperfect, not-quite-unison of their feet. The feel of it beat through the packed earth, up into Emma's bones. Every voice was raised to its own pitch, without regard for harmony, for to make a pleasing sound is to be vain. The forceful unloveliness clutched at all her senses and she felt all at once, with a flush like fever, a heightened awareness of God. She felt Him bend with curiosity, lazy interest piqued by the din. His eye fell on the tent as a boy's eye falls on an ant scrambling across a stone.

The Shakers sped their dance. Their limbs jerked in the lamplight, and the words of their song crashed all around her.

Shake, shake out of me all that is carnal!

Faster and faster still, until any suggestion of rhythm was gone, and the earth thundered with disorder.

I'll take nimble steps, I'll be a David,
I'll show Michael twice how he behavèd!

By the time she crept back to the snag, even her mare was frightened. Emma took the long way home, and kept her horse to a walk, afraid the beat of its hooves would direct God's attention to her—wearing nothing but a nightdress, and fled from her house without her mother knowing, and with nothing carnal, she knew, yet shaken from her.

She could sense far beyond the road, past Harmony Township and the great spreading forests of hemlocks and pines, that the night was livelier still. The northeast was afire, burning for God in all His variant forms. Emma knew their names. The Shakers and the Campbellites, the Methodists and Millers, the Second Advents and the Seventh-Days, the Disciples, the Friends, the myriad Churches of Christ. Some preachers called that place "burned over," as if a roaring blaze of fervor had swept the countryside, scorching every live and fertile thing, leaving rural New York and Pennsylvania as used up as the rocky soil of Vermont.

But in Vermont, Emma knew, the farmers dug boulders from their fields, and piled the stones in heaps, and generation after generation the heaps lengthened and became walls. The walls stretched like great pale snakes basking in the sun. And wherever the boulders were rolled away, the black earth yielded a fine and dogged crop.

Even as a girl, she knew the country wasn't burned over. The embers had been banked in lonely alcoves and forest dells. They glowed very hot indeed.

"We've found nothing yet," Joseph told her.

It was the deep of winter, an afternoon when the light hung pale just above the tops of the trees. They were walking in the snow, aimless, pottering along the hunter's path that wound from the rear of Hale House up among the hills. The snow lay in an icy crust, breaking and sliding beneath their feet, making their steps squeak faintly, as when one bites into a curd of new white cheese.

Snow deadened all sound. The world in winter draws in upon itself, and it had contracted that day around Emma and Joseph. They were isolated, made intimate by so much white. Her toes were cold inside her leather boots, but she didn't mind. It was pleasant to think of the warming up later, when she would sit in her room with her thoughts and her knitting basket. Then she would touch her bare feet to the copper warming pan, carefully, and think about Joseph's hair—the color of a deer's pelt—and imagine the tow-headed child he must have been. He walked with a limp so slight, it had taken Emma days to notice. She would think about that, too, later, when she was alone.

"You've found nothing?" Emma paused, lifting the edge of her skirt. The hem was done up in age-yellowed lace. She had tatted the lace several summers ago as an ornament for her wedding dress—not that she'd had any intended fellow. She had simply felt a great change come upon her that year, a transformation of the soul, and she'd known her marriage was imminent. She had known the man whom God wished her to marry would soon arrive, riding up the long road from Harmony to seek a night's lodging or taking her hand in the village street when she went for more sugar at the general store. But months had gone by, then years, and Emma had remained unmarried, and now the lace gathered little balls of ice which weighed down her skirt. She tried to shake the ice free. It remained stubbornly attached.

Joseph dropped to one knee. With a little laugh of apology—for it was presumptuous, maybe even shocking—he took her hem in his hands. Gently, he freed an inch of lace, then another, talking while he worked his way around her skirt, and soon his fingers were red from the chill, but he didn't stop until the last of the ice was gone.

"When I'm at Mr. Stowell's farm," Joseph said, "I can see gold under the earth. Or sometimes it's silver I see. But whenever we come close to the indicated place, the stone goes blank. I can see nothing at all. So our digging is in vain—all guesswork in the end."

"Why does your peep-stone stop working when you're close to the treasure?"

Joseph looked up, almost shy in that moment. "The enchantment on this place is too strong. It befuddles me, so I can't see anything but the enchantment itself."

When he stood, the knees of his breeches were dark with melted snow and mud. Emma laughed—she couldn't help it—and, grinning down at the stains, Joseph cut a caper on the trail, strutting as if that mud made him the finest gentleman in the valley.

His dance stopped abruptly. "You're pretty when you laugh."

Emma went sober then, and still.

He said, "You're pretty when you don't laugh, too."

"You seem very certain of your peep-stone." She moved past him, deeper into the forest.

"Do you truly not believe, Miss Hale?"

"You *may* call me Emma," she said, impatient. "After all. You may."

"Thank you."

"It's God I believe in. The Lord is my shepherd, not any spirit-stone or hex or doodlebug, all the things they claim are real out here in the valleys and dells."

"And I," he said. "I believe in the Lord."

He said it with such quiet force that Emma stopped walking. She stared at him. His great hooked nose did nothing to diminish his handsomeness.

"May I tell you a story?" he asked.

"Is it a true story?"

Joseph smiled. There was a certain brittleness to it. Thinking of her thin prospects and the lace at her hem and Joseph's ice-reddened fingers, she nodded before she could say something else cutting and ruin this prospect, too.

He told her of his childhood: the dark hills of Vermont, his family's toil in the rocky earth.

Then how his family moved to New York, and how he had spent his idle hours watching the preachers rolling up and down the rutted roads in their wagons, with their throngs of followers grayed by dust. The air crackled around the revival tents, Joseph said, like the air before a lightning storm, and a smell of sweat permeated the clearing or the field, wherever the preachers set up their tents. Crowds came to listen to those men. The walls of their tents trembled with the force of their words. Which preacher is true, which is the path to God? Joseph asked himself that question more times than he could count. Which leader shall I follow? There were so many, a new preacher every week, and sometimes two or three. He didn't know which was right or wrong, so he gave the question to God.

He went alone to pray, walking in the woods far from the stamping and shouting in the tents.

Among the drip of water from the treetops and the slow uncurling of ferns, Joseph fretted his still, small fears.

"And God appeared," he said quietly. "Even the Lord Himself."

He told the story so simply, with such innocent directness, that Emma clutched her black shawl tightly at her throat. She could feel again the stooping weight of God, His unblinking eye staring down. Her family had been simple Methodists, until Isaac lost his feeling for God. Then Emma's mother, Elizabeth, had carried on teaching her children from the Bible. She had gone with her mother to church every Sunday and believed in the Lord as she believed in the ground beneath her feet, but she had never seen the holy presence with her eyes. Not as Joseph had seen.

Joseph asked the Lord, in his farmboy manner, Which preacher has it right? Which church ought I to join?

None, answered God. Not a one of them.

Emma wrapped her arms around herself. She couldn't look at her companion. Between the crunching of their hesitant steps, she could hear Joseph breathing in a calm, certain rhythm.

"Do you want to see it?" he said.

"See what?"

"My peep-stone."

Before she could tell him no, he pulled something from the pocket of his brown woolen coat.

His fist opened. The stone was smooth, round, smaller than a hen's egg. It was dark and veined all through with ochre-red. Emma stared with a clutch of fear. Joseph's peace was too complete, without the un-conscious signs of liars and frauds. The Lord truly had appeared before him. How could Emma doubt it? Why ought she to provoke God's anger by doubting? And if Joseph had honestly seen the Lord, then his scrying, too, must be real.

She couldn't take her eyes from the stone. "You said you can't see with it—not anymore."

His hand closed. The moment the peep-stone was gone from her view, the spell was broken.

Emma looked up at Joseph's face and found him smiling.

"I can't," he agreed. "The enchantment on this place is too strong."

The next morning, Emma decided, she would tell her father that she intended to marry Joseph Smith. Her mind was made up—or God's mind was made up. Perhaps there had been no decision at all, no divine ordainment. Perhaps she only wished for the decision to be made, be-cause she was twenty-one years old, and the lace at her hem had yel-lowed, and it was long past time.

What is the nature of belief? From where does faith arise? You'd do well to ask yourself now, and decide upon an answer, for none of this history will seem plausible until you've settled the question.

It didn't begin with Joseph Smith kneeling in the snow, with Emma's hem in his fingers. It didn't begin in a gray November yard. All the flow-ers of Creation start as tiny seeds, but the seeds also come from some-where. From the mother plants that made them, and the bee in the throat of the blossom, and a wind, just any stray gust, an unassuming wind shaking the petals and drifting the pollen and spreading it to a new, fertile bloom.

They came from Vermont, the Smith family. At least, that was where Joseph Junior was born. Before that, they came from Connecticut by way of New Hampshire, and long before those days, from England. Jo-seph's mother, Lucy, kept up the habits of her foremothers, the country-English ways: casting circles before the hearth to make her dough rise, lines of salt at the doors to drive back evil spirits. She hung above the kitchen window a four-pointed bundle of reeds. When she pricked her finger on a sewing needle, she hastened outside and let the drop of blood fall among her garden beds, and this was why the herbs always grew so green and strong for her; it was certain that nothing else grew so vigorously in the stony soil.

She counted among her most treasured things the old handwritten books her ancestors had brought from England. The writing was so strange and faded, like spider's webs upon the page, she could scarcely read the books her mother's mother's mothers had written. But even as a child she had traced the sigils of Saturn and Jupiter and the horned moon; she had felt the significance and power of those ancient markings, and watched her children trace them, too.

On a little shelf in the humble parlor her Bible took pride of place, but alongside it, pressed against its cover, were *The Magus* and *Cabala*, the *Book of Knowledge* and *The Art of Fortune-Telling Unveiled*. There was little else to occupy one's mind through a long dark winter in the hills. And there was no harm in it, for Lucy Smith knew—as all people knew in that time and place—that all goodness and all power proceeded from God. Any charm or hex or ritual of blood and smoke was righteous and Godly, so long as the power was never used for evil.

When Joseph Senior won Lucy's hand, she brought a fine egg for their nest. Her brother Stephen, whom God had blessed with great skill as a merchant, had fitted Lucy with a dowry of a thousand dollars—an astounding fortune. But her new husband had no head for money. Before many years, the thousand dollars had vanished, drained away by a dozen of Joseph's schemes, none of which had ever returned the investment. Lucy imparted to all her children the same longing that haunted her the rest of her life: a fascination with gold and riches—a yearning to know what might have been if the Smiths hadn't been forced to scrabble in the dirt for their living. She had felt herself only temporarily impoverished. She had known, as you know the beat of your own heart, that fortune would come again—and not only fortune, but renown. Whom the Lord loves, He also chastens. She bore His scourge with Christian patience.

But it wasn't Joseph Junior on whom Lucy had pinned her hopes—not at first. It was Alvin, second-born and the first to survive infancy, who had been Lucy's golden child.

Of ten living children, Alvin was best loved of them all, the jewel in the family's crown. He had always been a good boy, obedient, hardworking. He grew into all the strength and potential his pleasing nature had promised. He was always kind to his little brothers and kissed his mother and blessed her every day. When Joseph Senior vexed the neighbors with his wild, haphazard ways, it was Alvin who made excuses and tipped his hat, Alvin who came over early to milk the cows, so his father was always forgiven. What little fertility the Vermont farm could claim was due to Alvin, too, for he bent his back to the plow with all the vigor his father lacked. When he took up water-witching and treasure-digging, using his mother's old books for a guide, no one murmured or complained, for he did the work with quiet integrity, and every well he found was fresh and sweet and deep.

When his father squandered the last dregs of their money on a shipment of ginseng bound for China, Alvin saved the family from penury. He apprenticed himself to a carpenter and diverted every cent of his wages back to his parents, for they had other children by then, plenty of children, and no good brother or son allows his family to go hungry. When Joseph Senior's wild ideas caught up with him and the family was forced to leave Vermont in shame, it was Alvin who did the lion's share of the work, building their new farm outside Manchester, New York.

Yet, whom the Lord loveth . . . God Almighty gathered Alvin back into His arms before he could marry and start a family of his own. It was too much calomel that took him. He died in agony, which had seemed unjust for a man so young, and one who had been the very pattern of charity.

At Alvin's funeral, the minister—a Presbyterian—said that Alvin would burn for eternity because he hadn't been a Presbyterian himself. Despite his good works, his valiant heart, the care he'd lavished on his family, Alvin was bound for Hell, and there was nothing any Smith could do about it. Joseph Senior shook his fist and shouted down the minister, but it only turned the town against him. In mockery of the Smith habit of treasure-digging, and of their fondness for books of magic, rumor held that someone had dug up Alvin's corpse and cut it into pieces, and used those parts in some obscure ritual, the nature of which was never detailed. Joseph Senior was tormented by the stories. He couldn't sleep, for fear they were true. He repaired to the grave with a few of his friends—the small handful of men who still trusted him—and exhumed his son's body himself. A spade splitting the roof of a coffin, so the smell of corruption comes up from within. And prying back the lid to find the body still arranged, still dressed in its final suit, but the flesh gone to rot and the good shirt stained, the face you had known as the face of your beloved son a slack horror, a ruin of flagrant mortality.

Enough about poor Alvin—enough. It doesn't do to think of it, much less to tell the tale.

With Alvin gone, Lucy was obliged to choose another champion who would carry the family's hopes into the future and restore her fate.

When her third son, Joseph Junior, was a child of seven years—while Alvin had yet lived—typhoid fever ran unchecked through the farmlands of Vermont. One after another, the Smiths fell ill, but it was little Joseph who suffered the worst. The infection gripped him for weeks, then months, swelling his skin with fever blisters, sinking the disease deep into his marrow. He couldn't walk without a stick to lean on, without crying piteously in pain. His parents despaired, knowing he couldn't survive.

Alvin rode for the doctor in Lebanon, New Hampshire—a surgeon whose reputation for curing typhoid was unmatched. But when he finally arrived at the humble farmstead and saw the child moaning and suffering in his bed, even that skilled physician thought it unlikely Joseph would live. Certainly, the boy wouldn't survive unless the surgeon amputated his leg, for by that time the bone had become so hideously infected that Joseph could no longer stand.

Joseph refused to have his leg taken off. "Only cut into the bone," the unlearned farmboy said. "Cut into the bone and remove the part that has gone bad. Let me keep my leg; it will heal."

The doctor was amazed, for there was a new procedure that worked as the boy described. How had this rustic child known? With luck and prayer, the surgery might spare his life and limb.

The doctor's grisly instruments were readied for their work, but Joseph wouldn't be tied to his bed. Nor would he take any spirits to dull his wits or deaden the pain. "Only let my father hold me," he said, "and send my mother away so she won't hear if I scream."

He did scream. He shrieked in his father's arms and tried to twist away until the pain carried him to a place beyond weeping, a place where his bladder loosed, and his vision went red and he seemed to himself nothing more than one great tongue of fire. But when it was over, the fever blisters abated. The bone knit itself, and shards the surgeon had chipped away worked to the surface of his skin while Joseph lay for months in his bed, thinking, dreaming, reading his mother's books, living in a land of fancy whose borders reached far beyond suffering.

The ordeal left Joseph with a limp and a few scars, and in his family's estimation, a value far beyond what even the fondest parent could imagine. In rising whole from his bed, Joseph became the miracle of the Smith family. In Alvin's absence, he became their hope. And now, there was nothing the Smiths believed Joseph couldn't do, and nothing Joseph doubted in himself.

Was it faith, then, that led to this marriage? Did Emma see in Joseph the same fine qualities Lucy Smith saw—resilience, courage, a clever mind trained or at least accustomed to long and complex thought? Did she believe Joseph when he told her he'd had a vision of the Lord and Jesus Christ in a silent, lonely wood?

Ask her now or ask her then, her answer would be the same. She couldn't have told you what she believed. Belief to her wasn't a matter of a singing heart or a sudden flash of knowing, the conviction that can only come, they say, from God. Emma's faith was a shy retreat. She was like a fawn that curls in a thicket and lies still for hours, hoping it will never be seen. For she always felt a black rush of something coming up behind, something vast and primal: God's judgment reaching like a hand to seize her. There were moments when she felt light-headed and the world around her spun, because she had suddenly remembered the ever present threat of Hell. She was a sinner, made of sin, as were all women and men. Her heels rocked endlessly on the edge of a pit. There were days when she felt certain the sin of her father's doubt would be visited upon her—that no matter how righteously she held herself, she would pay the price for Isaac's unbelief. God would not be merciful.

When she thought of Joseph's vision in the woods—when she tried to picture the two figures he described—she couldn't do it. She could imagine a vague outline of two masculine forms—white flowing robes, an aura of light—but her mind would proceed no further. Her mouth filled with water and her eyes with tears.

One detail she could imagine, but only one, and that with fantastical clarity: The feet of the Lord and Jesus Christ, suspended above the loam. Hanging in midair, just above the boy who shrank back, afraid, with a hand shielding his eyes. The feet were limp, pointing down toward the earth. The wounds in Christ's flesh were beaded with blood.

There was a line, she thought—there must be—between faith and fear. She didn't know where it ran. And in her own heart, Emma suspected, it had always been hair thin.

So what was it that led her to marry Joseph Smith? Fear of what might befall her if she failed to believe, or simply the fatigue of waiting? She was twenty-one when she met him. And then she was twenty-two, still unwed, closing in on twenty-three.

The treasure dig near Hale House produced nothing. The men all went away, discouraged, with Isaac's curses ringing in their ears. But Joseph stayed on at Josiah Stowell's farm, working as a hand. Josiah liked the young man, and still believed in the power of his scrying. He hadn't given up hope of gold. Over the course of those two years they ventured out together many times, Joseph and Josiah, with pickaxes and peep-stone, but neither grew any richer.

In March, Joseph was called before a judge, accused of being a disorderly person, of glass-looking and vexing young women wherever he found them. Josiah testified on Joseph's behalf. He staked his reputation, insisting Joseph was a good man, and never looked into any glass. By the letter, Josiah's testimony was true. It was a little brown stone Joseph used for his divinations, not a mirror.

When he was cleared of the charges, Joseph came back to Hale House again and again, whenever he could be sure Isaac wouldn't catch him (for Isaac had told him off, swearing he would never marry Emma, layabout and liar that he was). But they did manage a strange sort of courtship. Joseph was pleasant to look at and radiant in his enthusiasm, so Emma convinced herself she felt love enough—and anyway, she was almost twenty-three. If not this treasure-digger from New York, then who?

On a January night, when the moon cast a frigid blue sheen on fresh snow, Emma waited beside a window on the first floor of Hale House, watching the road to Harmony. The snowfall was a day old, and no one had come to board for some time, so the road was perfectly smooth, an undisturbed blanket of moonglow cutting through the forest like a slow, wide stream.

Her mother stirred in the kitchen. Emma could hear the scrape of a broom against the hearth. She turned just enough to see her mother from the corner of her eye. Elizabeth Hale brimmed with a restless, sad energy, as if she would like to hum a tune but didn't dare intrude on Emma's pensive silence. She put her broom aside, folded lengths of clean linen towel and stacked them on the butcher-board. She picked up the broom again, stared into the hearth for a long moment, silent and sober.

"Mother," Emma said.

Elizabeth came to the window. She parted Emma's curls, rested a warm hand on the back of her neck. "All will be well," Elizabeth said. But even her kindly voice was thick with disappointment.

Emma felt it all the time now, her mother's worry. What would Elizabeth do if no one would marry her youngest daughter? Emma, the best and brightest of her children, would be forever condemned to a life of lonesome waste.

From the road there came a rhythmic jingling—a bright, buoyant sound. Emma and her mother peered out through the frosted glass. A smart cutter, black with shining runners, came whisking up the lane. It skimmed over the icy crust, throwing up rooster tails of snow.

"Mr. Stowell's come," Elizabeth mused. "I wonder what for."

"It's not Mr. Stowell, but Joseph Smith." Emma turned away, so her mother couldn't see the blush of shame and triumph creeping up her cheeks. She busied herself with her coat.

"Your father told you off, miss: you're not to see that young man anymore."

"It's only a supper party at the Stowell place."

"Do you want to bring down your father's anger? You know how he feels about Joseph Smith."

"Several people will be there, Mother—all sorts of young women and men from around the valley. It's only natural for the season. What else are we to do for amusement on winter nights? Anyhow, it's not as if Joseph has come courting. He's only brought the sleigh to fetch me. I can't make it out to the Stowell place on foot in this snow."

Her hand was already on the door. She glanced back at her mother. The sudden flash of fear in Elizabeth's eyes made Emma hesitate. She rushed back and caught her mother in her arms—the familiar warmth of those soft, rounded shoulders, and against her cheek, the neatly arranged hair going coarse and gray.

"Your father and I only want what's best for you, Emma dear. Can't you see that?"

"I can," she promised. "I'll be back before midnight. Don't let Father wait up."

Joseph helped Emma into the sleigh. Her heart quickened at the feel of his hand in her own. He presented her with a fine fox-fur rug, which he must have borrowed from Mrs. Stowell for the ride. He never could have afforded such extravagance himself. Emma bundled the fur around her legs and soon, between Joseph's smile and the ringing of the harness bells, she was warm.

The forest slid by. Breath trailed in plumes from the horse's nostrils. They reached the Stowell house, all its whitewashed clapboard muted to blue by the moonlight. The barn beyond had been shut up tight; the snow around the Stowell place was almost as undisturbed as at Hale House, with no tracks to show where any sleigh had come or gone, except the one in which Emma rode. She looked at Joseph, speechless with surprise.

"It's not a supper party tonight," Joseph admitted. "Not exactly."

Dazed and quiet with caution, Emma took his hand again and walked by his side up the small rise to the Stowells' door. The two dark pines in the yard dropped crystals of ice from their branches. In the silence, the ice chimed faintly as it fell.

The door opened before Emma and Joseph had reached the first step. Josiah nodded a polite but nervous welcome. He took Emma's coat and woolen scarf, and Joseph—grinning now, cocksure—ushered her into the kitchen.

An old man waited beside the table with one hand on his Holy Bible. His shoulders were draped in the silk of a Methodist minister.

Emma took a long, deep breath.

"I figure," Joseph said, squeezing her hand, "we're both old enough to make up our minds."

She turned away. She gazed out the nearest window at the fields. Somewhere past the thick line of forest she could feel Hale House waiting—her home. Her narrow bedroom, its window glazed in bubbled glass, the kitchen with its smell of toasting bread and soft butter. Her mother was filling a warming pan with embers. In the barn, her favorite mare blew into the darkness, remembering a nighttime ride and the tall grass of summer.

Her father wouldn't wait up—not that night. And Joseph was still holding her hand. In a few months, she would be twenty-three.

Emma turned back to the minister. "Yes, all right," she said, and simple as that, it was done.

II

Treasure in the Earth

1827

Emma went walking once in a valley. Which valley doesn't matter, for they're all the same—a green valley somewhere in New York or Pennsylvania or perhaps it was Ohio. All along its floor there were farmsteads and clapboard houses, and furrows in the soil, and a smell of woodsmoke and under that, faintly, a smell of onions simmering over homely fires. She walked past cultivated fields and split-rail fences, and cattle in their pastures, and everything was flat and tame, the world was a world she could recognize, throwing open arms in welcome.

By and by, she left the valley and wandered beyond the fence line of the farthest settlement, where plowed ground gave way to open meadow. There were no cattle or sheep anymore, but there were deer bursting from thickets at the sound of her approach, bounding high with white tails erect. And there were ravens croaking in a sly line of woodland, and blue smoke rising from the trees. Twilight was well on its way. There was a certain smell hanging all around her, a damp suggestion of wild things, wolves or bears. The farther she went from human habitation, the faster it receded. The wilderness crowded around. It was only a matter of a few paces, a few minutes' walk in any direction, and she was cut off entirely from the Christian world. She never knew how short God's reach was until she found herself suddenly beyond it, in the wild places, in the shadow and thrash of unsettled land.

The most disturbing thing about the place beyond the fence line was not the isolation or the speed with which the great arrogant edifice of human habitation fell away. Rather it was the certainty that gripped her there. For she knew she wasn't the first human to listen for the laughter of crows in the black pines.

She knew because of the mounds. They were everywhere—everywhere white men hadn't dug into the earth, and in a good many places where they had. No hill God made was ever so regular in shape. Emma found them everywhere, whenever she was foolish enough to go wandering. Sometimes the mounds were small, little taller than a man and only as wide as a modest house. Sometimes they were practically mountains, rising abruptly from the edge of a forest, taller than the canopy. Some were rounded like a turtle's shell or flattened on top, as if trimmed by some gigantic knife. Whatever their dimensions, whatever their shape, she couldn't help but feel a cold, instinctive dread when she stood in their presence. Sometimes the mounds stretched for miles, long grass-covered serpentine curves. They lay along the earth like the stone walls of Vermont, with no discernible meaning unless one could view them from the sky, like the ravens, like a curious, inscrutable God.

Who made the mounds, and why? There wasn't a soul in the Burned-Over District but longed to know. The bravest and boldest men ventured up those eerie, even slopes with pickaxes and spades. They dug into the earth and brought up mysteries: ornaments of beaten copper, necklaces of gold, breastplates, spear tips, human bones.

Emma woke early in the farmhouse's upper story, in a small room under the eaves. A pale red wash of early-morning light crept across the room's only windowsill. Outside, beyond the walls of the Smith family farmhouse, the fields lay rounded with snow, and beyond the fields, ranks of dark hills cradled the valley—wooded hills, black with winter wherever a canopy of ice had fissured. A fir-dark, New York valley.

The Smith farm stood somewhere between the townships of Manchester and Palmyra. It felt very far indeed from Harmony—a distance too great to be measured in miles. A chasm yawned between the life she had known and the unknown territory where she found herself now. Marriage had changed her forever. She had changed herself, transformed by the sacred rite, no longer her father's daughter, no more her mother's child.

Sleep had relieved some of the pain that had followed her from Pennsylvania—an ache of loss and shame, for Emma was almost as frightened of her father's anger as she was of God's. Isaac Hale would be furious over her audacity. Never in her life had she openly defied her father, but done was done. She must trust to God and face her future with clear, open eyes.

She lay still in the attic-room bed, watching the window and what lay beyond. The dawn was pale as a goose's wing. Dust on the window-pane and a strip of crocheted curtain softened the sunrise, so there was no harshness to its sideways slant, no glare. Light filled the room in a gradual, unobtrusive way, swelling softly, laying a hand on Joseph's face so every plane and angle of him could be seen.

Emma watched him as he slept. She could hear every breath he took, the long, slow rhythm. This man breathing beside her. This husband. Joseph was peaceful when he slept, as he never was when awake—his face relaxed into a slackness that made him seem almost dull-witted. She touched his hair, very gently, and then his cheek. Even so light a touch was enough to wake him.

"Good morning," he said. A pause. He added, "My wife. Are you well rested?"

All the neutrality of sleep was gone in an instant. That question—simple words, but the way he'd asked: he had a peculiar habit, a way of being solicitous that drew people to him. That morning and every morning to follow, all the rest of her life, Emma would never decide whether Joseph did it with purpose, to bind others to him with loyalty and affection, or whether it was simply his nature. He may have been, for all she knew, as unaware of his charm as a bird was unaware of its song. Joseph had worked his curious spell on Josiah Stowell and his wife. And on the Stowell children, inducing the boys to steal molasses taffy from their mother's kitchen and bring it to Joseph in the farmhand's shack. He had worked this quiet magic on Uncle William during the treasure-digging days, which seemed now to Emma like an episode from someone else's past.

"I slept well," Emma said. "Did you?"

They had arrived at the Smith farm late in the night, long after the family had gone to their beds. Joseph had led her quietly through the front door, into a dim interior, which had smelled of new-split lumber, dry sap, and carded wool. Hand in hand, without any candle, they'd crept up the stairs and found their bed. Her whole body had shivered with the effort of silence, and with the delight of their secret arrival. She had shivered, too, at his body so close beside her own in their bed. The feather tick had smelled faintly of mildew, but it was soft and deep, and on that first night home, she had drifted into sleep with Joseph's arm heavy across her body.

"Guess it's time we got up," he said. "I can hear the little girls downstairs, chirping away. Come on; a man likes to introduce his pretty wife. It's one of a few pleasures in a dreary world."

She wanted to ask, *Do you really think I'm pretty?* But it was a foolish question, weak and womanish, so Emma held her tongue.

They turned away from one another while they dressed, and contended with the pitch of the roof, elbows and foreheads bumping against the sloped ceiling. His feet tangled in the legs of his breeches; he fell across the unmade bed with a burst of rough laughter. By accident, she saw him—shirttail sliding up over bare skin, the long, lean strength of a pale thigh. They were making enough racket to wake the household.

When Emma's hair was as neat as she could manage without a mirror, Joseph led her down to breakfast. The sun had risen higher over the fields. All the world seemed to dance with a glitter of light on snow, and the distant trees stood with palms raised like white-garbed women at revival.

In the kitchen, Joseph's mother, Lucy, worked over the stove. The strapping Smith boys loaded their plates with ham, for even in midwinter there was work to be done on a farm of eighty acres, and men must have their strength. A little girl perched on a stool beside the fire, braiding the hair of another, who sat on a bright rag rug, wincing, knees pulled up under a felted skirt. The eldest sister of the Smith family, only a few years younger than Emma, sang while she buttered the bread. She was hollow-cheeked and plain, but her voice was lovely.

"Oh," the singing girl said, looking up, "it's Joseph. Look, Mother; Joseph has come home."

With a little cry of gladness, Lucy hurried to her boy and kissed him on his cheek. Joseph's smile was tense, faintly embarrassed. He squeezed his mother's hands.

The old woman turned to Emma. Her expression was warm enough, but there was a spark in her eye, almost amusement. "You've found what you sought, at last."

Joseph introduced her: Emma, my wife. It was the first time he had called her wife in anyone else's hearing. She blushed, for the word carried a certain implication, an acknowledgment of an act she hadn't yet grown used to. But in another moment, she cast aside the foolish thought. Past time she was about a woman's business—long past time.

The family crowded around. The little girls kissed Emma and called her sister; the boys lined up and took turns punching Joseph's arm. Lucy Smith pressed Emma's hand. The old woman's skin felt thin and cold. Her fingers trembled. She told Emma she was beautiful, so very beautiful, which wasn't true, and at that moment the front door opened, and a man called "Hello!"

"Hyrum," the eldest sister answered. Her name was Sophronia, Emma had learned, though the little girls called her Sophie. "Come and see what Joseph has: a wife!"

The eldest surviving son of the family, and married almost two years, Hyrum lived with his wife in a log house at the far end of the field. But it was the family's custom to take their breakfast together, the whole clan gathering under one roof, so each morning Hyrum led his wife, Jerusha, across the fields to his parents' home. Hyrum was a match for Joseph in almost every respect—tall, broad, well suited to hard work; the Roman nose; a fondness for boyish pranks and for his mother's raisin porridge.

Jerusha trailed into the kitchen. She was meek and tiny, chestnut-haired, with wide-set eyes that were keen and piercing when she lifted her face long enough to look at anyone directly. She looked at Emma only once. Jerusha's eyes held an unmistakable desperation. The honesty of her stare was the first indication Emma had that something was amiss among the Smiths.

The family came to the long table in a bustle of conversation—all except Jerusha, who took her place in silence. The patriarch, Joseph Senior, had gone away, seeing to some business in another county—business about which the family wouldn't speak, smoothly abandoning any questions Emma asked, turning instead to subjects they found more cheerful.

In his father's absence, Hyrum led the morning prayer—and after, it was he who guided the conversation. He beamed down the length of the table at Joseph, at Emma beside him. She felt suddenly, absurdly embarrassed to be sitting so close to her husband, conscious of the warmth of his body while some other man assessed her and grinned.

Hyrum didn't mean to be audacious. By nature he was coarse as a handful of gravel, and perhaps he was just as bright. But he meant no offense with his leering grin. Emma told herself that, several times over. After all, what had she to be ashamed of? She was a married woman now, wedded by a preacher before the eyes of God. She had done nothing shameful with her husband.

"At last." Hyrum folded his buttered bread. "At last Joseph has a wife."

Emma's hands went very still in her lap. Those words plucked at her.

Joseph has a wife. As if there had been some urgency in the matter. As if any wife would do.

Lucy's hands joined as if in prayer. Her fingers were lean and hard as hen's toes, the knuckles thick and rheumatic. "I knew this day would come. Praise God, amen and amen."

"You all seem so very pleased," Emma said.

She was about to add, *I am the one who is pleased to join such a welcoming family.* But Lucy spoke again: "Now our Joseph can go and fetch the plates!"

Down the length of the table, porridge steamed on a dozen plates of good, simple yellowware. No one had been left without his breakfast. Lucy seemed young for it, but perhaps she had already begun to lose her wits. It happened sometimes to women her age, especially if they'd borne many children. Emma looked to Hyrum, then to Sophronia, finally to Jerusha, who met her eyes with that same grim intensity, the subtle look of warning.

Emma said, "I don't understand. Which plates do you need? Shall I fetch them for you?"

Lucy smiled—soft around the edges, her eyes not quite focused, a woman lost in a pleasant dream. "Joseph had a vision, you know."

"Yes," Emma said. "He told me."

Joseph laid a hand on her wrist. She glanced at her husband and found him pale.

"He saw an angel," Lucy said.

The children swayed on their benches, rising to the lure of a story they knew as well as they knew the Nativity. Jerusha alone remained detached. She lifted a spoonful of porridge and ate resolutely.

"Joseph saw an angel of the Lord," Lucy said, "who showed him the place on a high hill where a marvelous treasure is buried."

"Amen," Sophronia burst out with sudden passion.

Across the table from where Emma sat, Don Carlos cut a solemn look at Joseph and his new bride. He was perhaps thirteen years old, but despite his obvious youth, he lacked all the mischief of his elder brothers. He seemed a man already. Don Carlos excused himself from the table, abandoning the raisins half-unearthed in his porridge.

"What sort of treasure?" Emma demanded.

Hyrum answered. She could feel him crackling with enthusiasm. "A Bible, Emma, written on plates of gold."

"Why," Emma said, "should anyone put the Holy Bible on plates of gold, and then bury those sacred words under the earth? I call it blasphemy, to throw dirt on the Good Book."

Quietly, Joseph said, "It isn't the Holy Bible—not exactly. It's a history of the Moundbuilders."

"The what?"

"The people who lived on this land, many years ago, and their doings with Christ."

"Their doings with Christ? Come now, don't play." Not about this. To twist the word of God was to provoke His wrath.

Hyrum leaned toward her—the best job he could make of looming, given their arrangement. "We don't play, madam. Joseph has gone back to the appointed place, trying to retrieve the plates year after year. But each time, he is prevented."

She tried to imagine what it must be like to see an angel of the Lord and hear its command, its voice like bridled thunder. She tried to imagine, and then tried not to imagine.

Hyrum said, "The angel has always told Joseph he isn't ready yet. He must come back when he's properly prepared. Last September"—Hyrum turned to Joseph, grinning—"the angel said, 'You must marry, and bring along a wife!' And there you have it. Now that Joseph has got himself a wife, he'll finally be allowed to take the golden plates!"

"And you saw these plates of gold," Emma said to Joseph.

Hyrum answered again. "Not I—not anyone. Only Joseph is ordained to look upon them. It's death to anyone else. You'd fall down dead on the spot; that's what the angel said."

The whole family had gone still. The place where Don Carlos had sat seemed very empty. Lucy Smith gazed at Joseph, softly proud, softly beaming.

Emma's laughter broke the silence. She giggled behind her hand; she tapped Joseph's knee under the table. But he, too, was still.

"A prank," Emma said. "It must be. I know how boys are, with their freaks and tall tales. I wasn't a schoolmistress for nothing."

"It's no tale," Joseph said. "It's true."

"Very well. Then show me. Take me to the hilltop and show me these golden plates."

"You can't look upon them," said William, Joseph's younger brother. "It's a curse to see them, unless the Lord has prepared you."

"I don't believe it," Emma said. "If you say I can't look upon the plates, then show me this angel, if it's true."

Joseph picked up his spoon. He attended to his porridge, as if breakfast were all that mattered in the world. "When the time is right," he said, "I will."

Night settled hard upon the land, sinking a chill down to break the earth like the coulter of a great, dark plow. In the attic room that was hers and Joseph's now, Emma's candle made a spot of brightness on the windowpane. She couldn't see out through the glass, so she blew out the flame, and the room filled with a scent of singe, the oily warmth of melted tallow. Her sleeping-dress was wool, of her mother's finest spinning and Emma's own weaving. She'd sent a letter home explaining herself and asking for her belongings. Her clothing and spinning wheel and a few sticks of furniture arrived a few days later, but no word of forgiveness from her father, and even her mother's best wool couldn't keep the cold away. She pressed close to the pane, staring into darkness.

The Smith house lay silent. The little girls had gone to their beds and the men had carried lanterns over the snowy fields to Hyrum's cabin. They would talk there over the Gospel, as was their habit on long winter nights. Emma had pleaded a headache and so had won herself a few precious hours of peace. She had been married two weeks now, and already she found the relentless faith of the Smiths exhausting.

Alone, she wondered about Joseph's angel and his golden plates. She wondered about his peep-stone. She hadn't seen the stone since that day years ago when he'd knelt in the snow to pull ice from her hem, and now she found she couldn't picture the rock at all. Did it shine? Was it dark as deep water? Was it flecked or pitted? Did God's eye peer out from the stone's center, to watch Joseph watching Him?

The image unsettled her. The smell of the blown-out candle was suddenly too close, and her nightdress constricted at her throat. Despite the cold, Emma lifted the window's sash and let the winter come in. The air carried a sharp, smoky bite. More snow was coming. The snow wouldn't arrive that night, perhaps not even the next, but soon. She breathed frosty air. It stirred inside her, alive in her chest.

A faint, tinny, broken sound rose from the dark forest and faded away. She waited. The sound came again, as she knew it would: a distant wail. There was no pain in the cry, but even miles away, across Manchester's muddy brown acres, she could feel its urgency, its heat—the same fire that crackled in Uncle William's eyes and made the spittle fly from his lips, the same fire that burned around the Smith table at every meal. Somewhere on the fringes of civilization, a tent was glowing with light. Somewhere in the valley, a traveling circuit preacher was shouting and stamping his feet, Holy Holy Holy, and the flames of fervor were rising.

Emma had heard the tale of the girl in Rhode Island who fell ill with typhoid fever—a Quaker girl, given to silent worship. When she recovered, she rose up shouting. The spirit of God had entered her and burned away all that once was—and now, she proclaimed, she wasn't the humble child Jemima, whom her family had known, but the Universal Publick Friend, in whom the triune God rode like a knight on a steed. The Friend had not one word of literacy—couldn't even write her name, they said, yet she could recite the Bible from memory, identify any fragment of scripture, chapter and verse. Her followers grew in number and passion day after day; the Friend's recitations were proof that her frail, girl-child body was the boardinghouse of the divine.

When she died, so Emma heard, her followers waited for a miraculous resurrection. None came, and so they hid her body in a cold, dark cellar where the newspapermen couldn't see the corruption of her flesh, the plainness of her corpse—the frank stillness of a final death. And there the Friend remained, slowly returning to the earth, returning to Jemima, while in the sunlit yard aboveground, outside the cellar walls, her apostles sang to Heaven and shook their limbs in her name.

The story still turned Emma's stomach, months after she'd first heard it, and sent a shiver of dread up her spine. Those true believers tingling in anticipation of a resurrection while the smell of decay came up from below the ground.

One night she and Don Carlos found themselves outside while the family supper went on, the talk of signs and portents carried on along-side more mundane discussion of the plowing and planting to come. She told him the story—the Quaker girl, her followers whose faith wasn't shaken, not even while her body rotted into dirt.

"Do you believe it?" Emma asked him.

Don Carlos tucked his hands under his arms to keep his fingers warm. Across the road, across the deep ruts carved by an endless stream of preachers' wagons, an owl called once, and was still.

"I don't believe in much, Sister Emma," the boy said. "Only what I can read for myself in the Bible, and that ain't much anyhow. I never was too good at reading."

Summer. A thick, hot breath rising from the Erie Canal, from the ponds and irrigation ditches, even from the damp places in the forest, hidden groves spiced by a smell of rotting wood and living leaves. The air was thick with rumor—stranger tales than that of the Universal Publick Friend, or if not stranger, then more immediate.

Well before summer, in the first flush of spring, Emma had come to dread her trips to the hardgoods store in Palmyra—a trek she made weekly with Jerusha or Sophronia. Every stop at the store's counter brought new rumors of Joseph's dealings. And every story vexed Emma more than the last.

Joseph looked into his peep-stone, the shop girls said, and told Mr. Capron from the Dell that a quantity of gold watches was buried in his back acreage. Under Joseph's instruction, the Caprons drove stakes into the earth, a circle five feet wide, and while Mr. Capron dug for hours between the stakes—till his back was just about broke from the work, Mrs. Smith—his son marched around the perimeter waving a sword to frighten back Satan and his devils. No gold watches were found. Nothing was found but a turkey's tail feather, and what can you buy with a feather?

Worse was the story circulated by William Stafford. Joseph told him to cut the throat of a black sheep and lead the beast in a circle until its blood drained away and it fell down dead. Whoever dug inside the ring of blood was sure to break his spade on a cache of buried treasure. William Stafford found nothing. His spade was still intact. And he was forced to eat mutton for days; he never could abide the taste.

Week after week, on the carriage ride home, while Sophronia chattered and sang and drove the horses, Emma clutched at her own hands and turned her face toward the fields and tried to watch the countryside slipping past, but she could see nothing but the images those foul rumors had planted in her head. Her husband meddling with things ungodly. She couldn't allow herself to believe those wild accusations. If she admitted that her husband made circles of blood to conjure up treasure, then she must also admit that Joseph was a sorcerer or a liar. Neither was less sinful than the other.

Whatever else he may be, Emma knew her husband was no man of malice. True, she had known him only a little when they'd married, but by the summer of 1827 she was certain of Joseph's finer qualities: his kindness, his gentle nature. He would never deceive—not intentionally, or if he did deceive with intent, he meant it only for a game, and played that game with a light, innocent heart. He would never recommend such blasphemy, this witch-work, cutting an animal's throat, casting circles of blood. Nor would he challenge the Devil with a sword. The rumors went beyond the realm of common hearth magic, the Old World charms and superstitions deployed by farmers and their wives—hexes painted on barns to ward off fire and bad luck; water witches dowsing in the fields.

On a hot night in August, when the brook had run dry and the frogs had ceased to sing, Emma claimed the heat had affected her and excused herself early from supper. In truth she was no weaker than at any time since coming to the Smith farm, but the leaden ball in her throat was too heavy to bear. She couldn't abide the Smiths' boisterous talk about the Last Days. She waited in her small room upstairs until the family had begun their litany of signs received and salvations found—until old Mr. Smith was thumping the table with a callused fist. Then Emma drifted down, quiet as a ghost, and let herself out through the kitchen door, unnoticed.

She walked through fields hip-high with horsetails, through tangles of wild pea with their pods already black and shattered. The odor of the grass was sweet. The earth still held a warm remembrance of the midday sun. A last, thin wash of light clung to the western sky, low, a suggestion of gold lingering amid the blue advance of dusk. She wondered whether her father had cut his hay yet, and whether her mother had forgiven her for leaving.

She made her way toward a grove of trees: slender maple saplings and white birches, a few gnarled oaks that stooped like old women under heavy cloaks of green. A figure moved between two trunks and disappeared into the shadows of the grove.

"Hello," Emma called.

The figure reappeared, thin and hesitant, peering shyly around a maple bole. "Sister Emma." It was Don Carlos. His voice was still soft and high, yet it had begun to mellow at the edges, the first notes of a man's tenor.

She lifted her skirts above her ankles and hurried to the grove. Don Carlos waited on a stump. The boy's shoulders sagged. Labor was long and weary in summer, when the days were hot and almost endless. But she had never heard him complain. Nor had he shirked his duties to go off fishing in the creeks or to wrestle with his brothers, nor go with his friends up into the hills to dig for treasure. In the furry twilight, the resemblance between Don Carlos and Joseph struck Emma with a queerly poignant pain. She thought this must be exactly how her husband had looked when he'd been a boy, huddled in a grove of trees, freshly awed by his vision of the Lord.

"You look sad, Sister Emma." Don Carlos scooted to one side, making room on the oak stump.

She sat, smoothing the skirt around her legs. She closed her eyes. Beneath her palm, the oak stump was faintly damp from a day of shade. The hissing chant of night insects surrounded her. The sound stabbed with a hundred tiny blades. A tide of regret rushed in through the places where the song had cut her, rushed in and filled her until she gasped for air. Behind closed eyes she could see a black ram staggering, its legs buckling, a final crimson thread draining into blood-soaked soil.

"Don Carlos," she whispered, "I have been deceived."

"Deceived, Sister Emma?"

She wiped away the tears. She didn't wish to hurt Don Carlos with unpleasant stories about his family; he was only a boy. And he hadn't chosen this life, after all. He hadn't asked God to make him a Smith.

"I mean only," she said, "that I have come to a hard place."

Don Carlos held a simple cloth bag on his lap. He delved into it and pulled up a heel of bread, still warm from his mother's oven. He broke off a piece and placed it in Emma's hands, and she cradled it—the rough, wholesome crust, such a simple kindness. She was hungry, but her mouth was too dry to eat, so she said again, "I have come to a hard place."

Quietly, Don Carlos answered, "I know."

Summer subsided, the heat of each afternoon giving way to a clear violet chill that rose as a mist from field and forest. In the evenings, vaporous columns moved like ghosts between the trees—spirits hanging in the branches, caught and distracted among golden leaves. Sunset gave way to long, deliberate twilight. The air smelled of woodsmoke, the last cut of hay.

Emma finished her evening chores—shutting the chickens up in their red-painted shed, tossing the scraps from Lucy's stewpot over the stone wall of the pigsty. The hogs watched her in the fading light with small, shrewd eyes.

In the kitchen, Emma loosened the ties of her Sontag shawl and hung it on a peg beside the hearth. Someone had banked the coals for the night. In the ruddy glow, she examined the shawl. It had picked up the night's damp and the wool was acrid, alive with a smell of the animals from which it had come. A moth or a thorn had torn out a stitch or eaten it away; the shawl was threatening to unravel. She must take up her knitting basket that night and repair the damage. She had worked all day on her new family's homestead, but knitting was more pleasure than work, so she could almost rejoice. Lucy was in the sitting room—Emma could hear her crooning to her children or to herself while the youngest girls giggled over their needlework. If she could wait until the children had gone to bed—Lucy, too—she could enjoy an hour of silence in the rocking chair beside the fire.

She heard footsteps on the narrow stair. She turned and found her husband coming down into the kitchen. Joseph wasn't dressed in a farmer's linen trousers and loose summer shirt, but rather his dark woolen leggings and a coat Emma had never seen before: black, with broad lapels that he had turned up close to his cheeks and fixed in place with the knot of a black cravat. The lapels nearly hid his face. He wore his knee-high work boots, too, the leather pitted and scarred, but he had cleaned the boots meticulously and polished them to a high shine.

"Tonight," Joseph whispered. "We must go out tonight, to retrieve the plates."

Emma dropped the torn edge of her Sontag. She raised her brows first, then her chin. "Will I see your angel?"

"You'll see whatever the Lord wills." If Joseph noticed the challenge in her words, he'd chosen to ignore it. "Now go and dress. Wear dark clothes—black, if you have it. We must be as secret as we can manage."

In their small room, Emma found a bonnet of deepest blue—the darkest one she had—and knotted it under her chin. She slung a cape of black worsted around her shoulders. This matter of the golden plates was folly, some long jest thought up by Joseph and Hyrum, nurtured between the brothers who were still more boys than men. When the time came—when they had spread their play so far it grew thin—Joseph and Hyrum would admit their freak and share a good laugh over the looks on their family's faces. Emma had decided to cooperate only so that she could laugh *with* Joseph when he finally admitted the golden plates had been a game all along. She would never allow Joseph or Hyrum to laugh *at* her.

Joseph slid like a shadow into the bedroom. There was a briskness to him like the night itself. He examined Emma in her dark clothing and nodded, then sat stiffly on the edge of the bed. He was resolute, like a man expecting some dreadful trial. The mattress still smelled of age and damp, just as it had on their first night under the family roof—though in the spring, when Emma had turned the feather tick, she had mixed handfuls of dried lavender with the goose down. A wry thought came to her: *Perhaps I ought to have marched around the mattress with a drawn sword.*

Despite his air of hesitation, Joseph remained calm, and so quiet he made Emma's skin crawl. He blew out the candle but didn't leave the room. Loosely, he held Emma's hand. Beyond the warped pane of their narrow window, the last vestige of sunset vanished over the hayfield. The night was all disorder and darkness, shapes melting black and in-nominate into shapes. Only the stars offered any light, but they were small and scattered like salt spilled across a table.

Faint sounds of activity came up from the rooms below—the family making ready for bed. Just when she had begun to shiver—when she felt herself on the verge of speaking, merely to dispel her anxiety—Joseph shifted on the mattress and leaned forward, listening. Emma could hear nothing aside from the rustle downstairs, but at some particular moment—an instant indiscernible from the one that had come before—he stood and offered his hand. Whatever Joseph had heard, he had taken it as a sign. She followed him down the stairs.

They found Lucy at the fireside, rocking slowly in her chair, drawing a white thread through a hoop of white cloth. "Going?"

"We'll be back tonight," Joseph answered. "Keep a light burning."

Outside, the surrey was waiting, its canopy removed, the old black plow horse patient between the shafts. Joseph helped her clamber up into the front seat. Then he took the reins and drove out between the fields to the Stafford Road. He muttered a few words, too low for Emma to hear, but by their rhythm and force she identified the words as prayer. The carriage jolted, settling into the deep ruts of the road.

They drove for a long time—east or north, Emma couldn't be sure. Starlight spread and revealed some of the land—or her eyes grew accustomed to the darkness. She could just make out the posts of pasture fences, and in a silver distance, a flock of sheep moved slowly against the black fringe of the forest. The animals bleated at the sound of a wagon on the road—plaintive voices, thin and muffled by night.

After a time—when the light Mother Smith had left burning vanished behind them—Joseph left the Stafford Road and turned up a dry, rocky lane. The lonely track twisted into the woods, and then Emma noticed a darkness deeper than night cutting a wedge from the sky. A high, sudden hill had sprung up from the fields—pointed at its summit like a hunter's cap. Starlight limned its hide of trees. The heavens above were silent.

Joseph drew rein. The black horse stamped and shivered.

Emma turned to look over her shoulder. She knew this was all a jest—she knew it—yet she couldn't help but fear the angel. What would she do if it lurched up from the soil? What would she do if its face was wreathed in flames, its tongue barbed like the lash of a whip?

"Here?" Emma asked.

Joseph nodded at the hill. "Up there."

She gathered her skirts. "Very well. Help me down and we will climb to the top."

"I must go alone. You're to stay here, with the horse."

"You said—you told Hyrum and *everyone* that you were to bring your wife to the place. Am I not your wife?"

Through some trick of the starlight, Joseph seemed more illuminated than anything else around him. "Of course you are. It's enough that you're here, at the foot of the hill. Someone has to stop the horse from running off, or how will I carry the plates home again?"

"I should think the Lord can manage to make one horse stand still, if He has a mind to do it."

"Emma, dear heart. You're always so clever." He kissed her cheek, then bounded down from the carriage. He pulled something from behind the seat. It slid along the carriage floor with a heavy, metallic vibration. "God willing, I'll be back soon."

He moved away before Emma could speak again. She could see a shovel propped on his shoulder—that was what he'd taken from behind the seat. Emma gripped the reins and scowled after her husband, but she couldn't force herself to move. What had tethered her to that spot? Was it only a deeply bedded fear of the Lord's presence? Or was there an enchantment on that place—some sly magic in Joseph's voice that had bound her to his will?

She waited for a quarter of an hour, then a quarter more. Cold and immobility stiffened her body, but she dared not rise to stretch her limbs. The most she dared was to retrieve a rug from the box below the seat. The night was beyond chilly; unseasonable cold sank into her flesh like frost working into the cracks of a stone. Some small creature called from the brush beside the road—a shrill, repetitive chirp. The black horse flicked an ear.

When he'd been gone almost an hour, the curious restraint lifted. Emma remembered her father, growling at the treasure-diggers, *You know I don't hold to such nonsense.* She stood—slowly, for the chill had made her stiff as an old woman—and made ready to step down into the road, but in that moment, she saw Joseph returning.

He stood out plainly in the darkness, pale in his shirtsleeves—the black tailored coat was gone. Joseph flickered as he descended the hill, passing in and out of copses and groves. The shovel was nowhere to be seen. In his haste, he lost his feet and slid partway down the slope. The next moment he was up again, running. Even in the darkness, Emma could tell he was trembling. And now she could see his black frock coat hanging from one hand. Something weighed the coat down—some hard, heavy mass, swinging ponderously as he turned this way and that.

Emma called his name. He scrambled to the carriage and the horse stepped back, suspicious of the thing Joseph carried. He set the frock coat on the carriage floor, beneath the rear seat, and arranged the coat's folds so that whatever it concealed remained well hidden. Then he climbed up into the driver's seat and let out a long, shuddering breath.

He took the reins from Emma, hands shaking so badly that he fumbled with the leather. She could smell his sweat. Like an animal, she could taste in the air around him an acrid note, an emanation of victory or fear.

"Are you well?" she said.

He made no answer, only slapped the reins on the horse's rump, and the carriage leaped into the night.

As they hurried back to the farm, Emma looked over her shoulder at the thing Joseph had carried. At first, she could see nothing. Then the carriage passed from violet shadow through a veil of starlight. The frock coat came to life before her eyes. Whatever it concealed was solid, blocky, heavy as an imp on the surrey floor.

She follows Governor Ford closely, down the road from the great square
hulk of a house they call the Mansion, which has been her home and Joseph's these years since the church fled from Missouri. There are soldiers
all around the governor, armed with swords, shouting at people to keep
back, a wall of men and blades between Emma and her people. Yet the
Mormons come out from their homes and shops, from the Masonic Hall
that serves as the temple. Their faces are drawn, hands trembling. They
press as close as they dare to the governor and his men, calling, "Sister
Emma, what news? Give us good news if you can." Ford moves on to
the town square with the speed and determination of a man carrying out
some unpleasant task—filling the pit of an outhouse, dispatching hogs
at slaughter.

By the time they reach the town square, the commotion has drawn
half of Nauvoo into the streets. Ford takes the steps up to the top of the
wooden platform, mounts them as if this is his own God-given territory,
and Emma has no choice but to follow. It's late in the afternoon. The sun
is low and blinding, a hard dazzle between the chimneys which, she feels
now, are like hands thrown up in shock. She narrows her eyes to hold
back tears. She turns her face down to the planks underfoot because she
can't bear the faces in the crowd.

"Ladies and gentlemen." Governor Ford's voice carries over the town.
The assembly falls quiet, a suspicious silence. "As most of you know by
this late hour, I have placed this city under martial law. The *Expositor*
press was destroyed, a crime that cuts at the very heart of America. A severe atonement must be made. Prepare your minds for the emergency."

Heat rising up from her middle, striking her face. But fear is a familiar sensation by now—years of it, years. How many times must they
prepare for the emergency, how many times will their people cower under threat of retribution? God of mercy, wasn't Zion enough, and after
that, the trials of the star-fall—and Far West, and Haun's Mill? And here
she stands beside this man who doles out threats like rations of flour,

stands beside the governor as if she endorses every word. He has used her, Emma sees, to keep the Mormons in line.

She looks up, only for a moment, to learn how the crowd takes her, whether they hate her now. She sees Porter Rockwell at the front of the assembly. His eyes, small and hard, lock with her own, but his mouth is obscured by the tangled beard. She can't read his expression. His long hair hangs in two braided ropes down the front of his body. He nods once, comfort or encouragement. At least Porter knows she is no creature of Ford's.

"Another cause for excitement," Ford says, "is the fact of your having so many firearms. The public are afraid you are going to use your guns against my men, and against the other towns and settlements. I know there is a great prejudice against you, but you ought to be praying Saints, not military Saints. You have brought yourselves to this point, this sad state of affairs, with sixteen of your men in the Carthage jail, including the one you're pleased to call Prophet. Depend upon it: a little more misbehavior from the citizens of this town and the torch, which is already lighted, will be applied. This city can be reduced to ashes. I know how the governor of Missouri handled you. He wrote an order of extermination. It gives me great pain to think that there is danger of so many women and children being exterminated here in Illinois, too. Yet that is what I shall be driven to. I shall issue against your people another such writ if anything of a serious character befalls the lives or property of the persons who are prosecuting your leaders. You will be held responsible. Let there be no misunderstanding on that count. I am here as a guest of the honorable Mrs. Smith, and I know you will treat me, and my men, as befits guests of the Prophet's wife."

With that, the governor leaves the platform. His men draw their swords, forming rank around him. The crowd falls back; the crowd leaps away. Ford makes for the eastern edge of town, where the horses have been picketed.

She feels exposed there on the boards. Like being paraded naked through the streets, every shame laid bare. She pulls her shawl tightly around her shoulders, though the afternoon is warm, and descends the steps as quickly as she can.

The crowd surges toward her, crying out for answers, but Porter reaches her first. "Back," he shouts, "get back, you pack of dogs. Give the woman some room."

Gratefully, she takes Porter's arm—clings to his stoic presence, his flesh like stone. Only then does she realize she is shaking with fear and rage. She could curse herself for it. She had thought the days behind her when she would display her frailties to the church and the world. What good have these years of suffering been, if not to temper her spirit?

"I'll take you back to the Mansion," Porter says. "Stick close beside me, and don't say a word to anyone if it pleases you. If they don't like it, let them complain to me."

"Thank you," Emma answers softly.

The Saints fall back. Before they've left the square, there is room to speak freely.

"Sister Emma," Porter says, "I've a terrible suspicion that the Prophet is already dead."

"You mustn't speak that way," she says. "You mustn't believe it."

But she believes it herself. The same blunt knowing has come upon her, too. Joseph was already a dead man when she found him in the orchard—dead to himself and to God. Over the cries of the Saints, she can hear the metallic whisper, the rhythmic hiss of Joseph's scissors cutting through white cloth. She hasn't been free from that memory, that vision, since she found him there under the trees. A summer breeze, gentle as the breath of Eden, had picked up the scraps of white linen and scattered them across the orchard. The pieces had tumbled and fetched in the tall grass, in the glossy leaves of saplings.

Porter says, "Let me ride to Carthage and learn the news myself."

"It's too dangerous. If Ford sees you slipping out of Nauvoo, he'll assume you've gone to raise some army and break his siege—though where we might find sympathetic friends, I cannot imagine. Joseph has left us without a single ally for miles in any direction."

"Ford won't spot me. I won't let him."

"There are some things even you can't manage. How many men has the governor brought? Five hundred or more. There are Gentile eyes everywhere, and none look upon us with mercy."

"If we only had some word, if only we knew—"

"Ford was kind enough to deliver Joseph's letters to me. I haven't had a chance to read them, but at least we know he still lives. The devils haven't done for him yet."

"He's been in that jail two days, Sister Emma. I can't rid myself of this terrible feeling—like a stone in my guts. The Prophet is in danger. I know it's true, and if there's anything I may do, any way I may protect him—"

"You're his most loyal friend. And my friend now, too."

When they return to the Mansion, Emma finds the girls waiting in the yard. They are strung along the line of the paling like quilts hung out to air. Like dogs waiting for their master.

"I must tend the other women." She is weary to her soul. "Go and take some rest, Porter. Ford has gone back to Carthage on business, but he'll only bring a few men as guards. The rest will stay here; you can be sure of that. Ford's men will be like wolves around the sheepfold tonight. We need you here—you and Brigham both—to keep our men from despairing. This night will be a trial, and it's only by your example that we shall last until dawn."

When she has led the girls back inside and told them all what she knows—which is nothing, or close to it—and after she has comforted them, as far as she can stand to touch them, she finds she has an appetite after all. The other women leave to weep or pray in their rooms, or drift out into the orchard behind the house. Emma is left alone beside the laden table. She takes a slice of bread, covers it with cherry preserves. The clock continues its relentless measure of the day. Each small tick of its hands leaps under her skin. When she bites into the bread, the preserves are so tart they bring tears to her eyes.

She takes Joseph's letters from her pocket and unfolds the first. It is dated: *Carthage jail, June 27, 1844, 20 past 8 a.m.* She presses it briefly to her heart and wonders why she does it.

Dear Emma:

The Governor continues his courtesies and permits us to see our friends. We hear this morning that the Governor will not go down with his troops today (to Nauvoo) as was anticipated last evening, but if he does come down with his troops you will be protected, and you must instruct the people to stay at home and attend to their own business, and let there be no groups or gathering together unless by permission of the Governor.

There is no danger of any "extermination order." Should there be a meeting among the troops (which we do not anticipate, excitement is abating) a part will remain loyal and stand for the defense of the state and our rights. Should the last extreme arrive, but I anticipate no such extreme, caution is the parent of safety.

Joseph Smith

P. S. Dear Emma, I am very resigned to my lot, knowing I am justified and have done the best that could be done. Give my love to the children and all my friends, and all who inquire after me; and as for treason, I know that I have not committed any and they cannot prove one appearance of anything of the kind. So you need not have any fears that harm can happen to us on that score.

May God bless you all. Amen.

She regrets eating a single bite, for now her stomach roils. What is it about Joseph's letter that has upset her? Governor Ford told Joseph he wouldn't go to Nauvoo, yet the governor came with a militia at his back. And the postscript feels melancholy, for all its reassurance of innocence and justice to come. Joseph wrote his true meaning in the spaces between the words. He doesn't expect to leave that jail. He doesn't believe he will see Emma or their children again.

And it was she who made him surrender, she who forced him to go.

Twenty past eight a.m., a thousand years ago, an eternity. She understands Porter Rockwell's need to learn the truth and learn it now. She rises from the table, goes out into the hall. There's no need to call for any of the girls, for they have come to Emma. Melissa, Nancy, and Helen cling to one another, eyes red, faces swollen from their tears.

"The Governor has returned," Melissa says. "We saw him ride back into town when we were out there in the orchard."

"Returned—so soon? Scarcely an hour has passed."

The girls draw themselves more tightly together. They hold one another up.

"Melissa," Emma says, "wash your face and go into town. Find Porter Rockwell. Tell him I say he must do as he pleases—only he must be careful; he can't be seen. He will know what the message means."

III

The Leatherwood God

1827–1828

Emma bent with timid care at the edge of the garden where the split-rail fence met the road.

She brushed away the leaves that had gathered around the squash vines, performing even that simple task with deliberate slowness. A rich, earthy smell of frosted loam rose up around her. The dimples of the squash leaves held remnants of the previous night's rain and glittered in the early sun. The solitude of the garden was a comfort to her. Green vines, still growing even in the cold tail end of the season, seemed a promise the Lord had made to Emma alone. She cherished her small, new hope. Some boys only settled into manhood once they had a boy of their own to raise. This frail leaf folded inside her, or curled like the fiddlehead of a fern, might be the very thing to bring Joseph around.

A wind hastened down the valley, sudden and cold. She picked the last of the squashes quickly, dropping them into her basket. When she straightened, she heard a low chuckle beside the garden fence. It was Mr. Ebens, one of the nearest neighbors. He nodded a furtive greeting. Warily, Emma did the same.

"I hear there's treasure," Ebens said.

"Treasure, sir?"

"Dug up by your husband. He is your husband, isn't he? Joseph—young Joe. You married the boy. Yes, there's treasure, all right. The whole valley has heard."

His whiskers, white and gray, put Emma in mind of some bestial thing, a wolf slinking around the barn. "Sir, I don't know what you mean."

"He dug it up, that boy you married. Dug up some gold."

"You are mistaken."

That was no lie, by Emma's reckoning. She couldn't have said what had been wrapped in Joseph's black coat—gold or common dust. And he might not have dug it from the ground. She couldn't swear to its origins, whether it had come from above the earth or below it, or fallen from the sky like Wormwood.

"Then is he a liar, that Smith boy?" Ebens grinned, showing brown cracks between his teeth.

"You offend me," Emma said, more mildly than she felt.

He rattled a dry laugh and wandered away down the road.

The Smiths were no good at keeping secrets, that was the trouble. She wondered which of them had told the story, and to whom. Lucy with her unfocused eyes, or Hyrum, with something to prove. Sister Sophie, letting the tale slip to the shop girls while she pawed at the bolts of calico. Rumor of a treasure might land Sophronia a husband, if the town of Palmyra believed her brother the greatest scryer in the valley.

Was a husband worth all this? Ask Jerusha. Ask Emma Hale.

The shopkeeper tapped the last of the coffee out of his grinder's drawer into a sackcloth bag. The bracing scent of the grounds filled the mercantile, pushing back its usual odors of damp wood and grain dust. He weighed the bag, scratched a note in his ledger, then added the coffee grounds to Emma's basket alongside a packet of bicarbonate soda, a pot of molasses sealed with yellow wax, and a bar of hard soap. "Twenty-eight cents."

"It's to go on credit," Emma said. "The Smith account."

Beside her, Jerusha had folded herself up again—a habit whenever they ventured into town. She held herself so tightly, it seemed as if she feared someone might try to pry her open.

A yellow-haired girl in a pink dress sat beside the stove, darning the heel of a sock over an apple. The girl raised her eyebrows. She leaned toward the counter so intently, Emma half expected to see her ears prick up like a dog's. *Is this the shopkeeper's daughter, or his young wife?* She frowned at the girl, who tucked her chin and busied herself with the needle again.

"No credit," the shopkeeper said. "Not for the Smith account." He was a stout man with gray hair and a stiff, neatly trimmed mustache. Light from the window flashed on his spectacles, obscuring his eyes.

"But why?" Jerusha said. "We always make our payments. My husband, Hyrum, is a good man, a worthy man. There's no reason to deny—"

"Madam," the shopkeeper cut in, "is your husband the treasure-digger?" Jerusha cast a helpless look at Emma, who dropped her palm hard against the counter.

"If you won't take credit," Emma said, "you'll take payment in kind. I've good salted butter at home—"

"Too much butter already. No use for more."

"Wool, then. I'm the best spinner in the valley. It isn't boasting if everyone knows it's true. You'll take my spun wool as kind. I'll send Don Carlos down to you with twenty-eight cents' worth, and you'll accept it, and that will be that."

"So it's *your* husband who has the treasure."

Emma tossed her head. "Show me a man in this valley who claims he never hunts for treasure in his idle time, and I'll show you a liar."

"She's right, Papa," the girl said. "Digging is the best pastime these days. Why, just last week Billy Martin went digging up in the hills and he found—"

The shopkeeper snapped his fingers once. The girl blushed. She lifted the sock close to her face and stabbed it roughly with her needle. Emma could smell the pierced apple.

"Is that why you won't carry an account for us any longer, because young men think it jolly to go digging in the hills?"

"I've heard," the shopkeeper said, "some young men have found digging profitable indeed."

"Sir, what do you imply?"

"Word has been going 'round that the Smiths have found a great treasure and are hiding it away. That's why I'll give you no more credit. I figure, if the Smiths are rich now, they can pay up their account and do their custom in cash from here on."

Emma picked up her basket. "My husband found no treasure, sir. He found a book—just that, and nothing more."

"A book, buried in the ground?"

"Yes," Jerusha said meekly, "the history of the Moundbuilders."

The daughter's eyes flashed up from her sock. Not a soul in the valley didn't yearn after the mystery of the mounds—who built them and why.

A history may not have been the kind of treasure that could pay an account, but it was still a thing of value.

"Good day," Emma said flatly, turning for the door.

On the mercantile porch, the shopkeeper's daughter caught her by the arm. "Please, Mrs. Smith."

She spun to face the child. "Your father is an arrogant man. A shopkeeper oughtn't to think so highly of himself, behaving as if he's God on high!" She handed the basket to Jerusha, then brushed her palms together, concluding a dirty business.

"Mrs. Smith, if your husband truly found a book in the ground—only that—then you ought to tell people as much. That's to say, there's young men in the valley spoiling for adventure, and they've all got the idea that it'd be fine to go and raid the Smith place and take the treasure for themselves."

"Raid us?"

"If they knew it was only a book," the girl said, "not silver nor gold, they'd leave off. You should tell everyone how it really is before the talk grows any wilder. You know how boys can be when there's naught to keep them busy. I'd think it such a shame, if they was to run all over your farm."

Jerusha had already climbed up into the surrey. She hissed in disgust. "If idle boys think to make mischief on our farm, they'd best pray Hyrum doesn't meet them with his gun."

"I even heard tell," the girl said, "that someone means to go and get a peeper from over in Palmyra."

"A peeper," Emma said. "Why?"

"To look in a peep-stone, of course, and learn where you've been hiding your gold. Well, if they have a peeper, they're sure to find it, ain't they?"

Emma stomped to the rear of the surrey. A horse was tied there, a fine bay with a short back and good hocks. Hyrum had asked her to retrieve the animal from the horse-trader, but the horse-trader, too, had passed insinuations about the Smiths and their gold. *A fine day this is*, she told herself, checking the knot on the new horse's rope.

"We must be going." Emma climbed up next to Jerusha. "I'll send the wool down tomorrow. Tell your father not to fret about it. Contrary to rumor, the Smiths are as good as their word."

They set off down the Stafford Road. The cold, wet mud of Manchester soon gave way to broad fields, the white blanket of the year's first snowfall pocked and tented by irregular patches of stubble, all that remained of the autumn harvest.

Jerusha tucked a lap robe around them both, then retrieved her bar of soap from the shopping basket. "I shouldn't have," she said. "Five cents. But how was I to know there would be no credit?"

Emma watched her sister-in-law from the corner of her eye. In a better light, on a better day, Jerusha's face would be as fine and delicate as porcelain, all soft angles, smooth and pale. Now she looked merely breakable.

"I shouldn't have, but . . . oh, I only wanted something nice for a change."

"You should have," Emma insisted. "You deserve something nice."

"We didn't even have the money for it. Lord of mercy, I've never been so humbled in all my life. No credit!"

"Through no fault of ours. No credit, because that shopkeeper is a rumor-mongering scoundrel. We've done nothing wrong, nothing to deserve such treatment from our neighbors." She almost added, *Neither have our husbands.* She stopped herself at that.

Softly, Jerusha said, "What's to become of us, we two?"

Emma could think of no answer. She leaned closer; Jerusha lifted the soap to Emma's nose. It smelled of roses and hyacinth. It smelled like summer and peace, like someplace a thousand miles from the valley.

Jerusha said, "They tell Joseph he must translate the plates, don't they?"

There was no need to ask who *they* might be. Two months had passed since Joseph had slung his coat into the back of the surrey. In all that time, the Smith family hadn't ceased to talk about the treasure.

"Joseph is supposed to use some stones to translate," Jerusha said. "That's what Hyrum told me. He said Joseph will access some miraculous gift of the Lord. With stones."

"There's nothing to fear in using peep-stones."

"Isn't there?"

"It's a common practice."

"Common doesn't mean righteous. To me, it seems rather close to idolatry."

For a moment, Emma could feel Joseph as if he rode in the back of the cart, though he was miles away, at the farm. His towering conviction reached for her; it came into her heart through the ingress made by their physical connection. The acts of marriage had built a conduit between husband and wife. The sharing of their flesh had made them one—of one body, if not a single mind—and now she could almost hear his thoughts, even at a distance. Joseph with a stone in his hand. Joseph's awe at his own potential. He could sense his destiny unfolding, blooming like a waxy flower, petals too bright and scent too sweet to be pleasing.

"Peep-stones are not idolatry," Emma said. "At least, Joseph's stone is no idol. He only speaks to the Lord through his stone, not to anything else."

Jerusha sat up, staring down the road. "Who in the world . . . ?"

Someone was running toward them, arms and legs pumping in a desperate rhythm, breath so thinned from exertion that barely a puff followed in the crisp air. The figure was narrow-shouldered, young. She stopped the carriage. The figure drew closer, and the cart horse whickered, recognizing the boy a heartbeat before Emma did.

"Don Carlos!"

"Trouble at the farm," Jerusha said. "Already?"

By the time he reached the surrey, Don Carlos's face was livid. He stumbled in a crust of snow, then pitched forward over his knees, heaving for breath.

"Land sakes," Emma said, "get up in the cart." She slid down the seat, pulling Jerusha along, making room for the boy. He was dressed in his flannel shirtsleeves, no coat, no hat. "You look fit to catch your death. What were you thinking, running that way in the cold and damp?"

"Has something gone wrong at home?" Jerusha said. "It's not a fire, is it?"

Don Carlos shook his head, gasping. "Came to find you. Heard a rumor."

Emma drove on. Hyrum's new bay snorted from behind the carriage. "Imagine running off over a rumor, without even a coat. You don't have jelly for brains, Don Carlos."

Jerusha put a hand on Emma's shoulder. "Wait a moment. What rumor exactly?"

"We know what rumor," Emma said.

"Willard Chase from up the valley," Don Carlos answered, "and his friends. They got Willard's sister, Sarah. She's a good treasure-seeker— the best, they say—and her peep-stone never fails. They're on their way to the farm right now. They plan to toss the place. They'll find Joe's golden plates for sure, Sister Emma, with Sarah looking into her peep-stone."

Emma fixed the boy with a hard stare. In his flushed cheeks and glittering eyes, she saw the words Don Carlos didn't dare speak aloud, not even to her. *They'll find Joseph's golden plates if there are any plates at all.*

"Damnable fools," she muttered, and didn't know whether she cursed Willard Chase and his friends or the whole wide-eyed Smith clan. "How did you hear this story?"

"Jesse told me. You know Jesse—Franklin Scott's boy."

"Jesse Scott is a hell-raiser. He tells stories just for the pleasure of watching them spread. He's no different from the boys who set hayfields afire for the fun of it."

"He wasn't lying, Emma—not this time. I could tell by the way he smiled."

Emma urged the cart horse into a trot. Any speed was risky, for the roads were slick with ice, but the Smith farm was still a good ten minutes away. The Lord knew where Willard Chase and his friends were at that moment—all of them clamoring and spoiling for a wild time. The carriage hit a deep, frozen rut and slammed down on its springs. Jerusha tumbled against Don Carlos; the boy barely kept his seat. He might have fallen under the wheel, or under the hooves of Hyrum's horse.

Emma reined the cart horse back to a plodding walk. "Blast this cold! Blast everything!"

Since marrying Joseph, she had faced any number of indignities, but they had all been quiet and contained. What one suffered in privacy, one could bear, with God's grace. If the Chase boy succeeded in his mischief, the shutters would be thrown wide on all the Smiths' windows. Her life, all its perplexities and quiet fears, would be like a book left open for any passerby to read. She was strong enough to bear much, but she couldn't endure that.

"Where is Joseph?" Emma said.

"In the back field, cutting wood. Hyrum and Father are there, too, with Samuel and William. There's no one at home except Mother and

Sophie and the girls. Willard is on his way now, with his sister and her peep-stone. Jesse said it was true and I believe him."

Emma stopped the cart again, passed the reins to Jerusha.

"Where are you going?" Jerusha cried.

She didn't answer, only climbed down from the surrey. Was it only the cold that dulled the nerves in her hands, Emma wondered, so she couldn't feel the weight of her wool skirt as she lifted it—or had fear numbed her, body and spirit? She strode to the new bay horse, untied it from the back of the carriage, and looped the damp rope through the horse's headstall, knotting it into makeshift reins. The horse puffed its curious breath against her hands. It seemed a tame enough beast, and gentle.

"You can't," Jerusha said.

"Certainly, I can. It's a long drive home on this frozen road, but a short ride over the field."

"Without saddle or bridle?"

"I'm an excellent rider."

She maneuvered the bay closer to the surrey and stepped up on a spoke of the wheel. Her skirt flapped as she swung her leg over the horse's back and settled into its warmth. The animal tensed. Emma clutched the reins, fearful the bay would buck and spill her onto the hard earth. She thought of the baby growing inside her, a small, curled thing. Never in her life had she felt so frail.

"This is too dangerous," Jerusha insisted. "Get down, Emma."

"I won't be made a fool. Willard Chase can choke on his sister's peep-stone." She turned the bay toward the field. It obeyed smoothly, and Emma allowed herself the smallest flutter of hope. She called over her shoulder: "Get Don Carlos home quickly or he'll catch his death."

The horse broke into a smooth gait, ambling and swift. Ice-crusted stalks cracked like eggshells under its hooves. Emma didn't look back at the surrey. Instead she kept her eyes on the distant forest. She prayed as she rode. *Please, Lord. Let me get there in time. Let no harm come. Let the horse put its feet surely on the ground; let me not fall and lose the precious gift you've entrusted to me.* The horse stumbled. Emma buckled with the momentum, shouting in wordless fear, but she caught herself on the crest of the bay's neck and didn't fall—she would not fall. If she could only make it to the rear field in time, if she could raise the alarm and send the men running for home . . . Perhaps it wasn't too late, perhaps she could still spare herself from base humiliation.

The trunks of individual trees resolved from a blue mass of shadow. Their leafless tops held shrouds of vapor and glittering ice. Emma slowed the horse and turned, listening. The Smith homestead lay far across the rutted snow, the red buildings small and remote. From somewhere close, near the forest's edge, came the rhythmic pop of axes cleaving wood.

Emma called out for Joseph. The horse whinnied with excitement, dancing sideways; she twisted its mane around her fist, but never stopped shouting, nor urging her mount ahead. The men appeared at the field's edge. Their faces, their fair coloring, stood out against the dark of the forest. They looked like wax poppets brought to life by some covert magic.

Joseph dropped his axe in the snow and ran toward her, arms outstretched as if he thought to catch her, as if she might already be falling. He caught the horse's rope instead. "Emma! What in the Lord's name are you doing?"

"You must go back home, all of you!"

Joseph Sr. laid a hand on his son's shoulder. He was solemn with fear. "Illness? What has happened—who's stricken?"

"No one. It's not illness, nor fire, but something that may be worse. Joseph, mischief-makers are coming to discredit you. They're bent on rummaging through our home until they find your treasure."

Joseph shook his head slowly. His eyes were dull, uncomprehending. "My treasure?"

"The plates, Joe," Hyrum said. "You can't let them have the plates!"

Slack-faced, Joseph turned to stare at his brother. Then, slowly, he broke into a foolish grin.

Hyrum punched his shoulder. "Be quick! Think of all we'll lose if they take the plates away. Go back! Wood can wait. The trees will be here tomorrow."

Emma stared down at her husband—his glazed eyes, the fading trace of his smile. Then he blinked, reached up to the horse's back, and leaped like a trout in a stream. He scrambled, kicked—and suddenly he was mounted behind her, body pressed against her own. Emma's face burned, but there was no time for modesty. He reached around her waist to take the reins, and the horse lurched toward the farmhouse.

They reached the trampled front yard just as two carts came up the lane—Jerusha and Don Carlos in the surrey, and four strangers in a rattling wagon. Three of the strangers were smooth-faced young men, scarcely older than boys. The fourth was a girl of sixteen years, bundled in shearling and scarves. Jerusha sawed on her reins, trying to halt the surrey and block the wagon's path, but the cart horse had caught the scent of its barn. It threw up its head and hurried on. Only Jerusha's cry of dismay lingered in the yard.

Joseph sprang from the bay and ran at once for the house. Two of the strange boys had already thrown themselves from the wagon. They sprinted to catch him, and in the doorway of the rust-red house they wrestled, shoving one another, hammering at Joseph with cold-chapped fists. The boys pulled him back. He twisted and broke free, reached for the handle of the door, but they had him again. They swung him about in the yard, laughing like children at a barn dance.

Emma slid carefully from the horse. Her legs trembled when her feet struck the ground, but she couldn't fall. She was too rigid with indignation. The girl in shearling stepped down from the wagon to meet her. Emma paused long enough to look into the girl's eyes—impudent, clear blue, sparking with mockery. Wisps of orange hair had escaped her tight wrapping of tartan scarves. The locks twisted away from her face like a tangle of weeds.

The girl opened her mouth to speak, but Emma shouldered her aside. The boys had cast Joseph out into the yard, where he slipped in the snow and almost fell. They seized their chance and burst through the door, laughing and hurling insults.

Inside, Lucy and Sophronia were huddled at the fire, arms wrapped around the two little girls. Joseph tried to shove past the jeering strangers, but they bounced him back toward the door. He stumbled hard into Emma's chest. She felt a lurch inside her, a flutter somewhere below her navel. The child was afraid.

"What do you want?" Lucy asked calmly. The note of confidence in her voice took Emma aback—a certain dry pleasure, as if she knew she would soon be rewarded after a long bout of suffering.

The strangers only smirked and thrust at the girls to see them cringe. A light tread at the threshold silenced them all. The red-haired girl in the shearling coat stood in the doorway, haloed by weak winter light. She opened her fist to reveal a jagged white crystal. The girl glanced down at the stone once, dismissively, then looked around the room, considering the humble furnishings, the dim light, the faded rugs. Her eyes lingered on a long, low chest beside the fire. It was too small to hold blankets or kindling, too rough and hastily made for any heirloom. She pointed with the hand that held the peep-stone. "There."

Sophie and the girls screeched as they were shoved aside. But Lucy moved away with dignified complacence.

"Do something," Emma said quietly. Joseph's eyes had gone flat, almost colorless in the dim light. Emma couldn't read a word of him.

One of the boys fumbled inside his jacket. He produced a small hand axe, raised it over his head just as the back door flew open. Hyrum burst in, panting, the rest of the Smith men close behind. "No!" Hyrum bellowed.

The axe slammed down. The chest buckled. Dry wood scattered shards across the room; Emma threw up her hands before her eyes.

A stunned silence followed the blow. In that stillness, she heard a soft, whispering hiss.

Slowly, Emma lowered her hands. A pale substance spilled from the staved-in chest. She stumbled past the red-haired girl and fell to her knees beside the broken chest, plunging her hands inside.

One of the boys rounded on Joseph. "What's this?"

Sand. Only sand. Emma stretched her fingers until the skin between felt ready to split. She clawed through running sand for something— anything of substance. She found nothing but dust.

"I had a revelation from the Lord," Joseph said. "He told me you were coming here to take what has been trusted to me. I've moved the book to a safe place, where you can't defile it. You won't take my treasure, Willard. If you want to read the book, you'll have to wait till I've finished translating it, like everyone else."

The fire crackled. Lucy drew a long breath, and Hyrum grunted with satisfaction, but Emma remained on her knees, groping for the thing that wasn't there.

"Now get out," Joseph said, "all of you, or I'll send for the sheriff. I'll have you hauled away for disorderly conduct."

When they had gone, Joseph leaned his forehead against the door, breathing deep and slow. No one made a sound until they heard the

wagon rolling down the lane. Then Hyrum let out a whoop of glee and
the Smith boys laughed, pounding each other's backs. The little girls
giggled in relief, still clinging to their mother's skirt.

The last of the sand spilled from the ruined chest. Pale dust settled in
the woodgrain of the floor, sank into the cracks between planks. Joseph
knelt at Emma's side. She scooped some of the sand in her palm, let it
run through her fingers.

"I was given a revelation, Emma." He took her hand, brushed the
grains from her skin. "I've hidden the plates elsewhere. I had to; don't
you see? Or Willard Chase would have taken them, and we would never
learn what the plates say."

Emma couldn't speak. Something hard and cold had expanded inside
her, pushing the breath from her body. Only a fool would believe such a
tale. Yet revelations came all the time. The newspapers reported visions
and miracles, common as weeds in a ditch. She had read about the man
in Ohio, the one they called the Leatherwood God. He shattered the
peace of Sunday worship with a tearing, hollow boom like the snort of
some enormous stallion. *Salvation!* he cried—a huge man dressed in a
tailored coat and a fine beaver hat. No one had seen him before. In a towering voice, he commanded the congregation to come at him, fly at him,
try to touch a hair upon his head. Eager hands reached. They burned
with need, in these terrible Last Days, to grasp one hair-thin strand of
salvation. But the congregation fell back senseless, rebounding from the
force of his presence, dropping to the floor of the chapel to grovel for
his mercy. Surely that tale—or perhaps some other—was God's honest
truth. Every report of miracles couldn't be a lie.

If Joseph were telling the truth, then only Satan could have induced
Willard Chase to fall upon the farm. And if Satan had set his sights on
Joseph, then might he not also come for Joseph's child?

"We aren't safe here," Emma said, "not anymore. We must find a
place of safety, before . . ."

No one else knew about the child, not even its father. Emma was
determined not to speak of it until the small life had taken root and
couldn't be shaken loose—not by God or the Devil, nor any other power
under Heaven.

"What place is safer than this?" Joseph said.

Someplace far from the Smiths. That was where Emma needed to be, long before her baby arrived. Someplace where Joseph could take up an honest man's work, where a family's good name and solid repute would stand as bulwark against rumor. A place where Joseph and Emma could both sink into blessed anonymity.

"Harmony," she answered. "We must go back to my parents' home—assuming they'll have us."

All through the long drive to Harmony, Emma and Joseph hardly spoke a word. Their borrowed wagon was laden with all their worldly possessions: a few chests of clothing; the quilt Emma and Jerusha had made; her spinning wheel and cards; and the history of the Moundbuilders, wrapped in layers of cloth, stored at the bottom of a trunk where no one would find it, where Emma couldn't see.

Three days before they'd left the Smith farm, Emma had sent a letter to her parents—paid a boy to ride all the way to Harmony, carrying the note. The price had been dear, but she couldn't simply drive up to the yard of Hale House unannounced, without the least warning—not after the way she'd left. *Joseph and I are coming to stay*, the note had read. *This is the way it must be. Try to understand. I pray for peace among us.* Only God could say whether the boy had made the ride honestly, or whether he had absconded with Emma's money and left the letter lying in a ditch. If the letter never found its destination, then Isaac would have no warning. He would be confronted all over again by his daughter's rash betrayal almost a year before. Time moved in its endless march, wearing down all things like grist under a millstone—all things except Isaac's memory.

At last, on the fourth weary day of their drive, the wagon climbed the final rise and Hale House came into view. Emma laid a hand on Joseph's wrist. He drew rein. She could hear the faint squeak of her spinning wheel revolving on its axis. There was still time, perhaps, to turn and flee. Perhaps her parents hadn't noticed the wagon. She and Joseph might find welcome on the Stowell farm. There was a cabin at the back of Josiah's land, half swallowed by advancing forest; Emma and Joseph had spent their first night as husband and wife in that damp, cold place. They might live there again. They could pass the winter in the cabin. They needn't cross Isaac's path at all.

Next moment, as if her misgivings had summoned him, Isaac appeared around a corner of the house, arms full of wood. He saw the wagon and paused. At such distance, there was no reading his mood, no telling whether the letter had found him in time.

Joseph drove on, then halted again in the yard. Isaac dropped his burden on the front step and approached the wagon, but he wouldn't speak. He only stared up at Joseph. Rage had darkened his face, but as Emma watched, his anger gave way to wounded disbelief—an emotion she had never seen in her father, not in all her life. Isaac sniffed. He pinched the bridge of his nose. She realized her father was crying. He had never wept before, as far as Emma knew. The impossibility untethered her from the world. Light-headed, from a hazy and mobile distance, she felt as if she were floating past the scene, watching from someplace above and beyond. Joseph frozen with shame; her father—her father!—weeping.

"What nerve you have," Isaac finally said, when he could marshal his words. "What gall, to come back here after what you've done. You're a fraud, Joseph Smith. A fraud and a liar. I would rather see my Emma in her grave than married to you."

Joseph jerked as if Isaac had slapped him. He was weeping, too. The tether reconnected; Emma was pulled back to earth in a sudden clutch of gravity, back to the sting of the moment. A sharp snap.

Joseph spoke quietly, as if he feared someone might overhear. But there was a calm resignation about him, too. Surrender. "I am indeed a fraud. I've never had a vision, Mr. Hale, nor seen treasure in a peep-stone."

The starkness of winter crowded in—a white world, blank and bitter with cold. Was it true, or had he only said it to appease Isaac? Either way, Joseph had lied: to his family and all of Manchester, who believed he had found treasure in the earth. Or to Isaac, then and there.

Weariness like a stone fell on her, a stone dropped from a great height. It collided; it cracked against her soul, and she trembled under the blow. *I will bear it*, she told herself. *This humiliation, this deception.* What choice did she have? Her marriage had been an act of impulse bordering on desperation. But all the same, she had sworn holy words before the eyes of God, with her hand upon the Bible. She had cast her lot with Joseph Smith, and now she must play the part of his faithful wife, whatever trials would come.

On a portion of the Hale acreage, near a broad bend of the Susquehanna River, there still stood an old cabin—not as damp or drafty as Josiah

Stowell's, thank God. The Hale cabin had been, in fact, the first home Emma's parents had made. Isaac had built it himself mere weeks before he'd married Elizabeth and taken her from Harmony proper out there to the forest. But Elizabeth had always yearned for a finer home, so Isaac, smitten with his youthful bride and willing to sacrifice anything to see her smile, built the beautiful two-story clapboard residence that was now a landmark between Harmony and Great Bend, and the best boardinghouse west of Poughkeepsie.

Long after Hale House had begun taking in boarders, Emma's brother Jesse had returned to the farm with his new bride, a girl as white and laughing as a daisy, and the old family cabin had passed to their keeping—the cabin and thirteen acres of cleared land that surrounded it. But Jesse and his wife had departed years ago, taking their young children across the river to run a new-built sawmill. The cabin and land would be Joseph's now, Isaac declared, on one condition: he must take up an honest man's work, renounce his treasure-digging, throw away his peep-stones, and forget all talk of visions forever. He would work the Hale land like a respectable man, like a proper husband, or he would find himself out on the road, without a roof above his head and without his wife, too, if Isaac had anything to say about it.

Joseph agreed at once to Isaac's terms. What choice did he have? Emma had told him on the drive from Manchester that she was with child. The urgency of the moment had sobered him to his core.

At first, the cabin felt too dark and small. It held in its corners a damp smell of winter, and frost had laced itself up among the rafters. But Joseph cut wood diligently, stacking the cords higher every day, and soon Emma had driven back the cold—even some of the dimness—with constant fires in the old iron stove and bright things hung here and there, red linen curtains at the window, the quilt she and Jerusha had made spread across a narrow bed.

By the first thaw of early spring, the cabin had begun to feel like a home. Emma was glad for its silence, the long hours alone with her thoughts. What a contrast that place made to the Smith farmhouse, with its noisy mornings, the tramp of boots across the floor, the endless discussion of God's word and the preachers on the road. Emma thought she might write to Jerusha, ask her to come and stay—perhaps until the baby was born. Jerusha, but no one else.

Joseph had worked all season without complaint, clearing new tracts of land, finding nothing more alarming in the earth than ordinary stones, which he piled into long walls wherever Isaac directed. Honest work agreed with him—or at least, it agreed in those early times, the gray months of winter and spring. At day's end, when he came inside to warm himself and take his supper, he fairly glowed with good health. He went to bed each night eager for the morning, anticipating a new day's labor.

By and by, even Isaac came to accept Joseph. He seemed resolved to tolerate his son-in-law and make the best of a great disappointment. As winter receded and the days grew warmer, Emma often looked up from kneading dough or sewing a shirt to find Isaac and Joseph working together. Through the window she would catch sight of them in the field, her father and husband side by side, and she would know she had done right in bringing Joseph to Harmony.

In the evenings, Joseph brimmed with cheer. He came inside smelling of old snow, a chill reaching out from his body like a halo. When he laid his hand on Emma's stomach, its growing swell, he only spoke of hopeful, ordinary things.

Those happy days were not to last. Years later, in a world transformed, in a distant place she hadn't yet dreamed of, Emma would sit alone at her kitchen window, wondering why she had ever thought her gladness could last. Perhaps in those days she had still been more girl than woman. But when had the Lord ever granted her mercy?

The days began to linger. The sun reclaimed its power in shy advances, minutes of purple dusk. Hard snow receded from the fields. The icicles that had hung from the eaves all winter dripped even at night, filling Emma's dreams with a pattering sound. As warmth returned to the land, a restlessness overtook Joseph, more day after day, like the creep of thaw down the frosted walls. Every morning he went more reluctantly to his work. He dawdled at the edge of the forest for hours without raising his axe. Emma told herself she had no right to expect anything else. A man as bright as Joseph couldn't remain satisfied for long—not with a farmer's simple occupation, these predictable routines.

As the bare earth revealed itself, Joseph began to show his resentment.

How eagerly the soil yielded to his spade, how brightly the fields colored for him, how unchallenging the rhythm of seeds sprouting and growing. The honest life was too simple for his liking. The days lacked astonishment. It was the sort of life any man might expect to lead—just any sort of man, one you might see in the streets and nod to in greeting and forget about the moment you'd passed. The Lord had been cruel to make Joseph Smith a simple fellow, the kind who might only hope to make his living with axe and plow. Where might Joseph be now—who might he be—if God had made him the son of a wealthy family, with every opportunity in reach?

Emma watched the crocuses rise from the snow, the buds swelling on the branches of quince and cherry. Vigor spread across the land; circles of ice melted around the crocus stems. And Joseph lingered motionless in the field, slumped over his plow, moving slower with the passing of the hours.

A perse night in April, a night when the timid stars were almost the same color as the sky.

Emma stirred a kettle of porridge at the hearth while her husband came in from the fields. She offered him a greeting, but he was long-faced and vacant, stroking his chin with a grimy finger.

"Joseph?"

He pulled back the curtain on the cupboard, a small cellar of sorts built into the cabin wall. The chest lay inside—an old parcel-box Joseph had got from a glazier up in Manchester. There the golden plates had lain all the months since they'd come to Harmony, so thoroughly neglected that Emma had convinced herself the plates weren't there at all. They had vanished some night—neither she nor Joseph had noticed—whisked back up to Heaven by a capricious God. Or they had never existed in the first place. Joseph had never told his stories nor climbed that hill in the night. It had all been some perplexing dream, a vision half-seen, only partly remembered, a figure in the fog.

He slid the chest from its cupboard. Emma moved as if to restrain him, but Joseph was already lifting the lid and firelight was spilling inside.

There was something in the chest. An object covered in white linen—the box wasn't empty after all. Emma recoiled, for suddenly she could smell the revival tent again—the salt of eager sweat, the dry summer grass. Her heart pounded like the feet of those Shakers, faster, faster, and then, with the slow inevitability of decay, God's eye opened.

He took the plates from the cradle of straw in which they had slept all winter long. Inside the linen shroud, the plates were like a mason's block, heavy and flat with sharp, square corners. Joseph carried the block to a chair beside the fire and sat with his treasure in his lap. Silent, he withdrew a silver medallion from his pocket—a protective talisman his mother had given him long ago, when he'd been a boy confined to his bed. Joseph had carried that old trinket every day from the time Lucy had first pressed it into his palm. He stared into the flames, one hand resting on the linen-wrapped plates, the other turning and rolling and polishing the medallion. He never spoke a word, though his face was eloquent with longing.

The next evening, he returned early to the cabin, even while a blush still hung in the western sky. He took his old papers from the hidden chest—the papers he'd penned in Manchester in the attic room, the translation he'd made with his peep-stones. He leafed through the pages.

"Why don't you read to me," Emma suggested. "I'd like to hear your History of the Moundbuilders." She didn't know why she asked it. Perhaps she only wanted Joseph to be happy again, as he'd been in those first blissful weeks at the cabin.

He obliged, but shyly. Where had all his boldness gone? He was halting, stumbling, and Emma couldn't keep her mouth from twitching at his poor grammar and awkward prose. She hadn't been a schoolmarm without consequence.

After two pages, he trailed off. His face had gone red. "I guess I don't write much better than I talk."

"It's only because the words don't flow smoothly," Emma said, apologetic.

"I do the best I know how, but I never was much good at writing."

Eager to relieve his embarrassment, she spoke before she could really consider her words. "Let me rewrite these pages for you. I will correct any mistakes, so it all sounds smooth and pretty."

"Would you, really?"

"Why, certainly. I've time enough to see to it."

Whenever idle time presented itself—when the dough was rising, while the kettle came to a boil—Emma turned her attention to the pages.

The work was simple enough. She had only to copy out Joseph's story in a more elegant mode. She found she even enjoyed the respite, for the child was growing rapidly now and her back ached all the time. What pleasure it was to sit for an hour with only paper and ink, and the comfortable silence of an empty cabin.

Joseph's story described a lineage—the members of a single family, a king called Lehi and his many descendants, a king called Mosiah, a king called Benjamin. King Benjamin ruled the land of Zarahemla, to which the Lord had guided him after his forefathers had left Jerusalem. Emma liked the sound of the names. They were musical, ancient, familiar as her Bible. Were it not for her own hand moving across the paper, she could have believed Joseph's pages had come from the Bible indeed, torn out and lost in centuries past.

When she had mended the last of his work, Joseph read her revisions from his chair beside the fire. The field was only half plowed.

"You must act as my scribe, Emma. I'll read the words directly from the plates and you must write them down for me—write them as I speak."

"I can't. I've too much work of my own to do, with the baby on its way."

"Don't you see?" He struck the papers with a knuckle. "This is why the Lord instructed me as He did. This is why He brought us together. I couldn't retrieve the plates until I'd married—until I'd married you. God wanted you. He chose you for this work."

Emma shook her head. "Not me."

She began folding towels on the table, stacking them just so, restacking them, avoiding his eye. She remembered—could never forget—Hyrum stuffing buttered bread into his mouth. *At last, Joseph has a wife. Any wife would do.*

"Come now," he said, "don't be bashful. God has called you to a great work. It's not every woman who's called. Not every man, for that matter."

"Has He called me?" She laughed lightly, hoping it removed the sting from her words. "It seems to me the Lord only required you to take *a* wife, not this wife in particular. I'm not suited to the work."

"I declare there's no one better suited in all the world, in all of God's creation."

Her parents were only a few acres away. Perhaps Isaac's habitual doubt had crept into Emma's soul, infecting her by proximity. She imagined the marrow of her bones, thin black lines like ink on a page, but the words inside her weren't the words she had written for Joseph. They were her father's words. *Why should I believe you, Joseph, when you admitted you were a fraud? You told my father you'd never found treasure, nor seen any vision in the forest. Why should anyone believe?*

But his smile was so boyish, so trusting. She remembered him on his knees in the snow, the redness of his fingers as he'd picked the ice from her hem. And when he'd stood up and cut his caper, there had been dark patches on his trousers where the snow had melted through. Her heart expanded in her chest, yearning toward him, longing for the approval of her husband. The child turned over in her belly.

She began work as Joseph's scribe that very night. By the light of a single candle, Emma wrote the words Joseph gave her.

Where did he find those words? In darkness, in a whisper. In the silence of his faith, its dogged determination, his great need reaching down into the black place where his brother Alvin lay buried. Joseph dropped his two peep-stones into the bottom of an upturned hat—the very stones he'd promised Isaac he would toss into the river. With his hands, his work-hardened hands, he wrapped the brim to block out every hint of light and pressed his face down into darkness. He could see, he told her, words and images forming in the black. Like rocks under moving water. The very thought made her skin creep and her stomach quiver, and yet she longed to try it, too—plumb the darkness for visions, beg God to grace her with cascades of light. She imagined glowing words blurring as they flew by, like the flick of a bird's feathers, like trails of insect flight above the river in the evening, the luminous calendered wings.

But Emma had her task. She ignored both fear and curiosity. Her hand dashed over the page, cramping as she tried to keep up with the rapid flow of the narration. She was a conduit for his words, moving at his command, and he—he must be a conduit, too, bending to the will of a far greater power. For the language that poured from Joseph was so unlike his native farmboy drawl. The words Emma inscribed came without hesitation, and when he paused, lifting his head to roll the tension from his neck, she read back the passages and found they held all the mystery and rhythm of a sacred text. In music and meaning, they were kin to the Bible.

Each night for two weeks, they took up the translation. The world woke to the coming season—sunsets warmed the sky between trees; the trees jeweled themselves with buds and dangled fat drops of rain from their branches. Swallows built nests under the eaves. She could hear the birds, scratching and shuffling, when she took up her pen and sat poised at the table, ready to inscribe the words.

Days and weeks flowed like tributaries broadening a river, and spring expanded into summer, the abiding light, the smell of dry earth and barley. It was a wonder the crops grew at all, for Joseph had only given them half his attention, and less than half. But they would bear the fruits God had made them to bear—Joseph and the land. One could as easily stop the book from being written as coil stem and root back inside the seed.

The History of the Moundbuilders flourished. The stack of papers on the kitchen table rose a foot high. The baby would arrive within weeks, so Emma rarely played the part of scribe any longer. The child's eagerness for life had drained the strength from her body. She was tired out by midday, back and hips aching for a rest. She was content to leave the scribe work to Joseph's friends while she sat on the bed, propped up by a few old cushions, listening to the story unfolding. His voice was muted and small inside the upturned hat, like a shout cupped in a palm.

By that summer, Joseph had his pick of scribes, for he had never found himself lacking friends. His easy laugh, his amiable grin, his spark of appealing energy drew men to him—women, too. He picked up new companions everywhere he went—the store down in Harmony, the churches hidden in the dells, along any anonymous road, calling greetings to the boys in the fields. He sorted through his comrades with the discernment of a jeweler, selecting the best and brightest for his work. The lucky fellows who found themselves in Joseph's confidence gathered in the cabin three or four times a week, taking their turn with the pen while the hidden history rolled from his tongue.

In all that time, through the weeks and months of summer, not one of his friends saw the golden plates. Emma knew because she had asked them—bold and outright, meeting their eyes—when she served warm bread or water with mint leaves, a refreshment after a long spell of scribing. The plates had long since gone back into their box, concealed behind the curtain in the cellar cupboard, the hiding place only Joseph and Emma knew.

"Never," the scribes told her—each one, to a man. "Never have I seen the plates, Mrs. Smith, for Joseph told me it was death to look upon them. He reads by a holy light, your husband—by a holy power. God has blessed that man."

When their work was done and the last useful light had faded from the sky, Joseph and his scribes often sat together on rough-hewn benches in the yard, or on Emma's upturned laundry kettle. The thrill of holiness drained from their bodies, replaced by a hoarseness of the voice, an aching of the wrist. They watched the fields in the blue dusk—the fields that had somehow managed to sprout and thrive, though Joseph had paid them little mind since early spring. Under the stars, or under the clear, blue-white halo of a full moon, tassels of oats and the flat, wrinkled leaves of potatoes bent and whispered in the wind.

Those moments of peace brought Emma some hope. When the wind stirred, she felt the child stirring, too, stretching toward its future. It longed, like its mother, for simplicity and quiet. For Joseph to hold them both against his heart and stop all this talk of a book, a translation—all talk of salvation and sin.

On one particular night, Emma knew she would have no peace, although the breeze was gentle, and the sky was alive with diamond stars. But on that evening, Martin Harris had taken up the pen. With Martin for guest, the night was sure to be exhausting. The man's eyes were wide and urgent. A fever was upon him, one that made Emma feel burned to her soul and weary.

"It's the most extraordinary book I've ever read. Ever heard," Martin amended. "I can't quite credit it, Joseph, that I am taking some small part . . . that the Lord has blessed me not only to hear the book, but actually to take down your words!"

Joseph folded his arms tightly across his chest, as if to drive back a dreadful chill, though the night was warm. He sighed.

Martin's heavy white whiskers were glowing in the starlight. It gave him an air of fiery zeal. "I do believe that this book will change the life of every man who reads it. At last, we will know the truth! Why these mounds are here—why they are everywhere, in every valley, on every plain. Not a man in this region hasn't dug up some bit of brass ornament or the points of old weapons and wondered who made them. Now we know, thanks to your miraculous discovery."

Joseph glanced at Emma. Ruthless, she held his eye. Joseph could endure her look only for a moment. Then his gaze slid out to the fields again, to the ink-black forest beyond. He looked worn beyond reckoning, and with good reason. Emma had pleaded with him to find some other scribe, to stop imposing Martin Harris upon her. Enduring that man's company was like flogging one's own back.

Martin hadn't ceased to talk; he never ceased. "And thanks to the Lord—let us not be slow to offer praises for His blessings. Why do you suppose He chose this time to reveal the truth to you? Have you any idea?"

"None at all," Joseph said shortly.

"This marks some significance," Martin said. "It must. Some inscrutable working from On High. There is a code to read in the timing. It's a sign, is it not?"

"Seems everyone finds a sign in this or that," Joseph said. "The whole world has gone to portents."

"John Wesley wrote that Christ was to return in 1836," Martin said. "The blessed date is only eight years hence. I've always been a great one for John Wesley. I set store in his writings, I will tell you that much. Perhaps this revelation, Joseph's discovery, is to be our first preparation for Christ's return. Now we know the true history of our land—who built these great mounds, and why, and of course . . . of course, it could only have been the Hebrews! I have long suspected that we are a special, chosen people, we Americans. And now at last we may understand the origin of our greatness. This land was settled by the Hebrew tribes who struck out from Jerusalem and sailed across the sea! It nearly defies imagination. Yet here we have the word of God to prove it. Little wonder we are a great nation, with a history such as this."

Never mind, Emma thought, *the colonies—and all our ancestors taking ships from England. Never mind the Indians, who were here long before we came.* It wouldn't do, to argue with Martin Harris. The man was incapable of understanding nuance. If one were to ring a frying pan on the crown of his head, he would look around wide-eyed and ask, *Did you hear a church bell?* At least he wrote with a legible hand.

Joseph sat up on his bench. Those sharp eyes narrowed on Martin. "Perhaps you're right. Perhaps this is the time for preparation. Making the world ready against the great return."

Unused to being correct, Martin only stared, waiting for Joseph to say something more.

"Yes, of course," Joseph went on. "I see it now. God gave me the plates and showed me how to read them so I could reveal the history of this land to its inhabitants, and in so doing, bring them closer to God while there's still time." He sighed again, heavily this time. He seemed to diminish in the darkness. "But how am I to spread the news? That's what I can't work out. If we're to save souls in only eight years, then we must find some way to share the History of the Moundbuilders with a great number of people—all the people in America, if we can contrive it."

Martin said, "You must have the book printed, of course, when we've finished the translation."

Emma turned discreetly on her bench, rubbing the great swell of her belly. She didn't want to look at Joseph now. She could already sense his plan, the subtlety of his working. She never could bear to look at him when he lapsed into one of these moods of mastery.

He said, "But printing is expensive. We're only poor farmers, Emma and I."

"Surely it can be managed," Martin answered.

"I can't see how. This August will be our first harvest. Even then, we may not produce or sell enough to see us through the winter. And you can see Emma's condition for yourself—pardon my speaking of it, darling. We'll soon have a baby to look after, on top of all our woes. I'm afraid it will be several years before we can think of printing a book. I'm a man of faith; I know God doesn't err. But I really must wonder what He was thinking, appointing me to such an important task when I haven't a penny to my name."

"The Lord doesn't make mistakes, young man. He chose you especially for this work."

"So you say. Yet how will we afford it?"

From the line of the forest, a whippoorwill called. Emma couldn't quite bring herself to put a stop to it all—Joseph's insinuations, this luring of Martin, step by step, into a snare. Martin Harris had plenty of money; he could have done with a lick more sense. But what Joseph had said about the farm and the baby—that was all true enough. It frightened her to think of their precarious dependence on the first harvest, the uncertainty of her child's future. Everything could be lost in one freak storm, one cloud of locusts.

"Why," Martin said, "I can pay the printer's fee."

At once, Joseph raised his hands, as if fending off the very suggestion. "No, no. I could never ask such a thing."

"You haven't asked. I've made the offer myself."

Joseph lowered his eyes, suddenly bashful and young. He drew lines in the dust with the toe of his boot. "It's mighty generous of you. You fair-about take my breath away with such goodness. I'm blessed to have a friend like you. And God will reward you, too, by and by."

"Will He?"

"Such a kindly gift, and freely given—I tell you, Martin, that one day you'll be blessed to look upon the golden plates with your own eyes."

The man burned all the hotter. "Now, Joseph?"

"Not now. The Lord must prepare you first. It's dangerous to see them if you haven't been ordained."

"But Dolly," Emma said quietly. "What will she say?" Martin's wife was famed all over Harmony for her temper and stubbornness.

"Dolly will make do," Martin said. "It's my money, after all. The husband is the head of the house." Reluctantly, he stood. "But talk of Dolly reminds me of the hour. It has been a marvelous day. All the same, I must hie me home, to supper and to bed." He settled his hat, then lifted the brim in Emma's direction.

Warmly, Joseph gripped his shoulder. "I'll never forget your kindness in agreeing to pay the printer's fees. We'll speak again soon—very soon, my friend. May God be with you till then."

After Martin had gone, a curious heat bloomed in Emma's chest. She couldn't decide whether it was shame or relief. She hadn't the least idea how much money one could expect to earn from the sale of books. But even a few copies sold might prove a welcome bulwark against poverty. *Let Joseph make enough money to keep my child safe and well*, she prayed. A mother could ask for nothing more.

Midday. Joseph had gone outside to drag the plow, to break the earth for planting. Emma watched through a window. He rippled through the warped glass. He moved slowly, disenchanted, resenting the earth, the mule, all birdsong praising the season. He wished he were back inside. He wished he were reading from the golden plates, watching the glyphs of the Almighty pass before his eyes, the fire and fade of holy writ, the lingering echo, a purple glow, elusive in the dark.

The plow stilled in its furrow. The mule stopped; the singletree sagged to the earth. Joseph in the field. Joseph, standing still.

She couldn't watch him any longer—the man who had promised, for her sake, to turn his head and heart to sensible work. She tilted her face down so Joseph couldn't see her if he chanced to look back. She ran her dust-rag along the sill.

Joseph had left his treasure on the table, the golden plates in their linen shroud. Why hide them away, now that he and Emma conspired together, working against Isaac's wishes? But the plates remained wrapped as ever. They were always covered, even when Joseph read from them. Such was the way of the old fathers of true religion—that was what he'd told Emma. Moses, Abraham; they hid what was sacred.

"And Mosiah," Emma had said. "King Mosiah of Zarahemla."

He had grinned at her then. His smile was always radiant. "That's it exactly. The great fathers of religion. A man can read through linen when he sees with the eyes of God. A man can read through anything if his faith is strong enough."

She thought of a spill of sand, dust pouring from a broken chest, running across the floor.

The mocking eyes of the peeper with her wild, red hair.

What is he, Emma asked herself. *Is my husband a liar or an honest man?*

Quickly, before fear could stop her, she reached out to touch the shroud and the blocky thing underneath. She could feel a cool, hard mass through the linen, smooth and even as metal ought to be. It would be so simple to whisk the cloth away and look directly at whatever it covered—to see with her own eyes, to truly and finally believe.

She ran a finger up the covered plates. Through the linen, she could feel thin, compressed pages vibrating, the edges jumping beneath her fingertip. The plates gave off a faint metallic rattle. She pinched a corner of the cloth and tightened her hand, ready to pull it back, determined to know. But God's eye shifted; its pupil expanded. A black void yawned before her, dark as running ink. Shake, shake out of me all that is carnal, the men and women sang, and the cabin filled with the memory, the stench of zeal.

Emma let the linen fall, undisturbed. She wiped her hand on her apron, as if to remove the stain of sin. The plates rested in their shroud, and out in the field, Joseph leaned against a motionless plow.

The moon rose fat and full over the treetops. Emma stood in its golden light, in the first faint breath of a cool breeze, with her hands braced against the small of her back and the sweat running down between her shoulders. Evening was the only time she could bear to move, yet she was obliged to do a woman's work in the stifling heat of day. There was still so much left undone, so many preparations to be made, and the child was eager to be born.

Inside the cabin was Emma's domain. Outside, the furrows of the field belonged to Joseph. The season of first harvest was only weeks away, but between the brutality of late-summer heat and Joseph's neglect, the crops were weedy and thin. He and his friends had reaped bushels of paper, sheaves of pages. But God alone could say when Martin Harris would find a printer, and even then, a book was a fragile thing on which to hang a family's hopes. And so Emma convinced Joseph to write to his father, and beg him to send one of the boys to Harmony, to manage the first harvest and the second sowing.

Emma had expected Samuel or William—they were both strong boys, robust, with Joseph's towering frame and broad shoulders. But it was young Don Carlos who arrived that night, riding the bog-spavined sorrel from the Smith farm, whistling as he came down the path beside the barley field, backlit by a heavy orange moon. He had grown since Emma had seen him last. His legs hung down past the horse's belly and the cuffs of his trousers rode up to expose the dirty skin of his ankles, the sharpness of his shins. His hair was longer, untrimmed, falling across his eyes. There was a new angle to his jaw, a melting away of boyish softness, a slow emergence of the aquiline features that were the hallmarks of his clan. But though Don Carlos had grown, still he seemed too small and thin to handle a proper man's work.

Emma rolled her tense shoulders. Her calico dress was damp with sweat. The baby dragged, a constant weight, a ceaseless demand. She

went out to catch the horse's rein. Don Carlos stopped his whistling
when he saw her step into the lane.

"Sister Emma."

"How good to see you again, little brother."

"My pa sent me down to do the harvesting."

"We'll be grateful for your help. Any help you can give."

Don Carlos glanced past her to the cabin. The window was ruddy like
the moon, a square of candlelight. Emma could hear Joseph's voice rising and falling, reading out the translation of his History of the Moundbuilders.

"The house is small," she said, "but we've a good, comfortable cot for
you, and I'll feed you three square meals a day."

"That's plenty for me. Sam and Will eat so much I can scarce get a
crust to myself."

"I'll feed you up properly, and before you know it, you'll have out-
grown your brothers. You'll be able to throw any one of them in a
wrestling match. Won't that make a fine surprise at next year's harvest
festival? Are you partial to apricot jam? I've a good pot inside, and fresh
bread to spread it on. Get down from that horse; you must be hungry
after such a long ride."

Don Carlos took readily to the work Joseph had neglected. Emma
couldn't help but admire the boy's industry. The farm called to him—
the private seclusion of the Hale land, blue forest shadows circling the
fields like a castle wall. From morning till dusk, the boy bent his strong,
wiry back over furrow and plow, picking stones from the soil, plucking
beetles from the leaves. He was restless at midday when Emma brought
his meals. He paused long enough to bolt down bread and cheese right
there in a row of oats or among the withering potato vines. When she
brought water in the old clay jug, he scolded her for carrying such a
heavy burden, and the dipper spilled water down his chin. Though
nights found Don Carlos weary and ravenous for his supper, he seemed
to resent his bed.

She thought, *Here is a Smith the Lord fitted for a farmer's life.* She longed
to join the boy out there in the fields, if only she had the energy for
the work. Now seemed the time to revel in the subtle miracles of the
season—the ripening of grain in its husk, each seed already fat with a
new plant yet to emerge. The cabin had become cramped, intolerable,

filled as it was by Joseph and his friends. Fresh air would have done her a world of good, and most of all, the gentle world outside the cabin—wind sighing over the barley, the deep, low hum of the river beyond the trees. But the child had drained her pluck. She could only watch Don Carlos while she rested on a bench in the meager shade, sewing dresses for the baby.

In the evenings, Don Carlos proved good company. Emma found she could lure him in from the fields with strawberry preserves, or with the apricot jam he favored. As long as Emma had something sweet to offer, the boy would linger on the bench beside her, talking while Joseph remained closeted with his scribes.

And what did they speak of in those gentle moments—on evenings that felt stolen from the world? The crops, the birds calling in the forest, the rusted old tin can that Don Carlos had half-filled with beetles today. They spoke of Isaac and the bears he hunted; the adventure stories Isaac had told Emma when she'd been a little girl. They spoke of the baby to come, whether it would be a boy or a girl, and what its name ought to be. Horse races, dances at the Harmony Hall, the sounds that carried by night, shouts from the revival tents in the hidden dells. They spoke of anything but the Smiths, anything but Joseph and his plates.

"All my brothers grew up and moved away while I was still a girl," Emma told him, "but God has given me a brother in you."

One morning when she rose early to fix Don Carlos's breakfast, she sensed a new heaviness to her body, a tension of waiting. It was a feeling both poised and resigned, settling deep into the self—flesh, bone, and spirit. She had three weeks at most, and the baby would come.

Since that change, she never allowed herself a moment of idleness. Emma sewed while talking to Don Carlos, so the baby would have all the dresses and blankets it needed. Joseph had hung a curtain across the cabin, partitioning the bed from the hearth, for he thought it improper that his scribes should be too near Emma in her obvious state, improper for them to notice her body as she lumbered from stove to table.

On an afternoon bright with glare, she propped the cabin door open even though the flies were thick—for the heat was a worse torment, sending sweat down her back where she couldn't reach to wipe it away. She worked in silence over a pot of strawberry preserves, staring down over the vast swell of her body, over the spattered apron stretched across her girth. She listened to the talk behind the curtain.

"Miraculous. Miraculous. The world has never seen such a thing as this. A revelation granted in our time, handed down from the Lord Himself right before my eyes." Martin Harris again. Emma liked him less than she ever had before. Recently his zeal had begun inflaming Joseph in ways Emma couldn't understand. After a day spent with that man, Joseph was quiet, distant—and sometimes after Martin had gone, he went walking alone in the dusk, down beside the river, and stayed away for hours—well past midnight.

Whatever reply Joseph made never reached her ears. The humming of the flies was too close.

"I will have the money," Martin said. "Never fear on that count."

"I can't help but fear," Joseph answered. "The months are slipping by, my friend. If we're to do this great work—save precious souls before the hour of Judgment—then the book must be printed in all haste."

"The manuscript isn't finished yet. You said yourself—"

"All too soon, it will be finished. We're nearing the end. God has told me as much, when I've consulted Him in prayer. You said you could pay the printer's fee, but if you can't, well—"

"I can, Joseph, I can! It's only my wife who holds me back."

Emma let her wooden spoon rest in the pot. She wiped the sweat from her brow.

"Dolly," Martin said, "is most fearfully set against the idea. She thinks this History a foolish endeavor."

"You're the man of the house. It's your money, not Dolly's. It's for you to decide when and how your money is spent."

"Right you are, of course. But—er—Joseph, you and your dear Emma have been married not quite two years. Matters change over time, over the course of a life and a marriage. You'll see what I mean as you grow older."

Joseph's reply was lost again to the flies.

"I know my Dolly will be in agreement if she can read this book for herself. Once she hears the words—once she sees them on the page and feels their power—she will no longer trouble us. In fact, she will be eager to help."

The curtain moved. Martin and Joseph stepped out together, side by side. Emma grappled for her spoon, missed, caught the handle of the pot instead. She flinched away from the pain and put her fingers in her mouth.

"Only a few pages," Martin said. "I needn't take them all. If Dolly could but read the first chapter—"

"Perhaps," Joseph said slowly.

"Nothing better to convince my Dolly than her own two eyes."

"Better still," Joseph said, "for a man to be a man and tell his wife 'This is what I will do.' Didn't God Himself say that the husband is the head of the wife?"

"Why, of course," Martin said, "yet I think even God never reckoned with a woman like Dolly. Nevertheless, I know how to bring her around. I haven't been married to her all these years for nothing. The first chapter or two—that's all I need. Then we'll have Dolly's complete agreement, and the printing will proceed with haste."

Only a fool would trust months of work to Martin Harris. Emma took her burned fingers from her mouth. "Mr. Harris, my good man, Joseph and I are grateful for the aid you've given. This History isn't much, as it is now—only some handwritten papers. Yet the History is the only thing of value Joseph possesses. You know I'm to have a child any day now. Surely you understand why we're so reluctant that even a few pages should leave this cabin."

Joseph cut her a swift, strained look, half gratitude, half caution. He couldn't deny Martin's request. If he lost that man's support, there was no hope the book would be printed—and not one penny would appear to feed and clothe their baby.

"The first chapter," Joseph finally said. "You may take the first chapter home with you, but those pages only. Let's pray it'll be enough to bring Dolly around."

Joseph watched, dazed and silent, as Martin separated the first chapter from the stack of pages and wrapped it in a large cotton kerchief. Then he was off, all but skipping down the lane.

"A fine mess you've made of things," Emma said as soon as Joseph had turned away from the door.

"I've hardly made a mess."

"Oh, haven't you? I call this folly, Joseph Smith."

"Martin means us no ill. He's a bit strange, but he's good-hearted, and he believes in the History like no one else."

Like no one else. Not even you, Joseph. "And you've entangled yourself with all of Martin's wild beliefs. You've left the fields to ruin for the sake of this book. You've hung all our hopes on a gamble—Martin Harris and his money. He holds your future in his hands now. Your future, and mine, and our baby's."

"Emma, don't you see? I've got him exactly where I want him. All this talk of Judgment Day and saving souls—he's eating from my hand like a tame pony."

"It's dangerous to use a man's faith against him. Men do terrible things for the sake of God."

"A just God would never require His followers to do terrible things."

"Is that what you think?"

The preserves were burning. She turned back to the pot, scraping furiously with her spoon. It was all she could do not to curse aloud.

"You're fretting over nothing." He reached around her from behind, an embrace meant to be comforting. But the heat and the pain in her head made his touch unbearable. Emma shrugged him off.

"Martin is a loyal friend," Joseph said. "He knows his wife best, after all."

"Martin is a fool, and you know it. His folly is what you like best about him."

"He'll bring the pages back home, safe and sound. You'll see."

She stepped back so Joseph couldn't try to hold her again. She wanted nothing of him just then—his oppressive nearness, the strength of his grip. She wondered about Dolly Harris, a woman she had never met but whom village gossip painted in her head. In imagination, Dolly loomed like a temple spire, bigger than any man, casting a hard and certain shadow. She must be a woman of uncommon mettle, to speak so boldly against her husband. But then, if Emma were married to Martin Harris, she would find no difficulty speaking against him, either.

Then she could say to her husband without fear, *I don't believe a word of this book. Prove to me it's true. Prove it's really from God. Show me the evidence, if you can.*

She was carrying water to Don Carlos in the field when it happened. A lurch inside her, the drag of gravity, something hot and wet rushing down. Dumbfounded, she stopped and stared at the furrow below her feet. There were grains of barley lying on the earth. They shone from the wetness, a dark wetness. Dark-brown water. She remembered the birds she used to feed, rushing in around her feet to snap up the barley— the urgency of the hens, their aggression. That was blood down there, soaking into soil. She had never borne a child before, but all the same, she knew something had gone terribly wrong. Shock pulled the jug from her arms. It shattered among the stubble of the harvest, and clear water flooded away the stain. Emma screamed.

By the time Don Carlos reached her, the pains had begun. He turned Emma toward the cabin; he shouted for Joseph, for Emma's mother, who was thirteen acres away. Grief was already shouldering in where joy should have been. Don Carlos could feel it, too. He sobbed and tried to hide it. He urged her to hurry. He pressed his cheek against hers and said "My poor sister Emma" between his cries for help.

Joseph spilled out of the cabin with Oliver Cowdery behind him, one of his loyal scribes. At a word from Joseph, Oliver went sprinting to the corral for his horse, and Joseph came to take his brother's place.

"Run over to Hale House," Joseph said. "Fetch Emma's mother."

Don Carlos was off like a hare between the rows.

Emma's mother was beside her in minutes, pressing a cool cloth against her forehead, driving Joseph from the cabin. An hour later, the midwife came from Harmony, summoned by Oliver Cowdery, and Emma was made to tell it all again, how she had seen the waters black with blood. She couldn't understand how she spoke so easily, as if it were all very simple—but surely this couldn't be reality, plain and naked as it was. She saw the grief and fear in her mother's eyes. The midwife set her jaw and rolled up her sleeves.

Emma labored through the day, into the night. She went on striving past the next sunrise.

When the baby came, with one last scream of despair from Emma, she fell back on her bed, shaking with anger and relief. Her mother wept, offering thanks to God for sparing Emma, at least. Weak and defeated, the baby choked out one ragged cry. He lay an hour at Emma's breast, but he had no strength to suck. In the oppressive brown shadows of the cabin, he seemed to fade to near transparency. The too-pale pink of his wrinkled skin dimmed to white. His small, thin body went slack. His hair was golden like his father's. His lashes like filaments of bronze rested on his cheeks. His eyes never opened.

When she realized her son was dead, Emma struggled to sit up. Her torn body protested with a flash of fire. She held the motionless baby out to her mother, mouth open in a silent question, but her mother said nothing. What words exist for this? She pushed the little body back against Emma's chest. The baby was heavier than it should have been, pulling toward the earth as if it saw itself already buried.

Don Carlos was found and sent out to locate Joseph wherever he may have been. Joseph, Don Carlos learned, had spent that morning and the previous night down on the bank of the river. He had intended to sleep at Hale House, but sleep had evaded him, so he'd passed the cruel dark hours in the forest and down beside the river. Between Emma's desperate cries, he had skipped stones across a moonlit pool.

Joseph came into the cabin with his head hung low. He dragged a stool close to the bed and sat there in silence, holding Emma's hand. He smelled of damp earth, of green shadows under the trees. Her hand was motionless and cold, and after a time he let it go and took his son in his arms. He cried then, rocking the small body. Emma saw a shattering in his eyes, a slow breaking apart, and she understood there was more news to come, more than the loss of their child, as if this tragedy weren't enough to satisfy a hungry God.

"What is it?" Weak and hoarse as she was, her voice hardly carried to Joseph's ear.

"We have been deceived."

Joseph told how he had learned the news. Martin Harris had come to him, shame-faced, that very morning while Emma had been trapped in a sphere of pain. Martin had confessed how his wife had wrestled the first chapter of the History from his hands. She had thrown the pages on the fire.

"Burned," Joseph said. "Burned up and gone."

So they would lose the money now, too—and with it, all hope for survival. Emma would be reduced to a beggar. This double blow was surely a punishment from on high. She didn't know whether God had struck over Joseph's hubris, or for Emma's own sins.

And what were her sins? Pinned in place by agony, hollowed out by grief, she could do nothing then but enumerate them all. She had lusted after Joseph when they first had met, that November morning in the yard of Hale House. She had defied her father, marrying against his will. Perhaps the greatest sin of all had been her doubt—questioning Joseph and the origin of his book, questioning its very existence.

She took the dead child back and kissed its cool cheek. Cynicism and her relentless questions had brought this chastisement from the Lord. This was Emma's fault; all of it. She must believe it was her fault, or else her baby's death would serve no purpose, and God would be a senseless thing. She must believe. She must fear. She must wonder what else the Lord would take away unless she made herself a pattern of Christian virtue.

IV

The Thunder of Heaven, and the Fierce and Vivid Lightning

1829–1830

April. Locked in a dreary fog, the days wet and dark with cloud. The previous autumn, Martin Harris had given Emma a few coins with which to make a garden, hoping that it would bring her some small joy. She had planted jonquils at the cabin door, and now they'd come up. Day after day the flowers turned their yellow heads, searching for the light.

Emma bent over the jonquils with her kitchen knife, cutting a bouquet for the baby's grave. Joseph had fashioned a small box of pinewood, not unlike the chest in which he kept the golden plates. They had named their son Alvin and laid him to rest in a cold bed under the apple tree.

And then, scarcely a week later, Joseph had bounced back from the tragedy with his characteristic energy. He'd insisted they still had both Martin Harris and his money. He had prayed beside the river and a solution had come: he would tell Martin that God would allow him to retranslate the chapter burned in Dolly's stove, but the work would take time—and more funding. Mortified at the part he'd played in the destruction of a sacred text, Martin was all too eager to give Joseph money—for feeding Emma and Don Carlos through the winter, for new clothes, for a good horse—for anything Joseph desired.

Joseph and his scribes had worked through the ragged remnant of summer, then through autumn's chill. Winter had arrived in gusts of pale gray, and then the scribes had worked by candlelight, huddled close to Emma's hearth. By the end of winter they'd restored the lost chapter of the History of the Moundbuilders and had written the book's ending, too. The manuscript had grown fat while Emma's belly remained intractably empty. God hadn't graced her with another chance. Perhaps she had lost that hope forever. But no more ill luck had befallen the Smiths since Emma had willed herself to believe—to accept without question her husband's work, however improbable it may seem. She may have longed for a child, may have craved the blessings of motherhood more desperately than the desert wanted rain. But now she was resigned to contentment, to perfect obedience.

In March of 1830, with Martin's money and Dolly's spite, the History of the Moundbuilders was printed at last. Emma held the tight, black-bound volume in her hands. She traced with one finger the bossed leather cover, the gold-leafed words, the final title Joseph had chosen—or the Lord had chosen, depending on whom you believed. *The Book of Mormon.* She held the book while she watched Don Carlos growing out there in the fields, sheltered by the sanctuary of honest work. She held the book beside her child's grave. It felt like a Bible in her hands, and the few times she'd opened it to leaf through its whispering pages, it had sung like the Bible in her heart.

"My brother Hyrum is coming for a visit," Joseph told her. "He's bringing Jerusha."

She straightened with her bouquet. "Where will they sleep?"

"I'd thought to put them up at your mother's house, in one of her boarding rooms."

"How will we pay the fee?" She would never ask her mother to board anyone on good graces alone—especially not Hyrum Smith.

"Martin will pay, of course."

Hyrum and Jerusha arrived in a cart some three days later. Don Carlos came in from the field and stood beside Emma, who stood beside Joseph, who waited for Hyrum to speak first.

"It's been too long, Joe," Hyrum boomed.

Joseph stepped forward to shake his brother's hand. Together they helped Jerusha climb from the cart, then Hyrum turned his attention to Don Carlos. "What a fine fellow you're growing up to be."

Don Carlos said nothing. He didn't even smile.

Jerusha hadn't changed, unless it was to sink further into herself. Her eyes were wider, more staring than Emma had remembered, her cheeks hollow as broken eggshells. Emma kissed her hair, which had dulled like aging wood.

"Look at this," Hyrum said eagerly. "Look what we've brought you from New York." He went to the back of the cart where their travel trunk was strapped, opened the lid, and retrieved a stack of newspapers. "Not only from New York, I admit. We picked up papers along the road, too, in Pennsylvania, in every township we passed."

He handed the stack to Joseph. Emma read the headlines over Joseph's shoulder as he leafed through the papers.

FRAUDULENT "BIBLE" PRINTED IN PENNSYLVANIA.

BOOK OF MORMON IS OUTRIGHT CHICANERY.

TREASURE DIGGER JOSEPH SMITH JR. A BLASPHEMER.

WRITER OF SO-CALLED "BOOK OF MORMON" A KNOWN LIAR.

Worst of all was the final headline: *Joseph Smith, the Antichrist.*

"Merciful Heaven protect us," she whispered.

Joseph all but capered with delight, rapping his knuckles against the papers. "Now word of my book will spread, all right—and quickly, too."

"This isn't the kind of word one wants spreading," Emma said. How had the people of Harmony found out about Joseph's book? She wondered only for a heartbeat. Then the answer came to her. *Martin Harris. Of course.* From Harmony, rumors had raced down the road to other villages. She could feel her face burning. Never had she imagined that she might be at the center of some infamous tale. "You must do something to set the record straight, Joseph."

"Goodness, why?"

"They called you the Antichrist!"

"Let the papers call me anything they please. It'll pique a fellow's curiosity." He threw an arm around Hyrum's shoulders. "That's all we need—for folks to feel curious enough that they'll buy the book. Once they read it for themselves, they'll see it's true enough."

True enough, Emma thought, *which is not, strictly speaking, the same thing as true.*

Hyrum and Jerusha were to stay for two days. The first thing Jerusha did—once the men had gone off to the riverbank to talk over the book— was to gather flowers from the side of the lane. She took them to the grave under the apple tree and laid them at the foot of the tiny wooden cross, beside Emma's jonquils. "I'm sorry," she murmured.

Later, the family rode together into town. At first Emma was eager for the trip, happy to regain some of the old friendship she had enjoyed with Jerusha. But in Harmony, the people spat into their path. They made the sign of the cross, as if to ward away evil, or crossed their fingers, drawing hexes in the air. "Mormonites," someone shouted. The people in the street took up the cry as a mocking chant. The jeering crowd blocked the road. Hyrum stopped his cart.

A man shook his fist up at Joseph. "Antichrist!"

"Sir," Joseph said with quiet dignity, "I forgive your slander against me. I will pray for your soul."

Hyrum turned the cart. There was no getting through. On the drive back to Hale House, Joseph held Emma's hand, murmuring in her ear: This persecution was a sign that they were doing God's work, a sign that the Book of Mormon was true. She would see. Word would spread, and followers would come—men and women wise enough to know the truth when they saw it.

They did come. Two nights later, after Hyrum and Jerusha had departed under dark of night (for they feared Harmony's scorn), Martin Harris came to call with a lantern in his hand and new friends in his wake. Emma couldn't imagine where the man had found them. The strangers gathered on stools and benches around the hearth. With burning eyes and tight voices, they discussed Joseph's book—they had all read it—and some discreetly left donations on the table. Their contributions amounted to little more than a handful of coins, but every penny was a boon just then. Even pennies were precious now that Joseph and Emma had been shunned from proper society.

Week after week, rumors of the Book of Mormon spread, and the visitors increased in number. Discussions at the hearth grew more solemn in tone, until Emma felt as if she were sitting in congregation. How odd to see her husband, who after all was no more than a farmhand, leading a flock like a shepherd of the hills. But didn't God call the humble to His service? In the valleys of Pennsylvania and the fields of New York, true religion still lived. In the thundering voice of the Leatherwood God, the people had heard His words. They had seen His presence in the fluent recitations of the Universal Publick Friend, and in the shouts of the Shakers, in the hundred new religions that sprang from fertile soil. No one doubted that shepherds walked among the sheep—not in the place they called Burned Over.

In Harmony and other towns, the people still jeered and called Joseph's followers Mormonites.

When he heard that news, Joseph took the mocking label and bestowed it with pride upon his flock. If the world would call them Mormonites, then Mormonites they would be, and the congregation laughed with joy because it's good to have a name, it's good to know who you are. They were Mormonites, and then they were Mormons, and laughter was music to them all.

At dawn on a bright spring day, Emma followed her husband through the forest to the banks of a stream. Hyrum and the rest of the Smiths had come again from New York, and the night before Joseph and his brothers had dammed up the stream with stones. A train of Mormons walked in his wake—the true believers, those men who had sat beside Emma's fire, their wives, their children. They were forty in all, each silent with anticipation. An air of holiness pervaded the party and made even the forest seem reverent. The birds were a choir in the pines.

But when the congregation arrived at the stream, they found their dam unmade. The baptismal pool was gone. The stream ran shallow and fast between its banks, and the shore was trampled and pocked by countless bootprints, evidence of a mob.

"What's all this," Hyrum said.

Joseph turned to his followers. His countenance was gentle. The morning light coming down through the treetops seemed to fall on him alone, as if the sun itself were drawn to his presence. "Fear not. Those who wish us ill came by night and did their mischief. They don't dare move against us by day, for they are ashamed, and rightly fearful of God's judgment."

The congregation muttered. One of the women sniffed, dabbing her eyes with a kerchief.

Joseph threw his arms wide. "But they can't undo the Lord's work. Don't you see, my friends? This is only a sign that what we do is righteous and good, a sign our faith is true. Our enemies mock us in the streets of Harmony and spit on the ground where we walk. Why? Because Satan tells them to do it. He whispers in their ears. Satan would see God's truest work undone. He inspires men to raise their hands against all that is holy. But I say unto you, God is more powerful than the Devil. The Lord will make His true church live on this earth again. The time has come to restore what was lost. Let the Devil try to shake our faith. Let him vex us and torment us however he will. We'll show him, that Satan, the great deceiver! The faith of God's people can't be broken so easily!"

His followers cheered. They reached out their hands for Joseph. Their feet sank into the mud and stamped out the prints of the evildoers who had come in the night.

The boys waded back into the stream, shouting and laughing at the shock of cold. In minutes the stones had been retrieved, the dam rebuilt. The pool filled with violet water. The congregation stood in silence, pressed shoulder to shoulder in the early chill, watching the water rise until it was deep enough to immerse a body. Then Joseph bent his head. He raised his hands above the pool. Emma saw his hands in silhouette against the sun, the light flowing between his fingers, straight beams golden and sharp.

When he had blessed the water in the name of Christ, Joseph removed his simple wool shirt and passed it to Hyrum. He slipped his feet from his boots, took off his stockings, and splashed into the baptismal pool despite the cold. He didn't look back at his followers assembled on the bank. He only stretched one hand toward them, the hand a question: *Who will be first?*

Emma stepped forward to take that hand. She surprised herself, for it wasn't eagerness that moved her. But she didn't like that anyone might whisper, *Joseph's own wife hung back.* If this new church was to hold together—if Joseph's future was to be secure—then Emma must give every appearance of faith.

Water came up over her boot tops, cold gnawed her ankles. Her skirt dragged with the weight of sodden wool. The water was little deeper than her knees, but it was icy, and she dreaded the immersion to come. Joseph took one of her wrists and held it hard as if to restrain her, as if she might strike him. His other hand snaked to the back of her neck. Her mind reeled; the light spilled down from the canopy, blinding and harsh.

Between his hand on her nape and his grip on her arm, she couldn't move, couldn't shrink away.

"Emma Hale Smith," Joseph intoned, "I baptize thee in the name of the Father and the Son and the Holy Spirit, amen."

Then he thrust her back, pushed her down. The water closed forcefully overhead. Cold flayed her skin, cutting so deeply it seemed to reach everywhere at once, into her very spirit. She opened her mouth in surprise, but thank God, she didn't gasp and suck the baptismal water into her lungs. She tasted earth—bitterness stirred up by the feet of the men who had come by night to unmake what Joseph and God had made.

He pulled Emma up, back to the surface and the light. She coughed, fighting for breath, face hot with the terrible excitement of the moment. She broke away from her husband, pulling her thick, clinging skirts through the water, striving for the safety of the shore. There was a roaring sound around her feet as she thrashed her way to the bank. There she stood alone, holding herself tightly, shivering while the others went into the water, one by one.

When the last of the disciples had been immersed, the congregation made its way back along the trail. They wrapped their arms around their bodies and walked close together, singing in chorus to distract themselves from the vicious cold. But before they reached the shelter of Emma's cabin, shouts rang through the forest, loud enough to drown out their hymn.

"There they are," someone called. "I can see them, the whole damned lot—the blasphemers!"

A crowd emerged, so numerous they couldn't keep to the trail. They must have numbered near a hundred. There was no chance Emma's parents hadn't seen that mob coming up the road. And no chance, Emma realized now, that Isaac hadn't read the stories in the newspapers. She had avoided her parents since the printing of the book, certain they would scorn her or pester her over her husband's reckless endeavor. Now she understood that avoidance had been a grave mistake. Isaac must be bitter over the spectacle Joseph had made. It could only have been Isaac who'd told the crowd where to find Joseph Smith and his Mormons. Her throat tightened at the betrayal.

"Wet as half-drowned rats," one of the townsmen said.

"And fit to catch their deaths," said another. "But who'll mourn for a few dead blasphemers?"

Emma hurried to Joseph's side. "You must do something."

He looked at her. Just that, his brows pinched together, an expression of mild confusion or disbelief, as if he couldn't countenance that God would allow such a thing to happen.

"They've threatened us," Emma said, louder, urgently.

The men from Harmony—some women, too—shook their fists and hurled insults. Shrinking against the wet bodies around her, Emma found she couldn't count them all. They seemed to multiply—a hundred, a thousand. Their teeth and eyes flashed like the teeth of barking dogs. Children shivered, clinging to their mothers' wet skirts. Some began to cry.

"Don't be frightened," Emma said to the little children. But she was frightened herself. And heartsick, scoured to her bones by Isaac's part in this. "Let's have a song," she said. "Come, sing with me."

She groped for a hymn, even a simple nursery song—anything to brace herself up and stop the little ones from crying. "Soldiers of Christ, arise," she sang, "and put your armor on."

The others soon took up the music; even Joseph sang. He seemed incapable of doing anything else, too stunned to speak out against his tormentors.

The mob from Harmony didn't disperse, but they quieted somewhat and glanced at one another. A few turned away, gazing off into the forest, unwilling to look at the Mormons they'd come to vex—the small, huddled church still dripping from their baptismal rites.

The song swelled as the Mormons found their confidence. Emma's bitterness hadn't abated, but a fragile pride had risen up to stand alongside dismay.

The men from Harmony parted. Two figures advanced through bands of light and shadow: men wearing the double-breasted frock coats and high, round hats of the police.

The song died on Emma's tongue. One by one, the Mormons fell silent.

"Police?" Emma said. "You've brought the law into this? What cowards you are, the whole lot of you!"

"We won't see Harmony degraded," someone shouted. "This folly with your Book of Mormon has made a mockery of us all."

Hyrum said, "Do you send the police chasing after every circuit preacher who rolls through your village?"

"Not so long as they preach true religion," someone answered.

The police pushed through the last of the crowd. One smiled at the sight of the bedraggled flock. He covered his mouth, struggling to master his amusement.

"You're Joseph Smith Junior, are you not?" said the other.

"I am."

The police stepped forward, seized Joseph by both arms.

"Wait," Emma cried.

He restrained her with a look.

"You are arrested as a blasphemer," the first policeman said.

Emma rounded on him. "Did Isaac Hale send you?"

He ignored her question. "You will stand before a judge, as is your right, but until then, you will stay as our guest in the Harmony jail."

The mob cheered. They bared their teeth.

A new fear ran through her, a terror she didn't understand. Joseph in a jail cell—Joseph caged. The very idea seemed momentous and final, as if fate itself had made a fist and was already swinging its arm. It was too late now to dodge the blow. She threw herself at Joseph; she clung to him. "But we're to be confirmed," she protested. "He hasn't confirmed us yet. Please, you must allow him to bless us and seal us to our faith!" She feared what might happen if that thread was left to hang. Every girl who had grown up with hexes and hedge magic knew a rite must be carried through to its end. What evils might come in if the circle wasn't closed?

There was no fear in Joseph's eyes. There was, in fact, a light of amusement. "Wait for me at home, Emma. I won't be long."

He would be long. He would end in jail. She knew it, and the knowing sickened her, how heavily it sat in her stomach, how thickly it hung in the air.

Before she could protest again, Joseph nodded to his captors. He went willingly, walking tall and proud between them, and the jeering mob followed, leaving the rest of the Mormons alone. Emma stood with the shivering congregation. She watched until the mob and Joseph were lost to sight, until the forest closed around them. Only the sound of their laughter remained.

Joseph returned home that very night. He startled Emma—struck her to blind terror for one wild moment, for the scrape of the door opening was so unexpected that she leaped up from her rocking chair. The sock she'd been half-heartedly darning fell to the ground. She upset the candle, spilling hot wax across the tabletop. Only just in time did she snatch the candle up again, before the wax could catch alight and take the cabin with it.

Joseph laughed to see her fumbling. It was the sound of his laughter that brought her back to herself—a familiar, boyish chuckle.

"Land's sake," Emma scolded. "You frightened me."

Even in the dimness of night, she could see his radiance. He was beaming with victory.

"They've let you out already," she said.

"You seem surprised."

"I am. Those men in the forest—they held no affection for you. Not for any of us."

"Were you afraid, here by yourself?"

"Of course I was afraid. Don Carlos has gone back to New York with your family, and after the others put on dry clothing and returned to their homes, I couldn't help but know that I was one woman by herself, with only the forest around me."

"Why didn't you go across the field to your parents' home?"

Emma looked away.

"I preached from my window." Joseph stared as if he could see right through the walls of the cabin. "From the window of my jail cell. It was hardly wider than my hand, but I could speak through that gap, and so I did. The Lord sent me a sermon then and there, Emma, and I gave it out, exactly as He directed. And do you know, some fellows came and listened. I think they had it in their heads to mock me at first, but once they heard my words, they hung about in the yard below my window and listened. I think that's why they hurried me to the courtroom." A sheepish laugh. "I think the police were concerned that the crowd would grow, and they'd soon be clamoring for my release. Well, I stood before the judge to face my charges of blasphemy, but the judge declared me no more a blasphemer than any other prophet who plagues the land. And just like that, I was free. But I had no horse, and no one would drive me, so I was obliged to walk all the way home."

She went to Joseph, allowed him to hold her. He was warm and solid, not an apparition. Her terror of that jail cell, her stark certainty that Joseph would be taken from her forever—all had been for naught.

He took her by the shoulders, smiling. "Your confirmation—shall I give it to you now?"

Emma stepped back. For hours she'd sat alone in the cabin, with only her fears for company. When she hadn't fretted over Joseph in his cell, she had thought about the golden plates. She had never seen the holy treasure. And she had acted as Joseph's scribe, his first scribe, yet he had forbidden her to look upon the plates. Martin Harris, Oliver Cowdery, John Whitmer—Joseph had promised them all that they would one day see the plates with their own eyes. Why did he find those men worthy of witnessing such a miracle, but not his own wife?

The mob and the police had done their work and done it well. She hadn't been a member of Joseph's church for a full day, and already her faith was shaken. The circle had been left open. Chaos had come in.

He noted her hesitation, kissed her forehead. "It makes no difference, Emma dear. The Lord has something else for you—something better than a confirmation."

He led her to the chair beside the fire.

"Bow your head."

His hands came down gently on her crown. Joseph began to pray.

"Hearken unto the voice of the Lord your God, while I speak unto you, Emma Smith, my daughter."

Her heart expanded in her chest.

"A revelation I give unto you concerning my will, and if thou are faithful and walk in the paths of virtue before me, I will preserve thy life, and thou shalt receive an inheritance in Zion. Behold, thy sins are forgiven thee, and thou art an elect lady, whom I have called. Murmur not because of the things which thou hast not seen, for they are withheld from thee and from the world, which is wisdom in me in a time to come."

Her eyes opened. How had Joseph known of her doubts? A tremor wracked her body, and she didn't know whether it was awe or fear—couldn't have said where one ended and the other began. She only knew that these were the Lord's words, His true words, flowing through her husband—issued in Joseph's voice, but God's without question.

He sees my doubt. He knows I'm unworthy. How could she have fallen into doubt again, so soon after losing her child? What would she suffer now—how would the Lord chastise her?

"And the office of thy calling," Joseph said, "shall be for a comfort unto my servant, Joseph Smith Junior, thy husband, in his afflictions—with consoling words, in the spirit of meekness."

He prayed on, instructing Emma to go wherever he went, to scribe for him when the men could not. She bore the commands in trembling obedience. How quickly she had forgotten the promise she'd made while she'd rocked her dead son in her arms, that vow never to doubt again.

"And thou shalt be ordained under his hand to expound scriptures, and to exhort the church, according as it shall be given thee by my Spirit. For he shall lay his hands upon thee, and thou shalt receive the Holy Ghost, and thy time shall be given to writing, and to learning much. And it shall be given to thee, also, to make a selection of sacred hymns, which is pleasing unto me, to be had in my church. For my soul delighteth in the song of the heart; yea, the song of the righteous is a prayer unto me, and it shall be answered with a blessing upon their heads."

A hymnal. Emma would have shaken her head in wonder if his hands hadn't kept her still. *The Lord wishes me to compile a hymnal.*

"Wherefore, lift up thy heart and rejoice, and cleave unto the covenants which thou hast made. Continue in the spirit of meekness and beware of pride. Let thy soul delight in thy husband, and the glory which shall come upon him. Keep my commandments continually, and a crown of righteousness thou shalt receive. And except thou do this, where I am you cannot come. And verily, verily, I say unto you, that this is my voice unto all. Amen."

Joseph lifted his hands. She turned on the chair, staring up at him. She couldn't have spoken a word in that moment, not even if it had meant her life, for the feel of divinity pervaded the small room—a slow, insidious enchantment. Joseph himself was pale, so he seemed almost translucent, cupped by light, as when the first glow of morning falls on a marble statue. The sight of him astounded Emma. Peace was upon him, a radiant assurance. His eyes held her own, unblinking and serene.

The Lord had called her an elect lady. The King of Heaven Himself had said it. It sent a thrill deep into her heart, a quiet vibration akin to pride.

I mustn't be prideful. I must remain humble and meek in all things.

"Now," Joseph said, "will you accept the confirmation, Emma?"

She shook her head. For a long moment, while Joseph continued to look down at her, Emma didn't understand why she denied the confirmation—didn't realize, in fact, that she had denied it at all. But then her own peace and certainty came, a sure knowledge of what must be.

"I can't," she answered. "Not while I still hold such doubts in my heart."

"Can you truly doubt, after the Lord Himself has blessed you and charged you with a great work?" But he was beaming, so warmly affectionate that Emma couldn't help but return his smile.

"I am unworthy to enter my name on any church's roles," she said, "and will remain unworthy until true belief settles on me."

"And what must the Lord do, my darling, to have your belief?" He stroked her hair, ran his fingers through the long dark curls.

She didn't know how to answer. She couldn't say what feat or miracle would stir her frightened heart. She must tread carefully. If she angered God again—if she crossed Him . . . Well, she had seen already what the Lord could do when He was displeased. The small grave under the apple tree was only a few steps away.

"Belief is a wayward thing," she said. "It comes and goes with a will of its own. We cannot summon it, nor make it stay."

"Wise words. True words." He withdrew his hand. Already she missed his touch. Then he laid his palm gently against her cheek, both cradling her face and holding it still, so she couldn't look away. "But sooner or later, you must accept the confirmation. If you persist too long in this wavering, you risk being banished from Heaven forever."

The cold reached up for her, the cold and the dark from the chasm that always seemed to yawn at her feet, the pit of doubt that followed her like her own shadow. Emma shuddered. She knew Joseph felt it, the current of fear that wracked her body.

"You will have a sign," he said. "The Lord will send it. But the next time will be the last. If you turn away from God's true church again, Emma Smith, your soul will be damned forever."

The days advanced with inexorable slowness, a deliberate dragging of the hours. As she went about her work, Emma glanced over her shoulder, cautious as the crows in the field. Every moment she expected the promised sign, and yet none came. Or perhaps the threatened miracle had come and gone already, and she had been too careless to see it, absorbed in the small work of a country wife.

By night she lay unsleeping, rigid in her bed. With painful clarity, she recalled every mundane detail of the day that had gone before—the pop of an ember in the stove, the curl of a cloud in the sky—and wondered whether *that* had been the sign, or that, or the other. Had she missed the workings of the Lord, and so destroyed her only chance at salvation? She feared to sleep, for God might move around her in the darkness. The Lord worked by increments and degrees, with subtlety and a sly will to trap the unwary.

It was on a night like the others, a sleepless night, that Emma's sign came. She lay listening to Joseph's breathing, parsing the sound for messages from God. His breath, his dreams, were steady and confident, comfortably assured. In the tall grass outside, the crickets sang madly, delirious with the approach of summer. And she listened to the night, too—the buzzing of the insects, the calls of whippoorwills by the river—fretful she would miss the signal. Her soul was already damned.

It was because Emma lay so desperately alert that she heard the slap of running feet out on the lane. She rose, careful not to disturb Joseph's rest, and stumbled to the door. Outside, the sky was deepest blue, almost black between the stars, and the stars seemed very bright and close, as if they had stooped from the heavens to observe the little cabin beside the river. The barley field moved in a gentle wind, rippling in the starlight. She could still hear someone running.

Emma stared toward Hale House, but all was still. Then she turned and peered into the forest. Could it be an animal? From the east, from the track that cut through the woods to the farms in a neighboring valley, a small, pale form came hurtling down the lane. Only very slowly did she realize it was a child—a young boy, running as if the Devil were on his heels.

"Joseph," Emma said. She called for him again, louder, a rising note of panic.

He bolted upright in bed. "What's wrong?"

"Someone is coming. A boy, I think. Running over the ridge."

"At this hour?"

He joined her at the door, peering out with bleary eyes, scratching his chest through his nightshirt.

The boy stumbled into their yard and saw them in the doorway. He gave a wordless cry. The poor creature was breathless, far beyond his strength.

"Merciful Heaven!" Emma rushed out and caught the child as he stumbled and fell. He hung limp in her arms, heaving and sobbing.

Joseph was beside her now. He took the boy carefully, helped him stand on his feet, but the child quaked with exhaustion. "What has happened, son? A fire?"

The boy shook his head.

"He can't speak," Emma said. "Let him catch his breath."

She ran inside and fetched a cup of water from the kitchen pail. Joseph held the cup to the boy's lips. He drank, and some of his strength returned. He took the cup in his own hands, gulping down the water.

"Who are you, boy?" Joseph said.

"Aaron Knight." Wheezing and red-faced, he panted out his message. His father was having a fit. He didn't know what to do.

"Newel Knight is your father," Joseph said.

Aaron nodded. Fresh tears came to his eyes.

"I know Newel. Don't cry, young fellow. We'll set everything right."

He flashed a worried look as he lifted the boy in his arms. Emma followed him to the corral.

Aaron sniffled and wiped his eyes while Emma helped Joseph hitch their mule to the dogcart. The cart was scarcely large enough to run the simplest errands in town, but it was the only vehicle Joseph owned. Emma sat in the back with her arms around Aaron while Joseph drove, goading and cursing the mule into a rough trot. The poor boy wept against Emma's breast. Now that he was in friendly company, all his determination was replaced by terror, and he wailed and sobbed, certain his father was already dead.

"Be brave, little soldier." Emma stroked his fine, soft hair, longing with sudden force for her own child, Alvin, whose hair had been golden like this boy's. "Be brave. We'll help your papa; you'll see."

They reached the Knights' farm a few minutes later. Joseph leaped down from the driver's seat and lifted Aaron from the cart. Emma followed them into the house, close on her husband's heels.

Newel Knight had indeed taken a fit. Emma shrank from the sight—an otherwise sturdy man convulsed on the parlor floor, back painfully arched as if by some devilish power. His lips were pulled back from his teeth in an animal snarl; his face was a mask of terrifying vacancy. Newel thrashed and twitched, rolling in and out of a circle of candlelight, the only light in the room. Mrs. Knight was kneeling on the ground beside him, but she could do nothing but beg God to spare her husband. Emma could just make out the trembling forms of two little girls in a dim corner, clinging to one another, sobbing with their faces pressed against the wall.

Joseph stood helplessly over Newel. He was pale, obviously frightened by the unsettling fit, the demonic grin Newel wore while he shook and writhed, the emptiness of those wide, staring eyes.

"Joseph!" Emma shouted.

That seemed to break the spell. He knelt beside Mrs. Knight, and she looked at him, startled, mouth hanging open in despair.

"Now, Sally," Joseph said, "don't you fret. All will be well, by and by."

He reached into the pool of candlelight to lay his hands gingerly on Newel's head. He frowned at his own hands as if wondering what had possessed him, as if he thought himself every bit as afflicted as the man twisting on the rug.

"Joseph," Emma pleaded, "you must do something."

He drew a deep breath. The light flickered and danced; the circle around him constricted.

"Newel Knight," Joseph said, loudly, decisively, "in the name of the Father and the Son and the Holy Ghost, I command you to be well. Amen."

Newel's body fell still on the instant—so perfectly and thoroughly still that Emma pressed a hand to her mouth, certain he had died. There was no sound, save for the whimpering of the girls and Aaron sobbing against his mother's neck. Then Newel gasped—a great, tearing, shuddering breath. He moaned and rolled away from Joseph's hands.

"Newel! Thank God!" Sally released her son and crawled on hands and knees to her husband.

"Leave me be, Sally." Newel, when he spoke, was hoarse and weak. But he was speaking. The man had regained his faculties. He pushed himself up to all fours. A thread of saliva dangled from his lip; it glittered in the candlelight. Slowly, he sat back on his heels and wiped his face on a sleeve. Then he stared across the room at Joseph, who was still crouched on the rug with his hands outstretched. "By God, Joseph Smith. By God."

Joseph looked up from the parlor floor. Emma knew him well enough to read the startled disbelief in his eyes. He hadn't really thought his prayer would work. But it had. He had healed a man with a word and a touch.

When Sally and her children had been comforted and Newel was seated beside the kitchen fire, sipping watered ale to firm up his limbs, Emma and Joseph drove home together. They were both silent, sunk in their private wells of thought and revelation. Only when the mule had been returned to the corral and Joseph had opened the cabin door did Emma finally speak.

"Give me the blessing, Joseph. I'm ready now. I believe. Confirm me a member of your church."

When he laid his hands on her head, Joseph still trembled from his ordeal, shaken by the force of his power. But Emma was as solid as stone.

The light of early evening hangs dense over the branches of apples and plums. Between the trunks of the young trees, dust moves in lazy eddies; it sparkles in the declining sun. On another day, in an ordinary time, she would find the view of the orchard soothing. But that dust out there, the shining dust, has been kicked up by the feet of the governor's men, patrolling the streets of Nauvoo.

She stands at the library window, watching light stagnate between the trees. Joseph's letters are in the pocket of her dress. She can feel them as a great weight pulling her body down, a gravity of remorse. There is nothing in the letters to indicate that God has moved His terrible hand and taken Joseph away, taken him in a burst of gunfire or at the sharp end of some Carthage Gray's knife, by rope, by fall, by disease. But all the same she feels it, the ineluctable certainty of the Prophet's death.

This has always been the way with prophets. They die a martyr's death. Or else they are exposed in the end as charlatans, or at best, as good men led astray by Satan's enticements, who were themselves deceived. You die in glory or you live in shame.

She thinks, *Joseph planted this orchard when he still had hope for a future. And now he will never see the trees bear fruit.*

She is waiting, waiting in a passive light. For her heart to break or lighten—either would be preferable to this suspended state, the long pangs of silence. She is waiting for Porter Rockwell to return, though she hasn't the least idea how long it might take to ride to Carthage for news. Come to that, she doesn't know whether Porter was successful in slipping past Ford's men. They circle Nauvoo like a palisade. And if he got out of the city, he may not come back so easily. There is nothing to do but wait and watch and pray for Porter, and for Joseph, and for herself, if God is feeling generous.

Rustling in the hall. The sound of the girls retreating, quickly, as if startled—then the heavy tread of the governor's boots. She knows the sound of him already. He comes into the library without asking her leave. She doesn't turn from the window.

Ford sits in the green velvet armchair, which is Joseph's—which had been Joseph's. She hears the small click of a metal case opening or closing, the murmur of the women in the hall, just outside the library door. The girls haunt the place like ghosts—spirits cut loose by some sudden tragedy to drift, stunned and disconnected, from their bodies.

She says, "I hear you out there. Leave us, all of you. I'll come to you when there is news of the Prophet, and not before."

The women disperse. The hall is empty again, and silent. The emptiness expands to fill the library and then all of the Mansion, all of the town, Emma's heart.

When she turns away from the window, she sees that Ford has propped one ankle on his knee. His boots are dull with grime from the road. He has taken a cigar from a silver case and put it in his mouth, unlit. He toys with the case, turning it over and over, rotating it on his palm, as if in touching the thing he might find reason not to speak to Emma again. They watch one another in silence. Ford's expression is a study in neutrality. She sees no pity in his eyes, but no mercy, either, and certainly, no sympathy.

At length, he says, "Those ladies out there in the hall—the other wives. They leap to obey your orders."

She lifts her brows.

"Well trained, I suppose. Is that a part of it, this . . . practice you people hold? Training women like dogs?"

"It seems to me, Governor, that all women in every church, in every corner of the world, are trained like dogs. Are we so different in that regard?"

"But for a man to actually wed more than one woman—"

"Do you find adultery preferable to an honorable marriage?"

He laughs. He takes a match from his pocket and lights his cigar. The thick, too-sweet smell strikes her in the face. She has never abided tobacco smoke in her home, but she's in no position to do anything about the governor's habits now.

Ford says, "Is that the excuse you use to justify your bigamy—which is against the laws of the land, might I add? And do you call this lustful practice, this chasing after five women, ten women, a hundred for all I can tell—do you call that honorable?"

She won't answer. She can't entirely understand her own feelings about celestial marriage, the Restoration of All Things. She has never understood it—her rage, her despair, her envy. The deep trust of sisterhood, the love for the children who have Joseph's face but not her own—that shocking, instinctive, repulsive love.

"Have you nothing to say in defense of your peculiarities?" Smoke hangs around the governor's head. It half obscures his face, and she is glad of it.

"What can I say that you will believe?"

"Speak the truth, of course."

"What good will that do me now?" What good will it do her husband?

Ford waits. His foot wags in a lazy rhythm.

She says, "Our peculiarities, as you say, belong to us alone. Our practices are a matter between ourselves and God. We owe no explanation to any man."

"You owe an explanation if those peculiarities violate the law. You owe an explanation if that man is the governor of your state and is tasked with upholding the laws of Illinois and of the nation. All I ask, Mrs. Smith, is that you explain your customs to me so that I may understand. It may be that there is some statute or provision I can extend over your church. I may be able to protect you from legal action. I may save more of your men from prison, but only if I can understand."

"Is Joseph charged with bigamy, then?"

Ford's eyes go flat for a moment just before he answers. There is a stillness of regret as smoke rises past his face. In that moment, she knows Joseph is surely condemned, if he isn't dead already.

He says, "No, madam; there's no charge of bigamy against your husband—only the charge of assault against the First Amendment, for destroying the *Expositor*'s printing press. But I can't promise the rest of your men will be spared. You know how the papers enjoy reporting on your community."

"Rumors. Lies."

"Not all the reports have been false, it seems. And you Mormons have done little to endear yourselves to your neighbors. Bigamy charges may be forthcoming, now that the surrounding settlements feel they've gained the upper hand. But as I said, if you help me understand this . . . custom . . . there may be some provision in the law."

"The Restoration of All Things was a commandment from God. Ours is a living church. We receive divine commandments, and we obey."

"The Ten Commandments in the Holy Bible are sufficient for most men."

"We are preparing the way for Christ's return. These are the Latter Days, Governor. If a new world is unfolding, why should we not receive new laws?"

"And does it suit you, this edict that men should marry all the women they please? This commandment from God?" He flings those final words at her. There is no mistaking his derision.

"It matters very little what suits me and what doesn't." She has learned that much over the course of her marriage.

"I think it does matter." Ford takes the cigar from his mouth, leans toward her. "I think it troubles you rather a lot, Mrs. Smith."

"God matters to me. Doing righteous works in service to God—that is what concerns me."

"So this . . . restoration . . . suits you."

She holds her tongue.

"I don't believe you're telling me the truth, Mrs. Smith."

"Of course I am—a form of the truth."

Ford laughs and pulls again from his cigar. "A form of the truth? There's no such thing. There is truth and there are lies. There's nothing between."

"On the contrary. The world is painted in shades of gray."

"How so?"

"If enough people believe a thing to be true, and act as if it's true, then what is the difference between truth and lies? If a people reshape a city or a state or a nation—if we reshape the world, Governor, around our faith—then haven't we made our own truth, whether or not it agrees with yours?"

He sits back in the velvet chair, watching her with new respect. His brow is furrowed in contemplation.

She turns back to the window and the orchard beyond. A woman is there now, dressed in mourning black. Emma watches her, curious, lifted for the moment out of her present perplexities. She focuses on the woman and nothing more—the back turned to the Mansion; the slow, trembling way she moves between the young fruit trees. She walks without aim; she is lost, perhaps blinded by grief.

I am not lost, Emma tells herself—*nor am I blind. I never have been, not even when I tried my hardest to shut my eyes to the truth.*

The woman in the orchard presses hands to her face—weeping. She sinks to her knees out there among the eddies of dust, the glow of a warm summer evening. The grass is almost as high as her shoulders now; it half obscures her, and at the same time it frames her in her dark dress and shawl, so that she is stark and present as a revelation, as God's own hand.

The woman turns. Her face is contorted by misery. Eliza Snow. A sharp pain strikes Emma in the chest; she is gripped by a sudden longing to go out and put her arms around Eliza, help her to her feet, make her stand fast against the storm to come. But she doesn't love that woman, not anymore. She has decided she will never love Eliza again.

Eliza lowers her face. She finds something caught in the tall blades of grass, the grass already drying to pallid gold as the season advances. She takes the thing in her fingers, whatever she has spotted, and presses it to her lips. And now Emma can see that it's a small scrap of white fabric, and Eliza is kissing it, more avidly than Emma ever kissed her husband's hand or lips.

She turns to Ford again. She says, "It's your turn now. Tell me something true."

He waits. He nods.

"Is my husband alive or dead?"

Ford keeps his silence. He breathes out, and the smoke veils his face so Emma cannot see.

V

The Things You Have Not Seen

1830–1831

Emma bent to retrieve a crate full of clothing from the floor, but Sally Knight stopped her with a hand on her shoulder. "You mustn't strain over anything, dear. Not in your condition. Let me carry that box for you."

"My condition? However did you know? I've not told Joseph yet, never mind anyone else."

Sally patted Emma's cheek—a gesture Emma would have found condescending in another woman, for Sally wasn't five years older than she, but that soft, maternal warmth was merely her nature. She was the most comfortable, motherly creature God had ever made, and in the months since Joseph had healed her husband of his mysterious affliction, she had grown as close to Emma as a sister. "I've birthed seven children and have three living," Sally said. "One knows the signs." Then, noting Emma's baffled expression, she laughed. "Your bosom, dear. It does swell when a baby is on its way."

Sally set the crate on the table and paused beside the window. The early summer's day was bright and cloudless. She stood in a shaft of golden light, vivid against the blankness of the cleaned-out cabin, all the colors of her calico gay as a garden in bloom. She was the only live thing in a place emptied of life, and looking at her, Emma felt a pang of loss. She hadn't known how dearly she had missed a woman's company until she'd found it again. And now she and Sally must part. She stood beside her friend, heart aching even in the blessed summer warmth—the magnified heat of the sun through the glass, the heat like a hand on her chest, her eyelids.

Outside, Newel Knight and little Aaron were helping Joseph pack crates and carpet bags into the back of a borrowed wagon. David Whitmer, one of Joseph's scribes, had brought the wagon down from Fayette.

"How has your husband fared?" Emma said.

"Healthy as can be. We've seen no sign of a fit since Joseph blessed him. He's up to the work on the farm; hasn't even considered hiring a boy to help him this summer, and won't, I think, till harvesttime." She turned to Emma with a sober expression. "I never saw a miracle like the one I witnessed that night. I haven't stopped thinking about it, all these months." Sally and Newel, along with their three children, had joined Joseph's church as soon as Newel had recovered enough to withstand the cold of baptism. You don't witness a miracle, do you, and simply let it pass?

"What a shame to leave you now," Emma said, "when we've just come to know one another."

"We won't be separated long. Newel intends to sell the farm after the harvest. Then we'll come and join you."

"In Fayette?"

"Wherever you may be. After what happened that night, Newel thinks it best to remain close to the Prophet, and I agree."

The Prophet. Members of the new church had begun calling Joseph by that name—hesitantly at first, trying out the new title with care, half afraid the Lord might disapprove and send down a bolt from Heaven. Now they all but shouted Prophet from the rooftops of Harmony. Emma found herself unable to use the title. Joseph was her husband, first and above all. And she was Emma Smith, the same woman she had always been, not Sarah from the Bible, no prophet's wife.

"There are two riders coming," Sally said. "Look—do you see?"

They went out to greet the newcomers. Oliver Cowdery, mounted on his showy piebald, and Hiram Page came trotting into the trampled yard. Oliver was of an age with Joseph, as fine-looking a man as Harmony had ever seen. He had broken hearts throughout the valley, for he never made time for dances or fairs, nor any gathering where he might enjoy the company of marriageable young women. He concerned himself only with matters of the spirit. Emma suspected they had Oliver to thank for a good many of the church's young female converts, for it was known in Harmony that if you hoped to catch Mr. Cowdery's eye, you had best be well versed in the Book of Mormon.

Hiram Page cut an entirely different figure. At thirty, he was the eldest of Joseph's most dedicated men, saving Martin Harris. Hiram was stocky but not robust, better suited to scholarly pursuits than physical work. He jounced on his horse and all but fell from the saddle.

"We thought you could use a few more strong backs to help with the move," Oliver said. He noticed Emma stepping through the cabin door with a lightweight bag of wool in her arms. He offered a deep nod, almost a bow. Emma's face burned. Prophet's wife or no, it wasn't every day you received such courtesies from a fine-looking man.

"Strong backs—right enough." Joseph cut an amused glance toward Hiram. "It's a long ride to Fayette. Are you up for it, men?"

"We're up for anything," Oliver said. "You know we would follow you to the ends of the earth."

David slung an arm around Oliver's shoulders. "A long journey, but worth the effort. This is an endeavor blessed by God; I've no doubt about that. Why, I was just speaking of the miracle I witnessed yesterday morning, when I left Fayette to fetch our Prophet."

Emma said, "A miracle?"

"Yes, Mrs. Smith—oh, yes. I left my farm when dawn had scarcely arrived and drove out past the twenty-acre plot. Those acres have lain fallow for two years. But would you guess, an entire swath of that field had been freshly plowed. Seven acres or so, I'd say. Spread with fertilizer, too."

"Perhaps," Emma suggested, "one of your farmhands did the plowing the afternoon before, and you never noticed until you'd driven by."

"Impossible. I would have known if any mortal hand had guided the plow. It was an angel's doing—it must have been."

Little Aaron looked up at Joseph. "What does it mean, sir?"

"The Lord promises fertility." He rested a hand on the boy's head. "He means to grow a great and lasting church from this humble congregation. That's why I've decided to move the church up to Fayette, son. We can grow more steadily there. David's father, Peter, was kind enough to offer his home. Emma and I will live there until we can build a place of our own. God willing, our church will increase and thrive in New

York, the way the crops thrive in that good, dark, freshly plowed soil of David's farm."

David flushed with pleasure or zeal. "Fertility—just so. We've much to look forward to. God is good, my friends!"

Joseph took the wool from Emma. As he did, she thought, *Surely this decision to flee to Fayette has nothing to do with Harmony's hostility.* She had hoped the town's ire against the Mormons would abate with time, but it seemed the people she had once called her neighbors would never tire of their accusations. Blasphemy was their favorite charge. A simple trip to the general store for a pound of sugar or a handful of brass nails had become nothing less than a religious ordeal, complete with all the sufferings of a martyr. And though many residents had joined the church, the greater part of Harmony was still staunchly against them. Emma was exhausted by it all. She welcomed the move to Fayette, whatever Joseph's true motivation—for at least in another town she could expect a fresh start and a measure of peace.

And if the Lord had truly promised fertility . . . She let her hand rest for a moment on her belly. Perhaps this new child would have a better chance in Fayette. Perhaps, far from the dark cloud of Harmony's scorn, this child would survive.

The men arranged the final crates in the bed of the wagon. Joseph and Aaron laughed together, tossing a rope back and forth across the load to lash it in place.

"Tell me, Joseph," David said, "which of these boxes contains the golden plates?" His unsuspicious country face was bright with devotion.

"The plates will be carried to Fayette by someone else," Joseph said.

David wilted.

"They'll be carried by a special messenger. There may be trouble on the road. You know too many people of Harmony wish us ill. I couldn't risk such sacred things to robbers or mischief-makers."

"But who will carry the plates?"

Joseph regarded David with an air of cool detachment. "You'll know the bearer of the plates when you see him. The Lord has decreed."

Emma and Sally laid out a simple lunch of bread, hard cheese, and smoked venison. The men tucked in, gathering on the rough-hewn benches under the cabin's eaves. It would be their last meal before they stopped for the night at an inn somewhere in the south of New York, midway between Harmony and Fayette. By and by, Hiram and David wandered off to have a last look at the dammed-up stream where the first baptisms had occurred.

Watching them go, Oliver said, "I can't help but feel as if we're on the verge of something great. We're writing a new page of history—a new chapter."

"A new book," Joseph said, amused.

"And what new understanding will we bring to God's people? This revelation, that the Lord may speak to any man directly . . ."

Emma caught Joseph's eye and found her own misgiving reflected there. If any man may receive the word of God, then the church had no use for a leader. And if Joseph didn't lead his church, then he had no livelihood.

He put paid to Oliver's musing straightaway. "You've done invaluable work, my friend. No one acted as my scribe more frequently than you—not even Emma. But you're mistaken if you believe the Lord will deliver revelations to any man."

Oliver stared at him, so dumbfounded his face had gone pale. "Isn't that the very foundation of our new church? A restoration of the ways of the old prophets, a restoration of righteousness to the land, so that God will speak to us directly?"

"God will speak to His prophet, Oliver."

"And all righteous men. The Book of Mormon says—"

"The Book says God will speak in a language each man can understand."

"Does that not imply that God intends to reveal truth directly to our hearts?"

"Certainly," Joseph said, "through His ordained prophet."

Oliver frowned. "I like not that you should cut us off from our right as disciples, as Mormons."

"I cut you off from nothing." Joseph was mild, unruffled. "You especially, Oliver, my truest friend."

Still Oliver persisted. "But we who have heard God's restored word—we know how to receive His truth."

"What do you mean?"

"You have your peep-stone. So do many."

Joseph went still. Emma's heart pounded; the tense silence might combust any moment into anger.

At length, he said, "Oliver, have you been divining commandments through a stone?"

"I've tried it a time or two. I will admit I met with no success. But Hiram Page has done it. He has written out three or four revelations the Lord gave him through his stone, a little black one with two holes—"

Joseph rose to his feet. "This divining must stop."

Bewildered, Oliver stared up at him.

"It comes not from the Lord," Joseph insisted. He had drained of color. A pallor came over him whenever he was in the grip of a revelation, of any wave of emotion. It made him luminous, set apart from ordinary men. The effect had always unsettled Emma.

Oliver didn't seem to notice the shift in Joseph's mood—or if he had noticed, he ignored it, pressing his point with rising passion. "Are we only to hear the word of God from you, then?"

"Until God decides otherwise."

"You, who are no ordained minister?"

"Hiram Page is no ordained minister, yet you'll take any dark thing he scrawls down for the word of God."

"Hiram is a good man. He would never deceive me."

"Nor would I, Oliver Cowdery, and yet you doubt."

Emma shook her head, a covert gesture—yet Joseph saw. *You cannot lose Oliver,* her level stare said. His popularity and erudite bearing had brought far too many steady-minded people to the church. Without his influence, Joseph would be no better than the wandering preachers who tramped from town to town with unwashed, wild-eyed apostles squalling in their wakes.

Joseph moved at once to salvage his best asset. He stepped forward, laying his hands on Oliver's head. "Behold, I say unto thee, Oliver: thou shalt be heard by the church in all things, whatsoever thou shalt teach them by the Holy Ghost. But verily, I say unto thee, no one shall be appointed to receive commandments and revelations in this church excepting My servant Joseph Smith Junior, for he receiveth them even as Moses. And thou shalt be obedient to the things I shall give unto him, even as Aaron. And if thou art led at any time by the Holy Ghost to speak or teach, thou mayest do it. But thou shalt not write by way of commandment, but by wisdom; and thou shalt not command him who is at thy head, and at the head of the church, for I have given unto him the keys of the mysteries, and the revelations which are sealed, until I shall appoint unto them another in his stead. And thou shalt take thy brother, Hiram Page, and tell him that those things which he hath written from that stone are not of me, and that Satan deceiveth him. For all things must be done in order, and by common consent in the church, by the prayer of faith."

Joseph fell silent. Slowly, he withdrew his hands. Emma kept herself so perfectly still that she couldn't tell whether she was breathing.

After a long moment, Oliver lifted his face. Tears streamed from his eyes. "I felt the power of the Lord's presence. I will do as He commands."

"Of course you will." Joseph's voice hardly rose above a whisper. "You have ever been the Lord's faithful servant. And He directs me to appoint you to the office of Second Elder. None shall stand higher in the church than you, except for me."

Trembling, he took Joseph's hands in his own and kissed them—first one, then the other. "I am not worthy of such an honor."

Joseph laughed then, boyish and easy. The air of the sacred dispersed. "Nonsense, my friend. There's no man worthier. And it's because you're so worthy, Second Elder, that I must send you away."

"Send me away? I can't be separated from the church now, with a new start in Fayette."

"Oh, you'll be back. The Lord wills it. Once we've gathered our numbers in Fayette, we're to take the Gospel west. We must go out there, to the Indian tribes—the Lamanites. We're to bring them God's word, save their souls. And it's you who'll find a suitable place for us to settle. This isn't a task the Lord would entrust to any man."

Oliver shook his head rather dazedly. "I suppose it is not."

"You'll choose the site of our Zion—a New Jerusalem, a righteous home from which we may bring the Lamanite tribes to Christ. You spoke of writing a new history, and so you shall. But first, you must speak to Hiram and dissuade him from his wickedness."

They left Harmony shortly after noon, when the day's heat was at its worst. Oliver mounted his piebald horse and headed west, eager to begin his mission. From the back of the wagon, Emma waved farewell to Sally Knight. She would see Sally again, by and by, but beyond her friend was the old familiar vision of Hale House, the only real home Emma had known, with all the tender memories it contained. She hadn't told her mother or her father that she and Joseph were leaving. Since the day of her baptism—since Isaac's betrayal—she had spoken to her parents rarely, and only when pressed. She would see them again someday, she told herself as Hale House disappeared around a bend. Likely very soon. That thought should have comforted her, but she couldn't rid herself of bitterness and regret. Those shadows followed her all the long way from Harmony to New York.

But David Whitmer spotted a man walking north along the forest's edge. He had the look of a grandfather, with a long white beard, yet bore himself powerfully and carried with ease the great bulging pack on his back. And David, at least, was satisfied.

She wondered—she went on wondering, many years after—whether she first came to love Joseph on that journey to Fayette. It may seem strange, that any woman should admit she didn't love her husband when she married him. But since we are discussing the truth, since we are speaking of things we understand to be true, whether they are understood by others or not—then let us be clear on this.

She married Joseph Smith in an extremity of despair. She married him because Harmony was a small place, a tight confinement, and she was known by then as a cold, offish woman. But what came after, what happened in Fayette and beyond—the way Joseph wounded her with his actions, great and small—perhaps such wounds can only be inflicted on a heart that loves. If she had remained indifferent to her husband forever, or merely beholden to him because he was the Prophet and she a member of his church, then she wouldn't have come so close to breaking.

A heart, like stoneware, is both fragile and resilient. Years leave spider cracks across its surface, all the times it's set down hard or used carelessly so its edges collide with the iron of the world. A heart chips and wears. Its pretty surface dulls. It threatens to shatter in a hundred places. Maybe someday it will.

At the inn, she found herself clinging to Joseph's hand when he helped her down from the wagon. And when a woman passed by on the street and smiled at him, something opened wide inside of her, a pit that felt like hunger.

That was love, she thinks now—a kind of love. Or jealousy, which was, perhaps, the only form of love this strange life would permit her to feel. It opened its greedy self because they were leaving Harmony together, and she had no one else but Joseph. Or it grew because of her pregnancy, her stony determination that this baby would survive. Perhaps it grew because she believed Joseph truly was the Prophet, and God worked through him.

One way or another, the gall of love swelled and dripped its bitter sap. She can't tell you why. Joseph was never an easy man to adore—not for Emma. Because their love was uneasy, it was always difficult for her to understand. And harder still to describe.

In Fayette, Emma did not find the warm reception she had hoped for. To be sure, Joseph was welcomed with open arms and great cheers of Hallelujah by the men of the Whitmer clan—by Peter especially, the patriarch, an early convert to the church. But Emma was passed at once to the care of Peter's wife, Mary Elsa, who, with sour face and studied silence, made her feel the weight of her imposition every minute of every day.

The Whitmer home was beautiful. Made of split logs that alternated with stripes of clay caulking, it was large enough to put the cabin on the Hale acreage to shame. The upper story—what luxury—held two bedrooms, narrow and cramped but warm in the night. The lower floor was dominated by a river-stone hearth. Emma stared in open admiration at its graceful arch, the impeccable cleanliness of the smooth stones, as perfectly pale as when they'd first been dredged up out of the water, a testament to Mary Elsa's housekeeping.

"Your home is nothing short of perfect," Emma said, trying surreptitiously to work the ache of long travel from her shoulders and back.

Mary Elsa only looked at her with a pinched expression.

"It will be my honor," Emma said, "to help you keep house. I'm sure it will never feel like work, in a home as lovely as this."

"Plenty of housekeeping already." Mary Elsa spoke with a slight Prussian accent. "And me worked plain to the bone, but here you come, you two strangers from goodness knows where, expecting me to cook for you and clean up besides."

"I'll be glad to take on all the cooking and cleaning, if you like, Mrs.

Whitmer. You've been generous enough already, in agreeing to put a roof above our heads."

"Raised eight children. Eight! And now they're off and married with children of their own, but can I take a little of my well-earned rest? Never! I must play innkeeper, Peter says, to some preacher or whatever he is and his wife."

Emma thought it best not to tell Mary Elsa that she was expecting a child of her own. She would keep the truth to herself for as long as she could conceal it, and pray Joseph could build a house sooner rather than later. The old woman wouldn't rejoice to hear that a baby was on its way.

As the summer waned and the land turned golden, Emma worked tirelessly beside Mary Elsa, doing all she could to ease the burden. But Mary Elsa wouldn't be satisfied. She sighed over household chores—the sweeping, the washing, even the kneading of dough, which Emma had always found enjoyable, a time for meditation and meandering thought. Emma took on more work every day, but no matter how she applied herself, their hostess only seemed to resent her and Joseph more.

Once, she caught Mary Elsa muttering while she, Emma, was scrubbing the stairs. She didn't think Mary Elsa had intended her to hear. "What is this church? This church—this folly, I call it. Peter has done it this time, gone and made himself a laughingstock. The whole valley will mock us now." She lapsed into her native tongue. Though Emma had no Prussian, she could guess the meaning easily enough.

Mary Elsa's spite wasn't entirely unjustified. Joseph had predicted that Fayette would be fertile ground, and almost at once, he was proved correct. In Harmony he had tallied forty church members, most from his own family and the families of the men who had acted as his scribes.

But the Whitmers were popular in Fayette, and contrary to Mary Elsa's fears, Peter's love for the new church brought curious neighbors by the score. Within weeks of their arrival, the church roles had swelled to a hundred—then two hundred, and Joseph was obliged to deliver his sermons in a field behind the Whitmer home, standing on a makeshift stage made from apple crates and planks. Before autumn was out, the church seemed likely to grow to a thousand members strong. Emma would have been astonished at Joseph's success if she'd had time for reflection. But she and Mary Elsa hurried from one task to the next, baking bread to feed all the congregants, then cleaning up after Joseph's most trusted men, who sat at night before the arch of the fireplace smoking their pipes and discussing the nature of God. Emma worked so diligently, from sunrise to well past dark, that when night came, she fell gratefully into bed, though it was hard and small, and slept so deeply that more often than not Joseph had to shake her awake by morning. Even the crowing of the Whitmers' rooster couldn't cut through her exhaustion.

That autumn, Martin Harris left his wife, Dolly, having satisfied her with eighty acres, a new house, and a fat purse. Emma mused that if she were Dolly Harris, she would have found it satisfaction enough to be rid of that dull-eyed groveler, with or without the compensation. But Martin had followed the congregation to Fayette, and made it his daily business to remind Joseph of the promise God had made, that he should be permitted to look upon the golden plates.

The Lord evidently chose Fayette as the place for His great miracle. After an especially trying evening with Martin, when the man had wheedled and prodded more doggedly than he usually did, Joseph rose early and took Martin and David Whitmer into the forest to pray. They carried no food for their breakfast, and only a little water in clay jugs. Joseph wouldn't tell Emma when to expect them back, but the men returned an hour before sunset, staggering out of the trees, their shirts half unbuttoned and soaked with sweat. They wrung their hands in wordless awe at the visions they had witnessed.

Martin collapsed in the hayfield, rolling in the dust. Tears darkened his whiskers. He wouldn't be consoled until Joseph laid a hand upon his shoulder. Then he sat up, reached out and by chance found Emma's hand. "I saw the plates. I saw them. Beautiful—glorious—leaves of purest gold. They were covered by a white cloth at first, but then an angel lifted the cloth away and turned them over and over. He said: 'The book translated from those plates is true and translated correctly.' How they shone, those plates of gold! More brightly than the sun!"

That night, for the first time since coming to Fayette, Emma found she couldn't sleep. She lay with a hand on her belly, praying to feel the first small movements of her child. She prayed, too, for the will to obey God's commandment. He had called her an elect lady. He had summoned her to a great work, the compilation of a hymnal. But He had warned her not to complain of the things she hadn't seen. He would permit Martin Harris to see the plates, but not she, who had been Joseph's first and most encouraging scribe.

Emma might have learned to bear that bitterness. With time, she might have turned it sweet. But only a few days later, when she'd risen early to cook for one of Joseph's meetings, Mary Elsa came in from the milking shed without any milk—without even her pail. Emma looked up from the fire. Mary Elsa was wide-eyed and trembling. The old woman leaned heavily against the doorframe.

Fearing some dreadful illness had taken Mary Elsa, she rushed to the old woman's side.

"Go and fetch Joseph," Mary Elsa said.

"Ought I to send for the doctor?"

"No, child, no. Only help me to that chair, and then you go upstairs and wake the Prophet."

Joseph followed Emma downstairs, still dressed in his flannel sleeping gown, and knelt beside Mary Elsa. He held the woman's hand while she told her story.

"The mist is so heavy this morning. Everything white, white, as far as the eye can see. But as I came near to the barn the mist parted and a man came toward me. I was frightened at first; I thought to scream. But then I saw his face—a peaceful, kindly man. All my fear was gone in a snap, because of his countenance."

She swallowed hard, pressing a hand to her eyes, as if the memory was too much to bear.

"Go on," Joseph said.

"He had a white beard, and he wore a long white garment like your nightshirt, Joseph, and he said, 'You have been faithful and diligent in your labors, but you are tired because of the increase in your toil. It is proper therefore that you receive a witness, that your faith might be strengthened.'"

How richly Mary Elsa described the plates. Emma could practically see them for herself—except, of course, she hadn't seen them at all. The luster of gold, the sound the plates made when the angel turned them, a click like the sound of pearls, which Mary Elsa had handled once as a girl, when her cousin had worn them at her wedding. The light that surrounded those sacred plates, the glory—it had all made her forget herself, forget everything, and drop the milking pail in the mud. She felt as a girl once more, young and energetic, as if the holy vision had erased all her years and she was purified, as perfect as a pearl herself.

After that morning, Mary Elsa thawed in Emma's company. She was kinder, more forgiving, and she attended church meetings in the field behind her house, gazing up at Joseph on his stage of apple crates as if he shone like Moses himself. Mary Elsa even kissed Emma once, on the brow, and called her "elect lady." But Emma found herself unable to like Mary Elsa, despite her new hospitality, however she tried.

By December, snow drifted against the cabin higher than the downstairs windows, and Joseph's followers came over the fields two and three times a week to clear a path to the door. Emma watched from her bedroom as the snow fell. The curtains glowed in the directionless sunlight of winter. The world was muffled, reduced and clarified, transformed to something private and small. By now the child was lively in her belly. It kicked enough for two. She was grateful for every flutter and bounce, even for the pains in her chest at night, which could only be relieved by sleeping upright with pillows behind her back. She took every inconvenience for proof that this baby was strong enough to live. She spoke to the child in her heart—silently, the way she prayed—while she sat in those few moments of peace.

One afternoon, when the flakes flew like goose down past the glass, the wind abated briefly and the snowfall allayed. For a moment, Emma could see far down the Whitmers' lane, like looking through a layer of gauze or a virgin's veil. She saw, through a white world, not the angel Mary Elsa had met, but a man on a horse—solid and real, hooves churning, leaving blue tracks that stretched back into the snow's featureless blur. Then she recognized the horse's spotted hide, and she stood at once, calling down the stairs to Joseph. "Oliver Cowdery has returned!"

But it wasn't the Second Elder who swung down from the piebald's back in the icy yard. The man was a stranger—young, hardly past his youth, with heavy, sharp brows that nevertheless couldn't shadow his lively eyes. He fairly glowed with excitement as he came forward. When he shook Joseph's hand, he laughed in awe. "So you're the Prophet. It's an honor to meet you, sir—an honor."

"Glad to meet you," Joseph said. "But who are you, and what are you doing with my Second Elder's horse?"

"You mean Mr. Cowdery. I've come at his direction to speak to you personally, Prophet—to tell you what's waiting in Ohio."

"You ought to call me just 'Joseph,' fellow. Or if you like to be formal, Brother Joseph will do."

"Very well, Brother Joseph. My name is Parley Pratt, from Kirtland, Ohio. That's to say, I came first from Mentor, but I've found that Kirtland is my true home since learning of your Book of Mormon and the restoration of the true Church of Christ."

"You'd best put that horse away in the barn, then come on inside. Emma has made some fine porridge. It'll warm you up in a hurry, and you can tell us all about it."

Inside, Parley unwrapped himself like a parcel—stocking hat, long scarves, two woolen coats, two heavy sweaters. A smell of damp wool filled the cabin. "It was a long ride in the snow."

"And how came you to ride Oliver's horse?" Emma said.

"Ah, Mrs. Smith, that's a happy tale. I met Brother Oliver on the road between Mentor and Kirtland. I was headed there, you see, to deliver a few things to my preacher. A great preacher, such a fine man as the world has never seen. Sidney Rigdon is his name. It was he who taught me true religion and made me a Campbellite. At least, I was a Campbellite, until I met Brother Oliver. Now I've learned a better way, and so has Mr. Rigdon."

While he ate, Parley told how he had ridden beside Oliver, merely for the companionship of another young man on the road—but Oliver had preached to him, and Parley had felt a fire of truth burning in his heart when he heard about Joseph's book and its miraculous origin.

"Oliver rode with me all the way to Kirtland. I was apprehensive. I didn't expect Mr. Rigdon to receive him well. Mr. Rigdon is such a learned man, you see, and has been so dedicated to the Campbellite ways. He has built the town around Campbell's teaching. Every man, woman, and child in Kirtland numbers themselves among Campbell's Disciples of Christ. Or they did—but no longer. When we got to town, I took Oliver to Mr. Rigdon straightaway. Something told me, you see, that it had to happen. Those two men were destined to meet. And I watched Brother Oliver preach to Mr. Rigdon, just as he'd done on the road. Mr. Rigdon could tell it was God's truth. Well, a man as wise and righteous as he—how could he fail to see it? When Oliver finished preaching, Mr. Rigdon stood up from his chair and dropped away into a faint, straight off."

"My goodness," Emma said. "Was he hurt?"

"No, Mrs. Smith, not he. That's the way with Mr. Rigdon. The Holy Spirit comes upon him and strikes him into faints or fits or visions. We've all witnessed it, and rejoiced to see it. What a sign from Heaven! When he recovered, he told Brother Oliver that God had warned him years ago that He would send a messenger bearing a sign of the gathering of Israel. The messenger was to come just before the Millennium, when Christ will make His return. Well, Mr. Rigdon assembled the whole town that very evening and declared that the Book of Mormon was the sign he'd been waiting for. That was three weeks ago. We've finally finished baptizing all of Kirtland into your Church of Christ. Oliver sent me to you with this message, but he has remained to help record all those new names for the church rolls. One hundred and thirty-five new members for your church, Brother Joseph, and every one of them waiting for their Prophet to appear."

The trek to Ohio's northern lowlands took four long days by sleigh, through deep snow that mounded over everything—trees, farms, even the houses in the towns they passed. Kirtland sat on a distinctive rise above a bend in the Chagrin River. Everything lay white against white; there was no distinguishing near from far, land from sky, and the sky was a dense heavy blanket of woodsmoke and cloud, belly-down against the land.

"It may not be Zion exactly," Parley said, "but it's the best job we've made so far of building a Christian paradise."

They swept over a bridge. The river below was sluggish between its gray banks, clotted with ice. Someone must have spotted the sleigh as it came up the slope from the Chagrin, for a tin horn sounded, high and thin, strangely small in the deadening atmosphere of winter. By the time the sleigh had reached a flat swath of compacted snow that was the town's main street, men and women were already thronging the porch outside a great two-story mercantile. The mercantile sat at a crossroads, a towering construction of whitewashed board. Its twin chimneys, made from ruddy brick, were the only color in the world.

The people cheered when Joseph raised his hand in greeting. They shook their fists, they cried Hallelujah, they knelt in the snow and wept. Children ran behind the sleigh. The tin horn was drowned out by the cries of Joseph's new congregation, their passionate wails. If there had been any flowers in that barren season, they would have strewn petals in the Prophet's path.

Parley stopped the sleigh outside the mercantile. The people rushed in, shouting, stretching out their hands—and Joseph, bemused and almost hesitant, touched them and watched as those he touched fell back into the arms of their neighbors, red-faced and weeping. Here was a change from Harmony, and no mistake.

Oliver pushed his way through the crowd. "Brother Joseph!" When he reached the sleigh, he shouted at the crowd to stand back, to give the Prophet room to breathe. Then he helped Joseph down with a solemn air, as if he were a holy relic.

"You've made it in one piece," Oliver said. "Not that I doubted you would. But it's a long road from Fayette to here."

Joseph said, "When Brother Parley told me about the faithful people here in this good village, I knew we must come at once. You've done great work here, Oliver. The Lord is pleased—and so am I."

"I cannot take the credit. That honor belongs to Sidney Rigdon. A more righteous man the Lord has never made. Ah—here he comes now."

The preacher stepped down from the mercantile's porch and strode out into the crowd. Parley had whiled away several hours of the journey by recounting Sidney's most memorable fits and faints. Emma had expected a slight man, twitching at voices only he could hear. But Sidney was rather tall and robust, with square shoulders and a capable bearing. He wore a tailored coat of dark wool, a fine worsted fabric that almost shone in the brightness of his congregation's fire. His well-groomed hair had only just begun to gray around the temples. He had no need to push through the crowd, as Oliver had done. Even without looking, without ceasing to clamor for their prophet, the Kirtlanders sensed his presence and parted before him. An expectant silence descended. He looked at Joseph, taking the Prophet's measure from his woolen hat still dusted with snowflakes to the worn boots of scarred, slouching leather. Emma watched the preacher's eyes. They were pale, heavy-lidded. They seemed to look beyond Joseph, beyond the town to some distant place, a fixed point toward which no other person could gaze. His mouth bent in a prim, sober frown. His nose was sharp at the end like the beak of some great, solemn bird.

For a long moment, no one stirred within the crowd. Winter had frozen them all to their places. Then Joseph stumbled forward as if an unseen hand had pushed him. He reached up, making to catch himself on Sidney's shoulders, but by the time his chapped hands touched the man's coat it was Joseph who was holding Sidney up, Joseph who held the entire congregation.

"Behold," he said in a voice that carried, staring into Sidney's face, "verily, verily I say unto my servant Sidney, I have looked upon thee and thy works. I have heard thy prayers and prepared thee for a greater work. Thou art blessed, for thou shalt do great things. Behold, thou wast sent forth even as John, to prepare the way before Me, and as Elijah which should come, and thou knew it not. Thou didst baptize by water unto repentance, but they received not the Holy Ghost; but now I give unto thee a commandment, that thou shalt baptize by water, and they shall receive the Holy Ghost by the laying on of hands, even as the apostles of old. I have called upon the weak things of the world, those who are unlearned and despised, to thrash the nations by the power of My Spirit; and their arm shall be My arm, and I will be their shield; their enemies shall be under their feet, and by the fire of Mine indignation will I preserve them."

He removed his hands from Sidney's shoulders with a sudden jerk. The air crackled with sympathetic energy, as if the whole congregation had felt the Prophet's touch. The moment Sidney stood alone, without Joseph to hold him, his eyes rolled to white. He swayed on his feet; the people moved forward, moaning, to catch him as he fell. And because their leader had been struck mute by the force of Joseph's blessing, the people of Kirtland roared in his stead.

She would never be certain, in later years, whether Joseph's fight to keep control of his own church began that year or the next. She knew only that the struggle began in Kirtland. And how not? The town belonged to Sidney Rigdon. Not to Joseph—not even to God.

For years, the preacher had exercised a seemingly limitless patience, drawing in the most ardent believers in Christ's imminent return, locating them family by family or man by man in the valleys and hills of the

Burned-Over District. He called them. He reeled them in like fish on a line, and assembled an eager, hot-eyed flock on that unassuming bend of the river.

With a true believer's focus, he taught the ways of Thomas Campbell and made from his population the most meticulously faithful community among the Disciples of Christ. For Sidney had convinced all of Kirtland that it was right and proper to hold all things in common, that Christ would never return until the ancient ways lived again on earth. In that small Ohio village, thanks to Sidney's preaching, what belonged to one man belonged to all, for the Campbellites insisted that such was the custom of Abraham and Moses. Beasts and harvests and even homes, even the clothing on one's back—all could be claimed by a neighbor, and every gift, every charity would be given without hesitation or grudge.

She thinks of it now, a place where no man can claim one thing as his own, not even his Bible, and she can't help but wonder. Did the thought of holding all in common—even love, even women—first plant itself in Joseph's mind there, that winter, when he had scarcely arrived? Emma had no sense of what was to come, that first day in the new village. The congregation was wild with excitement, to be sure, but after the humiliations of Harmony and even Emma's difficulty in Fayette, she thought their fervor was a welcome change.

Oliver had asked the congregation to make a home for the Prophet. The crowd led Emma and Joseph to a small but beautifully made house, somewhat south of the mercantile. A merry-eyed, black-haired woman in a faded green dress opened the door and ushered them inside.

The house was elegant in its simplicity. A small kitchen against one wall boasted a cabinet stocked with dishes and a few copper cook-pots. There were wicker chairs with bright cushions and a rug made from braided rags, and someone had already laid a fire in the modest brick hearth, so it was warm on the inside, warm and inviting with a smell of sparks and smoke.

"This is to be our home?" Emma said to the dark-haired woman. "Truly ours?"

"What's yours is ours," the woman answered, "and what's ours is yours. That's our way—Christ's way. But you'll live here on your own, if that's what you mean. You and our Prophet. Newel Whitney built this place. He owns the mercantile, which is the post office, too. He and his wife had intended to live here, but they've given this house gladly to the Prophet for as long as he means to use it."

"I don't know how to thank you all. I haven't kept my own house in far too long, and even then, it was more rustic than this. I feel as if you've given us a palace."

"My name is Patty Sessions," the woman said. "I'm the midwife, thanks to God, so I suppose we'll be in one another's company in the weeks to come. How far are you, my dear?"

"Seven months, if I've counted correctly."

"And so big. Wait a moment."

Emma warmed herself at the fire while Patty returned to the crowd outside. A few minutes later she was back, this time carrying a large leather bag. She drew out what looked like an old metal goblet with its stem cut away, then bent before Emma's stomach, flattening layers of fabric over the taut swell of her belly. Patty laid the cup's mouth against the place where the baby dreamed; she pressed an ear to the narrow end. Emma held very still as Patty moved the cup and listened, moved it and listened again, and all the while Emma held her breath, wondering what the midwife could hear over the tumult of the crowd outside.

Finally, Patty lowered her cup and looked up at Emma, beaming. "Just as I thought. The Lord has brought you a great blessing. He has given us a sign of the Prophet's coming, and of the increase this church will see. I heard not one heartbeat, but two. You blessed lady—you shall bear the Prophet twins."

The Scriptures tell us that a thousand years are but one single day to God. And learned men can comb the pages of the Bible and prove to you the world was made six thousand years in the past. Six thousand years, six days of Creation, and on the seventh, God rested.

When Christ returns, we shall rest again—all of us who are faithful, who haven't been cast into Hell. The Millennium will be our great reward, an epoch of endless glory, when pain and suffering shall end. Whatever agonies have befallen us shall be forgotten. Whatever was broken shall be whole. What has died shall live again, and nothing shall trouble us, no illness, no loss, no falling away of husband and wife. Peace shall be ours—finally, peace.

Do you not believe that these are the Latter Days? It's a truth simply learned. Any Mormon child can lay it out for you—a boy chasing a hoop down a Nauvoo lane, a girl swaddling her dolls. On the second day, God brought the land forth from the waters. And after two thousand years there was the flood, the one Noah knew, when all the world was inundated, and the land had to rise again from the waters. Two thousand years—two days. And after two thousand more years, Christ and His Apostles came, as on the fourth day God made the greater and lesser lights of Heaven. What now? That was two thousand years ago, give or take a decade. We find ourselves in the twilight hour of God's sixth day. When the next sun rises, we will have our day of rest.

The coming of a Prophet, with his restored gospel and its miraculous provenance, only strengthened Kirtland in faith. Every hour they prayed for Christ's emergence, and expected to witness it the moment they lifted their heads. Joseph never held a meeting but the sermon was interrupted by shouts of fervor. His followers lurched to their feet or fell down in fits, which no man but Joseph could stop, and only then by laying his hands on their heads, those sacred Prophet's hands.

Girls lapsed into trance. They stared at the walls for hours or days. Young, healthy men would shudder on the ground and roll to the meetinghouse door, then through it, out into the January evening where the ground was hard and the edges of bootprints had frozen sharp as knives. The snow around the meetinghouse was rust-spotted from their blood. One night, a pack of youths became possessed of some strange, intoxicating spirit. They grunted like apes and loped on all fours through the streets, then out across a snowy field, howling about a parchment up above, a parchment unrolled among the stars, and they could read revelation in the sky. Newel Whitney's nephew climbed atop an oak stump, holding forth like a preacher before his congregation, only there was no congregation, and whatever sermon he gave was in no language anyone had heard before.

"Each man thinks himself a prophet here," Joseph said.

That night he was slumped in front of the hearth with his collar undone, his sleeves unfastened. The days were growing longer. Winter was subsiding, but who could notice when even a short February day left you wrung out and sick to your stomach from the latest news of another miracle.

"It's Hiram Page all over again," he said, "but a hundred times worse."

"You must bring them back under your control," Emma said. "If you aren't the head of this church—if any man may interpret God's word— then by this time next year, you'll have no church at all."

Bring them under your control, Joseph Smith, but how?

The widow Hubble had already proclaimed herself a prophetess. She issued revelation in the streets. Sidney Rigdon had given the widow his special salute, the Right Hand of Fellowship and the Kiss of Charity; she was sanctified by Kirtland's reckoning. There was nothing Joseph could do about it, unless he wanted to call the widow Hubble a devil.

A Mormon girl had predicted a devastating earthquake in the Orient, and that same year it came to pass. If Emma had known at the time exactly which girl had issued the prophecy, she couldn't tell you now, for predictions flew like wheat chaff and every hour someone cried out an omen. But the prophecy of the earthquake was printed in the papers, and the Campbells themselves took note—Thomas and his son Alexander. They came to the village to stand chest to chest with Sidney Rigdon, scolding him for the way his congregation had fallen. They preached against the blasphemy of this new religion. But Sidney's people ran the Campbells out of town.

The hotter the fire burned, the farther spread its glow. The moment the roads had thawed enough for travel by wagon, Joseph's Fayette followers came to join their Prophet, increasing the town's population tenfold. The little Ohio town soon looked as if it might become a proper city. Traveling preachers couldn't resist the chance to test Joseph's theology and, they hoped, discredit the Mormon Prophet before his very church. They meant to gather up the sweepings from a dissipated sect and swell their own numbers. The Methodists, the Campbellites, the Unitarians all tried, yet all were thrown back by the force of the congregation's faith. And all the while, the prophesies came, the seeresses wept, the stars opened their scrolls for any common man to read.

There was one power over which Joseph still had full command. None but he could heal by the laying on of hands. God knows they all tried, but fainting fits and spells of the shakes and trances that turned a body cold as ice—these afflictions couldn't be eased, except by the Prophet's touch.

"There," Emma told him one evening, speaking quietly even though they were alone in their borrowed house. "There is where you keep your hold: by healing. You must press whatever advantage you still have before it's gone forever."

Next morning, when a famous Methodist preacher arrived to accuse the Prophet of chicanery, Joseph summoned from the crowd a certain Mrs. Johnson, mistress of a serene and lonely farm more than thirty miles outside of town.

Mrs. Johnson's arm had been plagued by arthritis for many years; she was rendered half a cripple by the pain. Joseph put her useless hand in his own. "Woman," said he, "in the name of the Lord Jesus Christ I command thee to be whole!"

Mrs. Johnson raised her arm above her head with ease.

He had healed spiritual afflictions by the score—a dozen every day, so many the miracle had long since become commonplace. But never had Joseph healed a physical ailment, not since Newel Knight in the Harmony days—which no one in Kirtland had witnessed. The momentary shock of Mrs. Johnson's healing recaptured the church's attention, just long enough for the Prophet to announce his latest revelation.

"Behold," Joseph said, "the Lord has given unto me a great new work. Nowhere does the Holy Ghost live as He does in this place. And so, every man—yea, every one of you—shall be ordained a priest, as it was in ancient times, in the time of Abraham and Moses, when righteous men shared in the leadership of God's church."

The people cheered; they fell to their knees, tore at their hair in an excess of righteous passion. Some twisted on the ground. Like the snake of Eden, Emma thought, swallowing down her fear.

Joseph said, "Each man shall take part in the responsibility of guiding the Church of Christ—as deacon, as teacher, as priest, as elder, as seventy or bishop. Whosoever takes on the mantle of such an honor must work tirelessly for the church's good; God Himself demands nothing less. And each who takes the mantle, yea, even the least of these, shall acknowledge that no man stands higher in authority than God's ordained Prophet—be that Prophet me, or at a future time whosoever the Lord shall appoint to take my place."

When every man had sworn to uphold the hierarchy of the church, the Prophet lifted his holy hands above the town square. He declared

Kirtland consecrated ground. He told them all there was no place holier in the eyes of God, not even blessed Bethlehem.

What else could he do?

You mustn't think that Joseph was blind to his troubles. He saw them, perhaps more clearly than Emma did—more clearly, you may be sure, than Oliver or Sidney or any of his priests and seventies. Kirtland was his, and yet the town was a creature unto itself. It rose by its own power with Sidney Rigdon riding its back. It cried to the world, Come and see.

Emma saw. With a woman's watchful silence, she observed the Prophet struggling to keep his hold on the only livelihood he could claim. Like Jacob on the riverbank, he contended with a power far greater than he'd thought to find, and the fight exhausted him. The fight unmade and remade Joseph into something startling and new.

A black night in the Canaan desert. The stars like eyes, thousands of eyes, trained upon the riverbank, watching. A bright creature with which one humble man grapples, the terrible force of divine strength.

Joseph used every tool and weapon in his fight to shape his church. Often, Emma found him with a Bible spread open in his lap, or sometimes the Book of Mormon, but in those moments, she seldom found him reading. He only stared. Sitting beside the fire, watching through the window as an early night came down to hide the village behind its cloak. Or in the morning she would wake and find the bed beside her empty, and Joseph out in the biting cold, watching the sky, all his color stolen away by the pale-blue light of a late-winter dawn. In these moments he would mutter to himself as if composing a sermon, never loudly enough for Emma to hear. Sometimes she would find him pacing from one corner of the house to another.

He would draw the silver medallion from his pocket and turn it over in his hand.

Come and see. Joseph walking a circle around the table where he worked, trailing salt from his hand. Or drawing a circle in the air with his finger when he thought no one was looking. All the charms and protections he had learned from his mother, all the mysteries of his childhood whispering to him now, compelling him to try. Some of these rituals Emma recognized, as any country girl would—the twisted hickory stick hidden above the doorframe, a charm against enemies; the leaves of dried vervain scattered on the floor—vervain to amplify the will, to make one's thoughts manifest upon the world.

Other rituals were strange to her, and she found their evidence unsettling. A smear of blood behind the headboard on the side where Joseph slept. The scrap of paper she dislodged from beneath the cushion of his chair: It bore a cross with its lower end curved, an upward whip of a tail, and written on the obverse in Joseph's hand:

I.

N.I.R.

I.

SANCTUS SPIRITUS

I.

N.I.R.

I.

Come and see, the way Joseph's very presence transfixed her—not because of his beauty, which wasn't greater than that of most men, and was far surpassed by some—but because of his compelling power, a vexing, an infuriating, an outward spirit that turned you forcefully toward him when you most desired to look away.

Once she had been sewing, sitting on the edge of her bed, with wooden bobbins scattered all around. She took a heavy box full of fabric scraps from inside her old trunk, set it on the mattress, and at once the bobbins rolled toward the box. They sank into the depression around its perimeter. That was Joseph's way, and the way of people around him. He drew them in, by his secret workings or simply by his nature, and once you fell into the pit beside him, you couldn't roll away again.

What to tell you of that spring, 1831? Surely for someone in the village— for everyone else, perhaps—it was as bright and hopeful as any spring the world has known. The flowers bloomed for someone. The air was sweet with perfume. The sky was colored in delicate shades and the earth to match it, the initial pale green of tentative new growth, like the shades of green that appear sometimes in a button of mother-of-pearl.

You tilt the button in your fingers and the colors wink at you—and perhaps that spring was just as beautiful, as startling with delights.

It wasn't so for Emma.

It doesn't do to talk of it—not more than must be said. She bore twins, just as the midwife had predicted. She knew they wouldn't live, for neither baby cried, no matter how she or Patty tried to rouse them. The midwife called Joseph in before the babies drew their final breaths. Together, they held their children and kissed their satin cheeks. They talked to them, told them both how much they were loved, how they had been made in God's image and would live with Him forever in Heaven. The boy died first—they had named him Thaddeus—then the girl, Louisa, a few minutes later.

Emma never wept. The grief went too deep for tears—grief and refusal to believe this all could be real, the rage inside her, this new hatred of God's inscrutable ways. All more real than the feeling of her children in her arms, or in her womb. She was already forgetting them, losing that brief and precious memory.

She didn't cry, but she sat in her bed for three days or four. She had no reckoning of time. She listened while Joseph wept in another room and beat his fists against the walls and demanded of the Lord, Why, why make me a prophet and Your chosen hand if you won't give me the power to save my own children from death?

And she thought, from some vague, walled-off place where thoughts still could dwell, Oh, he truly believes in his own power. It isn't a game to him, after all.

Grief will take a man in the strangest ways. A man's heart is more delicate than he ever lets on, but the world won't allow him to show it; God knows why. When Joseph thought himself fit to leave home, he went directly to the meetinghouse and began to preach his sermons, though it wasn't the day or the hour for meeting. The congregation came anyhow, those who could take themselves away from their labors, and listened to the Prophet speak.

On what subjects did Joseph preach? It makes no difference now. The subjects of his sermons weren't the draw, in any case. It was the sight of him that brought his followers from the fields—the paleness of his face, white as the walls of a temple, white as an angel's raiment. And the way he glowed. A fierce power emanated from him when he spoke, the animation of his stifled pain. It was the look in his eyes that drew his congregation: a sacred desolation, enough by itself to move you to tears.

Joseph preached for a day and a night without stopping, pouring into any willing ear his insistence that God was great and could heal—would heal, if one's faith were strong enough. God could preserve you from the grave—even that—and nothing but the Lord could do it.

When Emma was strong enough to leave her bed, she went to the meetinghouse, leaning on Patty's arm. She sat on a hard bench at the back of the room. Joseph seemed not to recognize her across the rank crowd of his worshipers. He seemed unaware of anything, save his divine agony.

For hours, she watched. The women came and went, bringing the Prophet jugs of steaming broth and fresh-baked bread, which Joseph only touched when he became so weak from his efforts that he shook and would have fallen. They brought him tea and coffee to brace him up, and sweet cakes to cheer him, but he wouldn't be cheered until they brought the sick for him to heal.

He raised the lame to their feet with a touch and a shout. With spittle on his thumb, he cleared the clouded eyes of those half-blind. He made the deaf hear music, made a mute girl sing. And Lyman Wight, healed of his melancholy, jumped upon a bench and stretched himself, bending backward as if to embrace the whole of creation: "If you want a sign, look at me!" Joseph drove out devils and shook the doubt from those depleted of their faith. What was lost came crowding back again. What was darkened blazed like a midsummer fire.

The meetinghouse door banged open. Emma turned to see who had come—and her hand flew at once to her mouth. The breath left her chest; she couldn't summon it again, no matter how she pleaded or prayed.

A man stood in the doorway, face contorted with suffering. In his arms he carried a little boy, no older than five years. Emma stared at the child's waxen grayness. One small arm hung down, and hung too stiffly—the inert finality only death can bring.

Silence moved slowly through the meetinghouse, until finally it pressed the whole congregation down. The man approached Joseph at his pulpit. Without a word, he laid his dead son at the Prophet's feet. For a long moment, the two men looked at one another across the lifeless body—fathers who had each lost their children. Then the color drained from Joseph's face. That pallor came over him, the glow.

Emma staggered to her feet, ignoring the pain in her torn body. "Joseph, no. You cannot; you must not—"

But the congregation was murmuring now, their voices rising in a tide. The crowd demanded that their Prophet produce a miracle and prove that the Last Days were at hand.

Emma tried to fight her way to the head of the congregation, take Joseph by the arm and restrain him, but she was weak from the birth and from her suffering. The people spilled into the aisle, chanting, shuddering, crawling on the floor.

"Joseph!" Emma shouted. "Stop!"

He crouched. He laid the hands that had commanded so many miracles on the small, cold head. His voice carried like thunder, even over the excitement of his flock. "In the name of the Lord Jesus Christ, I command you to be healed—yea, be healed even from death! Rise and live again!"

The heat of faith was a swelter in the room. It made Emma lightheaded, but she held herself upright, she counted the heartbeats until the silence returned, eight, nine, ten.

The howling and weeping died away. Women picked themselves up from the floor. The child never stirred.

The stricken father gathered up his son's body. He pressed the poor dead thing against his chest. The congregation was so silent, Emma could hear every word he spoke, though his voice hardly rose above a whisper. "You're a fraud, Joseph Smith. You have deceived us all. You are no Prophet of God, and there are no miracles in Kirtland."

That night, Emma couldn't bear the sight of her husband's face, nor the way his breath would catch in his throat. She left him to his perplexity and his Bible, his talisman, his stones—left him to suffering and prayer. She took up her knitting and sat beside the fire, working stitches very slowly in the guttering light, wondering how she could do something so practical and mundane.

Someone rapped lightly at the door. Emma looked around, surprised. Who would call at this hour?

The tap came again.

She went to the door, opened it only a crack, just enough to see outside. She had half expected the grieving father with more accusations for Joseph, and by God, those accusations would have been justified. Instead, she found Patty Sessions at her door.

"Mrs. Smith—just the one I've come to find. Tell me, have you any milk still?"

The pain of losing two children in one terrible moment was still ever present, everywhere at once. That simple question alone was enough to buckle her under grief. She leaned against the doorframe. Sobs tore from her chest—and even then, she felt a tingle in her breasts, the flow of milk letting down. The night was cool. The wet stain spread across her bodice and made her shiver.

Patty saw the dark spots spreading. She drew in a long breath—satisfied, relieved. "Thank God; thank merciful God something good has come of this terrible day."

Only then did Emma realize that Patty carried a basket. It was wide and long, the sort of basket one uses to gather vegetables in the garden. But it was packed with blankets, and in the starlight, she saw the blankets move.

"Poor Mrs. Murdock," Patty said, "taken to the Lord an hour ago, and there was nothing I could do to stop it. Her husband is beside himself. He has three little children already and must raise them alone now. What could he have done with two newborn babes?"

"Two?" Emma blinked. She wiped her cheeks on her sleeve.

"May we come inside, Emma dear?"

Beside the fire, in its halo of warmth, Patty unpacked her basket. She lay the motherless twins side by side. They were so fresh and new, the cords at their bellies were still white and ringed by a rosy flush. They crinkled their faces, opened their precious mouths in red indignation, squalling loud and strong.

"Look," Patty said, "a girl and a boy. Poor dear Julia Murdock; how she would have loved them. But the babies are hale as can be, and you still have milk enough for two."

"I can't," she said—though what she couldn't do was take her eyes from the babies. The milk was flowing so insistently now that she itched inside her dress. She ached to feel those babies suckling.

"You can," Patty said. "I'm no prophetess. I can't claim to know the mind of God. I don't know why He took your babies, nor why He took

Julia Murdock tonight. But I do know He meant these children for you. You must take them, Emma. They are already yours."

Patty bundled the babies in their separate blankets and helped Emma with the buttons of her dress. By the time Joseph came to the surface of his grief and heard the voices by the fire, the twins were feeding contentedly. Such rapture Emma had never known—the sweetness of milk, the smell of the babies, which seemed to her more than a scent; it was like a hand that reached into her middle, into her heart, and clutched at her with a fierce, instinctive pressure. These were her children. Her daughter, her son. God had made her a mother at last, and she would never be separated from these two.

She looked up with a hazy smile, found Joseph there at the edge of the firelight, his sleeves hanging loose, his face long and uncomprehending.

"That man," Emma said softly. "That poor man at the meetinghouse. He was wrong about one thing. There are miracles in Kirtland, after all."

VI

But One Winter More

1831–1832

Joseph was a good father—the very best of fathers, whatever else you may say of him, whatever aspersions or sins you may lay, justly, at his feet. He took as much delight in the twins as if he had sired them himself. They were more precious than gold to him; he spent every moment he could spare holding the babies, cradling them one at a time against his heart, watching them learn and grow.

But Kirtland and the church had already changed him subtly, in ways Emma couldn't understand. Or perhaps the church—and the deaths of her natural twins—had altered Emma. She saw now with greater clarity—or through a glass darkly; even now she can't decide.

Joseph was a presence in her home, a presence in her bed, a hand on her breast in the darkness. And yet he was an interloper, a sudden intrusion upon a moment of motherly bliss or upon the staid routines of housekeeping.

He was the scraps of paper he left behind whenever he went to the meetinghouse; he was the strange inscriptions, the circles drawn in the air, and none of these were things Emma could reckon with, none added up to a husband she could comprehend. Because he was obliged to hide his true self from the congregation, he hid also from his wife. Or he had always hidden. Had he not told Isaac Hale as much when he confessed to his deceits?

She remembered the early days of their courtship. The secret visits he would pay, riding over from the Stowell farm when her parents had gone to town and she was alone at the house. He would take her hand and murmur that she was the loveliest, the worthiest woman God had ever made, and she had allowed herself to believe it. However she may find him an intrusion around the home, Joseph had still planted a longing in her to see him, to touch him when he wasn't there.

She ached for him then, in those Kirtland days, with an unabated hunger though she was his wife of four years. But this was no desire for his affection, nor for any carnal act. She longed for Joseph to become what he wasn't: a husband and father like any other. She wanted an ordinary life, and yet she wanted nothing of the sort. She found herself excited by his strange, compelling power. And because she saw him in every mood and every state of mind, she knew, or half-knew, that the Prophet was merely a construct—an image Joseph had created with his bright fabrications, his secret rituals, his towering force of will.

She half-knew this was all make-believe—the book, the visions, the commandments and revelations that came so readily to hand, straight from the heart of God the moment Joseph needed them. But she wanted to feel in her bones that prophets walked again, and a thousand years of peace were at hand, and God wasn't the cold and distant watcher she'd been taught to fear. She needed to believe that the souls of her dead children would live again. So she was resolved. If she must believe in Joseph's divinity in order to heal her heart, then she would believe. She would know the truth of his doctrines, right to the veiled center of her soul.

What is the nature of belief, after all? Is faith inborn, branded by some divine power on our spirits, or do we choose to believe, the way we choose to don a garment? You might think you know the answer. But look at the question from another angle and the answer changes like the Prophet changes when he steps outside his door.

On a dark night when the April rain beat heavily on the roof and hissed in the black mud, Emma and Joseph sat close beside the fire, rocking the twins to sleep.

"I fear we've come to a bad place after all," he said.

At first, Emma didn't hear. Her attention was fixed on her daughter, who blinked slowly in her arms and yawned. The babies had grown admirably in the month since Patty had brought them to the door. Pink and lively, they flourished like the fields as springtime advanced. They had named the boy Joseph Smith Murdock and the girl Julia Murdock

Smith, so the one who had given them life would never be forgotten. Emma traced with one finger the soft curve of Julia's ear, the silken curls of her hair, thin as drafted wool.

Only then did his words catch up to her. She looked up and found him staring into the fire, lips pressed, clutching their son as if he might use the baby as a shield.

"Kirtland," Emma said, "a bad place?"

She wanted to deny it but found she couldn't. Joseph had been forced to work ceaselessly to maintain his authority over the church. Even the advent of the priesthood had gone only so far in restoring him as head of the hierarchy. Emma suspected the novelty of priesthood would keep the men complacent for a small while. She had hoped the thousand new-comers from Fayette would temper the city's zeal, or at least dilute it. But Kirtland burned as hot as ever with longing for the Latter Days. The fever was catching. Even the humble Fayette Mormons had taken to fits of ecstasy, and each new day brought fresh talk of visions among the congregation.

The town had always been Sidney Rigdon's creation, his domain, and now his brand was burned into the flesh of the church. The mere presence of a prophet wouldn't change the people's habits. The world withered under a plague of prophets. What was one more, and what power did Joseph hold if he couldn't raise the dead?

That folly with the little boy and his grieving father—it had been a grave misstep. She held Julia more tightly, for a chill had come over her, even beside the fire. If the church abandoned Joseph as a fallen prophet, what would happen to Emma and the twins? Kirtland provided everything her family had, down to the food they ate and the blankets in which the babies were swaddled.

Without Sidney's favor, she and Joseph might be turned out on the road. Or they would be absorbed into the town, ordinary members of the church, subject to Sidney's authority.

"You can't allow the church to fall away from you," Emma said. "Without Kirtland's charity we'll have nothing to our names. We must think of the children now, if not ourselves."

"Do you think I don't know it? I've thought of nothing else since that day in the meetinghouse, that . . ." He shook his head, unwilling to speak of the dead boy. "But how am I to hold the church? How? They do whatever Sidney tells them to do, believe whatever he believes. All of them, even those who followed me from New York."

"Then you must bring Sidney more firmly under your control. Make him feel awe at your presence. Make him fear you, if you must, but keep his loyalty at any cost."

"I see that," Joseph said acidly, not looking at Emma. "I'm no fool."

The rain was a torrent, a roar against the roof. She asked herself wryly whether the ancient ways of the old prophets had been restored after all, and the world would be covered in water, and everything that displeased the Almighty drowned.

At length, he muttered, "It's like that business with Oliver and Hiram Page all over again—Hiram and his peep-stone."

"You handled that readily enough."

"Oliver is a different man from Sidney Rigdon. A breed apart."

"All men are the same, at the heart of matters. They like to feel important. They want to do great works and be remembered after they're gone."

He sat up straight, so suddenly the baby kicked and complained in his arms. "Great works. That's it, Emma. Oliver came to heel when I sent him on a mission, gave him a task to perform. But we've grown in numbers, haven't we? We'll soon outgrow this valley. We must keep moving west—spread the word of God to the edge of civilization. Oliver has done well in setting us up here, but I told him to establish a mission to the Lamanites, as well. He hasn't achieved that yet. It's work left to be done."

"Do you truly want to send missionaries into Indian territory?"

"Of course. The Indians should know the Book of Mormon. It's their history as much as ours."

"I don't believe they'll thank you for it."

"Of course they will. We can bring the Lamanites into Christ's salvation. Who wouldn't be thankful for that?"

Some challenge or denial was pressing inside her, fighting its way out, and she would have given it voice if she'd known which words to use. It wasn't that she didn't believe the history as recounted in the Book of Mormon—not exactly. She had witnessed the Book's translation. She had held the first printing in her hands, read from its pages, heard the rhythm of God's word, that distinctive music. But she also knew the Prophet as no one else did, no one in all Creation.

The rain abated some weeks later. The sky lifted its gray robes, revealing the tender blue of May. By that time, Joseph had already brought forth a new revelation. He left Kirtland with thirty of his best men—Sidney among them—to seek a certain place at the frontier's edge, which God had called Zion. There the Mormons would establish a second colony, a home from which they could minister to their Lamanite brothers, bringing the native tribes to Christ. In Zion they would build a temple to the Lord, and miracles would flourish. Even the dead would be raised. He had seen it in a vision, he told his rapt disciples: hundreds of converts waiting, yearning for the Gospel in the wild places where civilization gave way to frontier. The Mormons would go west, claim those souls, and gather to the church's bosom everyone who knew the Book of Mormon was true, and all who called its Prophet the speaker of truth.

Once the men had gone, Emma did her best to keep out of the public eye. She tended her children with Sally Knight or the midwife Patty for help and company. In the evenings, when she was alone with the babies, she wrote letters to her parents. She told her mother about the second pregnancy, the birth of her twins, how quickly they had died. She wrote to her father of Julia and little Joseph, how caring for them had filled her heart when she'd thought it hollowed out for good. But she had received no word from her family since leaving Harmony, and didn't know whether they would welcome news from the daughter who had broken their hearts. She wrote letters almost every night, but when they were finished, she fed them to the fire.

Emma left her borrowed home only when necessity required, for she thought it best not to remind Kirtland of Joseph's failure. Privately, she hoped Sidney's absence would cool a few brows, but the visions carried on as before.

At night there was shouting in the streets: *I have seen God and Jesus Christ; they stand even now on my rooftop, glowing, bright as the sun; come and see.*

It was given to me to know that a great storm is coming, a mighty wind as in the days of prophets, and six-sevenths of all our crops will be destroyed unless we repent, even this night, here and now, on our knees.

The widow Hubble was stricken blind for three days. When her sight

returned, she told what she had seen: the heavens opening, a great staircase coming down, and on the staircase the angels marched with swords
of fire drawn.

No less than four unmarried girls fell into fits on that same day, in
the same hour, at the four corners of the town, and on the Morleys' farm
an egg was dropped from the hen coop, and it broke to reveal a chick
half-formed in the shell, with two heads and scales like a serpent. The
monstrous thing was red as blood.

On the road headed west, Martin Harris saw Jesus Christ in the form
of a deer. It walked with him two miles, meek and tame, just beyond the
reach of his hand. The Savior's feet pressed into damp green moss and
every step, between the cleft of His hooves, brought flowers red from the
ground.

By the end of that summer, 1831, Joseph had returned to Kirtland with
all thirty of his missionaries behind him. Emma left the children in
Patty's care and went to the town crossroads in front of the mercantile
to welcome the party home.

When the men had dismounted and the calls from the crowd had died
away, the Prophet climbed the mercantile steps and looked out over his
congregation. Joseph wore an easy smile along with the dust of travel.
Sidney joined him on the mercantile porch but hung well back, his face
turned humbly down to the planks below his feet. Emma released a long
breath. The knots in her spine began to loosen. Only then did she realize
she had carried that tension all the months Joseph had been away.

"My dear brothers and sisters," Joseph said. "By the grace of God,
we've returned to you, and we come with good news. After we wandered
for many days, we were led to a town at the farthest edge of civilization,
a place called Independence in the state of Missouri. Just beyond the
town was a high hill. I climbed it alone, and beheld a vision there, a
sacred vision from the Lord."

The crowd seemed to lean as one toward him, shivering with anticipation as he recounted what he had seen. Even Emma could feel herself
drawn into the story. She could see the land he described as clearly as if
she'd stood on that hill beside him, witnessing it all with her own eyes.
A world that seemed promised to the church alone. The slope of the hill
obscured by the low, scrubby forest of Missouri country, and beyond the

woodland the broad, fertile valley of a gleaming river. The river was so wide, it seemed the only river God had ever made—a specimen of holy perfection, its surface bright and shifting with color under an endless sky. Beyond the river, a green land flat and empty, a page waiting to be written, and the distant peaks of the Rocky Mountains, blue like the sky, a flawless blue, but distinct in the white haze hanging where the sky bent down to the earth.

"I saw," he went on, "a great white temple, a House of the Lord. And a river of men flowing into that temple. White men, red men, all of them brothers, all at peace under the power of the true, reinstated word."

Someone called from the crowd, "What does it mean, Brother Joseph?"

"We will go west. Not merely to carry the word to the tribes, but to build that temple—yea, even the very temple of my vision. We shall be as Solomon's people in the days of old and raise a house of worship to delight the one true God."

After the crowd had roared its assent and Joseph and Sidney had shaken hands before the whole congregation—after they all had returned to their homes, Emma and Joseph included—she asked him how he'd managed it.

"Managed what, my dear—my own dearest of Emmas?"

Patty had just left, after offering her warmest welcome to the Prophet and tucking the sleeping Little Joe into Emma's arms. Joseph had taken off his riding boots beside the hearth. He padded across the room in his stocking feet to where baby Julia was crawling over a patchwork blanket, chasing the leather ball Patty had brought as a gift for the children. Joseph scooped Julia up and nuzzled her hair, kissed her small fat nose. She squealed with delight at having her papa home again.

"I mean," Emma said, "how did you put Sidney Rigdon in his place? He looked almost contrite, standing behind you and holding his tongue right there for the whole town to see."

He gave her a cool smile. "Sidney was a problem easily solved, once I got him away from the congregation. Every night, whether we stayed at inns or slept out under the stars, we shared our supper and then the whole company discussed Scripture or listened to one teaching or another from the Holy Bible. Sometimes I led those talks, and sometimes Sidney. Now and again, I invited some other fellow to take the lead. But most often it was Sidney or I, and before we began our nightly teaching, he and I would repair together to some private spot and pray. That was how we came to share our vision."

"A shared vision? With Sidney?"

"He saw what I saw,"

Joseph said it so calmly that she couldn't help supplying the words he'd left unspoken. *He saw what I wanted him to see.*

Once more, Joseph described the vision so vividly, she was half convinced she was witnessing it herself. She saw—as Joseph and Sidney had seen—the sky with its greater and lesser lights. The sun, the moon, the stars. And when he suggested that the lights in the vision represented three kingdoms that waited for mankind after death—each kingdom greater in glory than the last—Emma thought, *Of course. What else could it mean?*

"Sidney was so moved by what he saw," Joseph said, "he was stricken to weakness. He could barely stand and couldn't speak for a full day after."

But Joseph had risen unshaken from his knees. "Brother Sidney isn't as used to it as I am," he'd told the missionaries. And Sidney, having been emptied out by the power of the Lord, had declared when he could speak again that Joseph was the Prophet, the only true Prophet to walk this earth.

Emma sagged with relief when he finished the story. Kirtland was back in the Prophet's hands, more surely than ever before.

"Sidney agrees that we must move the whole church to Missouri." Joseph sat easily in the rocking chair, bouncing Julia on his knee. "So that's that, my dear. We'll go to Zion and build the temple and bring the Gospel west. We'll remain in Ohio but one winter more."

"Leave Kirtland?" Relief left Emma in an instant, pinched out like a candle flame. "Are you mad? You've only just regained your church, and it was hard-won. Now you would throw your congregation away again."

"I'm not proposing we throw anything away."

"You told your followers that Kirtland is holy ground. They believed you."

"So it is."

"And God's people should—what—up and wander off from a consecrated place? A place you declared pleases the Lord more than any other?"

"It's the people gathered in a place that make it holy, not the dirt beneath their feet."

"Your church won't see it that way."

"They will when I explain. We've been called to a great work. We're to build a temple in the west."

"Build a temple here."

"God hasn't commanded me to build a temple here."

"The people will follow you as long as Sidney trusts you, but the moment he comes to doubt you again, you'll lose him, Joseph, and this time you'll lose him for good."

He stopped bouncing the baby. He set Julia on the floor, allowed her to crawl away. Joseph rose stiffly and began pacing the room, to the window and back to the fire, neither looking at Emma nor speaking.

"Build your temple here," she said again.

"It's Missouri where we ought to build. Zion is waiting for us."

"Yet here you are in Kirtland, with more than a thousand members in your church. You can't command them like a man telling his dog to sit and heel. They are too many. Matters aren't as simple as they were in Fayette."

At the window, he pinched the bridge of his nose. His eyes were screwed shut. In the silence, Emma could hear someone crying in the town: *I've had a revelation; come and see.*

Finally, Joseph looked at Emma with their son in her arms, and everything in him that was hard and calculating fell away. The tension eased in his face. A wistful look came over him—perhaps it was sorrow. The change took her aback. He hadn't looked at her that way, that soft and longing way, since before they were married.

"I miss Harmony," he said.

Emma laughed. She couldn't help herself. "Harmony, where they called you a blasphemer, where they called you the Antichrist?"

"Not that. I miss the cabin—our home. It was so quiet there. I could hear my own thoughts. The fields in the sunshine, the little trails through the woods. Whenever I felt troubled in those days, I could walk down to the river and stay as long as I liked. I could skip stones across the water."

"There's a river here, not so far away."

"But if I tried it now, if I went down to the river, they would crowd around me begging for a miracle."

"You're a prophet, Joseph. What else should a prophet expect his followers to do?"

For a long moment he didn't answer. Then, quietly, he said, "I doubt I could still do it—skip a stone. I think I've lost the knack. It's been so long since I've tried."

You see, Joseph was retreating by that time. Retreating from what he had made, for it had grown far beyond his reckoning, beyond what size he had imagined a thing could grow—and faster, much faster than anyone could countenance. The church had become a force and a monolith, a solid density like the black walls of a dream, the way some ill dream takes hold of you, so even when you wake you can feel it still, the stifling way it had pressed around you and cut off your breath, the way you had tried, your dream-self, to walk through it, but its heaviness was all you could comprehend. A vague, unspecified threat.

Sidney had begun exhorting Joseph to write down all his revelations and make another book, or if he wouldn't write another book, then revise the Holy Bible, flesh it out with new understanding. He retreated from the constant murmur that moved through Kirtland, the cold look in some of his congregants' eyes, their silence when the Prophet passed by. Word had gotten out that Joseph meant to move the church to Missouri, and Kirtland was no longer the holy land.

Despite anticipation of the temple on the Missouri frontier, half the town chilled around Joseph, just as Emma had feared. If not for the fact that Sidney still believed—bound tightly to Joseph by their shared vision of the three lights and kingdoms—the church itself might have driven Joseph away. Emma was no fool. She understood that Joseph held only the loosest grip on his livelihood. And so she didn't complain when, late in the summer of 1831, he decided to move outside Kirtland, to the Johnson farm, where he would pass the winter writing the texts Sidney had demanded and preparing for the journey to Zion.

The Johnson farm stood thirty-five miles beyond the city. The white clapboard house with its brick chimney and twelve-pane windows crowned a gentle rise. Split-rail fences, weathered to silver, flowed like cheerful brooks down the sides of the hill into fertile fields. A stand of oaks graced the property, and in the blaze of summer's final, most determined heat, the ground below the trees was blue, inviting with its shade.

All the Johnson family came out to the drive, waving and calling while the Smith carriage rolled into the yard. John Johnson had been a loyal adherent since Joseph had healed his wife's useless arm. Now the whole family had been baptized into the church. His youngest, sixteen-year-old Nancy Marinda, stood holding her mother's hand, dabbing away tears of excitement at the Prophet's arrival. His son Eli, aged twenty-three, had just purchased an adjoining lot on which to build his own farm. Eli, too, came out to welcome the Smith family to the Johnson home.

"We're honored to offer our roof," old John said, clapping Joseph on the shoulder. "You bless us by your coming."

"It's we who are honored," he answered. "I've another book to compile. I hope to finish it before winter's out. Kirtland has grown so big, a man can't hardly think there. It's peace and quiet I need to carry out my work."

Emma noted, as John's wife, Elsa, led them all toward the house, that the woman's afflicted arm still hung limp at her side, the fingers thin and curled, half-hidden in her sleeve.

"There's plenty of room here." Elsa's gray head bobbed in a ruffled cap. "Plenty of *rooms*; we raised nine children in this house, years past. We've set aside the little room upstairs, first on the left, for the Prophet's study. You may have your pick of the others, but I do think you'd be wisest to choose this one here on the main floor. It's the biggest and best."

The bedroom was spacious indeed. Two windows let in the light of early afternoon. The place seemed to breathe easily, glowing and serene, with a cascade of sunlit motes glittering against the dark-paneled walls. A large bed with an intricately stitched counterpane dominated the room. Emma could see a trundle underneath, just the place for the twins to sleep. Outside there were no shouts about omens, no seers proclaiming visions—only a sustained whisper from the oak leaves, nothing more.

"This room will do nicely," Emma said. "Better than that—it's everything I could have dreamed."

That first evening, and every evening to come, while Elsa served up pie or ginger snaps after a hearty supper, Joseph sat beside the fireplace preaching his small, intimate sermons. The Johnsons were enthralled from the start. By the end of the first week, John's grown sons hurried over in the fading light with their wives and babies. They pulled ladder-back chairs and old milking stools and even cushions into a rough circle—and all of them, even the smallest children, listened to Joseph's teaching. Kirtland with its fervid hunger seemed a thousand miles away. Emma recalled those early days at the Harmony cabin, when she had first seen the potential of the church. The memory carried a pleasant pang. If only the church had stayed as it once had been—small, neigh-borly, only forty members in all.

By day, when Joseph was closeted in his study, Emma delighted in the companionship of old Mrs. Johnson and her young daughter. She found it invigorating to turn the twins over to someone else and pass the hours baking bread, or perfecting a stew in Elsa's great black kettle, or sewing new shirts for the children—they grew with astonishing speed. Elsa seemed glad to relinquish the bulk of her housework to another grown woman. Miraculous healing or no, the lame arm troubled her from time to time—perhaps more often than she cared to show. And her daughter Nancy Marinda, though a good and earnest girl, was neverthe-less plagued by dreaminess, and couldn't always be counted on to see her work through.

Emma found Nancy Marinda a great help with the twins, however. The girl was enraptured by babies. She would spread out a blanket in the sitting room, before the double-sided hearth, and play with the twins for hours. The babies had begun to sit up on their own, and Little Joe rolled from place to place across the floor. He drove Emma to distraction, for he would often roll under some piece of furniture, then shriek with frus-tration, and he couldn't always be extracted easily. Nancy Marinda kept the child neatly corralled and out of trouble while Emma worked in the kitchen. The girl made little dollies out of corn husks, and balls from scraps of old leather, and brought the twins to Emma for feeding when-ever they began to fuss.

She was a pretty girl, Nancy Marinda. Years later, Emma couldn't recall what she looked like in precise terms—the shape of her nose, the color of her lips, the way she fixed her hair. But she remembered that Nancy Marinda was pretty. That fact was seared forever into memory. A day would come when Emma would dwell on the girl's beauty, and other things—specific memories, isolated moments that intruded on her thoughts, sudden and horrifying as thieves in the night.

There was an evening in late October when the Johnson clan had gathered around the fireplace to hear another sermon. And Nancy Marinda had come down the stairs at just the right moment, when everyone else was already silent with anticipation. The tread of a foot on the stair. The slow emergence of the girl into view—she had changed into a new frock, deep claret red with a little white lace at her throat. She was vivid, hair neatly plaited so it shone in the lamplight, and that red dress had skimmed over her body with its latent curves. The girl had pressed against her small, new bosom a copy of the Book of Mormon. She looked down shyly, with one white hand on the bannister, but she glanced up and caught the Prophet's eye. Her cheeks colored; she smiled.

And there had been the day, sometime after Christmas, when Nancy Marinda had been strangely quiet while she tended the twins. Emma had been sewing at the fire, and Nancy Marinda was cross-legged on the floor, rolling the ball absently back and forth between her hands. She caught the ball and went very still, and without looking at Emma, said, "What's it like being the wife of the Prophet, Mrs. Smith?"

At the new year, the twins fell sick with measles—a wonder they'd caught it at all, isolated as the farm was. Old John fetched a doctor from town, and the doctor assured Emma the case wasn't serious. He expected Little Joe and Julia to recover without much fuss. Still, two sick babies had worn the entire household to distraction. Emma would have been beside herself, ground to the bone, if not for Elsa and Nancy Marinda. Between them, the Johnson women saw to it that Emma got her share of sleep. They never complained of the extra work.

"Get them each something nice," Emma said to Joseph, "when next you go to Kirtland. Some gifts to show our thanks."

He did just that. When he returned from his next sermon in the city, he took from the pocket of his frock coat three silk kerchiefs for Elsa. And for Nancy Marinda, a necklace made of white beads. He fastened the necklace around the girl's slender throat. From that day on, Emma never saw the girl without her simulated pearls.

Sometimes, after the spring thaw, Eli Johnson would ride to Kirtland beside Joseph, accompanying him to the Sunday meeting. Eli hadn't a wife or family of his own, not yet, and he and Joseph were so near in age that they made natural companions.

But if Eli found himself too weary after a hard week of building, it was Nancy Marinda who made the ride. Emma saw them once, out beside the Johnson barn, readying their horses. Joseph, dressed in his smartest coat, checked the reins on the girl's mare. There was a mounting block in the yard, but he put his hands around her waist and lifted her to the saddle. He stood as close to Nancy Marinda as a brother might stand while she arranged her skirt over the head of her sidesaddle. She laughed, a shrill giggle at Joseph's strength and nearness. Loud enough that Emma could hear, even in the house.

That evening, when the meeting was over and Joseph and Nancy Marinda had returned from Kirtland, Emma asked how things fared in town.

"Fare?" Joseph said.

"Kirtland's mood and temper. Are they kinder to you, more willing to follow, now that you've removed yourself from their midst?"

But he didn't want to talk about Kirtland. He preferred Zion and a hopeful future, the great expanse of plains and mountains that waited for him out there, in the place God had made just for him.

When the weather was good, he went down to the creek at the bottom of the Johnson acres to skip stones over the millpond. When the weather was good, sometimes Emma called for Nancy Marinda to come and help with the children, but the girl wasn't at hand.

Late in the month of March, on a cold and brittle night, Emma found herself awake near the midnight hour. She was rocking Little Joe with a hot damp cloth held against his ear. The boy had continued to suffer with earaches and regular attacks of the croup since his bout with measles.

The doctor had warned Emma that her son may be susceptible to such maladies for months to come; some children recovered very slowly from the illness. The house was silent, save for the baby's breathing and Emma's soft murmur of nursery songs. John and Elsa had taken Nancy Marinda across the valley to visit a cousin on the bank of the Cuyahoga. Joseph had fallen asleep on the trundle bed with Julia beside him.

The silence of that night, the peace, returned to her memory time and again, as if to mock her for not knowing. As if to chastise her—she ought to have seen what was coming, sensed the danger long before it arrived.

Perhaps she did sense something, moments before. She remembered pausing. Rocking Little Joe, then not rocking—straining to hear over the pop and flutter of the fire. What had she heard? The scrape of a boot on the porch step, or the sound of hooves out in the night-black yard, too many horses for the Johnsons to have come.

Just when she settled back and began to rock again, the front door crashed in. Emma leaped to her feet. Little Joe screamed in fear; she whirled and there were men in the house, crowding in, bellowing and shoving. The men had smeared their faces with soot to hide their identities, but she recognized a few: Kirtlanders, all of them, and Eli Johnson among them. They swarmed across the house like hornets from a kicked hive.

Someone tore Little Joe from her arms. She screamed with rage but there was nothing more she could do; she couldn't even reach out to plead with them, *Give me back my baby, don't hurt him*, for someone was holding her arms behind her back and she couldn't move, couldn't break free.

Joseph was roused by the noise. He cursed—words Emma had never suspected her husband might know—and Julia wailed in terror. A moment later the men dragged Joseph out into the sitting room, into the light.

"Please," Emma wept. "Why ever you've come, don't hurt him. Don't hurt any of us; I beg you."

No one so much as looked at her. They ripped the shirt from Joseph's back while he twisted in the middle of the crowd. Over the bellows of the mob and the cries of her children, she could hear the smack of fists against flesh. "Strip off his trousers," someone said. First Joseph's trousers, then his undergarments were flung across the room. The baying pack made for the door and the cold outside. They dragged Joseph, naked and beaten, his bare feet scrabbling helplessly on the floor.

Whoever had held Emma released her. Little Joe was thrust back into her arms. She clutched her son instinctively, cowering against the hearth with her back to the crowd, afraid all at once that they would take her child again and beat him, too. After a few wild moments, she realized the mob had gone. But if that mob could come down so violently upon the Prophet, Emma had no reason to believe they would spare her or the children.

She rushed into the bedroom where Julia was sitting up on the trundle bed, screaming, red-faced and frantic. "Hush," Emma said, rapidly, impatiently, "hush now, be quiet!" She wrapped each of the twins in a small blanket, then scooped them into her arms and hurried through the house to the kitchen door.

It was no easy task to open the door with two frightened babies in her arms. She left it hanging open and ran to a little shed at the edge of the yard, where Elsa dried herbs and set her cheeses to cure. The night was so cold, every breath burned in her chest; her eyes stung with tears. She prayed as she ran. *Let me not fall, my God. Let me not fall upon my children. Let those men not see me and come after me. Please let my children be safe.* Only when she'd thrown open the door to the shed did Emma think to pray for Joseph's safety, too.

She crept into the dark of that shelter one hesitant step at a time. The children were quiet, startled out of crying by the shock of cold. Her thigh bumped into the edge of the long, deep shelf where Elsa stored her cheeses. She set the twins down, warning them again to hush, then groped along the plank wall until she found the small casement shutter and pushed it open, just wide enough that she could peer with one eye into the yard.

The mob had brought lanterns, tin-can lanterns punched with holes so the scene was all a whirl of light: spots of orange candle-glow, half-moons, jagged stars sliding over a tangle of limbs. The hectic lights illuminated a soot-covered face distorted with anger and disgust, now a boot flying toward Joseph's ribs, now the swing of a fist and now—now, with a flash of clarity that made her breath catch, Joseph's face buckled in pain, his arms raising, but how could he protect himself when the blows came from every direction?

"Hold him down," someone shouted. Eli Johnson—Emma knew his voice.

The men spread Joseph out naked in the yard, bare against the frozen ground. They knelt on his arms, they sat on his legs to keep him still and exposed. He howled in helpless shame.

"Where's the doctor?" Eli barked. "Come on; you know why we've brought you."

Someone in the crowd made a timid reply.

"And I tell you to castrate him." Eli's voice was hoarse with anger. "You all heard what he did to my sister."

Someone else shouted, "If he wants to behave like a he-goat, then we'll turn him into a wether!"

Still the doctor resisted.

"Tar, then," another man yelled. "Get the tar from the wagon!"

There was another flurry of activity, someone bending over Joseph. He arched his back. Even in darkness, with only those spots of lantern light to show it, Emma could see how his limbs tensed; he struggled to break free. The men backed away, jeering—all but those who kept the prophet pinned against the earth. And then she could see the warm tar falling in streams from their buckets. She could smell it on the night air, a hot, acrid stink.

Someone brought a pillow—from the house or the wagon, Emma didn't know. They tore it with their hands, ripped into it as if it were the carcass of some small animal they had killed. Feathers rained down on Joseph, sticking in the tar. Stray feathers lifted on the air and drifted past the shed, past the window where Emma watched, shivering and weeping. Finally, the men issued a few last kicks and retreated to their wagon. Joseph was alone, writhing in pain, sobbing from the savage cold.

Emma went to him as soon as the mob had gone. She fell on her knees beside him, the twins heavy in her arms. "Oh, Joseph, what have they done to you?"

He tried to roll onto his stomach, push himself up to hands and knees. He fell back, cringing. "Put the twins inside." His voice was weak. It grated in his throat. "Then come back and help me."

By the time she'd supported Joseph into the house, her dress was ruined with tar. He looked a sorry sight—battered, head hanging, smeared with pitch and feathers, and between the swaths of tar, where his skin still showed, livid purple bruises were already spreading. In the firelight, she could see that his lip was bleeding. It had been sliced by some weapon, or bitten through.

She brought a clean rag from the kitchen, made Joseph hold it against his mouth to stanch the blood. He said carefully, muffled by the rag, "Someone tried to force a glass vial into my mouth. Tried to make me swallow whatever was inside. I broke the bottle with my teeth, rather than be poisoned. Wonder I didn't break my teeth, too."

"Don't speak," Emma said.

Numb and clumsy with fear, she guided him to the hearth and made him sit on its ledge, so the heat would soften the tar. Neither Emma nor Joseph slept that night. She scraped patiently at the mess, cleaning away all she could. Blackish stains remained on his skin. She was weary to her bones by the time the sun came up. She sat back on her heels, looking dull-eyed at his naked body, the angry bruises, the bloody raw places where the tar had torn away his skin.

"That's the best I can do," she said.

"It's enough." He rose slowly, wincing, and limped to their room. "Come and help me dress."

"You need rest, Joseph."

"It's Sunday. I need to go and give my sermon at the meetinghouse."

She stared after him for a long moment, even after he'd disappeared into the bedroom where the twins were sleeping. Finally, she dropped the tar-stained rag and staggered after him. "You can't mean it."

"Indeed, I do. Let my followers see—let the whole church see what has befallen their Prophet."

"They'll ask why. They'll wonder what you've done to deserve such treatment."

"Did I?" He looked up sharply from his clothing trunk. "Did I deserve it?"

Emma didn't know how to answer. She wanted to demand of him, What did you do, after all? What did Eli tell those men about you and Nancy Marinda? And was it the truth, or a lie? But she couldn't be sure he would answer honestly. She didn't know if she wanted the truth or one of his casual stories. She said nothing at all.

He rode to town that morning, though he was weak from lack of sleep as much as from the beating. He went to the meetinghouse—Emma would hear of it later, from Sally Knight and others. He stood before his church with his sleeves rolled up to show the bruises, the bloody scrapes, the cut on his lip that would one day become a permanent scar.

He delivered God's word patiently, with quiet dignity, and never spoke of ill treatment at the hands of his own men. From that day on, the greater part of Kirtland was convinced—for better or worse—that

Joseph Smith was a good and humble man, a prophet worth respecting. A man who could be trusted in all things.

He had planned to set out for Missouri only a few days after that sermon. Sidney Rigdon was eager to leave, once he learned how poorly the Prophet had been used. But they couldn't go just yet. Little Joe took pneumonia from the cold on that terrible night when the mob had come for his father. Every doctor and midwife in Kirtland worked to save the Prophet's son. One of them, Emma knew, must have been the very same doctor who'd come that night with a knife in his hand, promising to make Joseph a wether. She didn't care. She never attempted to learn which man had joined in the attack. She would have forgiven him anything if he'd been able to save her child. She would have forgiven God anything, if He had kept Little Joe alive.

When Joseph departed for Missouri more than a week later, he left another small grave behind. Little Joe was laid to rest beside the twins God had already claimed. The Lord had demanded His price again, but this time, Emma hadn't the least idea why she had been made to pay it.

June 28, 1844
Nauvoo, Illinois

When she wakes from a dream, she is lost and frightened, sitting up in her chair beside a dwindling fire, with a stiff neck and aching shoulders. She had thought she wouldn't sleep that night, as she hadn't slept the two nights since Joseph was taken. At first, she believes there is no difference between dreams and the waking world, and what she sees in her mind, behind the merciful walls of sleep, is the only reality.

She was on a hill. A high hill with a peak like a hunter's cap, and it was night, the stars in their multitudes were like the members of Joseph's church, countless and blazing. She dug into the soil. The earth yielded before her, moving itself away, so the labor was easy, and when she uncovered the stone box, she knelt and lifted its lid. Inside, a creature moved, shrinking from the starlight, coiling in the dark. What was the creature? A toad, or something like it—pale, soft-bodied, wide mouth and staring eyes. She cringed, but when she looked again, it had transformed into an angel or a man. The creature had turned into Joseph. He stood with both his feet inside the stone box, knee-deep in the earth. He looked down on Emma unsmiling, his face sober and white. There was no sorrow in his eyes, but neither was there joy, nor triumph. He never spoke, nor moved his hand. But the sky above him opened, separating like the edges of a wound, and something thick and dark poured down, flowing over his face, hiding him from sight.

In the moment of waking, she'd thought that substance had been tar. Now, shivering, she knows it was the wax poured for his death mask.

She rises from the chair. Her dress feels stiff and confining, heavy with the grime of two days' wear, yet she can't seem to remove it. She can't move forward into this future, the new reality already shaping itself around her.

The Mansion is quiet, but not with sleep. Down all its halls, Joseph's women sit beside their windows or lie awake with faces turned toward the light. She can feel them, all of them at once, a collective agony thinned and stretched by the days. What one woman feels under

Joseph's roof, they all must feel. Such is the law of sisterhood, and whatever else this life has made them, they are sisters of a kind.

Porter Rockwell didn't return in the night. She sees the first soft blush of dawn at her window, picking the trees from a flat square of sky, and she knows Porter hasn't returned this morning, either—the third day since Joseph was taken and the Illinois militia laid siege to Nauvoo. And still the church has no word of its Prophet, no relief.

She hears a rustle in the hall outside her door. She leans out into the hall, prepared to scold one of the girls back to bed. She stops when she sees the figure moving slowly through the darkness: Eliza Snow. Eliza's arms hang limp at her sides. Her face is turned up, as if she looks to Heaven for mercy, as if she looks for the ropes that hold her upright when she wants nothing more than to fall down into her grave. She drifts from one side of the hallway to another, scarcely aware of the solid walls around her.

The grief on her face—in every line of her—is more than Emma can bear. And yet, what is her purpose, what has the work of her life been, if not to endure the unbearable?

"Eliza," Emma says.

Momentarily, the name recalls the woman from her misery. She straightens, and looks almost regal, as she used to look in the early days. She turns toward the voice; Emma can see the effort it costs her, to focus, to comprehend. When she realizes it's Emma who has spoken, she gives a little gasp, steps back as if she fears Emma will strike her. Perhaps she's right to fear it.

"Come here." Emma holds out a hand. She doesn't want to comfort this woman who has broken her heart more ruthlessly than any other has done. But this church is Emma's now, or will be soon. It's her task to minister to all who suffer.

Eliza approaches like a horse led to the farrier, gripped by an instinct to run. But she comes. She allows Emma to take her hand and lead her into the bedroom. Her face is gaunt; there are deep pits around her eyes. She isn't as pretty as she once had been. Grief and time have worn all beauty away.

Emma draws her to the fireplace. "Sit." She sinks at once into the armchair, the very one that lured Emma into sleep. Emma is flooded now by a restless new anger. She wants to pace. She wants to shout and

claw at something—at the walls, at Eliza Snow—but what would be
the use?

"I have heard." Eliza's voice is small, broken. "I have heard—"

"You should know better than to listen to rumor. You, a person of
such standing, leader of our women."

"It isn't rumor I heard, but an angel, or God Himself whispering in
my ear. He told me—"

"Don't say it."

Eliza has a certain faculty with words, almost a kind of magic. It's
a gift Emma has often envied, along with her many other blessings. As
a girl working charms by the hearth fire, Emma would have called it a
knack—Eliza's special power of translating thoughts and feelings into
words, and thereby making them larger than reality, more real than real.
She can't suffer the strange enchantment now. If Eliza gives voice to her
bleak knowing, then Emma will feel it, too. She can't admit that Joseph
is gone. Not until proof comes, and she can no longer hide from the
knowing.

Emma says, "You haven't slept."

"Not since they took him. I have tried, but sleep evades me. It's cruel,
Emma, for I might see him in my dreams."

"In dreams, you might not like the sight of him."

Eliza watches the last weak flames lick up from the cinders, the
ashen cinders expiring. She says, "And what about you? Have you slept,
Emma dear?"

Such simple, unquestioned affection in her voice, such love after these
bitter years. As if nothing had ever soured between them. Emma turns
away, looking out the window at the dawn light spreading so Eliza can't
see the tears in her eyes.

When she can be sure of her voice, she answers. "I haven't slept much.
Not more than an hour or two."

"Quite a pair we make."

What a pair they'd always made.

"I sent Porter Rockwell to Carthage," Emma says, "to learn what he
could. You can be certain Governor Ford will never tell us the truth—
not until extremity forces him. But Porter hasn't returned. It may be that
Ford's men have caught him. I can't think of a way to find out without
raising the governor's ire."

"Send Brigham Young. He can talk his way through anything, and when talking fails, he can knock any obstacle over."

"That's the trouble. Brigham is too heavy-handed, and this is a delicate mission."

"Brother Brigham can be delicate when circumstance demands."

Emma scowls. "I've never seen that man act with delicacy in all my life—not as long as I've known him, which is longer than you've known him, need I remind you."

"Brigham is dedicated to this church."

"To his version of the church. Which, as you know, is not the version Joseph wished to continue." Her heart catches in her throat. She hears her own words then, the past tense. Quickly, she amends: "The version Joseph wishes, I meant to say."

"You dislike Brother Brigham because he upholds the truth of the Restoration."

"I dislike Brigham because he's a dangerous man. And the Restoration has been stricken down, erased by new revelations. Or do you no longer believe the teachings of Joseph, the Prophet of God and your . . . your former husband?"

Eliza watches the cinders again. The pale morning light falls gently on her face; it pulls back the shroud of her weariness, reveals her in all her fine beauty, her confident bearing. At length, she says, "Joseph will forever be my husband, whether our marriage is recognized by the church or by the laws of man. Or by you, Emma. Our hearts have been sealed together. I am his wife and will be his wife in the world yet to come. Not even death can separate us."

"Death can separate you," Emma says coldly. "Be sure of it."

"Brother Brigham is not a dangerous man. You recall how he helped us. He got us out of Kirtland, and then Far West. He sent us here, to Nauvoo and safety, when the world was burning. Surely, Emma, you haven't forgotten."

"Have you forgotten the way Brigham has behaved more lately? Pushing Joseph to hazard, goading him into these rash behaviors. And accusing me of trying to poison my own husband. Mark my words, someday we'll learn it was Brigham's idea to destroy the *Expositor*. And so it's his fault that we find ourselves where we do, with our city under siege and the wolves circling the sheepfold. Joseph and fifteen other good men are in prison. Perhaps worse than imprisoned. They might be dead already."

Eliza buckles, as if those words were a physical blow. She covers her face with her hands and a sound comes from her throat—a moan, an extended breath—as if her very soul is tearing itself free, rushing beyond her reach.

"Brace up," Emma says. "You mustn't act this way. You must be strong."

"You were ever the strong one," Eliza whispers, "not I."

She wants to say, *Why did you ever think me strong? Why did you take my forbearance for granted, all of you, Joseph and all his women, Brigham and all his men? Why did you take and take from me, and never pause to wonder whether I was strong enough to bear it?*

But the words won't come. The light is expanding inside the room, a stark light, the kind of light by which all things may be seen. Emma maintains her silence. It would be cruel now to cast up these old grievances, the hard, cold pieces of her heart. Eliza is suffering, and well does she know what it means to suffer. There's no need to hurt Eliza now, when the world and God have wounded her so deeply. Or perhaps Emma doesn't speak because she knows now that Eliza is right. She possessed this strength all along, even when she never saw it.

VII

In God's Name, Look to the Heavens

1832–1834

What use in dwelling on sorrow? Thank God, we can speak of happier things.

In March, Joseph took his most loyal men to Missouri—and Emma, stung by shame, found she couldn't continue living with the Johnson family, though they welcomed her. The church may have been satisfied that their Prophet was innocent, but Eli still watched Joseph with the same hard stare. And the girl Nancy Marinda refused to remove her necklace of pearl beads. She had wept more bitterly than Emma when Joseph had made his farewells and struck out west for Zion.

Instead, Emma found a new home in the upper story of Kirtland's mercantile—in Newel Whitney's fine, white building at the crossroads. She had two small but pleasant rooms for herself and little Julia, each room flanking one of the brick chimneys, so they were always warm at night. There was a kitchen of sorts on the first floor behind the mercantile proper, where Emma worked alongside Ann, mistress of the household.

Ann Whitney was the steadiest, most sensible person in all of Kirtland, save for Emma herself. A fount of Christian charity, she was mother to six children of her own and had adopted six orphans besides. She and the eldest members of her brood worked from sun to sun. They sang all the while, the whole lot of them, for Ann had trained her children in harmonies, so Emma found work in the Whitney household more pleasure than exertion, with every hour brightened and blessed by music. The children moved around her, biddable and smiling, and like a choir of angels their harmonies lifted her sunken spirit, reminding her that the same God who punished the sinner also blessed the righteous.

Joseph was thoroughly occupied with his new settlement in Missouri. He sent frequent letters praising Emma as a good and patient wife, an elect lady indeed, and pining for Julia, the delight of his heart. He wrote, too, of the ways he had organized the church. Oliver, Parley, the Whitmer family, his brothers and his father had followed him to Missouri, eager to build the temple the Lord had commanded. Joseph had gathered new members into his fold, too, for wherever he went, people were drawn to his earthy charm. By that spring, more than three hundred members had left for Zion. Joseph's dignity in the wake of the mob's attack had restored their faith in the Prophet, and they longed to labor at his side.

Together, on the edge of Christian civilization, Joseph and his many priests guided the growing church into the future.

Emma found her husband easier to love when he was far from her side. When Joseph was near, so was the power of his station and the awe of his followers, which extended sometimes even to Emma. Sometimes they would kiss her hands or bow as if she were a queen, which had always struck her as vaguely sinful; she was no golden calf. And when Joseph was near, so too were the doubts she couldn't pluck from her heart. The roots of her misgivings had delved too deeply inside. She recalled her husband's face when he'd rested his hands on Newel Knight's head and commanded him to be healed—that expression of bewilderment, of mild pain, as if he'd been startled that his prayer had worked. The memory of that poor father with the dead child in his arms—the way the man had looked Joseph in the eye and said, *You're a fraud and a deceiver.* When Joseph was far away, she scarcely thought of him, except when she read his letters—and then he expressed his affection and praise in such familiar, charming terms, all thoughts of her husband were warm and furred around the edges, softened by merciful distance. She thought, *Have I come to love my husband at last, and only now, when he is no longer beside me?*

That summer was a sanctuary for the spirit. Julia thrived under the Whitney roof. She was walking now, even running a few steps with a stilted, precarious stride. She had already learned a dozen words. Beaming down at Julia as proudly as if she were one of the Whitney brood, Ann declared she had never seen a brighter baby. Emma gave herself entirely to the delights of motherhood, marking with wonder all of Julia's new achievements, savoring the quiet moments when those small eyes opened wide, wondering at a bright and gentle world.

There was no need to venture out into Kirtland. Let the seers howl in the streets about their visions and visitations. Emma allowed herself to hear the songs of the Whitney children and nothing more. The world contracted around her, became a small and ordinary thing, untouched by miracles, unless they were the simple miracles that occur between a mother and child—a new word, a laugh, time preserved in memory, hanging in filigrees of gold.

In that season of warmth, she set to work on her hymnal, the sacred task God had given to her alone. When the daily tasks were finished, she would lounge in a dapple of afternoon shade under the lilacs, writing lyrics and notations on a roll of papers she kept tied with a cotton string.

She had no difficulty in finding inspiration, for even if Ann and her children hadn't sung all day, Emma's heart sang enough for a hundred voices. There was the peace and privacy of her new home. And this newfound affection for Joseph, the warm pressure in her chest when she read his letters. Most precious of all, the knowledge that she would soon give Julia a new brother or sister—a gift Joseph had left just before he'd gone to Missouri.

The baby would arrive in November. When she was certain of the time, Emma wrote to Joseph and gave him the news. *I am sorry*, she told him, *not to have mentioned it sooner, but the Lord has taken so many of our children already. I didn't want to raise your hopes falsely only to break your heart.*

His answering letter arrived so quickly, Emma felt he must have written and posted it the moment he'd finished reading hers. *I will be back in time for the birth.*

But he wasn't back for the birth. Not, at least, when Emma's pains began.

By the time her travail had ended—a far easier birth than the others had been—a healthy new boy was laid at her breast, and she forgave Joseph his absence. She could hear the Whitney children clamoring downstairs. When their mother told them that Sister Emma now had a son, the children set up a great chorus of hurrahs, clapping their hands in time, and the baby mewled at the sound, pressing his face to her bare skin.

The song broke off suddenly. The children shouted, "The Prophet has come! Mother, come and see, the Prophet has returned!"

Emma eased herself up against the headboard. "Joseph is back from Zion?"

"It seems so." Ann went to the window, looked down on the street. "It is the Prophet, without a doubt. There's no mistaking him, tall and fair-headed as he is."

Patty Sessions wiped her hands on a clean cloth, began packing her tools in her bag. "Your son is very well, Emma. I've no fears for the baby or for you. Ann and I will go downstairs and keep the children quiet. You and the Prophet will have all the time together you could like. I know it has been many months since you've seen one another, and this is such a blessed day."

She heard him coming up the stairs—leaping two at a time, eager as a colt in clover. He burst through the bedroom door mere seconds after the women had gone. "Emma! God bless us all."

In that first moment, having not laid eyes on her husband since the terrible spring, Emma was a bird taken from its cage and tossed into the sky—a tumble of new possibility, wide hope stretching out like wings. His face—she had almost forgotten what he looked like. How was it possible to forget those little details, all his particulars—the sharp nose, downcurved, the sandy hair swept back at his brow by a brisk November wind, the brightness of his cheeks, flushed with a father's pride. And that singular intensity of his eyes. She remembered a different season, early and years gone by, the crocuses rising from rings of melted snow.

A man entered the room behind Joseph, close as a spaniel on his heels. Emma had never seen him before. He was a block of granite, broad across the shoulders, confident to the point of domineering. He had let his hair grow a little long; it curved around his ears. The stranger looked at Emma on the bed—she was disheveled, matted with sweat, with a new red baby in her arms. His eyes flashed with a brief light she didn't understand, a curious and thoughtful look. The stranger said nothing, only took himself to the dimmest corner and pressed himself there, as if a man of his size and bearing could simply disappear.

"Joseph," Emma said, tilting her chin toward the man in the corner.

He had forgotten all about the stranger. He was staring at the baby in Emma's arms, and took a hesitant step toward the bed, then another. Finally Emma turned the warm bundle so Joseph could see his son's face.

"I told you," he said, quiet with awe. "I told you, didn't I, that I would be here for my son's birth."

"You missed the birth," Emma said with a little laugh.

"But I came. Just when I said I would." Without looking away from the baby, he reached out and found the midwife's stool. He dragged it closer to the bed and sat, leaning on the mattress, almost close enough to kiss the baby's cheeks. "We must call him Joseph."

"No," Emma said at once. They had already lost one son by that name. A superstitious dread ran through her. If they gave this child the same name, the same fate would befall him.

"There's nothing to fear," he said. "This boy will grow up to be a man. God gave it to me to know."

She exhaled. Not a sigh, exactly.

He said, "Just as God gave me to know that I would return to you on the day our child was born. You must trust me and believe. I am the Prophet, after all."

At that, the man in the corner shifted on his feet. It wasn't an ostentatious gesture, but the floorboards creaked, which was enough to recall him to Joseph's mind.

"Come over here, now, and meet the elect lady. My wife, Emma Smith. And my son, Joseph Smith III."

The stranger shuffled out from his corner. He went to the foot of Emma's bed and stood with his hands clasped at his waist, looking at Joseph so as to spare Emma the embarrassment. His mouth moved a little, tucked itself up at one corner in a semblance of a smile. Emma felt as if she were being weighed and measured. Something struck lightly in the air around her, a soft, precise click like the sound of an abacus.

"This is Brigham Young," Joseph said, "the newest member of our church, and one for whom God has set great things in store."

Brigham lowered his gaze, an expression that would have been humble, even denying, if not for the sly glitter of his eyes. "You're too kind to me, Prophet." A deep voice, resonant, the kind of voice you can't help but listen to.

In the days just after Joseph's return, Emma would rise from her bed still painful from the birth. She would look down from the second story of the Whitney mercantile, onto the main street below. Always, Brigham Young was there. He had made himself a permanent fixture, lingering wherever Joseph could be found, as close to the Prophet as circumstance allowed. Whatever the hour, even on the Sabbath, Brigham found some excuse to pass by the mercantile or loiter on its porch steps. He was the first man Joseph saw each morning, the first to nod in greeting. He moved with that purposeful stride, up the street and down, into the store and out, claiming the space around the Prophet with his body—with his rough and palpable presence.

There had always been a fire in Kirtland, the force that ran through the congregation and made them fall to the meetinghouse floor. But the fire had cooled somewhat in Joseph's absence, settling the rapid boil to a simmer. Now, though, since the Prophet's return—since he brought that bull of a stranger with him—the flames rekindled in a gust of heat. Emma half suspected that it was Brigham who'd fanned the flames, not Joseph.

On the Sunday after Young Joseph came into the world, Emma felt well enough to attend the meeting, so she wrapped her new baby in a sling, took little Julia by the hand, and walked carefully over the trampled snow to the meetinghouse. She could hear the chanting, the cries of ecstasy, before she'd even reached the door. Inside, she found Brigham stamping and thundering up the aisle toward the pulpit, fists raised as if he sought to grab Heaven by its hem and tear it all to pieces. And what poured from his mouth—words, if you can call them that. A cadence of sound, hard edges, harsh rhythm like a drumbeat. The words had no meaning, yet they went on and on, and the louder he shouted, the more the congregation wept and dropped into faints, or fell to the floor with awe. And Joseph stood before the eyes of his church, watching Brigham handle the hearts of his followers, watching Brigham gather to himself what had been Joseph's by right.

When Brigham finally paused, the sweat running down his brow, Joseph said, "Brother Brigham was speaking the true Adamic language, the tongue of the first man." At once the meetinghouse erupted with sound. Every Mormon was possessed by the spirit of the Tongues.

The noise pounded in Emma's head. She gathered her children and fled into the pale November morning. She preferred that cold to the chill she felt inside the meetinghouse, and under Brigham's shadow.

"Your hymnal is perfect." Joseph turned another of Emma's pages and stacked it, facedown, atop the others. Julia was perched on his knee.

"Ah—'Once more, my soul, the rising day salutes my waking eyes.' That's a favorite of mine."

Emma looked up from the small loom in her lap. She'd been tearing old cotton rags into strips, weaving them into lamp wicks so Ann could distribute them to the congregation. The winter was long already, and the new year hadn't yet arrived. Kirtland was hungry for light. "The hymnal is far from finished, so you can't call it perfect yet. But inspiration has been close at hand these months since you went to Missouri. The Whitneys sing all the time like a flock of little birds."

"I'm glad you haven't been lonely."

"I have, now and then." She found she couldn't look at him anymore. This new way of seeing him, the flowering of affection since he'd gone, made her shy in his presence. He was a fine-looking man, finer than she'd realized before.

"You should come with me to Missouri," Joseph said.

"Are you leaving again?"

"Not straightaway, but soon—when the winter thins out, on the other side of the new year, and we can travel more easily."

"I don't want to leave Kirtland."

He heard the finality in Emma's voice, looked up from the hymnal. "I thought you didn't like this town. When we first arrived, the place unsettled you."

"I did like Kirtland, at first. And then, after a while, I didn't. But now I like it again."

He laughed in that way he had, big and sudden and loud, so Julia giggled along with him. "Your mother," he said to Julia, "might seem to be a very sensible woman on the outside. But inside, she's as changeable as any other."

Emma thought, *I could be angry at you for saying such a thing, except I'm too glad to have you near.*

"Kirtland is my home now," she said. "I've made friends here—Ann and Patty, and Sally Knight came all the way from Harmony to be near you."

"The Knights are determined to go to Zion as soon as the roads are clear. Anyway, you'll make new friends wherever you go. I must return to Missouri. You know they need me to guide the temple's construction."

"When you go," Emma said, "you must send Brigham Young away."

She never knew where such insistence came from. She only knew that she feared to be left alone with the man. She feared even more that Brigham and Joseph would go away together, where she couldn't reach her husband and guide him to his better senses.

"Brigham?" Joseph chuckled. "Why should I send him away?"

Vaguely, she shook her head. "Give him a mission. Up to Canada, perhaps, to find new members for the church."

"He's one of our best and brightest. Dedicated to the church—you ought to have heard him recite from the Book of Mormon on the road. He knows my book like he knows his own mind."

"All the more reason why he ought to lead a mission."

"I want him close beside me. I like Brigham."

"He's a danger to you."

He lifted Julia from his knee and set her on the ground. She scampered away at once.

"Emma," Joseph said, with an air of tolerance that infuriated her, "why do you think Brigham is dangerous?"

She didn't know how to answer. Menace hung like a curse around that man, around his very name. She couldn't admit, *I just don't like him. There's no reason why.* The church was Joseph's dream. And he had been so kind to her of late—those letters he'd sent from Missouri, full of affection and praise. His warmth had even convinced her that the affair with Nancy Marinda had all been rumor and misunderstanding. Joseph had been, after these past months of their separation, a real husband instead of a prophet. She felt new pride in his accomplishments unfolding. She meant to preserve what was his, and she didn't trust Brigham to leave the church in Joseph's hands. The man was too calculating, his eyes too keen.

"I'll admit," Joseph said at length, "I've wondered if it wouldn't be better to leave Brigham here, though I won't like parting with him. But he could act in my stead—keep things running smoothly while I'm building the temple in Zion."

"No," Emma said, "you mustn't do such a thing."

"I can't make heads or tails of you. Why are you set so terribly against a perfectly good fellow?"

"He's a threat to your authority. Like Sidney and Oliver before, but Brigham is far more powerful than they. I saw him at that meeting."

"He put on quite a show."

"This way he has of commanding crowds, of infecting them with a particular spirit—"

"My spirit."

"Can you be certain it's yours? I say it's not. I say it's Brigham's spirit alone—his will. And he'll make the people love him more than they love you."

"Nonsense. Brigham loves the gospel. He loves me; he has bowed his head before me and begged for my blessing. He calls me Prophet."

"And when he holds your followers in his hands, he'll declare himself a prophet, too. Your church will split. Brigham will crack it into pieces, and you'll be left with half of what you've made, or less than half."

"These fears," Joseph said, "they mean nothing. They aren't of God."

"They aren't of Satan." Emma drew herself up. "Do you dare say the Devil has any hold on me?"

"On you? Never! You of all women." He chuckled. "If the Devil ever tried to come for Emma Smith, she'd break her broom handle on his soot-covered backside. It's only the birth that has you feeling so anxious, dear. Of course you're on edge. Our son is only a few weeks old. God has put you through trials the likes of which most women couldn't bear, but once our son is a little older, you'll feel sure of the world again."

She looked at the wicker crib where Young Joseph slept. Fear did grip her then, a sudden black terror that the baby had stopped breathing and she hadn't noticed, or he had disappeared completely—she would go to his cradle and find it empty, the blankets cold. Then she heard, over the whisper of the lamp's flame, a soft sigh, an infant snuffling.

"Be easy," Joseph murmured. "Our son is protected by God. So am I."

He spoke then of the temple. Emma knew it was only a ploy to distract her and silence her objections, but she fell gratefully under his spell. There was a music to him, you see, an instinct for rhythm and sound that belonged to the great composers, the artists who capture with the stroke of a brush a sense and a mood. It's easy to say of a man, *He was born a poor farmer's son; what can he know of beauty?* As if beauty is a thing God reserved only for the few who have sat in lecture halls of great universities, and those who were born in the cities, in fine houses, whose cradles were draped with gold.

He described the white temple rising from the earth. The stones hewn to perfect squares, the symmetry, the harmony, the way the plaster glowed in the sun.

"Never have I seen such a thing on earth." He rested a hand on the hymnal. "Not the temple itself, which is beautiful enough—or will be, when it's finished. But the goodwill and love gone into the making. Everyone lends a hand and works to a common goal, in any way they might be useful. Old women bring bread and water to feed the builders. Little children gather chips of stone in baskets and drag them away. I'd thought a temple would please the Lord merely because it would exalt Him. Now I know He looks down with delight because it's a thing we're making together."

"We need a temple in Kirtland."

Joseph shook his head. "Now that I've declared the Lord's temple must be in Missouri, at the edge of the frontier, how can I say otherwise?"

"Call it something else if you must. A school for endowing the priesthood—anything. But give Kirtland a cause. Give us a reason to work together as one body. And let the commandment come from you, not from Brigham Young. Let this new temple knit us so closely, no man can tear us apart. It shall stand forever as a reminder that the Prophet will never abandon his people, even when he must be far away."

"Us," Joseph said rather sadly. "'Give us a reason.' You truly won't come with me to Zion?"

"No. At least, not while the children are small. I can't risk them on the road, especially not in winter. You know it would kill me, to lose another baby."

He folded his arms. He stared into the lamp's flame, and the light shifted subtly over the planes of his face, revealing and hiding his thoughts by turns, but never showing anything plainly enough that she could read his heart.

She thought Joseph would refuse the Kirtland temple again. But after a long silence, he said, "Then let it be done. Let Kirtland build a great house of exaltation. It will be good in the eyes of the Lord."

In the springtime, as soon as the fields were clear and the mud of the annual thaw had given way to firmer ground, Kirtland's temple began its long, slow rising. Joseph himself helped set the foundation stone. He laid his hand upon the block to bless the work, to endow the builders with God's protection. Emma stood beside him with their infant son in her arms. It was she who was at his right hand then, not Brigham Young.

Sixty-five feet long, fifty-five feet wide, three stories high with a white spire crowned by a shining dome—every feature, every aspect of its meticulous design was dictated by the Prophet and granted to him by sacred revelation. The temple would take three years to construct, costing every imaginable resource the people of Kirtland could scratch up— timber for the scaffolding, strong men to quarry the blocks and haul them to the site, lime and horsehair, plaster and pine, bread and meat to feed hungry workers. Women spun and wove and worked their knitting needles without ceasing to make the sturdy clothes the builders required. Children cleared the worksite of debris or drove away inquisitive dogs; they carried messages from fathers on the scaffolds to mothers in town or cut firewood or tended their fathers' stock so the men could be left to the building. Toil occupied the hands and backs and hearts of every soul in Kirtland. And day by day, the temple progressed.

Emma could see the construction from her south-facing window, the pale sandstone walls rising higher by the week, then sprouting a tracery of scaffolding, angular and thin like the legs of some strange insect. At night the sandstone was luminous, pale blue under a sailing moon.

On a June evening, when a spirit of restlessness took her, she left her children in the care of Ann Whitney's eldest daughter and walked alone down the Chillicothe Road. She drew her shawl tightly around her body, though the night wasn't particularly cold. The sky overhead was lively with stars. They seemed too large and prying. Crickets sang in the grass, and frogs beside the distant river, a bright, chiming hum. Save for those choruses, the night would have been quiet, untroubled by visions or omens. Everyone was abed, resting to meet the next day's labor.

Everyone except for one man. As she came nearer, Emma heard

a thin, wavering cry, almost like weeping. For a moment she feared wolves, though the voice was like no animal she knew. She paused in the lane that led to the temple and held very still. Every instinct shouted at her to run, and as her eyes tracked cautiously along the top of the temple wall, a lanky shadow detached itself from a column of darkness. The figure moved along a ledge of sandstone, two stories above the earth. It stooped; it rose and stooped again, genuflecting, arms raised in silhouette—thin, black, distinct against the stars, clawing at the sky.

Emma loosened her grip on the shawl. Her hands fell to her sides and she watched, she listened.

Sidney Rigdon staggered a few more steps along the sandstone precipice. He came away from a scaffolded corner. As if in a trance, he moved down the length of the wall, into a great blue wash of moonlight. There he swayed, and though Emma was certain he would fall, a drifting sense of curiosity had overwhelmed her. She could only watch to see what Sidney would do.

"Holy, holy," Sidney cried—he wailed, he keened. He brought his hands to his cheeks and pulled them away, held them out in the moonlight. His fingertips were shining. He bent and brushed his fingers on the wall below his feet. He washed the temple with his tears.

In the long, drowsy days of summer, with the help of Ann Whitney's cheerful family, Emma often found her chores quickly finished. She was afforded a few hours of leisure while the sun was still high—the first time since her childhood she could recall such luxury. For a mother with two babies, one in arms and one toddling at her apron strings, an afternoon alone with her thoughts felt like a miracle worthy of Scripture.

On one such day, in the fattest and hottest part of July, she walked alone to the temple site with her hymnal papers, a bottle of ink, and a fine new Perry's pen. The pen had been a gift from Joseph on his most recent visit to Kirtland. He had purchased it in Indianapolis, along with a few yards of gaily printed calico so Emma could make new dresses for the children.

She sat in the merciful shade under a stand of redbuds. The air was thick with humidity from the river. She breathed in that rich, subtle perfume, the vegetal odor of green things growing in a languid season. The spice of the river made a pleasant contrast to the builders' brisk hammering. Men moved along the scaffolds and the tops of the walls, chipping at sandstone, hauling baskets and pails up the temple's flanks with heavy ropes. Their voices merged with the intermittent chirp of some small bird just overhead, and with the distant bleating of sheep in Hyrum Smith's pasture, south along the valley.

The pages unrolled in her lap. A fitful breeze stirred, scarcely strong enough to be felt. Dapples of light and shadow played back and forth across the hymnal and the deep-blue cotton of her skirt. She allowed her eyes to close, allowed the hundred strains of a mother's day to lift from her and dissipate on the air. How long had it been since she had simply sat and listened to the world, and felt the sun on her face? She never could surrender to peace when Joseph was in Kirtland. The world circled around him in a bewildering spiral, as when you pull the stopper from a washtub and let the water run out into the yard—a whirl and clamor, a tightening rush, with one man the center of it all.

After a time, Emma took up her pen and leafed through her pages, considering the lyrics she had already collected, marking changes here and there. She had altered some of the familiar songs of Presbyterians and Methodists—from whose ranks many of the Mormons had come—to better suit the spirit of communal life. The sound of chisels made a cheerful accompaniment to her thoughts. The afternoon slipped by more quickly than she liked. By the time a woman's skirt swept into view—her eyes turned down to the pages—she looked up, blinking, and found that the redbud shade had spread itself far along the grass and the light was golden and low, aging toward sunset.

Ann Whitney stood before her. Ann's round face, usually placid and smiling, was tense with worry.

"Oh dear," Emma said, gathering her pages, "is there some trouble with my children? I'm sorry. I should have kept better track of the time."

"No, no. Don't get up, Emma. The children are well. My girls are looking after them. They've even fed your little darlings; we had goat's milk in the springhouse for Young Joseph. Sit, please. I came to find you. I wished to talk."

Emma rolled her manuscript and tied the pages while Ann sank into the grass. Ann seemed to be groping for her thoughts.

"You're troubled," Emma said.

"I am. At least, I think I'm troubled. It's difficult to know. Oh, I'm not making a lick of sense. I spend so much time in the company of children, I've forgotten how to speak to a grown woman." She laughed rather shakily.

"Is your husband well?"

"Quite well. Only I've a certain feeling, a tightness in my chest, and I don't know whether I'm worrying over nothing or whether we really do face a great danger."

"Danger? You had best explain if you can."

"Well," Ann said, "you know I've several friends and relations who followed the Prophet to Zion. We exchange letters often. This morning, while I was reading the latest bit of news from Missouri, it occurred to me that . . . that tensions seem to be rising. I don't know how to explain it any better than that."

"Tensions in Zion?"

Ann looked at her with no small amount of surprise. "Surely Joseph writes to you from Missouri."

"All the time. But he's made no mention of trouble." She felt rather embarrassed. Either she had just admitted that Joseph left his wife uninformed, or she had told Ann that Joseph himself was unaware of danger.

Ann said, "Zion seems a hard, unforgiving place. I could wonder why the Lord chose it as a land of promise, though I suppose He must intend to use it as a trial of sorts, to separate the wheat from the chaff, as the Scriptures say. Zion is the refiner's fire, I suppose, which will purify the worthy and make our people unbreakable."

"What has happened, Ann? You must tell me. Should I be worried about Joseph?"

"My friends and cousins say the people of Missouri are untrustworthy folk. They're the sort who found city life, even farming life, disagreeable. So they set out for the frontier, to live as far apart from proper civilization as they could manage. It used to be the habit of these homesteaders to push farther west when too many others settled near them, and in that way, they kept themselves apart. But three years back, President Jackson made that new law—you must have heard of it—establishing Indian territory."

"And now these strange Missouri folk are no longer free to move," Emma guessed.

"Yes. Now they must apply for special permission to go out into Indian country, and I hear that permission isn't often granted. I suppose this state of affairs has made the Missourians feel rather trapped. And because they feel trapped, it seems they look on everything as a threat—even the settlement at Zion."

"But Zion is a peaceful community."

"Of course—but it's growing. Brother Oliver and his men have been so active in their missions; they're bringing new members from Canada and the eastern states, more all the time. It's little wonder the Missourians have begun to murmur against us."

"What do they say?"

"Oh, I can't know the whole of it." Ann shook her head. "Only scraps, here and there; whatever I can glean from letters. First, I heard that Oliver preached some sermon to a Lamanite tribe—told them they ought to cease fighting and join in community with white men, and farm alongside Zion."

"Joseph has hoped to bring the Indian tribes into our church. It's little wonder Oliver sought them out."

"Yes, but the Missourians didn't like it one bit. They want no communion between white men and Indians. And with Mormons so plentiful, they've begun to fear that we'll have the numbers to sway votes and change the governance of the state to our liking."

"It seems very likely we shall do just that. I see no trouble with it. After all, that's the American way."

"The settlers on the frontier see a great deal of trouble in the prospect of a strong Mormon vote. If one believes the letters I've received, the newspapers in Independence have printed all manner of slander against us, insisting we'll use our votes to seize land from the Gentiles."

"But that's ridiculous. We've always paid for our land. We would never take anything by force."

"I'm afraid it's not an unfounded fear," Ann said soberly. "I've learned that some of the Zion men have taken to preaching in public squares, in the Gentile towns, in an effort to bring new members to the church. But such things they have said! 'This land is to be an inheritance for God's chosen people' and 'All those who don't come into the fold will be chastised by a destroying angel, and their farms and houses taken.'"

Emma stared up at the temple, though for a moment she saw nothing except a stark white blankness of shock. At length, she said, "Joseph would never teach his followers such terrible things."

"It matters very little whether the Prophet actually taught such a lesson or not. Word has gotten out. Whether the bad blood came from Joseph or some other man, the Missouri Gentiles hate and fear us now."

Emma pressed a hand to her mouth. Ann had rightly seen a pattern of escalating hostility, and if her friends' letters were to be trusted, Joseph and his men had done nothing to soothe the settlers' fears. In fact, they had done the opposite.

Quietly, Ann said, "I'm afraid the news gets worse. Missouri, you know, has always resisted abolition. They're all set against it; the very idea that every man ought to live free is enough to incite them to violence—so my friends say. Well, it seems some of Oliver's missionaries made a grave misstep. While in the north—Wisconsin Territory, I believe—some of our missionaries stayed for a few weeks with a settlement of freed people of color. You know how handily Oliver preaches. He was successful in convincing many of those good folk to join our church. One might say he was too successful. The new converts attempted to come to Zion. Oh, Emma, there was such a stir! It gave me a chill just to read it."

"I'd heard," Emma said, "that Missouri allows people of color to sue for their freedom."

"Certainly, but if I were a betting woman, I'd wager my last penny that the governor doesn't make it easy."

"If their law allows slaves to be freed—rare though it may be—surely they couldn't object to already-freed people entering their state."

Ann laughed without mirth. "The governor objected, all the same. Those poor new converts were turned back at gunpoint. Can you imagine it? Apparently, there's some obscure law that any Black person wishing to enter Missouri as a free man must have a certificate of citizenship from another state. Those new converts had none. They were only humble folk when our missionaries found them, living in cabins in the woods. I doubt they'd ever thought to apply for a certificate of citizenship, and who can say whether any state would grant it?"

"It's a shame," Emma said hotly. "I know some would mock me for being a naïve Northerner, but I see no good cause to hold men in bondage, no matter the color of their skin."

"Plenty in Zion agree with you." Ann covered her eyes for a moment, as if the afternoon glare pained her head. "Too many people, I fear. The Zion newspaper printed a declaration that was, I suppose, meant to smooth matters over with the Gentiles. Oh, Emma, it made everything worse! The elders intended to declare that our church holds no official position on slavery. But my friends told me the Gentiles took it poorly. They read the declaration as an invitation to all people of color, that they should come to Missouri in droves and take up with the Mormons, and now the Gentiles are boiling with fear. They think Joseph intends to raise up an army, drive them from their homes, seize their land, and take their slaves as members of the church!"

All the warmth of the afternoon had vanished. Emma wrapped her arms around her body. "God have mercy," she whispered. "Joseph has told me nothing of this. I don't even know whether he sees it happening around him."

"He must see it. He's God's ordained Prophet. Of course; of course, Joseph knows."

A subtle layering of cause and effect. One history riding another. You ask where it began. Not here, as all the tale that's come before has proven. But this was one beginning of many.

That summer, the Gentiles on the Missouri frontier assembled in mass meeting. They created a manifesto demanding that all Mormons must be expelled from their territory, lest the new recruits to Joseph's church should inspire slaves to rise against their masters. The Missourians agreed to give the Mormons ample warning and fair compensation for any property they couldn't carry over the state border—though who believes that compensation would have been fair? On such terms, the Missourians would allow the Mormons to abandon their temple and their land, walk out of Zion with their lives intact. Any who remained would be handled however the Gentiles pleased. Who signed the manifesto? Not only hundreds of men from the settlements that ringed Zion like the coils of a snake, but the judge of the county court, his clerk, the constable, the deputy, the jailer.

Someone in Zion—it may have been Joseph—instructed the editor of the *Evening and Morning Star* to publish a new declaration. This bold statement made clear the official stance of the Church of Christ: *We feel in duty bound to state that our intention was not only to stop free people of color from emigrating to this State, but to prevent them from being admitted as members of the Church.* The missionaries who had traveled far afield, preaching the Book of Mormon to freed slaves and to the Indian tribes, were disgusted and disheartened. But in the end, the *Star*'s retraction proved worthless, anyhow. The Gentiles did not soften. Damage done couldn't be so easily mended.

More than five hundred men descended on the town of Independence, bristling with guns, shouting for Joseph Smith's blood and the blood of every Mormon. They read aloud their demands: that no new Mormons should come to plague their county at any point in the future; that every Mormon already settled there must vow to sell his land and leave; that every business and storehouse operated by and for the benefit of Mormons must close immediately—especially the printing press, which had wrought so much evil already. Every immigrant from Ohio should be turned around on the road and sent back to the rat's nest from which he had come. And finally, as the crowning insult, the edict said that all who wouldn't comply with these reasonable requests should turn to their brethren in the church and allow them to interpret with their swooning divinations and muttering in tongues the exact meaning of the Missourians' words. For emphasis, the man who'd been reading the list of demands lifted his rifle above his head.

They marched as a mob to Zion. The bishop Edward Partridge and his friend Charles Allen went out to face those five hundred slavering wolves alone. They pleaded for more time. In mockery, they were given fifteen minutes to clear the county of Mormons. Then they were tarred and feathered, left beaten and bloody in a roadside ditch.

The Gentiles next fell upon the office of the *Evening and Morning Star.* They destroyed the machinery of the press, broke the furniture into kindling, and used it to set alight every copy they could find of Joseph's *Book of Commandments*, his new compilation of revelations, the holy word of God. The fire burned for hours outside the office, and all through the night the Gentiles cut down trees for rams and battered the building until it fell, until it was no more than a heap of bricks and a pile of smoldering ashes.

Imagine it if you can. All those families fleeing the noise and the violence, cowering through the night in the cornfields outside Zion. The women and children, the old men, creeping back to town as the first feeble light came down from a distant Heaven. The children dirty and hollow-cheeked, too exhausted for crying.

The Prophet arrived in Kirtland only a few hours before that shameful news came. The town was still celebrating Joseph's return when the letters poured in—dozens of letters, hundreds, pleading with Kirtland to send help, to send Joseph back as soon as he arrived, for he'd set out from Missouri only days before the mob came to Zion. They begged him for guidance: *What shall we do, how shall we make peace with our enemies? Send men with guns to defend the weak, send a skillful speaker who might convince the governor of Missouri to intercede. Send prayers, at least, if you can't send real help.*

Joseph sat with his head in his hands in the room above the Whitney store.

"For mercy's sake," Emma said, "say something. We can't leave our people to suffer."

When he finally spoke, his voice was so faint Emma could scarcely hear. "Go and get Brigham Young. I want to talk with him."

"What can he tell you that you don't already know?"

"I want his advice."

"You're the Prophet, not Brigham."

"All the same, go and fetch him."

She located Brigham at the home of a wealthy, unwed woman by the name of Vienna Jacques—a newcomer to Kirtland, an heiress in her early thirties who hadn't yet contributed her moderate fortune to the common goods of the town. Emma could easily guess what Brigham's purpose had been under Vienna's roof. What better new wife than a wealthy one? Brigham and Vienna sat rigidly beside an oil lamp, poring over the letters they'd received from their friends in Zion.

Shocked silence hung in the room; it made Vienna's airy home feel as cramped and dismal as a cell.

"The Prophet wishes to speak with you," Emma said from the threshold.

Brigham's eyes seemed to turn in upon his soul, or to stare far beyond Emma to some vast distance. Perhaps he saw all the way to Zion, flame-lit, the smoke of its destruction rising with the desperate cries.

He followed her through the darkness to the Whitney store. Inside, he bulled past Emma without excuse and climbed the stairs. She hurried after.

Brigham threw open the door to their private quarters. The children, whom Emma had only just coaxed to sleep, jolted awake. Young Joseph began to cry.

"You've brought me here to ask what you should do," Brigham said. "I'll tell you what to do. The Bible says, 'An eye for an eye.'"

"No," Emma said as she tried to quiet her son's cries. "You must listen to me."

Brigham sneered. "Listen to a woman?"

"I am his wife."

Joseph looked from Brigham to Emma and back again. Still he said nothing.

She scooped the baby into her arms and knelt beside Joseph's chair. "Zion is a powder keg now. One spark and it will blow apart. You must act carefully."

"You must *act*," Brigham insisted.

"Joseph, you will lose everything if you move with haste—not only your church, but the lives of your followers. Think of the women out there in Zion. Think of the children. Would you turn them over to the wolves?"

Brigham grunted with disgust. "The wolves are already circling. You were raised a farmer's son. What does a farmer do when wolves threaten his flock? He takes up his gun and goes hunting!"

Joseph drew a long breath. Some of the color returned to his face. He smiled at Brigham, and the smile was almost easy. "Perhaps I should send you out to Zion, Brother Brigham. You can organize the men, lead them in my place—"

"He's too hot-headed," Emma said, never caring that Brigham heard. "If you must send anyone, let it be Sidney Rigdon."

"That mewling old fool," Brigham said.

"Sidney thinks carefully before he acts—even before he speaks. What's more, his countenance is always peaceful. He won't incite the Gentiles to further violence."

"Nor can he protect our people when the Gentiles fall on them again," Brigham said. "And they will, Joseph. They will attack again."

"Joseph." She rested a hand on his knee. He looked down at her, wide-eyed, as if her touch had frightened him. "God brought us together for a purpose. Please be guided by me. I would never turn you awry."

For a long while, the only sound was Julia whimpering under the quilts, and the intermittent spitting of the flame in the lamp. The night, stunned to stillness, seemed to breathe around her—heavily, as Brigham was breathing, that great square chest rising and falling as he waited for Joseph's decision.

"I shall do as you counsel, Emma," Joseph finally said. "And if I err, then God will send me a sign."

Brigham roared in frustration. He stamped out the door; the building shook as he barreled down the stairs, out into the night. The children cried in his wake.

Emma said, "You ought to have gone back to Zion, too."

"What, and get myself killed by some mob? Are you so eager to be rid of me?"

"Petulance doesn't become the Prophet of God."

"Don't try me, Emma. I've had more than enough to vex me these past weeks."

She swallowed hard, willing herself to look at Joseph. She still couldn't do it.

"I've had a letter from Oliver," he said. "He has been writing to Governor Dunklin of Missouri but there's nothing the governor can do, no provision in the law, until Zion has its lawyers and can take our cause to the courts. What good would I do in Zion till then? Vienna is the likeliest person to carry out this work. It isn't only her money we need now. Vienna is sophisticated. She was brought up in a big city, raised by a family that understands how to speak to powerful men. She isn't some rustic farmer, like me. There's nothing I can do for Zion that Vienna won't do twice as well, and with half the effort."

"You are the Prophet. Your presence would bring Zion hope."

Joseph laughed bitterly. "What good is hope when an armed mob is just outside your door, ready to pick you off like a varmint in a vegetable patch as soon as you show yourself? I've read the letters. I know what they face in Zion."

Now, at last, she looked at him. "You claim to be the mouthpiece of the Lord, and yet you say, 'What good is hope'? Do you know what I think, Joseph Smith? I think you're afraid. You fear to face the very dangers into which you've sent your followers. That congregation trusted you. You asked for their faith, and they gave it."

"I asked for nothing!" There was such sudden passion in him that Emma stepped back. He was trembling. His face had gone pale—not with the eerie luminescence that came on him when he preached or doled out revelations. This was a pallor of another kind, the draining away of his very human, very ordinary blood. "I asked for nothing. This was never what I intended. This isn't what I set out to make when all of this began."

What did you intend, she wondered. *What did you think you had made?*

Because Joseph looked so fragile and frightened—because she pitied him—she answered only, "I know." She made herself take his hand.

Neither of them was accustomed to such gestures of affection; that wasn't the course their marriage had run. His hand was cold and inflexible. She found it easier to look away again than to meet his eye.

"I've heard," she said, "that Zion is having difficulty with their food stores. Ann has had more letters from her cousins. The situation sounds dire."

"That pack of rabid dogs burned up two of our storehouses. The people left in Zion have already been reduced to grating dried feed corn, cobs and all. They're making a sort of bread with it—can you imagine? And once the feed corn is gone, they'll have nothing. They can't go out hunting, surrounded as they are."

"We must take up a collection—food, clothing, whatever we can gather, and send it all to Zion."

"The wagon would only be taken by the Gentiles. Whoever drove it would be killed."

"We must try anyhow. We can't ignore this dreadful mess. Our people will starve. If you were to take the wagon yourself—"

"Then the mob would kill me. They would throw me on a fire, like they did to my books."

She let go of his hand—slowly, gently, so he wouldn't know how angry she was. "If God has anything to do with it, you'll be safe."

The Lord did provide one small mercy that terrible autumn and winter. The first snow of the season didn't arrive until the twenty-fifth of

November, so Zion was spared the bitterest cold a while longer. Emma rose from her bed that morning—early, as she'd done since the first grim news had come from Missouri, for her sleep was often broken by nightmares. She sat on the edge of her mattress, feeling a change in the air, a new dampness, a close, insistent pressure. Even before she went to the window and pulled the curtain back, she knew the snows had come.

But when she looked south to where the temple walls stood white above the white-dusted pines, she found three bedraggled riders headed for the crossroads.

"Joseph," she whispered urgently. She was afraid to speak, already aware that some new, dreadful fate had befallen the church. "Get up. Put on your clothes. There are riders coming from Zion."

David Whitmer. Parley Pratt. Charles Allen, who had already suffered once at the hands of the Gentiles, with hot tar on his skin and their hard boots cracking his ribs. The three men were so depleted by the long, cold journey to Ohio that they practically fell from their saddles. The Kirtlanders who'd gathered in the road rushed forward to catch them.

"Parley is feverish," someone said. "He needs a doctor, quickly."

"They all need a doctor. Nancy, go and fetch Doctor James. Bring Patty Sessions, too; she'll be of some use."

They carried the Zion men through the mercantile, up the stairs to one of the Whitneys' unused rooms. There the men remained for two days and two nights, groaning and shivering in narrow cots under mounds of donated blankets. The town physician attended them, giving his daily instructions to Emma and Ann—who, with the help of the midwife, nursed them every hour, wiping sweat from their brows, spooning broth into their mouths, and emptying their chamber pots until their wits had returned.

"Thank God," Emma breathed when the doctor declared all three would survive. She bowed her head over the nearest cot in a prayer of gratitude.

Someone took her hand. She opened her eyes. She had sagged over David Whitmer's cot, and now he clutched her fingers. His grip was hardly stronger than a baby's. When he spoke, Emma had to lean closer to make out his words.

"Where is the Prophet? We've come to find him. We must tell him everything that has happened." Despite his weak voice, there was fire in his eyes. "Fetch him, please, Sister Emma. There's no more time to lose."

Joseph was dark around his eyes from lack of sleep. The buttons were open at his sleeves and collar; the strap bow hung untied at his throat, limp and stained. Joseph settled at David's side, and Emma dragged a small milking stool to the foot of the cot. There she remained, shivering, going colder by the moment, while David told of Zion's fall.

"It happened on the last night of October," he said. "It was a cold night, and I remember the air smelled of woodsmoke. Otherwise we might have smelled them coming, those Missouri men. You can smell them sometimes, you know. They stink like animals. Like dogs ready to fight."

"How many men?" Joseph asked quietly.

"Fifty, or near that number. It's strange, that so few could do what they did to us. They were nothing like the five hundred who'd come the first time, when they destroyed the press and threw the *Book of Commandments* on the fire. But then, they didn't come to Zion proper. They went out to the little colony on the Big Blue River. It isn't much—only a few cabins, a couple of barns, twenty acres of fields at most."

"Wasn't that settlement protected?" Emma said.

"Of course, Sister—by its own men. But since the first attacks, we haven't had enough men to spare for proper sentries. All we could do was hope the Gentiles wouldn't learn about the settlement on the Big Blue. But they did learn. They fell on the place with torches and whips. Whips, as if the women and children were no better than dogs or cattle."

David was wracked by a fit of coughing. Joseph placed a hand on his brow to steady him, and after a moment, he recovered his breath and went on.

"Our men tried to stand against them, but the Gentiles stoned them till they broke ranks and fled. The Missourians chased them all—chased them with their whips."

Emma covered her eyes, but she couldn't drive back the vision in her head—women desperate to hold their children, the babies stumbling and tripping through the cold, the laughing men on their heels, like hounds after screaming rabbits. "God preserve us," she muttered.

The story went on relentlessly. Emma could see it all—the Gentiles firing the few crops that had been left in the fields, tearing the roofs from the buildings so the Mormons couldn't even take shelter against the weather. They found the last storehouse in the forest, where only feed corn remained—all the people of Zion had to see them through the winter. Those fifty devils took it all, every last cob and seed.

"A few of us went back to the storehouse to see if anything could be salvaged," David said. "We found one man breaking all the boards from the walls."

Parley caught the man, and, with a few other fellows, marched him to the Justice of the Peace in Independence. But it was Parley and his friends who were thrown in jail under pretense of unlawful arrest.

"We tried, Joseph, to raise a force of our own."

And this, too, Emma could see with sinking dread. Each man setting his jaw and joining the cause, even those too old to drag a plow. Even young boys, children, putting their feeble hands on anything that might pass for a weapon. Pitchforks, spades, the hafts of butter churns. They had twenty rifles at most, and precious few bullets, yet they stood against the onslaught with the reek of gunpowder in the air.

One of the Zion men was killed that night, and a pair of Missourians. David was sure he killed a Gentile himself.

Emma leaned back on her stool, as if she could separate herself from this fatal entanglement. With two Missouri men dead, the blood would never stop flowing. An eye for an eye for an eye for an eye, till the whole world went dark.

"We were only defending what was ours," David said, "but they didn't see it that way in Independence. The people of that town all convinced themselves that we planned to kill every one of them, or drive them away. They boarded up their houses, then they tore the boards away again, fearing we would burn their wives and children in their homes."

"Why," Joseph said, "when we've never lifted a hand against them? Only in defense, and only after their provocations."

"We can't lift a hand anymore," David said, "not even to defend ourselves."

"What do you mean?" Emma asked.

"They've taken all our guns. Every last one. That's to say, we were made to surrender our guns. Forced into it. Lilburn Boggs, the lieutenant governor, called up his militia, then sent word to Zion that Parley and the others would be shot like shoats in a pen unless we surrendered all our weapons and agreed to put someone on trial for the deaths of those two Gentiles. I was among those who went on foot to Independence, hoping to sue for peace. I was frightened—we all were frightened—for the town already outnumbered us before the militia arrived, and now there were more than a hundred Gentiles for every one of our men. But what could we do? If we'd left Parley and the rest to be killed in that jail, we would have answered to God for it. And to you, Joseph."

Joseph was silent for a moment. His gaze was fixed on David's blanket. Emma could see his eyes traveling, following a line of stitching along the quilt, following the path of his thoughts.

"Who is this Lilburn Boggs?" he said at length. "What sort of man is he?"

"He seemed respectable at first," David said. "He carried himself with the air of a man who demands obedience and knows he'll get it. I felt— well—rather timid when we stood in front of him. But when he spoke, I knew him for a devil. He spooled off talk of statutes and protections, the importance of the rule of law. He assured us that if we handed over our guns, he would see to it that our tormentors would leave Zion in peace."

"Surely you didn't trust him," Emma said.

"No, Sister—of course not. Though he did release the prisoners; I will say that in his favor. But we had no real choice but to comply with his demands."

"What then?" Emma asked. There was more to this tale. She could feel the weight of words left unsaid. There was yet something haunted in David's eyes.

"Almost as soon as Boggs had our guns, word raced through Independence. And then, I suppose, word ran beyond the town, into the farm country where the most dangerous Gentiles live. Before the sun had set, they were on us again, but this time there was no hope of fighting back. Boggs never had any idea of keeping the mobs from our settlement. He only wanted to disarm us and leave us to the mercy of our enemies."

She listened, stiff with terror, as David described the burning. The smell that hung in the air—so many houses and farms burned, the sunset was distorted through black smoke. When they'd taken a torch to every Mormon roof, they took their bullwhips to the men. They scattered families into the wilderness, driving them into the teeth of the night, never caring whether they separated mothers from crying children.

David spoke on, but his voice receded. The walls around Emma seemed to fall away, and she could feel it as if she ran among the displaced—as if she were one of them, all of them. A wind was rising, a violent storm sweeping in from the open plain. The storm was a dense black thing crouching at the edge of the world, darker than the smoke that had once been Zion. The wind flayed through ragged garments. The weather screamed at the refugees; it swallowed the desperate cries of the people as they staggered, soot-darkened and torn, into the brush and the forest.

Somehow—thank God for these lone, small mercies—the Mormons found one another in the darkness. A bleeding hand reached out to claw through a thicket and found, instead of thorns, another hand to grasp. All through the night, the remnants of Zion searched for one another, until every man, woman, and child were accounted for. Then they burrowed like rats into the brush on the bank of the Big Blue River. They huddled in the dark, pressed body to body for meager warmth, while the wind like a final judgment tore at the cowering world, while rain came down like the lashes of the whips that had already scarred their bodies. They could only pray the storm wouldn't scour them all to bone.

For two nights and three days, so David said, the people of Zion hid themselves in the river bottoms. Emma felt the agony of every bleak hour. The only roof above their heads was made of bare branches. When they looked up, the branches were like cracks running across the sky; the world was broken beyond repair. For food, they had only the bark of trees and the remnants of berries left rotting on brambles. They whispered when they spoke. Their children kept silent, even the babies, quieted by instinctive fear. And all the while they prayed for mercy. They prayed that Joseph Smith would send one word of hope or blessing so they would know their God had not abandoned them after all.

The fire shone more brightly in David's eyes. "On the third night, the storm finally abated. One of the young men ventured down to the riverbank. It was one of the Wight boys, I think—Lyman, maybe, though I couldn't swear to it now."

No, Emma thought, still with a terrible acceptance. *Who can swear to anything after days and nights huddling in the wilderness, after all the faces of the people around you have run together like ink bleeding off a wet page?*

But someone was crying out that night. She could hear the voice

ringing in her own head—the first raised voice the wretched had heard
since the screaming and sobbing had ceased. But these were no cries of
anger. Not even of fear.

"In God's name, look to the heavens! The stars are falling from the
sky!"

They crept from the shelter of their thickets and the low, damp lean-tos
they had made. They rose up from hands and knees and stood like men
for the first time since collapsing in despair on the forest floor. The river
cut a broad swath through the woodland, and the sky above was an un-
obstructed band of deepest blue, a perfect arc overhead. All the clouds
had gone. The night was alive with stars.

"And the stars moved, Brother Joseph. Upon my soul, they streaked
across the sky. They fell sometimes three and four at a time, or more,
and not a second passed without a star falling."

She could see that, too, with her eyes opened or closed. Great tails
of gold burning in the dark behind the plunging stars, so numerous that
the world was as brightly lit as by day. The river shimmered in bands of
orange and gold and a mobile, bending blue.

"We rejoiced to see it." David struggled to rise from his cot. Joseph
put another cushion behind his back, so he could sit up and look at him
directly. "We rejoiced, for it was a sign—the very sign we've been waiting for."

Tears streamed from the man's eyes. They fell, Emma thought, like
the stars he described, bright and endless.

"The stars are shaken from the Heavens. We haven't suffered in vain,
nor been driven from our homes and our temple without purpose. God
had tested us in the wilderness. He didn't find our faith lacking. The
tide of evil has turned. The Latter Days have come, and Christ's return
is at hand. What else can that sign mean? You were given the Golden
Bible. You restored the Gospel. And now, my brother and my Prophet,
our Savior will come."

Emma closed the door to their private room. She stayed where she was,
facing the door because it was flat and simple and plain and it was all
she could face until she'd gathered her wits and her words.

When she turned, Joseph had sunk into his chair at their small table.
Emma had left the lamp burning in case Julia woke. The light picked

Joseph out from the somber shadows; it set him apart, so he was the only stark and factual thing in all the darkened world. His arms were braced upon the table as if it was more than he could do, to hold himself upright.

"Those stars," Emma said. "I wonder if it truly was a sign of the Latter Days."

Joseph shook his head without looking up. It didn't seem a denial—only a gesture of bewilderment. He was like some small, helpless thing, an animal caught in a snare. "Why didn't we see the stars fall here in Kirtland?"

"I've been trying to work out the dates," she said. "As near as I can guess from what David told us, the people of Zion saw the stars fall on the night of November thirteenth. We had cloudy skies that day. Rain and wind."

"The same storm that lashed them. God sending His punishment here to Kirtland, I suppose, to scour me to the bone."

He covered his face with his hands. He slouched over the table, leaning his whole self against the dark place, his covered eyes, the not-seeing.

She came and sat across from him, though he didn't look up, not even when he heard the scrape of her chair. "I'll tell you what you must do," she said.

"It isn't your place to tell me."

"It is."

Now he raised his head. His stare was hard, rebuking.

"You can't ignore a sign like this," Emma said.

"The stars? They were no sign."

"What in mercy's name do you mean, no sign?"

He huffed, as if he wanted to laugh but had no mirth left inside of him, not even the small, dry pleasure of contempt.

"Whatever this is," Emma said, "this church of yours—whatever you thought you made, you haven't made it, Joseph. The church has created itself. It has become a creature of its own design, made after a pattern you can no longer see. If you could ever see it."

"You talk as if you believe it all," he said, "every word of it, back to the beginning."

"You talk as if you don't believe. As if you never did."

There was a tightness around his eyes, a readiness to lash out that would have frightened her if David's story hadn't burned all her fear away.

"I left my family," she said, "and my home, my parents, to follow you."

"You're my wife. It was your duty to follow me."

"An easy thing for you to say—you, who have your whole family here in Kirtland. They followed you because they believe in you. You and your golden Bible. And how many thousands of other people have come to join you, because they believe?"

He stood suddenly, almost upsetting the chair. He paced from the window to the table, back again. "It isn't my fault, that they believe. I never asked for this; I never wanted it—a church, and two entire towns hanging on my every word, and all of them waiting for me to open my mouth so some revelation will tumble out, and they can kick it down the road. I only wanted to write a book. I never asked them to believe."

Slowly, she said, "I won't ask whether you believe. In your own prophecies. In the doctrines you've established as God's truth. It's a sin to lie, Joseph—and whatever else you may or may not believe, I know you love and fear God, and have every wish to keep His commandments. If you've any hope of an afterlife—in that triune Heaven you and Sidney dreamed up, or in some other, more conventional realm—you won't damn your soul by lying. And I won't back you into the corner of your lies." That was her duty, as his wife.

He wrung his hands while he paced. "I don't know what I believe. That's the honest truth. I don't know whether to believe myself. I've seen visions, or things I've thought were visions. I've heard voices speaking, and I don't know whether they were in my own mind or came from outside of me. And sometimes I look back on everything I've done and said, and everything I've been, and it seems as if it couldn't have happened, as if it never happened at all. There are days when I can't credit what I've achieved. There are days when dreams and the waking world feel the same; there's no boundary between." He rubbed one eye with the back of his wrist. Emma realized he was crying.

"It doesn't matter now," she said, as gently as she could manage, though she wanted to shout at him. "It doesn't matter where it began, nor what your intentions may have been, nor the nature of your visions. This church has assembled itself around you and your book. God meant this church to be."

"I want nothing of it."

She laughed. Not because she was amused, but because the sudden impact of his words rocked her from the inside, shook loose some bat-winged thing that could only emerge as laughter. "It matters very little what you want. The people of this town and of Zion—what's left of it—believe with their whole hearts that you are the Prophet of God. And because they believe, you are. However this began—with a game or a jest or a fraud—God has taken it in His hands and turned it to His purpose. You told Brigham that if you had erred in judgment, God would give you a sign. And now you've had your message from Heaven. The stars fell."

"It was your idea to send Sidney to Zion. Brigham was right; I should have sent an army."

"Brigham was right," she answered smoothly, begrudging him nothing. "I was wrong. I'm woman enough to claim my mistakes. Are you man enough to claim yours? You must help Zion. You must go there yourself. You didn't ask to lead a church, but all the same, God has put you at the church's head. You've no choice but to do your duty and serve the Lord."

Late in the month of February, Sidney returned to Kirtland with another man in his sleigh. Parley and David both rushed out to greet them, clapping Sidney's companion on the shoulder. "Take me to the Prophet," the fellow said.

They led him to the room above the mercantile, where Joseph sat frowning over his letters.

"Brother Joseph," Parley said, "look who's come from Missouri. This is Lyman Wight."

Emma had been sewing near the window, making the most of winter's meager light. She looked up in surprise. The newcomer was tall, narrowly built—even thinner than he ought to have been, thanks to his privation beside the river. Despite his hollow cheeks and the dark circles under his eyes, Lyman was well groomed, with a neatly trimmed beard and a suit Emma recognized as one of Sidney's.

He came forward while Joseph was still staring up at him. He fell to his knees, bowing his head as if he knelt at the throne of a king.

"Come now," Joseph said, "there's no need for this. Parley, fetch that chair; sit, Lyman, and tell me how our people fare in Clay County."

Lyman fell gratefully into the chair. "Everyone from Zion has taken shelter in good, charitable homes. The Baptists have been exceedingly kind. No one has quite enough to fill his belly—especially not those Christian souls who've agreed to help us—but we've all survived the ordeal. And Brother Oliver asked me to bring you this news person-ally: Daniel Dunklin, the governor of Missouri, has had a few men arrested—Gentiles, I mean—some of the worst who led those packs of wolves this past autumn and winter. The Gentiles are to stand trial soon, and Dunklin has assigned deputies and lawyers to our case. There will be an investigation. The governor intends to root out more of these vil-lains and bring them to justice."

"That's fine news," Joseph said.

"There's more. Dunklin has promised Brother Sidney that Missouri's militia is ours. We need only call upon him, and he'll command his men to escort us back to Jackson County if we wish to keep our settlement there. Though of course, there isn't much left of Zion. Still, we may re-build if we choose, with the governor's blessing and protection. And," he added with a certain restrained glee, "our church may apply for public arms. Do you know what that means? We may form our own militia, as long as it acts in accordance with the law."

Lyman and his friends cheered, but Joseph passed a swift glance to Emma. She stuck her needle in a fold of the fabric, waiting for him to speak. He seemed to draw himself up, though he never left his chair. She thought, *Whatever Joseph believed, whatever he didn't, he's ready now to act as the prophet God means him to be.*

"What news," Joseph said. "You've made me a very happy fellow, Brother Lyman. This is exactly what I've prayed for—what we've all prayed for, this long winter in Kirtland. But thanks be to God, He has made the way clear. He has marked our path for us, and no mistake. The time has come to raise up an army of the Lord, to defend the land that was promised to us. Let no man take back what God has given."

Lyman pressed a hand to his heart. Hoarsely, he said, "You saw the stars fall that night, didn't you, Brother Joseph? You know what it means."

"I saw," Joseph said, though Emma knew he hadn't. "The Last Days have come. God's righteous people shall be exalted. All those who have been our enemies will turn to us with love, or they will feel the sting of our rebuke. The redemption of Zion is close at hand. It must needs come by power, with a stretched-out arm."

Joseph stood. He laid his hands on Lyman's head and blessed him.

A bright, clear morning in May found Emma with the rest of Kirt-land's women at the crossroads outside the mercantile. She held Young Joseph on her hip and Julia by the hand. Joseph's army, which was called Zion's Camp, milled and chattered with excitement, checking their horses' tack, accepting last-minute bundles of clothing and hard biscuits from the mothers and sisters and wives who had come to bid them farewell. A festival mood hung over the town. The sky was the optimistic blue of late spring, and the wind over the newly planted fields smelled wholesome and fresh. Birds trilled madly among the li-lacs, which swelled with pink buds as if to emphasize all the good yet to come, and at the southern end of town, the temple had been freshly crowned by a roof and a finished spire. The very house of God seemed to smile at Zion's Camp.

To Emma's surprise, it was Sidney, not Joseph, who mounted the steps of a hastily assembled platform to address the crowd. There he stood, clinging to his lapels and waiting for the Kirtlanders to notice him and fall silent.

When every face had turned to him, Sidney's clear baritone rang out over the gathering. "Brothers and sisters, our beloved Prophet has asked me to deliver a benediction on this fine day, and upon our endeavor: this mission of mercy and righteousness to our brethren who have been scat-tered and persecuted in Missouri."

Emma frowned to see him there, in Joseph's rightful place. She gave Sidney only half her attention as his oration went on, his insistence that the Last Days had come and they must march forth unafraid to strike at God's enemies. Her eyes darted around the milling crowd, searching for Joseph. It should have been he who addressed the people, not Sidney. She would serve him up a piece of her mind as soon as she found him.

"Brother Joseph and I have been together much in prayer and discus-sion," Sidney said, "these months since we learned of God's sign in the skies above Zion. That glorious star-fall was the banner of a new era. Therefore, Brother Joseph has decreed that our church and our people shall be known by a new name. No longer shall we be called the Church of Christ. Let all the people of the world know us from this day forward as the Church of Latter-day Saints."

The crowd raised a cheer. Emma had heard nothing about a change of name until that moment. She turned away from Sidney and her eyes fell at once on Joseph. He stood only a few yards away, among some of his men. When Emma caught his eye, he nodded coolly. What did this mean, that he had made such a momentous decision without consulting her? Joseph had always discussed the church with Emma—seeking her advice, working out the tangle of his thoughts by hearing what she had to say.

Emma looked around. One of Ann Whitney's daughters was kicking idly at a post on the mercantile porch. "Sara Ann," she called, "won't you please take Julia in hand? It's only for a few minutes. She's too small to take out into that crowd; I'm frightened she might get away from me and run under a horse's hooves."

Once her daughter was safely tended, Emma edged into the crowd, struggling to reach Joseph while her son writhed and complained in her arms. Joseph was jesting with Parley Pratt while they secured their saddle bags.

"Joseph," she said, "why did you not address the people yourself?"

He turned to her with some surprise. "Emma, dear. Merciful heaven, I'm going to miss you."

He kissed her cheek. It was all she could do not to pull away impatiently.

"Sidney is a fine speaker," he said. "It's important that the men of Zion's Camp should feel I'm with them—truly with them."

"Of course you're with them. You're their prophet and their leader."

"I must hold them together while we're out in the fields and towns, putting down the Gentile menace."

"You'll hold your men together best if you show yourself as a general, commanding respect—not playing among them like a schoolboy."

Parley and the other men turned away, which was more tactful than listening while Emma lashed God's anointed with her tongue. She swallowed the remainder of her complaints.

Someone whistled from the edge of the crowd, a high, rising pitch.

"Our signal to ride," Joseph called. "It's a new day, men—a new world. Let's go and do God's work!"

The riders made their last farewells and swung up into their saddles. Joseph led his horse closer to Emma. Optimism at what was to come rolled from him in palpable waves, like the ring of heat that ripples out from an iron stove. He kissed Young Joseph's forehead, then Emma's cheek. "Tell my little angel Julia I will miss her and will see her again soon."

Then he mounted his horse, laughing, and settled his hat on his head. He followed the men he was meant to lead south and west out of town. Emma stood for a long while. Young Joseph, sighing in her arms, leaned against her shoulder. Soon the crossroads were empty. Sparrows came down to scratch and peck through the mud and the pockmarks of hoof-prints, searching for crumbs from the hardtack the men had packed into their bags. She was curiously light in her chest, in her whole being—relief or something equally hopeful, something she couldn't name. She told herself it was a benediction she felt, God's blessing on Joseph's endeavor. She told herself this day was the first of a new era. Life would soon return to relative peace. No more would she hear of settlements burning, of men shot dead, of women and children abused.

It was the blue sky that made her so naïve, the birdsong that made her so damnably trusting. Two months later, when Joseph returned at the head of his hollow-eyed, bedraggled army, she would learn what misfortunes had befallen the Prophet, and curse the lightness she'd felt that day.

When Zion's Camp came limping back to Kirtland in the heat of July, Emma whisked Joseph up to their quarters above the mercantile before anyone else could speak to him. She pressed a bowl of broth into his hands and stood beside the window, leaning one hip against the sill, looking down on the streets because she couldn't look at him.

"Tell me," she said. "Tell me everything. Hold nothing back."

He was quiet. His voice scarcely rose above a whisper. "At first, it was almost like a holiday. We rode the countryside and camped at creeks and riverbanks, and in the evenings we drilled in the maneuvers we would use when we came upon those devils in Missouri. There was a feeling of brotherhood. And every night, when drills were finished, I would blow a note on a curled black trumpet made from the horn of a ram. Sidney gave me the ram's horn on our first day—a gift, a symbol of my leadership."

"A ram's horn," Emma said flatly. Had they thought this was a masquerade, this march against Missouri?

"When they heard the horn, all the men of Zion's Camp gathered to take my nightly sermon. We all knelt together in prayer. We kept peace among us."

"Spare me the foolishness," Emma said. "Cut to the heart of the matter. You came back looking like beaten dogs. And if I'm not mistaken, you're a few men short of the number you set out with."

"Fourteen," he answered faintly.

"You lost fourteen men? Who? Where did they go?"

She expected him to confess that the missing men had slipped off to start new lives in the towns they had passed. Fourteen who'd found the strength to escape the Prophet's orbit. She did not expect the ragged answer he gave.

"They went into their graves. Dead—all of them."

She spun away from the window. She stared at him, mouth open, but what could she say? Joseph didn't see her. He was looking through her, watching his memories play out again and again like a ghost pacing some dark hall.

"Cut to the heart of the matter." He spoke in a wooden voice, a hollow voice. "The heart of the matter is this: the Lord tested us and found our weakness. He found where we could be broken. It started with mosquitoes and biting flies. Then we ran out of what little meat we carried. The men felt that keenly, I can tell you. They started to murmur about the comfortable beds they'd left back home, and the company of their wives. Next a great storm came up and we were forced off the road, up into the hills to avoid the flooding. There were no settlements up there, no one to sell us meat to fortify us, and anyhow, the roads were impassable and the fields had turned to swamp."

"How long did you remain in the hills?"

"Days. First the flood, and then Martin Harris was laid out by snake bite. We had to wait for him to recover. And all the while we were delving into the bottoms of our provision bags, and the flour we'd brought was infested by weevils. It was all we had to eat, by then.

"Once the roads dried out a little, Brigham sent me down from the hills with the company's money to buy something more to eat."

"Brigham. Brigham sent you."

"He held the purse-strings," Joseph said. "Everyone agreed I was too free with my gratitude to keep charge of the money. I was liable to give it away as rewards for good service."

"Merciful Lord, Joseph. You would have been wiser to let Martin Harris hold the purse. Don't you see what you've done, putting power in Brigham's hands?"

Joseph only talked on, his eyes distant, his face long with remorse.

"The best I could find were a dozen cured hams—but the hams were old, and some had begun to rot along their bottoms. I told the men that all the rot could be pared away, and the meat underneath was wholesome. But I suppose the spoiled hams struck some of them as a final insult."

"I should think so."

"An entire squadron rebelled. They threw the hams in the mud at my feet. If that had been the worst of it, we might have repaired our wounded spirits, one way or another. But later that same day, every horse in the army foundered, and we were forced to cool our heels in that miserable spot till our horses had recovered."

He told Emma how he prayed over the animals, and preached to his men rather desperately, imploring them to humble themselves and remember their purpose, scolding that anyone who continued in a spirit of rebellion would be punished by God. With time, the horses mended—all but one, so at least Zion's Camp had fresh meat for a few days.

Emma listened with a sinking heart. As Joseph spoke, all she could think of was Brigham Young, riding somewhere behind Joseph, watching the Prophet's shoulders hunch, watching him sink lower in the saddle. She could almost see Brigham's small eyes glittering, the money swinging in his purse, his lip curling in a smile.

"When we finally reached the Missouri border, I sent Parley and Orson Hyde across the river to meet with Governor Dunklin. The mood lightened a little. All the men felt that the worst of our trials lay behind us, and everyone felt certain that when Parley and Orson returned, it would be with the news that Dunklin was prepared to roll out a grand welcome and guide us back to Jackson County under the protection of his militia, just as he'd promised to do. But Parley and Orson were told that the governor had rescinded the offer."

"Why?"

Joseph said nothing, only drew a long, shaky breath.

"Why, Joseph? Tell me. You owe me the truth."

"Word had already reached Missouri that an army of Mormons was on the march."

Of course. What else had any of them expected? Inwardly, she cursed herself for having failed to foresee this turn. Any of them ought to have guessed it would happen. Even Joseph.

"There were militias from four different counties waiting across the river. They were convinced we'd come to murder every Gentile woman and child. It was all Dunklin could do to give Parley and Orson safe passage back to our side. We had no choice but to turn back. If we marched into Missouri, it would have meant our deaths—every last one of us in Zion's Camp, and every Mormon still hiding in Clay County. It's a civil war waiting to erupt. We simply couldn't continue."

"Merciful Heaven," Emma said. "I hope you've learned caution from this, at the very least. I suppose it's too much to hope that you've learned some wisdom."

He squeezed his eyes shut. "Oh, Emma. If only my chastisement had ended there. The men all argued for a spell. Some wanted to pull back. I thought perhaps we might go north and find a friendlier crossing, then make our way in secrecy to Clay County, and somehow assemble the refugees."

"It would have meant your death if you'd gone through with that plan."

"Death came anyhow. I ask myself now what I could have done to stop it. I'll ask myself for the rest of my life."

The men fell to fighting, Joseph said, swinging their fists with every notion of brotherhood forgotten. And all the while, Emma knew, Brigham was watching—making his silent calculations. Joseph tried to assert his authority and bring his men back into some semblance of accord. But the moment he raised his voice, he was shouted down again. One of his men even cried, "You prophesy lies in the name of God! Your heart is corrupt as Hell!"

"I couldn't bear such an insult," he said. "Before I could think better, I took the ram's horn from the pommel of my saddle and threw it at the man who'd shouted at me. He ducked. The horn hit the ground and shattered. The horn that had called us all to prayer, destroyed in a flash. And I was the one who had thrown it."

There was nothing to do then but turn back for Kirtland. Yet even that journey was a trial. Cholera ran through Zion's Camp, laying every man out on the uncaring earth. There was no treatment they could find out there on the plain, save a good dunking in cold water and a gruel made from whiskey and flour.

"That was how they died," Emma said. "Those fourteen men."

Joseph said nothing. He still held the bowl of broth in his trembling hands. It had long since gone cold, and he hadn't drunk a drop. He stared past her, out the window that looked south from the upper story of the Whitney store, to the dome and spire of the temple.

"What did you tell them?" Emma demanded.

He shook his head vaguely, uncomprehending.

"How did you excuse this . . . this folly? How can you make them believe you're still a prophet now?"

"I told them God no longer required an army to fight for Zion's redemption." His words were flat, haunted. "'Behold,' God said, 'I will fight your battles. The destroyer I have sent forth to lay waste to mine enemies, and not many years hence they shall not be left to mar my heritage.' I told them, 'Sue for peace not only to the people that have smitten you, but to all people of the land.'"

He would speak no more. He seemed not even to know where he was, nor to feel Emma's presence. She watched him contending with those raw, close memories—and saw him then, truly saw Joseph, perhaps for the first time in her life. The distance and dullness in his eyes. The way he looked at the temple's spire, this thing he'd created by the force of his will. He was unblinking, unmoved.

She remembered a gray day in November, the hens scratching in the yard. She ought to have had some warning. A merciful God would have told her, then, how hopeless this all would become. If she had known, she would have made Joseph stop, one way or another, and hellfire be damned. Fourteen men dead, and Zion burned, a state eager to break out in war, to hang Joseph Smith like a dog. It had gone far enough.

But he couldn't have stopped it then. This church is a creature unto itself. It has long since slipped its leash and broken all its tethers. Before Governor Ford came to Nauvoo, and long before the governor had heard Joseph's name, the church had already run beyond the reach of the Prophet's hand. There is no catching it now. There is no taming it ever.

June 28, 1844
Nauvoo, Illinois

She wakes again. Groggy this time, with a heavy head, a sour taste in her mouth, under a sheet on her bed. She hasn't dreamed this time, or if she dreamed, she can't recall it. When she eases herself up from the mattress and pulls back the sheet, there's a fresh cotton nightgown on her body. It gives off a faint scent of lavender. The old dress is gone altogether— not hung over the back of her chair, where she leaves clothes in need of washing. She didn't put herself to bed. It must have been Eliza, but she has no memory of it, no memory of anything in that moment except for Joseph and his strange history. Outside, the sun is high. It blazes through her linen curtains. She would sleep again if she could be certain she wouldn't dream.

A knock at the door. Harder, more urgent—only then does she realize it was knocking that pulled her from sleep. She stands, and clings to the bedpost to remain on her feet.

"A moment," she calls. It may be Governor Ford. "Only give me a moment to dress."

The door squeals as it opens, a furtive sound. Emma darts a hand to her bed and pulls up the sheet, wraps it around herself so no man may see her in her nightdress. But it isn't the governor at the door. It's Porter Rockwell, Esno hat pressed hard against his chest. Wisps of hair have pulled out of his braids, a wild aura around him. His eyes are grim and stricken.

Softly, Porter says, "Mrs. Smith."

She sinks back down on her bed. She stares at Porter—the dirt and sweat of a long ride, the tracks of grief, pale lines down his face.

"I'm sorry," he says. "I've been to Carthage jail. If only it hadn't fallen to me to bring you this news."

"No."

But she knows it's true, even as she denies it. She has known for hours, for days. She realized what would come of this folly when she found Joseph in the orchard, those scraps of white cloth scattering on the wind.

"Our Prophet and his brother Hyrum," Porter says, "taken up to God. The bodies are being sent back to Nauvoo for a proper burial. At least they'll allow us that small mercy, those Gentile devils. At least Joseph will have a funeral."

She turns her face away. The sheet clings to her, tight like a winding-sheet on a corpse. "Have you met Eliza Snow today? Have you told her the news?"

"I've spoken to no one. I came straight to you as soon as I found my way past the governor's men."

"Go and get Eliza. Send her here, to me."

VIII

Ask, and It Shall Be Given

1835

"My! What a lovely new home!" This was Ann Whitney, who had let herself in because Emma had told her the latchstring should always be out for her. After the generosity Ann had shown in those early Kirtland days, free hospitality was the least Emma could offer. She was in the kitchen, scoring the tops of a few new loaves of bread; she called, "I'm here, Ann. Come and find me, for I'm all flour from head to foot and can't do a thing until the bread is baking."

As Ann came into the kitchen, she craned over her shoulder to see the wainscoting in the hall. She carried a basket of vegetables over one arm, pink radishes, a few early carrots. It was spring of the year 1835, a mild season. "You and the Prophet have certainly done nicely for yourselves."

Emma wiped her hands on a towel and took off her apron. She beat the apron with a palm, knocking free the worst of the flour. "This isn't so grand a house—not compared to the one I grew up in—a wayside inn back in Pennsylvania. I wouldn't allow Joseph to build anything too fine. It's better for him to be humble now. We should always cultivate humility."

"But it's pretty in the small details. That paneling down the hall is perfectly delicious. This is a home any woman could be proud of."

Once Zion's Camp proved a failure, Kirtland met Joseph with anger and mistrust almost as often as with praise. Men quarreled over whether the church had a prophet at its head, or merely a charlatan—or whether Joseph had once been God's anointed but had fallen out of favor.

Contention and division had crept in to replace the spirit of community that had been Kirtland's hallmark. Debating clubs were now the mode among younger folk, and the keenest subject for discussion was whether Joseph Smith still held the authority to lead the Church of

Latter-day Saints. The mere existence of the debating societies rankled Joseph, but what cost him sleep was the fact that the most vigorous and notorious club had been founded by his own brother, Don Carlos. Until the tragedy of Zion's Camp, Don Carlos had been content to keep his opinions to himself. But he was a man of twenty years now, with a home and acreage of his own. He was no longer a child, captive to the family fervor.

By Christmas, every man was for himself. Whatever private holdings had once been trusted to the church were taken back with jealous speed. If Joseph and his elders weren't quick to return assets, the church leaders were summoned to the county courthouse. Neighbor sued neighbor; apostles sued the Prophet. Bitterness hung like a fog in the air, stifling and thick.

Joseph took the change in Kirtland's temper with remarkable passivity. He understood there was nothing to be gained in fighting back. If he hoped to hold on to some small means of livelihood—and keep the remains of his church together—he mustn't become a tyrant. He even managed to find a little cheer in the change. Here was an opportunity to live as most men did—in a real home, where his wife could keep her own hearth. And so, as soon as the snows had melted, he built a beautiful home on a lot close to the temple with the help of his brothers.

Emma had loved the house from the moment she'd seen it. It was no elegant manor—only a simple, two-story, clapboard affair with a high-peaked roof and one brick chimney. But it was hers alone, and honestly come by, not given out of pity or duty. After eight years of marriage, she would finally live as any proper, respectable woman lived.

"It is pretty enough," she told Ann. "Joseph and his brothers have built so many houses together, they can fairly do it in their sleep. I'll put in a flower garden this summer."

"And Joseph's store." Ann nodded out the kitchen window, toward the small shop across the street. "Newel worried at first that his store would compete with ours, but he stocks different goods, and the town has grown enough to appreciate a second shop."

Building the house had been a balm to Joseph's soul. He could lose himself in the simplicity of labor, the wholesome ache in his arms and back after a day spent toiling at a fixed cause. Long before the house was finished, he'd come to crave the routines any ordinary man might enjoy.

And so he built the store, too, and thought to divide his time between a prophet's mysticism and the staid, earthy routines of keeping shop. There was a single small room above the store's main floor, which Joseph used as his office for prophetic work. But the church needed little of his attention now. He had long since established hierarchies of priests and apostles to handle the lion's share of organization and arbitration. With more time to himself, he settled gratefully into a shopkeeper's life.

Emma was content with the change. It made no difference to her whether her husband made a living as a prophet or a merchant, so long as she and the children were secure. And if truth be known, his flagging interest in spiritual matters came as a relief. Her life felt almost ordinary for the first time since Joseph had come into it. A weight had been lifted from her spirit. She wasn't sorry to feel it going.

"I'm glad Newel's business still thrives," Emma said, "and glad to see you. I've been so busy since we moved in, I've had no time to go visiting."

"My children miss you and your babies—though Julia can't really be called a baby any longer. Four years old, and pretty as they come. And so big! She's almost as tall as my six-year-old. Tell me, how do you like living so close to the temple?"

"This is a beautiful spot, and all the more lovely because the temple is near. I can feel it all the time, you know, like a friend standing close beside me."

Since Zion's Camp, many members of the church had fallen away. Some had left Kirtland altogether. Yet the meetinghouse was still crowded with congregants every Sunday. It was the temple that held them, Emma knew—a monument to the Saints' work and sacrifice, a shrine to the sacred bonds of community. Men had bruised their bodies to raise that spire. Women had crushed their grandmothers' china into dust, mixing the dust into plaster to make the walls gleam white as Heaven. The temple was a reminder of what Kirtland once had been—what it might become again someday, when the storm clouds had moved on.

"Busy as you are," Ann said, "with a new house and two growing children, I suppose you could use a real friend beside you—one with hands to share in your work."

Emma laughed. "Are you my volunteer?"

"Not I, sad to say—though nothing would please me more than to work with you again. But you've seen my household with your own eyes; we're an unruly bunch. I can't be spared."

"Your children, unruly? Never."

"I do know of someone, though. She just arrived, not two weeks ago—a good girl, seventeen, cheerful and hardworking. And an orphan, the poor thing. Her parents were lost to fever over in Mantua. I've taken her in. In fact, I've put her up in the very rooms you and Joseph once used."

"Dear Ann, ever the benefactress. Sometimes I feel as if I can never match your example of charity."

"The girl made her way to Kirtland by herself—on foot most of the way, if you can believe it. She could scarcely walk another step by the time she found us, and oh, she was thin. My heart broke to see her. But she'd heard Kirtland had mercy to offer, so she went on walking whenever there were no carts to carry her. And what do you suppose waited for her? By the time she found us, all communal holdings were dissolved back into private property. But I would never turn away any soul in need, especially not a child. And such a child she is! So gay and delightful. You might take her in, Emma. A girl of her age can't help but feel lonely and wasted, living in a little room above a shop, without any society. She's good with children, and yours are a handful each now, big as they are."

"That's true enough. I'm run ragged, looking after Julia and Young Joseph."

"Meet this girl," Ann said, "and see what you think. She needs an anchor in a storm-tossed world, and my house is full up."

Emma agreed to go and meet the orphan the next day. She packed a small basket with gifts: a loaf of new bread and a little pot of honey, along with a pair of linen kerchiefs that she had embroidered during the long, dark hours of winter. Ann came out to meet Emma on the mercantile porch, then led her up the stairs to the old familiar rooms.

"Fannie," Ann called as they climbed, "you've a visitor, my dear—a very important one."

The girl came out of her room. She was small and slender with a narrow face, but she wasn't unattractive. In fact, she was rather a pretty child. Her cheekbones were sharp from deprivation, but they held a bright-pink flush. And those hungry, longing eyes, blinking at Emma in surprise, were heavily fringed with dark lashes. She looked altogether enchanting, like a fairy spirit.

"Fannie Alger," Ann said formally, "I would like for you to meet Mrs. Smith—Sister Emma Smith, the wife of the Prophet."

The girl gave a deep curtsy. The hem of her pale-blue dress pooled on the floor. When she rose up, she was already chattering. "I'm pleased to make your acquaintance, Mrs. Smith. I won't ask if I may call you Emma yet because I only just met you, and Ann—that is, Mrs. Whitney—told me once it's not fitting for a girl of my age to seem too familiar with a nice respectable lady like yourself. But I do hope we'll be familiar one day, Mrs. Smith; honest I do. There are such a lot of nice folks in this town and I just want to know all of them. It's a jolly place, really— everyone is so good and friendly. I would almost feel all the way glad that I've come here, but I can't feel entirely glad because I'm an orphan now, and I miss my parents a terrible lot. I suppose Mrs. Whitney told you all about that."

"Yes," Emma said delicately, "Mrs. Whitney mentioned something of your hard times. I'm sorry for you, but pleased to hear you've been treated kindly."

"Oh my, yes. Ann's—I mean, Mrs. Whitney's girls are awfully nice, and all the gentlemen who come to the store tip their hats when they say hello, just like I'm a real lady myself. I guess I am close enough to being a lady now as makes no difference."

She certainly was. Her frame was slender, but the bodice of her dress fit snugly, revealing the curve and high carriage of her breasts. She ought to wear a lace capelet, Emma thought, for modesty's sake. But no doubt the poor girl had had little inclination to consider such things. She had only just lost her mother. Who was to teach her modesty?

"I like Kirtland real well," Fannie went on. "I even went down to the church last Sunday, and such a time I had! Your church here, it's nothing like the church we had back home. Such songs as we sang! They about made my heart feel like it was flying."

Ann said, "Sister Emma herself chose those songs. She is compiling a hymnal for the church."

"Are you a Mormon?" Emma asked the girl.

"Do you mean, am I a member of your church? No—not yet, but after

I saw how nice the meeting was, I made up my mind that I'd be baptized just as soon as I could find somebody to do it. Ann has been so good to me, and all you Mormons are so loving and gentle to one little useless orphan girl like me. I would like to call myself a part of this church, seeing as how it's made up of kindly people."

Ann said, "Fannie, dear, the man who preached on Sunday was Joseph Smith—our leader and Prophet, and this good lady's husband."

"Oh!" Fannie clasped her hands under her chin, a gesture that was almost pleading. "He was a real fine preacher. And such a handsome fellow. He wore his coat so well. I've seen a lot of good preachers, too, though I am so young. We had plenty who came through our church in Mantua. But this one—Mr. Smith—he spoke like no fellow I've heard before."

"You oughtn't to call a man so important as Joseph Smith a 'fellow,'" Ann said mildly. "It doesn't convey the proper respect."

"I'm sorry. Only I didn't think anything of it because he seemed so much like any other gentleman. But he has a real knack for talking about God, hasn't he?"

Emma handed the basket to Fannie. "I've brought you a few small things. I thought perhaps you could use them."

"How thoughtful—and me a perfect stranger to you. My, but these kerchiefs are pretty. Look at the flowers, Ann, just look! Pansies are my favorite."

"Fannie," Emma said while the girl dipped her finger in the pot of honey, "how do you do with little children?"

"I adore small children. Why, they're perfect angels as far as I'm concerned, even when they're carrying on. I was the youngest in my family, so I didn't get to play with babies much. Only when my cousins would visit."

"I've two small children of my own—a girl and a boy—and I would be glad for your help. Would you like to come stay with Mr. Smith and me, and live like an older sister to my little ones?"

Fannie looked up with shining eyes. "I don't feel as if I'm worthy of such kindness."

"All God's children deserve charity. I myself have had to rely on the kindness of others. Many times, in fact." She and Ann shared a look—Ann warm and giving, Emma misty with gratitude. "What better way to honor the mercies I've been shown than to extend those same mercies to another soul in need? As long as you don't mind the noise and fuss of children, Joseph and I would be glad to welcome you."

Fannie went home with Emma that very afternoon. It took the girl only a few minutes to pack her belongings in a small, tattered bag. She kissed Ann warmly on the cheek, promising to visit as often as her new duties allowed. Then they set off south along the Chillicothe Road. Fannie chittered like a starling all the while.

"Of course, I miss my mother and pa dreadfully, Mrs. Smith, but it's hard to keep a heavy heart all the time when you've come to such a pretty place. And oh, the temple is real beautiful. I've never seen a building so grand, not even the time I went with my pa to Cleveland. There were heaps of bigger buildings, of course, and some of them were prettier because they had such dandy carvings all along their tops, but your temple just has a feeling about it, doesn't it? It feels like a kindly grandfather watching over you, old-fashioned but good and reliable. And the sun looks so bright on those white walls, it makes you want to throw open your arms and holler about all the good things in the world."

"You're a cheerful soul," Emma said. "I think it will be good for me to be in your company. I find my spirits in need of lifting, now and then."

At home, Emma helped the girl settle into a small room tucked behind the kitchen.

Fannie turned slowly, taking in the humble furnishings and close walls as if she had stepped into a queen's chamber. Emma led her across the road to Joseph's store, where she'd left the children under their father's eye.

"Julia is four and a dear child, though she is sometimes headstrong." Emma held open the shop door, ushering Fannie in. "We call our son Young Joseph. He is two and a very good boy, most of the time. Ah, and here is their papa, Mr. Smith—though everyone in Kirtland calls him Brother Joseph."

Joseph closed his ledger book and rose to his feet. "Emma, darling, you look well this afternoon. The children, you'll be glad to know, are napping on their blankets in the storeroom. And who is this young lady?"

Fannie seemed at a loss for words—a remarkable change in her character. She blushed and couldn't quite meet his eye.

"Joseph, meet Fannie Alger. She has come to Kirtland as an orphan, seeking charity and mercy, for her parents are both dead of the fever. I told Ann Whitney we would take her in until she has married and settled down in a home of her own. She'll be a great help with the children, I think."

Joseph came around the counter to take Fannie's hand. "What a charming girl. And cast out by fate into a cold, lonely world. Well, of course we must take her in, Emma. There's no question about it."

Over the course of that pleasant, naïve spring, Fannie was a comfort and delight. She and the children shared an obvious affinity. Julia and Young Joseph loved to play with the cheerful girl, and would obey her requests to pick up their toys or put on their nightdresses far more readily than they obeyed Emma. Fannie seemed fascinated by kitchen work, peeking under the towels to see how the bread dough was rising, jumping up eagerly to tend the kettle whenever she heard it boil. She would join Emma at the washtub without being asked, and even seemed to find laundry agreeable work, never noticing how the hot water and lye soap chapped her delicate hands. Her endless questions and sunlit observations made the hours pass swiftly. In fact, Fannie was so industrious that Emma sometimes chased her outside, insisting she go and associate with people her own age.

"You can't spend all your time with me and the children," Emma said. "You need friendship with some good, fun-loving girls. And you're old enough to be married; you ought to meet the nicer boys of Kirtland. Make their acquaintance and decide whether any are to your liking. I'm sure there are dozens of young men who would jump at the chance to court you, pretty as you are."

When Fannie took the children outside and the house was quiet, Emma sat with the pages of her hymnal rolled out before her, reordering the songs, probing carefully at the tone and feel of each selection. The work was almost finished, yet she couldn't turn the manuscript over to Joseph for printing—not yet. Something was missing. There was a tear in the cloth, a sense of incompletion that tormented her subtly like a splinter under the skin.

Sometimes Emma thought the haunting sense of deficiency might not be in her hymnal, but rather in her home. Joseph had found such refuge in a shopkeeper's life that he had retreated almost entirely to the small, predictable world of his store. He came to the house for supper and to kiss the children goodnight, but the better part of his waking hours was spent with his ledgers and stocks, the accounts his customers owed, their payments, their requests. Those members of his church who'd remained in Kirtland still looked to him as their chief leader. But Joseph no longer saw himself in that brilliant light. Or if he was still the Prophet in his heart, then it was God who had drawn away, gathering Himself back into the unknowable confines of a distant Heaven.

Now and again, Emma looked up from her pages with a furrowed brow and stared through the glass to the store. And there was Joseph, across the road—the broad and empty road, an abyss between them. She would see him bent over his work, counting out some small items from a lidded jar or grinning in welcome as a customer came in. He was like someone else's husband, like some man Emma had never known. In those moments, great waves of sadness would sweep over her and steal her breath, and she would blink through a sudden pang, a hunger for affection and trust—things she and her husband had never truly shared, except by letter, and only across great distance. *How strange*, she told herself, *to miss a thing I've never known*. Now and then, she even convinced herself that she would prefer to have the Prophet back—restored to his former power, holding Kirtland in his thrall—just for the sake of having a Joseph who was familiar to her, a husband she could recognize.

It isn't that Emma was unhappy that year. She existed—as, it must be admitted, she had always done—in a place beyond happiness, outside its delicate and shifting boundaries, a place where happiness was so foreign as to be irrelevant. Her life wasn't all sorrow and longing—far from it. Her children thrived; they gave her the fierce, wild, protective joy of motherhood. And Fannie was a little lark—helpful, industrious, eager to please all summer long, a laughing, singing streak of color in the home. Emma wasn't unhappy, but neither was she whole.

She would pause, some evenings, beside the kitchen window. The children were in bed and Fannie had gone to some party or dance with the young people of the town. The house was silent and blue without any lamps lit, a cool, waiting blue. She stood alone beside her table with the unfinished pages of the hymnal spread around her, weighted down with cups from her cabinet. She looked across the darkened street to the shop. A light burned in the lower story. All she could see of that light was a stripe of gold, the thin gap between two curtains drawn like veils. The slash of gold disappeared and relit, disappeared and glowed again, blinking through a settled dusk.

Joseph was pacing. He passed across his window. He turned and retraced his steps and crossed the window again, but always he found himself standing in the same place as before.

Years later, when she examined the course of her life—when enough time had passed that the pain had dulled and she could bear to look through thickets of shame—Emma understood that this was the point where it started, this mess, this present peculiarity. It appears to her now like a mark on a map. A fat slash of ink, an X, the appalling destination to which all roads had been leading.

The end of summer. The long hot days, the withering heat, with the smell of the river close all around you and the damp from the river closer still, clinging under your arms. The children were limp and fussing. When Emma said she couldn't leave her cooking and tend to the children, Fannie Alger went very slowly, dragging her feet, casting her eyes to Heaven as if pleading for patience. The girl had never done such a thing before. Fannie had been quiet all day—a blunt, secretive silence. Emma had taken it for a young girl's natural impatience, her eagerness for parties at the finer homes in town, for the company of girls her own age, which on the best of days was preferable to the tedious questions the children asked, the endless cleaning up, the feeding and washing. On a day that made a body weak with summer heat, the children could scarcely be tolerated. Even Emma would admit that much. But Fannie, for all her petulant slowness, would spring up to do any task that would take her into Joseph's company.

She ought to have seen it much sooner than she did. The way Joseph, coming home from the shop or some meeting of the priests and apostles, would greet Emma first with a kiss on her cheek. But after Emma, always, without fail, he would go to Fannie and kiss her cheek, too. Emma took it for a brotherly kiss, but the girl would blush—the soft rose petals of her cheeks, her face like a rose opening to the sun. And she would look down in a display of modesty, but she would turn toward Emma while she did it, so Emma couldn't help but see the color rising.

All these things she noticed, and yet she did not. She witnessed the glances, the smiles, the lingering looks that passed between Fannie and Joseph, but she didn't truly see. Fannie in blue, the color she favored—cornflower blue, a shade Emma hates now—lifting her bright hem farther than her ankle while she climbed the stair to the children's room. And pausing on the staircase to pass some casual word to Joseph, so he would look up and see the smoothness of a stocking exposed, the slenderness of her leg before she seemed to recall herself and let her skirt fall. The way Joseph, when passing in the hall, would drag his hand over the small of the girl's back, so lightly it might have been an accident.

And those nights, the long mute nights when Joseph and Emma lay far apart in their bed, because the heat of summer or the long years had made nearness unbearable. He was insistently awake, tossing on the mattress, turning his face to the wall.

There came a day when Emma found herself overburdened with the cooking. The kettle was boiling, the children bickering in the parlor over some storybook or toy. Young Joseph gave a scream fit to wake the dead. She called for Fannie, asked her to look after the children and put a stop to their noise, or come and stir the kettle at the very least so Emma could see to it. But Fannie never came. There was no answer, no tread of her foot across the floor, not even one of the petulant moans Emma had come to expect.

The girl must have slipped out to the willows, Emma thought, where she often sat idle in the shade. Scowling, she brought the kettle back to a simmer, then turned her attention to the children, who by that time were red-faced, both of them flat on their backs, kicking their heels against the floor. Neither one could be soothed, except with molasses candy.

Emma dropped into her chair beside the kitchen window. She rested her elbows on the table and pressed the heels of her hands against her eyes. Her head was pounding. She stank of her own sweat. She wanted to retreat into her hymnal, take the roll of whispering pages and go down to the temple, as she used to do. She wanted to sit in the shade and let the music run through her mind until the throb in her head abated. But who would look after the children?

When she had composed herself, she stepped out into the yard, searching for Fannie in the green shadow under the trees. Emma shaded her eyes, looked north to the heart of town, but there was no sign of the girl tripping along the road.

Across the street, the door to Joseph's store was shut, the curtains drawn across the windows. Strange, that Joseph had closed to business well before the supper hour.

Curiosity overtook her annoyance at Fannie. She went back inside and took the children to her bedroom and locked the door so they could come to no mischief. Then she crossed the road, craning her neck this way and that as if she might somehow see through the heavy velvet curtains into Joseph's store. She tried the shop door and found it locked. A prickle of foreboding ran under her skin, a hot flush of caution that only doubled the day's misery.

Joseph never locked his door, except at night. If he'd gone to speak with one of his apostles at the other end of town—or if he'd left Kirtland altogether on some obscure business—he hadn't mentioned it to Emma.

She stood for a long moment with her hand on the door. Insects droned in the fields, a thick, lazy hum, but over that sound she could just make out another—a strange, sustained, rhythmic rustling. The muffled sound was coming from inside the shop.

"Hello," she called through the door. "Joseph, are you there? Where are you?"

She went to the rear of the building. A bar of shadow, blue as cobalt glass, slanted across the ground. Discarded crates from Joseph's shipments were stacked along the wall, some overturned or with their sides broken away. A pair of stray dogs nosed at one another amid the refuse. When they saw Emma approaching, the dogs hunched and scuffled away.

She made for the shop's rear door, hoping Joseph had forgotten to lock it. She passed a window as she went, but its curtain had been pulled hastily and the window wasn't entirely concealed. In the gap between the fabric and the sill, she could see something moving—a harsh, repetitive motion. The movement stopped her, struck her still and dumb. She could do nothing but stare in horrified understanding.

It was Joseph she saw. Moving that way. His trousers were lowered, his shirttail hanging down. Only a patch of bare thigh showed above his sagging belt. The backs of his thighs, white and stark—his hips moving

with an urgent, focused intensity against something pushed up and
bunched on the table before him, something voluminous and soft, cornflower blue. Fannie Alger had bent herself over the counter and Joseph
was working at her. She could hear, now, the girl's ragged breaths coming in short gasps, a slight sound through the pane of glass.

She was around to the front of the shop, pounding on the door before
she knew she had moved. Pounding, screaming—first accusations and
then wordlessly, like an animal snared, in pain. She kicked the door.
Kicked it again, hard enough she thought she might knock it from its
hinges, demanded that Joseph open, let her inside, explain himself, explain what he was doing, what he thought he was doing, who in God's
name he thought he was.

There was a wagon rumbling past on the Chillicothe Road. The
driver pulled in his team and stared at her. The driver saw when the
Prophet opened the door, red-faced, his eyes shifting away from his wife,
and hastily tucking his shirt into his half-buttoned trousers.

Her throat was raw by evening, bloody and torn on the inside. Everything
inside of her was bloody and torn, from screaming her accusations and
insults, from pleading. She had fallen to her knees once they were back
behind the privacy of their own walls. She had wept; she had begged
him to tell her why. Fannie Alger had come skulking into the house and
Emma had screamed at her, too, and driven her out. She had thrown all
the girl's belongings into the yard, into the dirt where Fannie belonged,
and the girl had gathered her things with a composed, haughty grace,
with all the righteous suffering of a martyr.

"You're mad," Joseph told her. "Don't turn the girl out. She needs
our charity."

"Is that what you gave her? Charity?"

"You didn't see what you think you saw. If you would only take hold
of yourself and listen!"

She wouldn't listen. And the only thing she could take hold of was
the great beast of pain that reared up in her soul. It was the monster of
Revelation, many-headed, all its mocking mouths agape. She clung to
her rage, and rage kept her standing long after Joseph had left the house
with his fists clenched, cursing her stubbornness, her madness.

She walked down the street, past the temple, south and south and southward still while the town grew small and distant behind her. Twilight was coming on. The fields, withering into the harvest, were rosy and orange in an early dusk. She walked to the little cabin Don Carlos had built at the edge of Hyrum's property.

She could see Don Carlos working at a patch of potatoes as she came near his fields. She stopped at his fence, wits dulled by exhaustion and sadness, watching him rake the soil with some long-handled tool. The hoe looked too spindly in the remnant summer light, Don Carlos's arms too strong. She remembered him as a boy in Harmony. She could see him so clearly, just as he'd been in those days, riding a sorrel horse with the cuffs of his trousers pulled up, exposing his dirty ankles. How long ago that time felt now. How far behind her Harmony lay.

Don Carlos had grown into all the potential his brothers had never achieved—strong of will, sure of heart, pure in spirit. He moved among the plants easily; he never seemed to tire. The fading light pulled away. Now a shoulder and now the straight plane of his back, now the angles of his face melted into the coming night. Just a farmer, any farmer, at one with his land. He had never wanted anything but that.

He straightened, glancing toward the road. He noticed Emma standing at the split-rail fence and paused, wiping his brow on a sleeve. He was the image of Joseph, tall and well made, with a face that would be fine and compelling, but for the size and shape of his nose. He ran a hand through his sandy hair, waiting for Emma to approach.

There was a little gate made of twisted willow farther along the fence line. She let herself through and walked between two rows of potatoes. Some of the vines had begun to die back. They crackled against her skirt.

"Sister Emma." Don Carlos didn't need to ask how she fared. He could read her face.

"Why did you come here," she asked, "to Kirtland?"

He looked down at his feet. Frogs sang by the river, calling mindlessly into the silence. At length, he answered, "I don't know."

"You do know. You must know why."

Helplessly, he shook his head. "I suppose because my family came. That must be the reason."

"Your family followed Joseph here. Joseph and his book."

He nodded. He looked disappointed to have found such a simple and obvious answer.

"Why didn't you go away, Don Carlos? Go somewhere else. There is so much more to you than there is to any of them—your brothers, your father. Joseph especially. You're a better man than they, better than all of them together."

"What has he done, Emma?"

She folded her arms tightly around her middle, as if she could hold herself together that way. She drew in a long breath. It seemed to come and come, the air rushing into her, the coolness of night making itself felt, finally; cold flooding into her body but never filling her up. Finally, she said, "I've chased Fannie Alger away."

He understood then. Even in the twilight, she could see the color draining from his face, the shock of her words descending. He came to her and put his arm around her as he'd done once before when her heart had been broken. She covered her face with her hands. She could smell his body, a sharper, cleaner odor than Joseph's smell. He was hot from his work. Beads of his sweat soaked through her sleeve and dampened her skin.

"How do you know?" he asked.

"I saw them, God help me. Joseph says I saw nothing, that my eyes played me a trick, but I know. I know what I saw. You sound as if you know, too."

"I only suspected. I'd hoped I was wrong. I thought I was wicked even to think that my brother—the leader of our church—could do such a thing."

"Why didn't you tell me?" She began to weep again and was surprised by it. She had thought her tears used up, but sorrow is a well that refreshes itself agony after agony.

"What good would it have done, for me to tell you? I had no proof. If I'd had any proof, I would have come to you, Emma. I wouldn't have let you suffer."

She sagged against him. "What am I to do now? What can I possibly do?"

Don Carlos didn't answer. His silence was just as well; they both knew there was no good solution to her predicament. The bonds of marriage aren't cast off so easily, not even when a wife is betrayed. And worse, Joseph was still the leader of their church, their community, the whole world as far as any Mormon was concerned. The majority of the church still regarded him as the Prophet, even if he had lost the will to lead, even if he had driven himself from the path of righteousness and into a place of shadow. If Emma were to leave him now, it would be worse than sinful. It would tear the church apart, cast thousands of souls adrift—souls who had given everything to build God's kingdom in these Latter Days.

Don Carlos said fiercely, "You may not be able to do much about it, but I can. Let my brother show his face and I'll teach him what a man is. He'll learn who's the better Smith; I promise you that."

"You mustn't," she said. "It would only make more trouble."

"Where are the children tonight?"

"I've sent them up to Ann Whitney's place. Ann came down to comfort me. She has heard already—the whole thing was witnessed, or my anger was witnessed, at least, by a driver on the road. Rumor will fly. There's no stopping it now."

"Stay here tonight. My cabin is very small and I'm afraid it's not comfortable, but I'll do my best for you."

She nodded. If she returned home that night, if she faced her husband—whatever Joseph was now, husband or not—her heart would break again. She couldn't bear to see Joseph or hear his voice. She couldn't remain in the home he had built for her, couldn't linger in the rooms where her children played, the children she and Joseph had raised and loved together.

"Come along." Don Carlos turned her gently. The sound of the frogs was almost enough to make her forget what she had seen. For one brief moment she gave herself up to the quiet of the evening, the simple comfort of a brother's arm around her shoulders.

"What are you doing with my wife?" Joseph's voice split the air. Emma turned and found him coming down the lane like a thunderhead, towering and cold.

Don Carlos stepped away from her. "What were you doing with a woman who isn't your wife?"

"Emma," Joseph said, "you will come back home with me."

"She'll stay here," Don Carlos said, "until she sees fit to return. If she ever sees fit."

Joseph scoffed. His hair was untidy, sleeves unbuttoned and wrinkled. "What, will you take my wife now?"

"Don't be a fool. She's my sister by marriage. I'll care for her as a brother ought to do when her husband refuses to tend her properly."

"The children need you, Emma."

Those simple words brought fresh tears to her eyes, another great swell of pain. She wanted the children near. More than that, she wanted to keep them far from their father's deception.

"I'll call on Jerusha," Don Carlos said. "She'll go up to the Whitneys' place and fetch the children. They may stay here, too, Emma, for as long as you please."

Joseph roared. "By God, you will not take my children and my wife from me, both."

Don Carlos stepped toward him, snarling in his face. "You're an impostor and a tyrant. Do you think I don't know what you are? I've always known; I've always seen."

"How dare you speak to me that way?"

"I dare. I'll say whatever I please in my own home. I built this cabin myself; it's mine. A man has a right to thrash a liar and a fraud if that fraud dares to trespass on his property."

"You built a cabin," Joseph said. "I built a church. I built a world."

Don Carlos pointed at Emma, who was weeping now, trying to call up some strength to shout at them, to beg them to stop. "Yes," he said, "look what you've made. You've broken the heart of a good woman, one of the best God ever created. Just look at all you've accomplished. Be proud, Joseph Smith."

"I ought to whip you," Joseph shouted. "Whip you before the whole congregation and have you thrown out of the church, driven out of town!"

"Come and do it, if you can."

Don Carlos didn't wait for his brother to swing first. He threw himself at Joseph.

Joseph had always prided himself on his size and strength, his skill as a wrestler. But he had never reckoned with an opponent like his brother. Every pain Don Carlos had felt since his earliest days exploded from him now. Emma could hear the solid smack of his fists against flesh, a grunt as the wind left Joseph's lungs. Joseph fell back, cowering, gasping for mercy with his hands crossed over his head, but Don Carlos went on thrashing until Joseph dropped into the furrows and curled in a tight ball—and even then, Don Carlos kicked and kicked with his heavy boots. Clods of mud flew from his soles out into the field.

"Stop," Emma screamed, "you'll kill him!"

Suddenly Hyrum was there, short of breath from running, and Jerusha, who threw her arms around Emma, dragging her back, out of range of the men's fists. Joseph moaned weakly. He rolled in the dirt, curling more tightly into himself. Tears streamed from his eyes.

Hyrum pulled both of Don Carlos's arms behind his back and hauled him away. Like a bulldog straining at its leash, Don Carlos leaned toward Joseph, avid to finish what he'd started.

"In God's name," Hyrum bellowed, "control yourself, boy!"

Don Carlos spat into the churned-up earth. He barely missed Joseph's face. "You're a false prophet. You always have been, and now everyone will know it."

The simplicity of that accusation made Emma shudder. She would have fallen to the ground if Jerusha hadn't held her up. But Jerusha's arms were tight around her body, and there was a tremor in her, too—in her breast, her throat, as if she longed to speak but didn't dare. The more tightly she held Emma, the more Emma could feel the defeat inside her, a spirit of silence and long hiding. It pressed into Emma's soul like a thumb pressed down to mark the dough.

The evenings were quiet, bewildering in their peace. Emma sat with Don Carlos at the edge of his field, each of them on an upturned bucket, the way they'd done so many years ago in Harmony, when he had been a child. Emma's own children were tucked into their uncle's bed, tired out from playing with Jerusha's brood. They slept contentedly—unaware, thank God, of how their lives had been torn up and remade.

"I would divorce him if I dared," she admitted. "It's a shame I would carry the rest of my life, but still I think it would be best. If only I could make myself do it. If only I could see myself as a divorced woman."

"You wouldn't be shamed if you married again," he said.

"Who, though? Who would have me?"

He looked at her and said nothing. The slight stir of his chest as he breathed was the most compelling thing in all the fading, red-violet world. In the Harmony days, when they'd sat talking in the night air, the windows of the cabin had glowed with lamplight, and Joseph had

pressed his face down into the darkness, but it had never been so dark
that Emma and Don Carlos hadn't seen each other plainly. And now
there was such need in his eyes that Emma felt foolish, because she had
never noticed it before. How could she not have seen, how could she have
seen anything else? The words he dared not speak came to her as clearly
as if he'd spoken them aloud. If he were to suggest it, she didn't know
how she would answer. Hope welled up in her. It made her hands shake.
This was a foolish hope, she knew, reckless and absurd. Something else
rose in her, too—a warmth she'd never had for her husband.

"If I had a wife," Don Carlos said, cautiously, "I would leave Kirtland. I would leave this church for good."

"You would leave your family behind if you went. They'll never abandon Joseph."

"It isn't Joseph who holds my family to this church. It's Alvin—the
memory of him. My mother, my father, they need Joseph's book to be
true. He has invented a version of God that will allow Alvin to find salvation. Life after his death."

"I never realized," Emma said. "I never thought Alvin's death could
still hold such power over your family. Joseph told me, of course, how
he died—how it broke your mother's heart to lose him, and how it hurt
you all, to think Alvin was condemned to Hell. But I never thought such
things could bend a person to another's will, all these many years later."

"You're a mother now, yourself. And you've lost children—more than
your share. It's a pain that never lets go. Not from a mother's heart."

She could find no way to answer.

"It's more than Alvin, too," he said. "We had money once—long before I was born. My parents have never forgotten how their chances for a
good life were dashed. With Joseph and his church, they've found a way
to be great again. Important. That kind of pride is a deadly sin, but they
can't seem to let it go. They've always wanted others to think highly of
the Smiths, and now they have that esteem. They're mother and father
of God's own Prophet." He shook his head. He plucked a long stem of
grass, chewed its tender end. "They'll never leave Joseph behind, nor admit any of his wrongdoings. It would make them paupers all over again.
It would make them no one, and they couldn't bear it, to be no one after
having stood so near the center of all things."

"You say you would leave Kirtland if you married. What would you do if that woman, that wife of yours, was many years older than you? And if she already had children by another man?"

Don Carlos had no chance to reply. Through the dusk, through a subtle plane of shadow, he had caught sight of movement on the lane. He stood abruptly. Emma could feel his readiness to fight. It hung around him like the stink of an animal provoked. Joseph was coming toward the farm. His white shirtsleeves stood out sharply against the night; he was luminous, otherworldly, like the angels he often spoke of, the angels he claimed to have seen. His limp was far worse than usual. As he came nearer, she could see the livid bruises on his face and arms, around his neck. She hadn't known Don Carlos had choked him.

Joseph looked at Emma silently for a long moment. His breath was short and shallow. Perhaps Don Carlos had broken a rib or two. She couldn't read his expression—resentment, regret? He'd always been adept at masking his feelings.

Joseph turned to his brother with great dignity. "You laid me out for days. I could hardly move."

"I'm glad to hear it," Don Carlos said.

"I came here to tell you that I freely forgive you."

Don Carlos folded his arms.

"You know my unshaken disposition," Joseph said. "I know in whom I trust. I stand upon the rock; the floods cannot—no, they shall not overthrow me."

"Take your false prophet act elsewhere," Don Carlos said. "It doesn't impress me. I see you for what you are."

Joseph went on as if his brother hadn't spoken. "You know the doctrine I teach is true."

Don Carlos gave a short, hard laugh.

"You know God has blessed me. I brought salvation to my father's house."

"You've deceived our family and countless others. You call it salvation; I call it sin."

"If at any time you should consider me to be an impostor, Don Carlos, for Heaven's sake leave me in the hands of God. Don't take vengeance on me yourself. You called me a tyrant, but you know I'm not. To take away men's rights is a thing that has always been banished from my heart, and ever shall be. David sought not to kill Saul."

"Leave my property," Don Carlos said.

"Not without my wife."

Joseph held out his hand to Emma. She could see how it hurt him to do it, how he shook with the effort.

"She will stay here with me," Don Carlos said.

"She belongs with me, and well does she know it."

For a moment, Emma imagined a life with Don Carlos as her husband instead of Joseph Smith. She pictured them leaving Kirtland together in a wagon, the springs creaking cheerfully as they rolled on to a new future. The children between them on the driver's seat, the feel of the town growing smaller, less significant behind them, until finally it vanished. Kirtland was nothing, the church was nothing, a past she hardly felt was her own. Then the flash receded, the light dimmed. She considered what she would look like, how it would strike others if she were to divorce her husband and marry his twenty-year-old brother. Scandal would follow them wherever they went. Newspapers all around the country still ran salacious articles on Joseph and his golden Bible, the Mormons with their strange practices, the blasphemy they called religion.

News that the Prophet's wife had left him for his younger brother would hang like a millstone around her neck. The shame of it would cover her children and mar their futures. And she must consider the gap in years between herself and Don Carlos. No marriage could be built on such a foundation. She was trapped there in Kirtland. For her children's sake, she had no real choice but to remain with Joseph. She must pray that God would humble him and prevent him from sinning again.

She rose from the bucket, though it made her sick to her stomach, sick to the pit of her soul. "I'll go with you, Joseph."

Don Carlos stared at her. "Is this really what you want?"

Emma shook her head. She cast her eyes down; her gaze fell down, sinking with the weight of her sorrow, and she couldn't look at Don Carlos again. She allowed her husband to put his arm around her shoulders.

"Send Jerusha up with our children in the morning," she said.

Joseph turned her away and guided her back down the lane—though he limped heavily, almost leaning on her for support. She found she could look at Don Carlos after all. He hadn't gone inside. He was standing at the edge of the field, watching her walk away.

I see you for what you are.

See this: imagine it. There is a forest, barred with light and shadow, a wood at the edge of a rocky field. The air between the trees holds a damp smell of moss, the spice of loam. In the canopy the birds are calling, and there are shafts of light, long and straight, green as a peeled twig. There are tracks in the soil where a deer has lately walked—passed through this glade and moved on, untroubled, because this is an ordinary forest, an ordinary day, there is nothing unusual here.

A boy enters the wood. He follows the deer path into the brush, past mounds of dogwood, past the places where the pinedrops rise from among the fallen leaves. The birds never cease to sing as the boy walks, not even when he sinks down suddenly in a place indistinguishable from any other clearing. He folds his hands.

What does the boy pray for?

Guidance, or grace, or a strength he has never had. A way to settle his mother's restless heart. A way to make his father proud, and some way, please merciful God, to pull himself out of the shadow his dead brother still casts, even from under the ground. He prays for greatness—what boy has not?

Ask, and it shall be given to you; seek and ye shall find.

If two luminous figures appear, dressed in white robes, and hang above him in the green-lit boughs—if they open their incandescent hands, you will see that they hold nothing. There is nothing to fall from their fingers, and the boy dreaming on his knees never looks up to see. He is looking inside himself to a place full of quiet knowing. Within, he has found the tools he may use to build a world around him: strength of will, imagination, an unshakable belief in his own self.

The robed figures lift like vapor on the air. Unnoticed, they rise, they disperse among the dazzling light of sun through the treetops, the flares like stars, their points sharp enough to cut.

She thought about Nancy Marinda, the Johnson girl, with the string of pearl beads around her neck.

These years, these long and burdensome years, Emma made herself believe nothing had happened between Nancy Marinda and Joseph. The mob who had fallen on him had been mistaken, their anger and violence misplaced. Joseph had held himself so serenely in the wake of the attack. Who but an innocent man could bear himself that way, without a trace of shame? The way he'd preached to his congregation, you would have marveled to see it. You would have sworn he was the most righteous fellow God had ever made—his lip fat with blood, his body welted and black from the tar.

After they returned home and Jerusha brought the children, Emma went to Joseph. He was standing out in the small yard of their home, which felt to her now like a foreign place. He was staring up over the willows, their green sway and whisper, looking at the temple, the dark dome and its spire.

"I would ask you," Emma said, "to apologize. You owe me that much. Apologize, and beg God for forgiveness, too, if you haven't done it already."

He didn't move. She wondered if he'd heard. Then she wondered if she had spoken at all or had only thought about the words she must say. But then Joseph turned, and his smile was so beautiful, so full of affection that Emma choked on her tears. Something warm and wholesome lifted inside her, a surge of openness and purity, and she knew she had never felt such love for her husband before. She was ready to forgive—for the children's sake, if not her own. He need only ask, and she would give him that grace, willingly.

"Emma, dear." He touched her face. His hand was gentle. "You know I would apologize—I would fall to the ground and grovel for your forgiveness—if ever I'd done anything that required it."

All the warmth inside her drained away. He was still touching her face. She couldn't understand why.

"I did not transgress against you. Whatever you thought you saw, you didn't see. It was a misunderstanding, nothing more. I did not commit adultery. I would never have such relations with a woman who was not my wife. Emma, you know it's true."

IX

The Weak Things of the World

1836–1837

In spring, the river fattened on the thaw, running swift and high between its banks. You could hear the water's rush, an ongoing sigh, early every morning before Kirtland had taken up the noise of daily life. That was how the Mormons came down to the temple, like a river in the thaw. The road was a watercourse, the fences and fields its banks; a lively current flowed down, the people murmuring and splashing in anticipation.

Emma paused in the little yard outside her home. With a pang of misgiving, she watched the congregation flocking past. Hardly a soul glanced at her, and those who did lifted their hands in greeting. There was no hint of judgment. She knew this. Even so, she couldn't help fearing the rumors. Since the previous autumn, whispers had passed from home to home like a miserable infection. The Prophet had committed some sinful act, an adulterous transgression, the details of which varied in the telling. But on one point, every rumor agreed: Emma Smith had been wronged.

She had kept to herself through fall and winter, as much as she'd been able. She disliked being the object of too much sympathy; it only made her dwell on what had transpired, and she was determined to forget Fannie Alger—Nancy Marinda, too.

"Where are they going, Mother?" Wide-eyed, Julia watched the congregation. She clung to Emma's skirt with one hand and Young Joseph with the other. The boy was staring with far more apprehension than his sister. He looked as if he wanted to cry but couldn't quite decide why he should.

Emma bent and tied Julia's bonnet under her chin. "They're going to the temple, darling, and so shall we. Today your father will dedicate the temple, and after today, we shall worship God in His own house every Sunday."

She lifted Young Joseph to her hip, drew a deep breath to steady her nerves, and led Julia out to the road.

If anyone pitied Emma that day, they didn't allow her to see. Several people called out greetings. A spirit of festivity pervaded the town. She could almost forget she'd been the subject of the greatest scandal ever to rock Kirtland. The people sang as they marched in one body, the whole church in harmony. All around her in the crowd, she saw copies of her little brown-covered hymnal peeking from men's pockets or pressed against women's hearts. The music Emma had chosen rang inside her mind, every note and lyric lifting her soul until she felt herself soaring high above the troubles that had plagued her through the winter. A new season had arrived—one of rebirth and redemption.

The crowd narrowed and compressed outside the temple, filing through one of its dark doors, which a boy of the lowest-order priesthood held open. Each congregant fell silent when they crossed the threshold and saw the temple's interior for the first time. The outer façade was lovely enough, with its gleaming walls and stately symmetry, but so great were the elegance and richness of the inner chambers, Emma thought Heaven itself might pale by comparison. Save for the polished wooden pews, every surface was white with plaster. Great pillars held up a soaring ceiling. Windows almost twice the height of a man allowed morning's soft gold to come pouring in; the light flowed along corners and curves like melted honey. At the east and west ends of the chamber, under two massive arches of carved and painted wood, rose the pulpits of the priesthood offices: a long altar capped in polished oak, and above the altar, three successive tiers of three interlinked, bow-curved rostra. Each pulpit was marked with the initials of a degree of the priesthood, the letters picked out in gold leaf. The men who held those offices already sat in their lofty perches, watching with solemn dignity as the flock arrived.

Emma made her way down the banks of pews to sit as close to the eastern altar as she could manage. A contented quiet filled the room. Even the children were reverent, staring around in wide-eyed fascination. *Let them see me today*, Emma thought—*Let everyone see, and let them all know I'm no longer ashamed.*

Joseph, for all his faults and sins, had willed this magnificent place into being. He had brought this community together and held them for six years, united in a single purpose, to create this wonder of a chapel. Everything she had suffered seemed justified amid the gold-and-white glories streaming in through those high Gothic windows. Every indignity, every doubt—they were prices she could well afford to pay. It would have been worth any cost, this bliss, this proof of the goodness the Mormons had made together. As she gazed up at the moon-white arch bending above her head, pride came upon her so powerfully that tears stung her eyes. She dabbed them away with her kerchief. It must be a sin, or nearly a sin, to feel such pleasure in what her husband had accomplished. Yet no man but Joseph could have made something so magnificent. No one else had his vision—the boundless imagination, the unshakable confidence. No one else had the force of will—such power, the unearthly gift to make others believe that they could build the kingdom of God on Earth. Don Carlos had called Joseph a fraud and a tyrant, and perhaps he hadn't been wrong. But Joseph was also something more: a leader of men; a maker of worlds.

When the last congregants had entered, Joseph emerged from a small side chamber, dressed in his finest brown coat, his collar held stiffly in place by a blue ascot tie. Her heart leaped at the sight. Time, reality, the solid walls around her seemed to bend and shift; she felt herself standing again in the yard outside Hale House, staring down the insolent boy who had grinned at her, the fog of his breath half-obscuring his face. Could this be the same man?

The invocations, the blessings, the hymns, the sermons, the assembly weeping with ecstasy. She watched her husband through it all. He was inexhaustible in elegance and grace. Her eyes had fastened to him the way a baby's stare attaches to its mother, through some unconscious, infrangible instinct. She thought, *Have I always loved him so? I must have seen him thus, always, but I never was aware until now.*

When morning had faded, Joseph excused Sidney Rigdon from the altar, where he had preached a most inspiring sermon, and stepped up again before the congregation. He looked down upon the assembly with that serene, loving smile. "Now," he said, "we must send our beloved women and children back to their homes. The men shall remain for further blessings. Go in peace, under the Lord's protection."

Startled, Emma leaned back in her pew. Why send the women away? Hadn't the women sacrificed just as much as the men for the sake of their temple? They had sacrificed more, in some ways. She thought of the china cups and saucers ground into plaster, the heirlooms that could never be replaced. *This place belongs to us as much as to any man.*

She glanced tentatively to her right, then her left. The other women looked around in stunned disbelief. *At least*, Emma thought, *I'm not alone in my dismay.*

No man returned from the temple that afternoon. Nor did they come home for supper, nor in the low gray fade of dusk. Emma put the children to bed by herself, then went out into the yard with her scrap-pail to feed the hens.

A handful of women passed by on the Chillicothe Road. They were wrapped in shawls against the chill. None spoke; it was no social outing. They moved with the stiff, determined air of soldiers marching to war.

"Sister Emma," one of them called.

She blinked through the dusk, trying to determine who had spoken. It was Phebe Carter, a tall, sturdy woman, almost as broad as a man. She was only a few years younger than Emma, yet she had steadfastly refused to marry. God would make it known to her, Phebe told anyone who would listen, which man He intended for her husband—if he wished her to have any man at all. While she waited patiently for that matrimonial revelation, Phebe made herself useful. She was the most reliable friend any woman in Kirtland could ask for. If rumor implied that a man had used his wife poorly or had made her cry, he was apt to find Phebe, with her acid tongue and strident voice, waiting for him the moment he stepped outside his door.

"Come and join us," Phebe said. "These poor girls have all been made to fix supper and put their little ones to bed *and* bring in the animals and lead the family prayers without any help from their husbands. And all that food gone to waste, waiting on men who refused to show. I ask you! We're going down to the temple to find out what for. And to give the men what for, if they haven't a good excuse!"

She joined Phebe's band on the road. The evening was dark, though the sun had only just set. There would be rain the following day—rain all week, if she guessed correctly.

The brigade rounded the willows and turned down the temple lane. The women paused, huddling close together, none daring to speak. The great white hulk stood silently before them, stark and pale against the encroaching night. Surrounded by darkness, the temple seemed to brood.

Emma could feel it breathing, a slow inhale. She could sense the mysteries gestating inside those walls, words whispering without a voice, the thrum of a chant in an ancient tongue, a language forgotten before this world began.

"Look," Phebe whispered.

They all strained to catch whatever she had seen.

Quietly, Emma said, "I don't see—" but in the next moment the windows of the first floor brightened with a sudden flash, bursting into life and gone in an instant. On the heels of the flash, a roar emanated from the temple, the sound of a tearing autumn wind—but the willows never stirred. They could hear the men now—one great concerted moan of awe, a wordless exclamation.

"Mercy," Emma said, caught somewhere between fear and exasperation, "what are they doing in there?"

Vilate Kimball caught her hand. She was trembling. "Look to the spire!"

Above the temple, a great heavy sag of cloud had thinned and parted, drifting away. A train of vapor dragged through the upper branches of the willows. The gap in the clouds let down a bright golden bar of moonlight. It fell upon the temple as if aimed by God's own hand.

"Mighty Lord." Vilate sank to her knees, hands clasped in frantic prayer.

Emma and Phebe held each other's gaze for a long, silent moment. Then Emma broke away from the fluttering, praying women and strode toward the temple with Phebe on her heels.

"Land sakes," Phebe said when she was certain the others wouldn't hear. "A lot of nerve these men have, abandoning their wives till all hours, leaving us alone to fend for ourselves. What should we have done if Indians had swept into town, I ask you? Or wolves. Or Missourians."

They were only a few strides away from the doors now. Emma held up a hand for silence. Inside, she could hear a wild revelry: laughing, shouting, singing. Someone was howling, a high, wavering cry like the baying of a hound.

Emma tried the door, but it was barred. She knocked, but the sounds of celebration went on unabated. She knocked again, harder this time—then pounded with all her strength, forgetting it was the door to God's own house. But the doors remained shut, the women alone in the dark.

She told the women to return to their homes; their husbands would be back in their beds before dawn's first light. But sunrise found Kirtland's men still closeted at the temple. Another day unspooled itself entirely in feminine hands. By the second evening, a far larger group of women had gathered to mutter darkly outside the temple.

Emma made her way to the front of the crowd, intending to pound on the door again—to shout for Joseph, if necessary—whatever she must do to recall the men to their temporal duties. But when she broke from the pack, she found another woman already standing at the door.

She was a stranger, a newcomer to town. She wore a long felt coat over a dress of dark-green velvet, finer clothes than anyone in Kirtland could afford. A well-made carpet bag stood at her feet, and she was gazing up at the spire high above, silent and still amid the hoarse shouts of Amen that carried from the building. Black curls spilled down her back, a tumble of hair like a waterfall seen by night.

"Hello," Emma said. "You must be new here."

She turned. Her eyes were large and brown, with a dreamy, almost sorrowful cast. The stranger was of an age with Emma, yet there was no hint of weariness about her, the habitual strain one sees on all mothers of very young children. She was refined, delicately polished—even in the dimness of night, Emma could see that much. With their dark hair in near-identical curls, they might have been two sides of the same coin: Emma, the rough and dogged country wife, and this unknown creature, elegant and graceful, the very picture of feminine ideal.

"Hello," the stranger said. "Yes, I've only just arrived this night. A charming town. My name is Eliza—Miss Eliza Snow from Mantua."

Emma took the proffered hand. Eliza's skin was so soft and fine, she thought at first that the woman wore satin gloves. "I'm Emma Smith—Mrs. Smith. Welcome to Kirtland; though I must confess, you've found us in an unusual state."

Eliza smiled. "Are those men I hear caterwauling inside this church?"

"We dedicated our temple yesterday. The ceremonies are . . . still ongoing."

"Your temple." Eliza gazed upward again. A rapturous expression came over her, eyelids sliding down heavily. "It is a moving sight to behold. We have heard of this church in my town. Who hasn't heard? I wanted to see it all for myself—your town and your temple. Churches we have in Mantua—churches aplenty. In Cleveland I have seen such beautiful constructions, the great stone palaces of the Presbyterians. But a temple is an entirely different sort of jewel, is it not? I've not seen one with my own eyes until today."

"You've a way with words." Emma held back none of her admiration.

Eliza clicked her tongue. She tossed her head, a polite dismissal, but Emma caught a flash of pride in her eyes.

The nearest door opened suddenly. Eliza gave a little exclamation of surprise; she and Emma stepped back and found themselves pressed close together while the men came staggering out into the night air. Eliza put an arm around Emma, just as if they'd been friends since childhood, as if they were sisters. They watched, bewildered, as the men lurched out from the building, belching, leaning on one another, singing in bleary discord. Most of them had cast off their coats. Their ties were loose around their necks or gone entirely; their collars hung open, revealing the flushed skin of their chests and primal patches of hair. Emma couldn't seem to close her mouth, so she covered it with a hand. Men reeled past in the moonlight, clutching at one another. Some crawled in the dirt. She could smell them, one uniform stink of sweat and whiskey and wine. Their wives hurried forward, scolding and grumbling, and took their husbands by their elbows or chivvied them back to their feet.

Eliza said, "I had thought you Mormons adhered to the temperance doctrines. I read as much in one of the newspapers."

"We do," Emma said helplessly. "We've done so for years. I've never seen such a display. I assure you this is not the way we comport ourselves in Kirtland—in this church. Mother of mercy, I can't imagine where they found the spirits, or why Joseph allowed such slovenly behavior. I'll give him a piece of my mind when I get him home. He'll wish I'd left him to Phebe Carter's tender mercies by the time I've finished."

"Joseph—he is your Prophet."

"Yes. I suppose you've read about him, too, in your city papers."

"There are more Smiths in this world than stars in the sky. But are you, Mrs. Smith, the wife of the Prophet?"

"I am. How did you guess?"

"No one but a great man's wife would dare speak of him so brazenly."

The last man emerged from the temple: Joseph himself. He saw Emma straightaway and came to her with a wide, unfocused grin. Joseph took her by the shoulders and held her, leaning against her subtly to stop his pitching and swaying. She could smell the whiskey under his arms, thickening the reek of his sweat. "Emma, my beautiful Emma."

"You're intoxicated." Her face was hot. Her whole body was hot. How long had it been since Joseph had called her beautiful, or touched her with such affection? And yet she was humiliated. How could he behave so boorishly, staggering about drunk where anyone could see? And to touch her with this familiarity in front of a stranger . . .

"Such glories we've witnessed, Emma, my dear, my good, best wife."

"You want your bed now. There's nothing for it but to sleep this off."

"We saw the Lord Himself." He punctuated the claim with a loud hiccup.

Emma glanced at Eliza, but she had taken little notice of Joseph's indecency. She was looking at the leader of the Latter-day Saints with an expression of detached curiosity. "So this is the Prophet. A remarkable man, if newspapers can be trusted."

"One can't be too certain of the papers," Emma said drily. "They've printed all manner of falsehoods about our church and our town. They lie scandalously."

"Even so," Eliza said, "I think I shall stay in Kirtland a while and learn the truth for myself. Your temple is a thing of great beauty. There is inspiration here for a poet."

Joseph pushed himself away from Emma until he stood upright. He grinned at Eliza, face red from two days of ecstasy. And Eliza, never taking her dreaming eyes from Joseph, smiled back.

There is no use trying to mislead you. By now you have discerned a certain pattern unfolding. Looking back, it's plain to see—the signposts and indicators arranging themselves, the foreordainment of what was to come. Perhaps it's human nature, the very essence of mankind's sinful self, to go on repeating whatever we've done before. Season follows season and sin follows sin. The only mystery left is why Emma was so long in learning caution.

What made her susceptible to Joseph's deceptions? Was it his smile, his way of putting a person at ease, of causing all those in his orbit to believe he was innocent? Or was the fault her own? A lonely heart will cleave to any solid thing that brushes against it, poor unwanted burr. There is no sense asking why.

The hardest part of learning the truth—the hardest part of what came later—was the great love she felt for Eliza, right from the start. There are times even now when she looks back on those early days with Eliza Snow and misses their spirit of sisterhood. It grew so quickly between them, trust and friendship unfolding like some miraculous flower, all its petals sweet and endlessly arrayed. She had been hungry for it—starving for a woman's friendship. And the companionship she found with Eliza was so satisfying, such a balm to her wounded spirit, that now and again she still thinks, to this very day, that she loved Eliza more than she ever loved her husband.

The morning after the men emerged from the temple, Eliza came to call. She wore another dress of tailored velvet, rich claret red instead of green, with a black shawl of knitted lace pinned around her shoulders. Hundreds of small jet beads winked among the lace. Emma was painfully conscious of her workaday brown wool, the stained apron, the untidy locks that had fallen loose from her bun. She smoothed her hair as best she could. "Come in," she said.

Eliza looked around Emma's home with an air of pleasant surprise. Evidently it wasn't quite as rustic as she had expected.

"I suppose you've come to see Joseph," Emma said. "He's gone for the day—over to Chardon to approve some new goods for his store."

Joseph had slunk out of the house almost before Emma was awake, hoping to avoid her scolding. She was prepared to save it up until the evening, when he came creeping home again.

"I would have liked to have spoken with your prophet," Eliza said, "but I'll gladly make your acquaintance instead, Mrs. Smith." She glanced down at Emma's apron. "If you aren't too busy to entertain for a few minutes. I wouldn't like to impose."

"Not at all. In fact, I would rather like conversation with another woman. I've had no one to talk to except my children for far too long."

"You have children? Oh, please, may I meet them? I'm so fond of little ones."

"They've gone out with their cousins and their aunt Jerusha to look for strawberries. But I expect they'll be home within the hour. Please take any seat in the parlor. I'll put on some coffee, unless you prefer tea."

While the kettle came to a boil, Emma took off her apron and retreated to her room, where she did what she could to tame her hair. She considered trading the old brown dress for something brighter, but she didn't want Eliza to suspect her of putting on airs. Instead, she tied on a shawl of her own—misty madder rose, without any beads to dazzle, but with lacework as fine as any in Ohio. Emma had made it herself.

She swept back into the parlor with two cups of coffee and a little pitcher of cream.

"Last night," Emma said, "you introduced yourself as Miss Snow. You aren't married, then."

Eliza sipped delicately from her cup. "I've never desired marriage. I have designs of my own. I hope you won't find me too preposterous, Mrs. Smith, if I confess to you that I am a poetess. When I heard the Mormons had finished building their temple, a spirit of longing was stirred in me—that spirit which makes me write about all manner of beautiful, wondrous things. I wanted to see your temple for myself. Now that I have, I shall turn my muse loose to play wherever it will."

"You mean to spend some time in Kirtland, then?"

"I should say as much. I mean to remain in Kirtland for a year at least. Now that I've seen this town for myself, I believe I may find plenty of inspiration among the Mormons. In any case, my living here ought to create a sensation, and sensation sells books—as you well know."

"So the city papers still print scandalous stories about our people."

"Everyone loves a spectacle."

"We aren't a spectacle. We're ordinary folk—a community dedicated to God."

"And serious in that dedication."

Emma placed her cup on the side table and looked up, startled. "Why, of course we're serious."

"That is spectacle enough. Darling, you've lived all your life in lonely places. But I grew up at my father's side in Cleveland. In the big cities, believe me, purity and honesty are rare as butterflies in winter."

"Tell me about Cleveland," Emma said.

"What would you like to know?"

"Everything."

They whiled away the better part of an hour, Eliza describing the cosmopolitan life while Emma tried to picture herself in a city, in another life altogether. Eliza was warm and generous, far earthier than her elegant appearance had led Emma to believe. She found herself liking Eliza more with each passing minute.

"As long as you intend to stay in Kirtland," Emma said, "I do hope you'll consider staying here, as my guest. I would be glad of your company, and you would be welcome for as long as you please."

"As long as I please may be a long while indeed," Eliza said. "If you grow weary of me, toss me out on my backside."

It's easy to say now that Emma should have been wary. She shouldn't have brought another woman into her home, not after that shameful business with Fannie Alger. But Fannie had been a girl—easily manipulated, prone to foolish infatuations. Eliza was a headstrong, self-possessed woman, more concerned with her poetry than with men. And she was delightful company. Much as Emma loved her children, she couldn't help craving conversation with another grown person. And even when Joseph didn't brood in his store until well after dark, she fetched up constantly against some blunt barrier between them—a coldness, a solid thing like a wall of stone.

Spring warmed to a lush, lazy summer. The air thickened with a smell of honey. Emma and Eliza worked side by side in the house and out in the new garden they'd planted together. The children adored her; they called her Aunt Eliza, and Emma hadn't the heart to correct them, especially since Eliza was so charmed by their affections. When the day's work was through, she and Eliza wandered the beds of their garden, picking berries to make preserves or gathering snap beans for the next day's supper, talking in the low, gentle light.

"Sometimes," Emma admitted one evening, "sometimes I wish I could leave Kirtland and go to a city like Cleveland. Or Philadelphia or Boston. You say city people don't lead godly lives, and I suppose it must be true. But all the same, it sounds a fine thing, to feel the world so large and free around you."

"I doubt Joseph would appreciate the cities," Eliza said. "Certainly he couldn't be a prophet there. City folk are too hard-hearted to put their trust in prophets."

Emma said nothing, only went on plucking the beans from their vines.

After a pause, Eliza said, "Do you know my secret wish? I would like to be acknowledged someday as a great poet—one of the best. I would like to be a lauded writer whose name is known all across the country. All around the world, in fact." She watched Emma. Her finely made, elegant face stood out sharply against a blur of approaching dusk. She seemed set apart from Kirtland, from the Mormons, from everyone and everything. She was the center of her own reality, the dazzling sun around which all her enigmatic planets turned. "Do you think me vain," she asked, "and is that vanity a sin?"

Before Emma could answer, Eliza ducked down behind her row, vanishing amid the broad leaves. An instant later, she popped up again. She held a long, curved bean across her upper lip. It drooped to either side of her mouth like a city gentleman's mustache.

When you have a sister, when you have a friend, you can face any trial. It is perhaps one of her greatest sins that she found Eliza nearer and more comforting than God. Perhaps, indeed, it was Emma's love for Eliza— her great reliance on one mortal woman to the exclusion of her Lord and her faith—that caused God to punish her and scar her as He did.

Even so, she can't hold herself too sharply to account. Without Eliza, she would have broken. There was that week, that dark and dreadful week at the end of the summer, the week when Joseph fell ill. Fit as he could be one morning, by the afternoon he closed his shop early and came staggering home, scarcely able to answer when she asked what was wrong.

She thought for a moment that one of his spells of revelation had come upon him. But there was sweat on his brow, a tremor in his limbs, and when he spoke, she heard a rattle deep in his chest. Shrill with fear, she called for Eliza, who came running in from the back lot, where she'd been reading to the children under the willows. One look at Joseph, and Eliza's hand flew to her mouth. That was when Emma first knew her husband was gravely ill.

They told her later—the women of the church, and Joseph's apostles— that the Prophet lay in bed for seven days. But when you tether yourself to a sickbed, time loses all meaning. You expect death every moment, and you don't sleep for fear you won't be there to hold the beloved's hand when the end comes. And if Joseph wasn't exactly beloved to Emma by then, he was a fixture of her life. She wouldn't have known who she was without him. At a sickbed, if you rest at all, it's in a chair beside the fire, and then you are hollowed out, wrung dry. Your eyes ache with the effort of keeping them open but you can't lie down and sleep.

The great stretches of nothing are the worst of it. When Joseph was sleeping, she sat dull-eyed and weary on a stool beside their bed, watching his chest struggle to rise, and watching the floor when she could no longer bear to look at him. She ought to have occupied her hands, but she was too worn out for needlework. She was preparing, as much as any woman can, for widowhood. The doctor came twice a day and shook his head over Joseph; Emma knew she would soon be without a husband. And she couldn't, she couldn't conceive of herself without him. She asked herself why. Why ought she to cleave to a man like this—a man who had wronged so many, and she most poorly used of all? No answer came, and no relief, and the hours went on passing or not passing; the days like stones in the earth went on, standing still.

If not for Eliza, she would have shattered herself against the hard walls of grief. Eliza had had the foresight to send the children away, to Hyrum and Jerusha, so they wouldn't take the sickness. And it had been Eliza who'd called for the doctor, first thing, the moment they'd stripped Joseph of his sweat-soaked clothes and bundled him into bed. It was Eliza who pressed bowls of broth into Emma's hands and steadied her while she brought the spoon to Joseph's lips; Eliza who wrung out the damp cloths and handed them to Emma, so she could place them on her husband's brow.

One evening—four days, five after Joseph had taken to his bed—or it may have been a hundred years after, for all she could tell—Emma stood with Eliza in the garden. She had no recollection of leaving the bedroom. Eliza must have led her there, out into the open air where the wind moved freely against her face and chased away the smell of sickness. The air was cool, rose-colored with a lingering sunset. It smelled of the hayfields ripening, a dry, earthen scent, and of sheep in a nearby pasture. That familiar, animal smell, the warmth of the wool, the grassy dung. Crickets sang under the willows. The sound piercing and melancholy because the singing went on and on.

Emma swayed on her feet. Her bones creaked as she looked up at the temple spire. The temple was almost vermillion in the light of sunset. She was detached, floating up and away from herself, and she remembered her father weeping in the yard, and Joseph weeping in the wagon seat, confessing everything.

She said, "I can't bear to lose him, and yet he has wronged me. He has wronged me terribly; I should be glad to be free of him."

"No one is ever glad when death comes," Eliza said quietly, "even if one has been wronged."

"You don't know, because you came to Kirtland lately. You don't know what Joseph did. Everyone else knows. It seems to me as if the whole world must know. They can all see my shame, every time I step outside my door."

She told everything while the red light crept down the face of the spire and the sheep called in their pasture, a distant sound and thin. She even spoke of Don Carlos, the offer he hadn't quite made. And when she'd said everything, she covered her face with her hands. The sound of the crickets sawed through her, cutting to the heart. She thought perhaps Eliza would judge her harshly, and would be right to do so, for what kind of woman can't hold her husband's attention? But Eliza's arm went around her shoulders, and Emma leaned against her, and all the fear and grief and dreadful waiting since Joseph had taken ill surged up inside. She wept, shuddering, choking for her breath.

"It has never stopped hurting me," Emma said between sobs. "I see the same thing every time I close my eyes—what I saw through that window. But he denies it. He says I never saw it at all. He says I'm mistaken. But if I were mistaken, it wouldn't go on hurting me so, after all this time."

"Why should it not hurt you? Any woman—any man, for that matter—would be wounded by such a betrayal. Oh, Emma, you poor, poor soul."

"I still love him." She thought she loved him. She felt something for him—possessiveness borne of long habit, or the dull, inevitable dedication that comes from being tied to a thing for years.

"My friends send me clippings from the newspapers," Eliza said.

Emma looked up. She wiped her eyes. Eliza was watching her face steadily, as if judging whether she was strong enough to bear what must be said.

"What do you mean, clippings?"

Eliza bade her wait. She went inside the house while Emma remained standing in the garden, for she was too weary to move from the spot. When she returned, she held a few letters in her hand. She unfolded one to reveal a scrap cut from a Cleveland paper.

Wild revelries at Mormon temple, the clipping read.

Eliza opened another. And another. Emma read each clipping with growing dismay. *The orgiastic rites of the Mormons. Kirtland church-town a cesspit of sin. Adultery is the order of the day among Mormons. Mormon men share communal wives. Bigamy and adultery plague Mormon town of Kirtland, OH.*

Emma pressed a hand to her mouth.

"I don't wish to cause you more pain," Eliza said gently. "I thought you ought to know what the outside world thinks of your church and your husband."

"But none of this is true, not a word of it. I would know if it were true. It would be . . . obvious."

"I came here to learn the truth for myself," Eliza said, "and the truth I learned is this: You are a good woman, Emma Smith—hardworking, steadfast in your morals, caring toward your community. You are an ideal mother, a beloved friend—and, I now learn, a patient and forgiving wife whose forbearance goes far beyond what any reasonable man should expect. If the outside world loves to point and laugh at your church, it is only because they don't know you as I do."

She looked up at the spire again. A flock of pigeons was circling, dark slashes against a remnant glow. Their wings clattered as they settled to the evening roost. Wild revelries at the Mormon temple. The newspapers had been right on that count. The men had spent two days in a shameful state of intoxication, neglecting their wives, their children, their work. If the papers had been correct in one report, might their other claims be true, as well?

Despite Joseph's denial, she knew what she'd seen that day, when she had looked through the store's half-covered window. But with a friend's arm around her shoulders, the truth didn't seem quite so inescapable.

Eliza linked her elbow with Emma's as they walked toward the heart of town, wicker baskets slung over their arms. The pantry was close to empty—the children were growing so quickly that Emma could scarcely keep up with their demands for bread and butter—and Joseph didn't stock all the necessary goods at his store. In any case, she didn't like to visit that store if she could avoid it, not since the incident with Fannie Alger.

"Joseph seems entirely restored from his fever," Eliza said, "though I suppose he'll be rather weak and wobbly for a few days yet. It's only natural, after an illness so severe."

"I thank God he wasn't taken. What should I have done, raising two small children on my own?"

"You wouldn't have been on your own, dear. The church would have given you every possible aid. And I—I wouldn't leave you to fend for yourself. What kind of a friend would I be if I were to abandon you in your hour of need? What kind of a Christian?"

"You've been friend enough already. More than a friend; you've been like a sister to me. Can Joseph truly have suffered through a week of sickness? It feels as if months have passed. If you hadn't been beside me, I would still be lying abed myself from sheer exhaustion. More likely, I would have taken the fever myself."

"Thank God we both were spared, and the children, too."

"It's strange," Emma said. "In a sense I love Joseph, and in a sense I don't. Or perhaps what I feel for him is a different sort of love. I've lived so long as his wife that I can't imagine being anything else. And yet he infuriates me. He frightens me, this way he has—the way he can take a man's heart and hold it without even seeming to try." A man's heart, or a woman's. "And I wonder: Is it a sin not to know whether I love my husband? What must God think of me?"

"The Bible does say that husbands should love their wives. It's silent on the subject of how wives must feel toward their husbands."

Emma laughed a little; she couldn't help herself. Eliza had spoken as if she'd long since puzzled out every inscrutable whim of the Creator.

But a sober mood had fallen over Eliza. "Why do you suppose God made marriage?"

Emma thought for a moment before she answered. "To guard our souls against the sins of lust and covetousness. I suppose that must be the reason."

"But a man may feel lust for a woman who is not his wife. A man may covet, whether he is married or no. Marriage is no barrier to sins of the heart. You know the sad truth of that, Emma."

"Come to that, a woman may feel lust, too, and covet a life that isn't her own."

There was still something inside her, a restless creature, that remembered the way Don Carlos had looked, standing at the edge of his field with night coming in around him. The gray night, the purple dusk fading, Don Carlos watching as Joseph led her away. Sometimes—more often than she liked to admit—that inner animal stretched, expanding to fill her spirit. In those moments it threatened to swallow everything that was careful and disciplined in her faith. She became on the inside a creature with a wide-open mouth and a hungry belly, a thing with teeth and claws to tear at everything that confined her. Tear them down and take and take until the great dark void of longing had been filled.

She realized Eliza had made no reply. A studied silence had come over her friend, a clipped sensation of waiting, as if she expected Emma to say more—explain herself, excuse herself. No proper woman spoke of lust so casually. *What must she think of me? A woman so cultured and self-possessed as Eliza Snow—surely she never has coveted any man in all her life.*

She reached for a new topic. "I do hope you haven't received any more newspaper clippings from your friends in Cleveland. I pray no one else in Kirtland will learn of the tales they tell about us in the big city."

Eliza answered sadly. "I believe it may be too late for that. I've attended some of the debating clubs, you know."

"Have you?" Emma looked at her in surprise.

"Out of curiosity. I wanted to learn what the debaters say about the Prophet. I wanted to take the temperature of Kirtland as a whole, so to speak. I never spoke against your husband, Emma. I never would betray you. You must believe that."

She felt as if she were girding herself for battle. "What have the debaters said about . . . this matter?" She couldn't bring herself to speak the accusations aloud. Adultery, bigamy, the decadent lusts of the Mormons.

"There are many people in Kirtland who have friends and relations in larger cities. And it seems as if the tales have spread. Papers from Baltimore to Charleston have printed rumors of ill doings among the Mormons."

"How has it affected them, Eliza? You must tell me whatever you know. Joseph will be unaware. That store of his—it's a realm of fancy;

that's what I believe. It's his hiding place, where he can make believe he isn't the Prophet and never was. If he's in danger of losing the church, then I must tell him. No one else can make him see sense."

Eliza paused before she answered, weighing her words with care. "The debating clubs are lively with talk about how the outside world views the church—what the Gentiles think of us. They discuss whether it ought to matter to any Mormon, how the rest of the world perceives us—or whether we are better off tending to our own affairs and leaving the Gentiles to form whatever opinion pleases them best. There are some who feel there might be a kernel of truth in the stories. There are some who feel there's a great deal more than a kernel—bushels of truth. And there are others still who insist the stories have been invented out of whole cloth by Gentiles whose hearts were filled with hate."

"We must pray," Emma said, "that the papers will tire of these rumors and move on to other gossip."

"I pray for that very thing, each night, each morning."

She looked at Eliza more sharply then. "You said 'us' and 'we.' Do you call yourself a Mormon?"

Eliza smiled. Emma was struck by those misty eyes, the way she seemed to look far beyond the present reality to a bright realm no one else could see. Her cheeks colored with a small, secret pleasure. "It seems that decision has been made for me. God has brought me to the place where He wished me to be. And He has spoken in my heart. I am adept at listening to my heart, and going where a just spirit directs me. What else does it mean to be a poet?"

As they neared the crossroads outside the Whitney store, Emma became aware of a rising disturbance—the hum of many voices, an expectant tension in the air. She looked down a nearby lane. A young woman dressed in a modest, dark-brown frock was weaving and staggering toward the main street. A crowd of onlookers followed closely, faces eager and voices goading. Oliver Cowdery was at the head of the pack.

"Dear me," Emma said. "Is that girl ill? See how she stumbles. Why are all those people not helping her?"

"That girl is Joanna Newcomb. You haven't heard her name? But you don't get out to the debating clubs; of course you can't have heard. They call her the Dancing Seeress. She slips into trances and spins and leaps until she falls down to the ground, and then she brings out some revelation or other. She likes to do it at the crossroads, where everyone can see."

"How long has this been going on?"

Eliza tilted her head, considering. "Two weeks; perhaps not quite as long as that."

Since Joseph had fallen ill. "Did the whole town believe Joseph would die of fever?" The people were hungry for the spectacle of revelation, and if their Prophet was unable to give it—or if he was unwilling—they would find it in any corner.

She watched the crowd as they followed their seeress toward the mercantile, and spotted more than a few familiar faces. David Whitmer, which surprised her, and Martin Harris, which did not. Oliver—Joseph's second counselor, who stood but one rung below the Prophet himself—watched the trance-stricken girl with an obvious hunger. Emma understood at once that he was in love with the seeress.

"You've gone pale," Eliza said. "Do you want to watch her dance, or—"

"No," Emma said quickly. "We might as well turn back. There will be no getting through that crowd to the mercantile—not until they've begun to disperse."

She didn't want to stand too near the seeress's followers, afraid she might feel in their ranks a stronger love than any they still held for Joseph.

A clean, biting smell of early frost still clung to Eliza's velvet cape when she came in one evening from her rounds of the debating clubs. An autumn sunset lingered at the corner of one window. Emma helped her off with the cape and took her gloves to dry them at the kitchen fire. North along the road, all the lamps and windows of Kirtland glowed against a fast-falling night.

"What news have you uncovered today?" Emma asked, half amused. Upright though Eliza was, Emma suspected she had too strong a liking for gossip.

"Grim news, that's what. There are two different women in town who have told their friends they want to divorce their husbands, but no one will say why. The women themselves won't speak of the reason—out of shame, I expect."

"Two? That sounds like unfounded rumor to me." One woman seeking to leave her husband would be strange enough. That two should turn to divorce at the same time strained credulity.

"I don't think it's rumor, Emma. The women who gave me this news sounded entirely sure of themselves."

"There's nothing in these stories. There can't be. It's one thing to feel wistful and crave an escape when your husband has made you angry. Goodness knows, I've felt that way myself. But to actually leave? Unthinkable."

Eliza made for the kitchen and Emma's kettle of stew. "We shall see whether there is any truth to the stories. If we hear of a divorce—or two—we will know. I'm sure I can't imagine what would drive a woman to want to leave her husband. Unless he beats her too hard, or too often."

Emma almost said, *I can imagine what would drive a woman.* She kept her silence. She had made up her mind to forgive Joseph and live an honorable life. It would do her no good to speak of the things that still pained her—the canker on her soul.

"Let me fix a bowl of stew for you, too," Eliza said. "And have a good piece of that lovely rye bread you made. I can tell you haven't eaten a bite this evening. You're washed out." But as she crossed to the cabinet to retrieve another dish, they heard a clamor outside. "What under Heaven could that be?"

The sound grew louder—a confusion of many voices. Men arguing, Emma realized. They were drawing closer to the house. Eliza and Emma peered through the lace curtains. A handful of men milled outside the gate. Brigham Young was prominent among them. His deep voice cut through the rest, shouting insults and accusations. He raised a fist, trying to stir the others to fight. Oliver Cowdery ignored Brigham's threats as if he were no more than a gnat.

"Let us pass," Martin Harris said to Brigham. "We must speak to Brother Joseph."

"I'll be shat on if I let you pass. Speak to Brother Joseph? Ha! You want to harangue him and browbeat him. Do you think I'm a fool?"

"Brother Brigham," David Whitmer said calmly, "we're no threat to the Prophet. Surely you know that."

"I'm not your brother, you serpent, you worm—not if you think to damage this church. Come on, fight me, if you're man enough. The whole lot of you, fight me! I can lick you all or lick you one at a time, whichever you prefer."

Emma shook her head. "That man has been a blight on this town since the day he arrived." She took her shawl from its hook beside the kitchen door.

"Where are you going?" Eliza said. "Not outside, I hope."

"Someone must talk sense into Brigham before he starts breaking noses. He won't harm me. He wouldn't dare lift a hand against me, especially not where others can see."

She swept down the path, calling for Brigham to wait a moment, to take hold of himself. Before she could reach the gate, however, Joseph emerged from his store and hurried across the road, tugging on his jacket.

"What's all this?" Joseph said mildly. "Come now, there's no need to fight."

"These dogs have come to bark at you," Brigham said. "Don't listen to them. They're disloyal, no true men of your church."

Oliver looked at Joseph for a long moment—sober, his fine face tense with consideration. Finally, he said, "May I speak with you alone?"

Brigham stepped between them. "Don't listen, Joseph. He isn't worth your spit. Not one drop of it."

"All right, Brigham, stand down." He laid a hand on Brigham's shoulder. "What a good friend I have in you—always on guard. Oliver, come inside, and Emma here will fix you something to eat. The rest of you, go on home. Oliver will be well. I won't bite his head off, if that's what has you looking sick with worry. Go on, now. Brigham, let them return to their homes. That's an order."

Emma ushered Oliver into the house. As they entered, she could hear Eliza retreating to her small room behind the kitchen, talking to the children as she went. At least Eliza would keep the little ones sheltered from whatever bleak thing Oliver had to say.

Joseph took his favorite seat in the parlor, the green velvet armchair. He gestured for Oliver to sit, too.

"I prefer to remain on my feet," Oliver said.

Joseph smiled, benign and peaceful. "Whatever you please, my friend—my oldest and dearest friend."

Oliver looked away. He shifted side to side, as if gripped by the urge to run or stride across the room and strike Joseph. Emma knew she ought to retreat to the kitchen and give the men their privacy, but her husband might need her. Who else but she could talk him into sense?

"Speak," Joseph said. "You know I'll always listen."

Oliver looked at Emma. Only that—looked at her, but there was such terrible agony in his expression. It took her some few ragged heartbeats to realize Oliver pitied her. He reached into a pocket and drew out a clipping from a newspaper. Emma felt the house turn slowly around her, felt the floor unmake itself below her feet. She put a hand on the brick hearth to keep herself upright.

"From a Boston paper." Oliver quoted the article: "'We have heard many reports already that the Mormon men make a habit of gathering "wives" in much the same way a shepherd gathers sheep. More such reports come to us by the week. There can be no doubt that the Mormon religion is but a mask used by charlatans to disguise their true purpose—which is, we must frankly state (shocking though it be), to make a commune founded upon the sin of adultery and the crime of bigamy; to practice the moral uncleanliness of passing women about for common use. How can such insult to decency stand? All good men and women must decry the evils of Mormonism wherever they find them and stamp out this moral cancer before it spreads to consume the whole nation.'"

He crumpled the paper in his fist.

Joseph sighed—a comfortable sound, the pleasant persecution of the righteous. "Will they never cease to print these lies?"

Oliver closed his eyes. His face burned red. "You know it's true, Joseph. You know this is no lie."

Then he opened his eyes and looked at Emma again—more sharply than before, an anguished expression. That was the first notion Emma had that she had betrayed her feelings. She had uttered a cry, perhaps—one she was too distressed to hear—or lurched against the mantel. She couldn't bear the weight of his pity. She turned her face away.

"I know nothing of the sort," Joseph said. "If there is adultery in this church, I haven't heard of it. And if it has come up from the Devil to plague our people, then I'm confident God will strike down the guilty."

Something hot and hard settled in her stomach. Joseph was choosing his words with meticulous care. What was he hiding, and who did he think he was deceiving?

Certainly not Oliver Cowdery. He laughed, a bitter sound. "Are you so quick to condemn yourself to Hell?"

"You may have heard stories," Joseph said. "I'll allow that. You may have heard rumors and misunderstood. There was a girl Emma and I took in last year, an orphan."

Emma covered her face. She couldn't endure the thought of Fannie Alger, couldn't suffer the memory, that vision repeating inside her head. The blue dress pushed up, the rhythmic rustling, the white backs of her husband's thighs.

Joseph went on calmly. "The girl developed an unfortunate infatuation with me. But anything more you've heard concerning that girl— well, it's simply untrue. You know how tales spread."

Oliver stepped forward so suddenly that Joseph's hands flew to the arms of his chair; he gripped it hard.

"For pity's sake," Oliver said, "for the sake of your good wife, tell the truth, I beg you. Tell the truth now and save your soul."

"I do speak the truth."

"You know there have been foul doings in your church, in this town. You know there's more to this than rumor. And you know, Joseph, who is guilty of the sin of adultery, and who is not."

Joseph pushed himself up from the chair. All pretense toward mildness was gone in a flash; he glared at Oliver with such hatred as Emma had never seen in him before. "I know you're in love with that devil of a girl, the Dancing Seeress."

"Joanna? What if I do love her? It's no sin to admire a good Christian woman. I've done nothing with Joanna that could shame me, or her. I've done nothing sinful with any woman who isn't my wife. Can you say the same?"

"You follow a false prophet," Joseph said. "You've thrown in your lot with a liar, a fraud. Your love for that girl has blinded you to the truth."

Oliver scoffed and turned away, but Joseph pressed on. "You've allowed yourself to be deceived. Even you, the Second Elder of this church—even you have defected from God's anointed Prophet and turned your back on truth."

"I will determine truth for myself."

Joseph's face blanched to that unearthly pallor. "You and your lover must leave Kirtland at once. Neither of you may return. You're cast out, Oliver Cowdery—cast out from the light of God. You have two days to remove yourselves from my city and my church."

"Your church? It is our church. It belongs to all the Latter-day Saints. I told you once you were no fit leader. You, never an ordained minister. I knew this could only ever lead to sin."

"Thus saith the Lord," Joseph spat. "Leave God's presence."

"Thus saith Joseph Smith. It isn't the same thing. Have you forgotten that? Or did you ever know there was any difference between yourself and God?"

"Please," Emma said. "Don't do this. Both of you—reconsider."

Oliver was already making for the door. He paused, gave Emma a long, sorrowful look. "No, Sister Emma. It's right that I should go. In fact, it's long past time I took my leave of your . . . husband. I pity you; that's the truth. You're a good woman. You deserve more than what this man has given you."

Oliver left Kirtland two days later, as Joseph had commanded. He took Joanna Newcomb, the Dancing Seeress—and a good number of her admirers, as well, perhaps sixty in all. He took David Whitmer, who had believed so purely in the Book of Mormon that he saw a miracle in a half-plowed field—David, who had suffered at the hands of the Gentiles in Zion, who had placed his body in the path of bullets and struggled through the snow to bring news of Zion's destruction. Once David's heart was turned, most of the Whitmer family went with him. Oliver and Joanna took Martin Harris, too, who had once been so thoroughly in Joseph's hands that he had beggared himself, given up his land and his wife to follow wherever the Prophet led. In two short days, Oliver Cowdery had eroded the foundation of Joseph's church almost beyond repair. His bitterness was a swift river biting at the banks. And as she stood by her garden gate, watching a train of wagons rolling out of Kirtland forever, Emma was forced to admit that her husband's church had always been built on sand.

Joseph didn't stand beside Emma to watch his life's work falling away. He had closeted himself in the upper story of his shop. When she looked up to the window, she could see him—a faint silhouette, a gray stain, a shape of a man against a lace curtain. He was looking down on the street, the procession of his broken congregation. He was looking down on Emma. She drew herself up, and folded her arms as she used to do, that posture of defiance, the withering look she'd used on schoolboys and young men of nineteen years who thought they could hold the world in their hands like a plum, like a penny.

She stared back at Joseph while the wagons groaned and the horses' hooves scraped hollow on the road, and the women in the backs of carts raised their hands in sad farewell and called out, God bless you, Emma Smith, and may He forgive your husband. And it was Joseph who withdrew. The silhouette moved on the curtain, rippled, vanished from her sight.

Early one evening, late in September, Emma stood in a halo of warmth beside the wood stove, stirring a kettle of apples stewed in cinnamon. The children were laughing and squealing in the parlor, where Joseph played with them, leading them in songs and clapping games with as much abandon as if he were a child himself. Weeks had passed since the exodus. There were times, there were entire days, when Emma cursed her husband for his lack of concern. He ought to have been more troubled by the erosion of his church. He ought to have taken a lesson from the loss, made himself a better man. The papers hadn't ceased to jeer at the Mormons. If anything, the articles that made their way to Kirtland felt sharper in tone, more critical, as if the outside world were rousing itself into one great passion of contempt. Joseph ignored the articles, or laughed and tossed them on the fire.

There were times when she cursed him, but that evening she only felt relieved that he could still play with his children. If he saw cause enough for joy, then perhaps the future wasn't as bleak as Emma feared. She stirred the apples in her old copper kettle. The sweet warmth of the spice filled her kitchen, and in the parlor, her family was happy and whole. What more could any woman ask? What more could a woman hope for in this unpredictable world?

The front door opened. The children left off their song, clamoring, "Aunt Eliza, Aunt Eliza!" Usually, Eliza greeted Julia and Young Joseph first, giving each a kiss on the cheek, and sometimes a peppermint candy. This time, she didn't pause. Emma could hear her urgent footsteps in the hall, the rustle of her cape as she pulled it quickly from her shoulders. Joseph followed her into the kitchen, asking whatever was the matter. The children, disappointed, whined in the parlor.

"I must speak to you and Emma both," Eliza said. "I'm afraid it's quite pressing. Julia, keep your little brother in the parlor and out of trouble; there's a good girl."

Emma took her kettle from the heat. Eliza held her cape over one arm; her hair was disheveled, her cheeks flushed, as if she'd run partway home.

"Land sakes," Emma began.

Eliza silenced her with a curt gesture. "I've just been visiting at one of the debating clubs. Some young fellow burst in—I don't know his name, though I recognized his face, and he is a Mormon, surely enough. He'd been riding back to town from Burton, and he met a whole troop of men on the road. They were wearing the uniforms of the Geauga County militia. They're headed for Kirtland this very moment. Joseph—they have a warrant for your arrest."

Joseph's eyes lifted, as if some unseen force had taken him under the chin, tilting his face up to Heaven.

"A warrant for his arrest?" Emma said. "On what charges?"

"Defaulting on one of the loans he took for the temple plot. And more." She lowered her voice, as if she feared the children might overhear. Or as if she feared Emma would hear it. "The warrant lists bigamy among the charges."

"Oliver is behind this," Joseph said. "I curse the day I met that man. He has a selfish heart."

Emma pressed her hands against her stomach. A wild pressure was building inside; she didn't know whether it would burst out as a scream or as laughter. "What will you do, Joseph?"

"I'll be damned if I stay here and let them haul me off to jail under false pretenses," he said. "I'll be damned if I give Oliver his fun."

"You can't run from the law," Emma told him.

"God will protect me. And God tells me now that I must go."

She took hold of his arm. "You can't play these games. You mustn't be so foolish."

"Let him go, Emma." Now that Joseph had invoked the Lord, all urgency had dissipated from Eliza. She watched the Prophet steadily, unshaken. "This is only a device invented by his enemies. If this warrant is a sham, then these county men will give up before too long. If it's a legitimate warrant, they will bring it again, and Joseph will meet the charges in court. He will be exonerated then. I'm sure of it."

He took Eliza's hand in thanks, held it for a moment. Then he broke free and made for the bedroom. "Little time to spare," he called over his shoulder. "Emma, come and help me pack a few things. Eliza, be so good as to saddle my horse, quick as you can. Don't forget my saddle bags. Put a little food and a canteen of water inside."

Emma stuffed a few shirts and several wool stockings into Joseph's old pack from Zion's Camp. She secured his bedroll to the pack's laces. Joseph delved into the bottom of his trunk and brought up a small leather bag. He poured its contents on the bedspread, counting out a meager supply of coins and paper banknotes. "It isn't much, but it'll have to do." He returned the money to his pouch and slipped it into a trouser pocket.

From the other pocket, he withdrew the silver medal—the protective talisman his mother had given him when he'd been a small boy. He held the medal in his palm, studying the engravings on its surface, scratched into the patina of years. A strange sensation moved up Emma's back, a sinuous, rising fascination, half curiosity, half fear. She had seen the medal before as flashes of light in his hand. He had told her once that it was nothing more than an old-world charm, kept as a reminder of the love he bore for his dear, superstitious mother. That excuse had satisfied Emma before.

Now, as she watched her husband—the intensity of his eyes; the resolute fixity of his expression—she understood that Joseph had given her one small part of the truth.

She choked back her fear and crept to his side, looked down at the thing in his hand. He made no move to conceal it. She frowned, trying to puzzle out the symbols etched on its face.

"What does it say?" she whispered.

"*Confirmo Deus Potentissimus.*" He didn't merely speak those words. He imbued them with power, the way he spoke the words of his sermons and revelations. The sound came from his throat, and it came from all around her; the words reached in from beyond the room, beyond the house, from some dark, vast plane she could neither see nor stop herself from feeling. "Strengthen me, O God most powerful."

He lifted the talisman to his lips so quickly that Emma leaped back, startled by the movement. Then he dropped it back into his pocket, lifted his pack to his shoulders, and hurried from the room. She was left to gather her wits as best she could, stumbling in his wake.

On her way out of the house, she recovered enough sense to dodge inside the pantry. She took an empty flour sack from a nail on the door-frame. Half a loaf of bread, a string of dried apples, and the remainder of an old wheel of cheese went into the sack. She retrieved two small jars of potted pork from the upper shelf, dropped them inside, too. It was poor fare for a journey, but the best she could manage on short notice.

In the yard, Joseph had already swung into his saddle. The horse threw up its head, dancing, sensing the women's fear and Joseph's eager-ness to be away. Emma held the bag of food up for him to take.

Dusk had already come. A heavy slab of cloud canted sideways over the town—deep blue, charcoal gray, almost a blanket of black, and un-der the belly of the clouds, a memory of sunset still burned, ember red.

"Where will you go?" Emma said, trying to sound unconcerned, and failing.

"I don't know yet. But God will guide me; you may believe that."

She clenched her fists, though she never meant to give any sign of anger, nor the wild new fear inside her. "Damn this foolishness, Joseph! Damn this talk of God."

He blinked in surprise. "It isn't like you, to use such language."

She wiped an eye on her sleeve, the first she knew that she'd been cry-ing. "What shall I do without you? The children—"

"You'll manage easily enough. You're a strong woman. And you've help from Eliza, if you need it."

She could feel Eliza lingering just behind her shoulder. There was a tension around the other woman, a stirring like words waiting to be spoken.

"I call it cowardice," Emma said, "to run. You ought to face this war-rant like a man. If there's no truth in the charges, then a judge will exon-erate you, as Eliza said."

"I'll face my accusers in court when God tells me to do just that. Right now, He tells me to run. I've always done as He directs; you know that."

Eliza laid a hand on her shoulder. "He must go now if he's to avoid the warrant. Every moment brings our enemies closer."

Emma threw herself back with a tearing gasp, as if some silent angel had drawn its sword and cut the bond between husband and wife. She reeled from the shock of that blow and found Eliza's arms around her. Together, they watched Joseph ride away. The dust from his running horse rose and spread on the wind. Before the last, low flush of red had faded from the sky, the Prophet was already lost to sight, swallowed by the coming dark.

Having left the children in Eliza's care, Emma passed two hours after Joseph's departure pacing fretfully from one end of the Whitney mercantile to another. The store was closed after sunset, but Ann had left a lamp burning on the counter so she wouldn't be without some light. The lamp cast long, wavering shadows along the floor and between the shelves. The stillness of the place unsettled her. When she heard the sound of horses at the crossroads—dozens of horses, scores of them—she left that solitude gratefully, preferring to confront Joseph's accusers rather than remaining alone for another haunted minute.

The night was heavily overcast, but enough lamps burned in the homes around the crossroads that Emma could see the Geauga County militia as they rode into Kirtland—fifty men all told.

Holding Ann's lamp, she waited on the porch for the sheriff to notice her. But another figure slipped along the side of the building and bounded up the steps before the sheriff could take note of Emma. The man was broad as a bear and moved with an unmistakable arrogance. She knew it could only be Brigham Young.

"You heard the news, too?" Emma said, more calmly than she felt.

"The whole damned town has heard. These dogs have come to carry off our Prophet under false charges, no doubt brought by Oliver and his friends. Joseph should have let me beat that shit of a man, beat him to a pulp. And now they think they'll spirit the Prophet off to prison—"

"Joseph isn't here."

He looked at her sharply. The lamplight caught him under the chin, throwing all his features into slanted relief against the darkness: the jaw like a mason's brick, the determined set of his mouth, the small, shrewd eyes narrowing, judging the truth of what she had said. "Where has he gone?"

Emma gave a little toss of her head, as if to say, *I wouldn't tell you if I knew.*

"I'm sure I needn't remind you that our situation is precarious, Brigham. You must keep your temper in hand."

Men and women had crept from their homes to stand at the edges of the crossroads. They carried lanterns on chains or held shaded lamps by their rings; some even cupped candles behind their hands. A hundred anxious faces glowed against the night. There were no children to be seen. No doubt, the children were hidden away in root cellars and barns, or sent across the fields to shelter in the hedges. No one had forgotten the lessons of Zion.

One rider maneuvered his horse to the mercantile porch. The animal threw up its head, groaning, and a rope of white froth dripped from its mouth. There was a golden star pinned to the man's lapel. "Abel Kimball," he said, "sheriff of Geauga County. I've come with a warrant for Joseph Smith's arrest."

"On what charges?" Brigham said.

"Bank fraud, conspiracy to commit murder, and bigamy. Where will I find him?"

Brigham stepped to the edge of the porch. "That's a damned lot of lies. Joseph Smith never did any such thing. I'd swear to that in court."

"You may have your chance to do just that. Now be so good as to tell me where I might find the man."

"He isn't in town," Emma said. "He has gone away—missionary work. We don't know when he'll return. His missions take him away from Kirtland for weeks at a time. Sometimes months." She hadn't told a falsehood since she'd been a child. She half-expected God to strike her down for the sin. But after the first ragged heartbeats, she composed herself. Was it really so simple, to look another person in the eye and lie to them?

"If this Prophet of yours has gone away," Kimball said, "then we'll wait for him in town."

"For how long?" Brigham was doing his level best to control his anger; Emma could see that much. He wore a studied calm that didn't suit him.

"However long it takes for Smith to return and face his charges." The sheriff turned in his saddle to address the milling riders. "Dismount, men, and dig in. We may be here for the long haul."

Rain set in, gray and monotonous, the morning after Kirtland fell under occupation. The Mormons moved furtively from their homes to the shops and businesses at the heart of town, holding their cloaks and Hanways up to keep off the worst of the rain. No one called out greetings to neighbors. If you passed a fellow you knew on the street you issued a curt nod and your eyes slid away, back to the road where the sheriff's men were passing, horses splashing through the ruts where the rain had gathered. A few men put on displays of valor—they called it valor, though Emma called it foolhardy bluster: cleaning their hunting rifles out on their stoops, where the patrols couldn't fail to see. The Saints kept up a near-constant presence at the temple, even at the old meetinghouse. Gray figures wrapped in capes and shawls filed through the rain to relieve their friends at prayer, so that every hour the Mormons beseeched a distant God to spare Kirtland from Zion's fate, and protect the Prophet wherever he may be.

Gathering turnips from her garden, Emma straightened to see another handful of congregants passing her home on their way to the temple. A couple of Kimball's men trotted out of a nearby lane and swung onto the main road. The passing Mormons pulled their cloaks more tightly around their bodies, hurrying on with their heads bowed. One of the riders jeered as he passed: "What use in being God's chosen people if you can't even pray this rain away?" Emma's hand tightened on the handle of her digging fork. She stood in the midst of that downpour, watching the riders until they vanished around a bend in the road. When she was certain they'd truly gone, she lifted the basket of turnips to her hip and went back inside.

Eliza came to meet her at the kitchen door. Julia was clinging to her skirt, clamoring for attention, while Young Joseph fussed in Eliza's arms. "The children are restive," Eliza said. "I've told them they can't go outside to play because of that terrible rain, but they won't hear it."

"I'm sorry. Only let me wring myself out and warm myself at the fire a few minutes; then I'll take them in hand." To Julia, she said, "I wouldn't allow you out of doors just now, even if it weren't raining. I don't trust those men on horses. You know this, Julia; I've told you. Until the bad men leave, we must all stay indoors, where we're safe. If you're wanting for fun, you may help me wash and cut up the turnips."

"Washing turnips ain't no fun," Julia said.

"Merciful Mary. Who taught you to speak so poorly? Never your mother; I'm certain of that. Start washing the turnips, Julia, while I put on a dry dress. There's wash-water in the pail. Once I'm dry, I'll come and help you. We can sing while we work. That always lifts our spirits. You may pick the first song, any one you please."

Emma retreated to her room and shut the door. She peeled the wet, clinging dress from her body, then unhooked her stays, let down her petticoats, and stripped off the damp chemise. A smell of wet wool filled the room. It made the walls feel close and stifling, as if someone were leaning over her shoulder, peering at the last vivid memory Emma had of her husband—Joseph making ready for his flight, the strange medallion in his hand. She was wearing nothing but her linen drawers and wool stockings. She crossed her arms over her nakedness and shivered, turning to look over her shoulder, but there was nothing there, no shadowed face leering at the window. In any case, the curtains were closed.

She dressed as quickly as she could manage, eager to be out of that room. She was just fastening the last buttons on her bodice when Julia cried from the kitchen, "Look, it's Papa! Papa has come home!"

"God help us," Emma murmured. "It can't be—not now!"

She ran from the bedroom, nearly colliding with Eliza as she came hurtling down the hall. Together they went to the kitchen window where Julia was peeking out between the curtains.

Eliza sighed. "Thank goodness, it's only Don Carlos. Silly girl—that is your uncle, not your papa. Can't you tell the difference?"

"Few people can, from a distance," Emma said.

She opened the kitchen door and called Don Carlos to the side of the house, but once he was in, he refused to remove his hat. Fat drops of rainwater rolled down his oiled coat and hung from the brim of his old Tyrolean.

"I've been speaking with Brigham," he said. "We both agree it's long past time you were away, Sister Emma. You and the children. Kimball's men have been asking about you—where you live, what's your temperament, all that sort of thing."

"Kimball knows my temperament very well for himself. I spoke with him three nights ago, when he first invaded."

Don Carlos frowned. "If the sheriff is so keenly interested in what sort of a woman you are, it can only mean he expects to be very much in your company. Brigham and I both think Kimball plans to take you and the children as prisoners."

Emma's hand flew to her mouth. "He can't imprison me," she muttered. "He hasn't any cause. I've done nothing wrong."

"Do you think that matters to him? The governor sent that sheriff here to arrest Joseph. If he must dangle some bait to get his man, then by God, he'll do it."

"He would answer to the courts for it," Eliza said.

"Oh, yes, certainly—long after he'd lured Joseph into his trap. And God knows what he might do before the law catches up with him. Men like Kimball don't balk at terrorizing women and children."

"Julia," Emma said, "go into the parlor with your brother. This is no fit talk for your ears."

When Julia had gone, Eliza said, "Surely Kimball doesn't intend to hurt Emma or the children. No man would do such a thing."

Don Carlos leaned toward the window. He tracked a pair of Kimball's riders as they made for the heart of town. "I'm afraid the Gentiles don't bear us any goodwill, Sister Eliza. It may be that I'm too cautious, but I don't like to think of Emma falling into Kimball's hands. Joseph has already vexed the law sorely enough. I don't believe Kimball will keep his patience much longer."

"Don Carlos is right," Emma said. "I should take the children and leave. The sooner, the better. I ought to have seen the danger for myself, but I've been distracted by worry. I don't know whether the sheriff would truly keep me or my children as his prisoners, but this town has become a tinderbox. You've seen those fools polishing their guns in the open, Eliza. You know a single spark could set the whole place ablaze. And Joseph might be witless enough to come back, if he thinks he might save me from the sheriff. If I leave Kirtland and take the children with me, he'll have little reason to return."

"I'm glad you see things my way," Don Carlos said. "It makes this easier. I was prepared to bundle you up in a sack and carry you off myself, if need be. I've already arranged a way to get you and the children to safety. You'll leave tonight, three hours after sunset, as soon as the usual patrol has moved north from this end of town."

He took a small paper packet from his coat's inner lining and handed it to Eliza. She opened it to reveal a fine brown powder.

"Valerian root," he said. "Patty the midwife prepared it. A strong dose, but it'll keep the children quiet till you're well out of harm's way. Two-thirds to Julia, one-third to Young Joe, an hour before we set out. Make sure they drink it all."

Eliza pinched the packet closed and tucked it up her sleeve. "But how shall we get out? We must know what to pack, how to dress ourselves and the children."

"We?" Emma said, surprised.

"You don't believe I would leave you to face such adversity on your own. You are my dearest friend. I will be with you, come what may."

Emma squeezed her hand. To Don Carlos, she said, "Assuming we can get out of Kirtland unseen, where will you take us?"

"It won't be me who spirits you away. I dearly wish I could do it, Emma—you know how I wish it. But once Kimball realizes you've gone, he may turn on the rest of my family—anything for leverage against Joseph. My brothers and I must stay here. Someone has to look out for our mother and our sisters. My father is too old and weak to protect them now."

When the appointed hour came, Emma and Eliza slipped from the house and hurried down the garden path. They'd dressed in their darkest clothing and wrapped themselves in several shawls each, for there was no telling what conditions they might meet, nor how far the road must run. The children slept in their arms.

Each carried a single bag filled to bursting with necessities and the few sentimental items they couldn't bear to part with. The rest of their goods—anything of the least practical or monetary value—had been packed into trunks or folded in scraps of canvas, then hidden away in the root cellar or under a loose floorboard in the bedroom. Eliza had rolled her poems and essays into tight cylinders, lashing them with twine, then slid those thick wands of paper into the back of her stays so they wouldn't take up space inside her bag. The women had left a single lamp burning at the parlor window, the better to make Kimball's men believe Emma was still at home. The light fell across the garden in a long, distorted rectangle. As they passed through the phantom glow, Emma could see Eliza's papers straining against the fabric of her dress. They looked like the bones of some hungry, hunted animal glimpsed through a hide.

Emma nudged the garden gate open. It squealed on its hinges; four or five chickens took fright at the sound and clattered among the young cabbages and the dying vines. Eliza had chased all the chickens from the coop. They would wander through the gardens of Kirtland until they joined other flocks.

The rain had abated shortly after sunset. A thin wash of gold showed where a half-moon hid itself from the world. The clouds were limned around the edges. No one could call it moonlight, but it was sufficient for making one's way from the house to the temple. Lamps burned in windows along the Chillicothe Road, but even those lights looked tentative and small. The town was already receding from Emma, already backing away.

They hurried down the short stretch of road to the temple and brushed past the redbuds where Emma had sat with the pages of her hymnal and a welling heart. She would never see that quiet sanctuary again. She knew it now, felt a certainty of separation like the ringing of a bell inside, a hollow shiver. The peace under the redbuds, the temple in bright glory, Don Carlos at the edge of his field . . . and her children's graves. She must leave them all behind. For what? For vows she'd taken on a reckless winter night. For words that bound her more tightly than love could bind.

Eliza stopped suddenly.

"What is it?" Emma whispered.

"I saw a man."

A ring of deep shadow surrounded the temple, made all the denser by the slight luminosity of its walls, the way they magnified the few beams of moonlight that filtered through the clouds. Emma squinted, struggling to make out whatever Eliza had seen.

Could Kimball's men have learned of their escape? Had the sheriff done something terrible to Don Carlos, and made him talk? Then she saw the man for herself—wide but not tall, waiting at one corner of the building. Even by night, his prideful carriage was unmistakable.

"It's only Brigham Young."

"Of course; thank God. I ought to have known, but my nerves, Emma—"

"Hush. Come along."

Emma fought down her dismay. She ought to have known Don Carlos would appoint Brigham to the task. But if Brigham could bring her children safely out of Kirtland, she would fall on her knees before him and kiss his bare feet. Though she wouldn't be surprised to find a devil's hooves hidden in his boots.

He waved them on. They followed him around the corner to the northern side of the temple, which was hidden from the road. A large dray stood waiting with two stout horses dozing in the traces.

"You took your time in coming," he muttered.

"Would you have preferred we'd walked out the door and into the path of the sheriff's men?"

"Stop this, both of you," Eliza whispered. "You'll have time enough for bickering on the road."

Emma clenched her teeth; she could have bitten through leather. Julia stirred in her sleep, murmuring against her neck. The children mattered; nothing else did, not this persistent dislike for Brigham Young—only the children, and Joseph's safety. She must temper her mistrust.

"Thank you," she said to Brigham, rather curtly, "for helping us now. I know it isn't easy."

He jerked his head toward the back of the dray. Several crates of potatoes and turnips had been stacked beside the rear wheels. The wagon's bed was three feet deep at most, and a canvas cover had been stretched taut as a drumhead from wall to wall, forming a low roof. "You'll ride in the bed," he said quietly, "you and the children, at least till we're out of town." He took Eliza's bag and slung it none too gently into the darkness below the canvas. "Inside, ladies. Move as far to the front as you can manage. Emma, give me that bag. Get the children in; quickly, now."

He lit the stub of a candle and fixed it with a few drops of wax to the wagon's lowered gate. By that feeble light, Emma and Eliza laid the children on the damp wood and pushed them into the depths of the dray. They followed first on hands and knees, then crawling on their bellies.

"Tell me when you're situated," Brigham said, "and I'll put out the light."

A smell of cold and mildew filled the space below the canvas. Emma fussed with the children's blankets, doing her best to make a soft, warm bed to hold them. She wrestled one of the shawls from her shoulders, rolling it to cradle Young Joseph's head. Eliza dragged their bags up and pressed them against the wagon's forward wall, beside a large wooden crate stenciled with the address of Joseph's store.

"What's in this crate?" Emma asked Brigham—more to distract herself from rising panic than because she cared to know.

"Joseph's papers—the revelations—his journals. Everything I could find in his office. I thought perhaps he might not have a chance to retrieve them, and I didn't like that his work should fall into the hands of our enemies."

Eliza brushed the crate with her fingers, softly, as if she touched a holy relic. "Thank you," she said.

"We'll take the north road" was his only reply.

"Through the heart of town?" Emma said. "The southern road is nearer and less populated."

"Men are watching the southern road, too; I can promise you that. If our ruse is to work, I've got to convince the Gentiles I'm headed for Lake Erie and the shipping lines. Otherwise, they'll wonder why I'm driving a wagon at all, this time of night. The patrols are especially busy just now. There has been some unrest at the crossroads, outside the printer's office, so you may be certain we'll be stopped and questioned."

Emma blinked back tears. She would not cry in front of this man.

"Lie flat until we're beyond Kimball's men," Brigham said. "If you move, you'll cause the canvas to bulge, and then the whole jig will be up."

He blew sharply. The light went out. A chill closed in. She was sickeningly conscious of the canvas roof, so low, just above her body. Brigham began lifting his boxes into the wagon's far end. He pushed the crates so deeply into the confined space that Emma was forced to pull her feet up, curling around the children.

Eliza's hand came down gently on Emma's arm, then patted along its length until she found Emma's hand. She squeezed. The wagon springs creaked; the bed rocked; Brigham had climbed up into the driver's seat. He barked a quick command to his team. The wagon lurched, then rolled. The rumble of its wheels shuddered through her body, threatening to shake loose her tears. She held tightly to Eliza. The children slept between them.

Emma knew they were nearing the crossroads when she heard men arguing, their shouts loud enough to carry over the groan of the wagon springs. "The press is ours, and we'll print whatever we damned-well please!" "How dare you think to turn this press against the Prophet!" "He's no Prophet of mine." "This is a city of Saints!" "Call Joseph Smith a saint if you like; I call him a devil!"

Emma rolled carefully toward the wagon's wall.

"What are you doing?" Eliza whispered.

There was no use answering. She didn't know herself what she was doing. She eased up carefully to her elbows, fearful she would bump against the canvas and ruin their disguise. Fitful lights licked along the slender gap between wagon and canvas. She pressed her face against the dray and found she could peer with one eye through the gap.

They had reached the crossroads. Men had gathered in a tight knot outside the printing office of the *Messenger and Advocate*, Kirtland's newspaper. She couldn't begin to guess their numbers, for the light from their torches and lanterns flashed and the whole scene seemed to fly like a flock of starlings, rapid and bewildering. Figures stretched and distorted like nightmare beasts with broad, hackling bodies and long faces, pointed teeth in wide-open mouths. The men shouted; they swung their fists. They called their brothers sinners, and adulterers, enemies of women or enemies of the Prophet; she couldn't make out more than that.

"Get down," Eliza whispered sharply.

Emma returned to her place. "They're fighting," she said. "Already. Joseph has gone and Oliver Cowdery has taken his friends and broken the church apart, and so soon—easily as that—they're at one another's throats."

The wagon rolled on. The sounds of unrest fell away. Eliza said, "Give me your hand."

They clung to one another in the cramped, stifling dark until they heard voices again—men calling for Brigham to halt. The wagon stopped. The sudden lack of that bone-jarring vibration felt more still than death. Eliza gripped her hand with fierce insistence, and Emma curled around her children, motionless as a fawn in the grass, scarcely daring to breathe. *Please, God, let the children sleep on. Don't allow them to wake. Protect Brigham Young; give him wisdom now, when he needs it most. Guard his tongue and hide his anger.*

"Where do you think you're going?" one of the men said.

"Up to the lake." Brigham's answer was neutral, pleasant—almost friendly. "There's a steamer expecting my shipment."

"At this hour?"

"The boat sails at dawn. If my load of roots isn't on that steamer when it leaves port, the whole crop'll rot. There won't be another shipment made for two weeks at least."

"Roots?" the other soldier said. "I've never seen anyone transport roots under a cover."

Brigham said, "What with all this rain we've had, I thought it best. Go on and have a look if you don't believe me. Let down the back gate; see for yourself."

Footsteps circled the dray. There was a clatter, a shiver; the gate squealed open. Emma strangled a whimper of fear. After a moment, the gate slammed shut again.

"Turnips," the man said.

Brigham chuckled. "You fellows don't think I'm tangled up in this Mormon mess, do you?"

"You live here in Kirtland—isn't that so? I've seen you in the town."

"Of course, but my family has been here for two generations."

"I saw you on the porch of that big white store the night we came. You seemed Mormon enough then—Mormon enough for two men."

"I?" Brigham laughed. "You've mistaken me for some other fellow. My family has been in this valley long before these Mormonites came swarming in. Like rats, they are, infesting the place. They've all but taken over the valley." He spoke with such perfect contempt that Emma felt cut to her heart. If she hadn't been lying beside a crate full of Joseph's papers, which Brigham had rescued himself, she might have believed his denial. "And now their leader has cut and run. Prophet, they call him." Brigham spat. "That's for the Mormons and their Prophet. Joseph Smith is a fool if he's not an impostor. Good riddance, I say. If he never comes back to Kirtland, then he'll be back too soon."

The men laughed. One said, "Why stay, though? If you aren't a Mormon yourself, then why live among the infestation? There are better valleys in Ohio for farming, and not so far away."

"What, and part with my father's land? My people were here before theirs. If I've got anything to say about it, my bloodline will continue on this land long after the Mormons have moved on. After we've driven them away. No, sir; the Mormons will be rid of me when I'm dead, and then they'll have to bury me under my own soil."

"Even so, we can't let you out of the city tonight. You've seen the situation for yourself. It's a riot waiting to happen."

"But I'm no part of it. Let those fools tear themselves to pieces and be done with it. The sooner the Mormons settle their scores with one another, the sooner they'll leave—or so I pray. Anyway, what can one man with a load of turnips matter? I've got a steamer to meet, fellows, and a long night ahead."

Someone muttered a few sly words, too low for Emma to hear.

Brigham chuckled. "You're a man who knows how to bargain. I respect that. All right; you let me pass out of Kirtland tonight, and tomorrow afternoon, when I've come back with my empty dray, I'll give you a cut of the shipping money. Five percent."

"Ten," the other man said.

Brigham grunted, a good-natured, half-amused sound. "You know, friend, I could drive off without any by-your-leave. You'd have to shoot me to stop me, and then you'd answer to Sheriff Kimball—and the governor after that, I guess. Is a noose around your neck worth an extra dollar in your pocket?"

"All right, five percent. Hurry up, now. Be on your way before the sheriff sees."

"He won't be looking in this direction for some time yet," Brigham said. "Got his hands full at the newspaper office, I'd say. Good night, fellows. Keep yourselves lively and keep up the good work."

The wagon lurched into motion. Little by little, Eliza's grip loosened. There was a hollow booming as the dray crossed the bridge at the northern end of town. Emma lay rigid with fright—afraid of the militia, of the violence boiling over at the crossroads, and most of all, the confined misery of the wagon bed, which made her think of the cramped black interior of a coffin, the little coffins where her dead babies slept.

Something giddy was expanding in her chest—something hysterical. It would come out any moment as a lunatic's wild laughter. She prayed for control, for her sanity until she felt the wagon bed tilt—and then she knew they were climbing the forested ridge above the bend in the Chagrin River. Only then did she allow herself to weep—quietly, for fear of waking the children. Great shuddering sobs wracked her body, beating at her from the inside until she was limp and wrung out, until she could do nothing but lie in the frigid darkness with the motion of the dray batting her from side to side.

When the slope leveled, Brigham stopped his horses and climbed from the driver's seat.

There was a scuffling at the edge of the canvas. Emma swallowed what remained of her tears and scrubbed her face with the corner of a shawl. Brigham pulled back the cover. Fresh air flooded in, the smell bright and bracing, laced with pine sap and rain. The clouds had parted since she'd last seen the sky. In the places between those heavy swags, the stars crowded in.

Emma and Eliza sat up, breathing deeply, savoring the air.

Brigham nodded, an oddly formal greeting. "You can ride sitting up properly now, if you like."

Emma rose to her knees, staring between the pines, down through the night. Kirtland lay far below. Pinpricks of light illuminated windows, small as glass beads, and far to either side, the land swept out, an endless black expanse. The earth went on and on without regard for what the church had made. But there was a forceful brightness near the heart of town, a smear of red against black. Eliza saw it and gasped, reaching across the children to clutch Emma's arm.

"What is that light?" Emma asked dully.

Brigham grunted. "The *Messenger and Advocate*, I assume. They're burning the press."

"But that's horrid," Eliza said.

Emma stiffened on her knees, raising herself higher. "Who is burning the press? Kimball's militia?"

"Perhaps," he said. "Perhaps not. It could be anyone. Kirtland has fallen into civil war, it seems." He sounded detached, merely interested—not frightened, not sorrowful in the least. Emma found she couldn't look at him. She recalled his mocking tone when he'd negotiated with Kimball's men. *These Mormons and their Prophet. Joseph Smith is a fool if he's not an impostor.*

"Where are we going?" She kept her eyes on Kirtland—the small, fragile town that had been her world for seven years. "Where will you take us now?"

"To the only place where we can reasonably expect to find some welcome. I'm taking you to Missouri."

She rounded on him. "Are you mad? We can't go to Missouri! The Gentiles will kill us!"

"Hush," Eliza whispered. The children had stirred at the sound of Emma's voice.

"They won't kill us if we deny we're Mormons," Brigham answered. "And that's exactly what we'll do. We'll give no Gentile any reason to suspect us while we pass through their territory. Once we've gone beyond Jackson County, we'll be as safe in Missouri as anywhere else. The remnants of Zion have gathered at a new settlement—haven't you heard? It lies on the edge of the frontier—well beyond Independence, that pit of Hell."

"I hadn't heard," she admitted.

"The place is still quite new. They call it Far West, and we shall call it home—at least until Joseph finds us. After that, let him lead us wherever God wills."

They drove on into the night. Emma and Eliza propped themselves against the crate of papers. They took turns resting their heads on one another's shoulders, catching whatever phantoms of sleep they could while the wagon descended the ridge and turned toward Lake Erie's shore.

She huddled close to Eliza throughout that long, weary night. The boundlessness of an unmoved world spread all around her, distending itself, unfurling into the dark. God had called upon the weak things of the world. She feared the weak things were too inconsequential to do God's bidding.

Missouri lay many days to the west. The journey wasn't a comfortable one. They slept in wayside inns whenever the opportunity arose—Brigham was supplied with plenty of money, the origins of which Emma could only guess at—but more often than not, they slept on hard, damp bedrolls under the wagon and woke cramped, poorly rested, wet with autumn dew.

All the while, she fretted about the congregation in Kirtland. There was no telling whether the fire at the press had spread to burn the homes of her neighbors. Bitterness like an infection had traveled through the city, ushered by fear of the occupying militia. Who could say whether Kirtland still remained? Perhaps it had torn itself apart on the night of their departure. Perhaps it had never existed in the first place; it had been only a dream, half pleasant, half terrible, vaguely recalled in that fleeting way dreams have of returning long after you'd thought them forgotten.

When they came at last upon the flat, gray expanse of the river—Missouri's eastern border—Emma found a new dread. This muddy shore was where Zion's Camp had met its fate. And beyond those waters, wrinkled and dull as the cast-off skin of some vast and cunning serpent, a hostile land waited. Missouri still thirsted for Mormon blood. She could feel it, the land's hunger, the people's hatred of her—of her children.

Brigham halted his dray a good half-mile downriver from a small village, a bare handful of homes and businesses clustered around a ferry's pier. He turned in the driver's seat, eyeing the women. "Let's work everything out properly, here and now. We must be in perfect agreement if we hope to move freely through Missouri. We mustn't give anyone reason to question us too closely. You'll be my wife, Emma. And you, Eliza, will be Emma's spinster sister. You look enough alike that no one will doubt you share blood. We've naught to do with the Mormons—nothing whatsoever, do you understand? We've never been to Kirtland, nor heard of Joseph Smith."

"But everyone has heard of Joseph," Eliza said.

Brigham tossed his head impatiently. "Very well. We've heard of him, but we think him a fool. That's what you'll say if anyone asks. And you must say it convincingly. You can't falter or look down when you lie."

"Lying is a sin," Emma said faintly.

"Then sin, and live. Sin to keep your son and daughter alive if you haven't enough sense to save your own hide. You know what happened at Zion. These Missouri men won't balk at killing little children."

Eliza pulled Julia's face tightly against her breast; she covered the girl's exposed ear with a hand.

"Now," he said, "have you anything in your possession which might give us away? We can't be sure our trunks and bags won't be searched."

"What about Joseph's papers?" Emma asked. "What if they look inside the crate?"

"We'll say they're Eliza's papers. She's a writer; they'll have no cause to doubt us. They'll glance inside the crate and see nothing but pages full of words. They won't sit down to examine every line."

"I pray you're right," Emma said.

"Of course I am. Anything else? Anything specific—something a man might recognize as belonging to a Latter-day Saint?"

"I've a Book of Mormon," Eliza said, "in my bag."

Emma glanced at her in surprise. Eliza had hardly spoken two words together about her interest in the church or in Joseph's teachings. Yet she had treasured the Book of Mormon enough to take it with her out of Kirtland.

Brigham extended his hand. "Give it to me."

Eliza delved into her bag and retrieved her Book of Mormon. It was bound in chestnut leather, front cover embossed and leafed with gold, a fine new edition. She placed it solemnly on his palm.

He stood in the wagon, whipped back his arm, and hurled the sacred book far out into the Mississippi. Emma gasped. Eliza gave a wordless cry. The Book arced above the water and hung for a moment, silhouetted against a pale sky. Its pages fluttered, a forlorn bird.

Then it plummeted, disappearing under the water with an insignificant splash.

"How could you," Eliza exclaimed.

"Stop this foolishness," he said. "I'll destroy a thousand holy books, and gladly, if it'll help me deliver the Prophet's family safely to Far West."

Emma was still shaken by the time they reached the ferry. The dray halted at the pier, facing out across the Mississippi. While Brigham negotiated with the ferryman, she could do nothing but stare over the water to the thin blue haze of its opposite shore.

"Where'd you come from, anyway," the ferryman said.

Brigham answered smoothly, "Outside Cleveland."

"Ohio, eh? What have you got to do with those Mormonite devils?"

"Not a damned thing," Brigham growled. "A pack of sinners and fools, they are."

"We've had some trouble with the Mormonites hereabouts."

"So I've heard. To Hell with the lot of them, I say." Brigham spat over the side of his wagon.

The ferryman slapped his thigh. "The devils won't trouble anyone much longer. Papers said their town of Kirtland has burned to ashes."

"Do you suppose it's true?" Brigham sounded merely curious, not concerned. Emma stared resolutely at the far shore.

"God knows," the man answered. "Papers ain't always reliable. But I wager the Mormons are just about finished. Their leader's on the run—that Joe Smith fellow. Dodged a warrant for his arrest. On that much, all the papers agree. I say it won't be long now till old Joe is caught by some posse and brought to justice. He'll be strung up by his neck, sure enough, and then the Mormons will be through."

In the back of the dray, Julia began to sniffle, then to weep. Emma heard a rustle as Eliza took the girl in her arms. She could hear Eliza whispering comfort, then singing softly, so low the melody almost blended with the great, endless sigh of the river.

"What's the matter with the child?" the ferryman said.

"Damned if I can say," Brigham answered. "You know how girls are, bursting into tears at a change in the wind."

The ferryman named his price, and Brigham agreed. The barge carried the dray over the rocking waves. The horses threw up their heads at the sound of water under their hooves. Brigham held them by their bridles and talked to them calmly, ignoring the women and children for the duration of the crossing. But when they reached the shore and he'd shaken hands with the ferryman—when the horses had been hitched to the wagon and they rolled on into that hard, bitter land—Brigham turned on the driver's seat and fixed Julia with a hard stare.

"Leave her be," Emma said. "She's only a child."

"She'll get us all killed if she isn't more careful."

What in this land wouldn't get them killed? Be as careful as you like; there are snares laid for the unwary, and trenches cast about you. Place one foot wrong, and you'll fall.

See us safely to Far West, she prayed.

If Joseph still lived, he would find them there.

Emma has dressed herself by the time Eliza comes, though her fingers are numb. Strange. Why should it strike her this way, take her like an illness? It's only a fact of the world, a thing she has known since Joseph first agreed to surrender. He is dead. But the world goes on turning.

Strange, that a body should go on living, hands go on working the buttons of a dress, and strange the way your feet slide into your boots and the petticoats fall down around your ankles, the way you can look into the glass and smooth your hair and see the old redness of your eyes, the hardness of your mouth and know what you've known all along is true. And your heart is still beating, and you refuse to stop breathing. You don't even need to think about it. Your body is hungry for breath, but it shouldn't be. The grief and guilt ought to be enough to kill you.

Eliza slides in sideways through the door. She almost doesn't open the door at all, as if she can pass like a ghost through a solid world. Once Emma had imagined Eliza could see into another reality, a realm misty as a dream and fitted for her remarkable, far-seeing eyes. Perhaps she'd been right, and Eliza was always a being from another world—this shell of a woman, this lost spirit, drifting silently in.

"You know Porter has returned from Carthage," Emma says. No break to her voice. There is work to be done.

Eliza nods. She can't look up, can't meet her eye.

"You must be strong," Emma says.

Eliza shakes her head. Her mouth buckles; her eyes close. She shakes her head, and then she nods—denial, acceptance. An angel told her, after all. She has known, even before Emma knew it.

For a long time, there is only silence, except for one little closed-lipped mew of pain from Eliza. Crows call from somewhere outside, out across the orchard. The Mansion is shuddering around them, the girls in their rooms, in their private spheres of grief, feeling what Eliza feels.

Emma says, "God's will be done. We can't know His meaning. We can't understand His designs. It isn't for us to know. It's only for us to obey with perfect faith."

"My faith." She can barely make out Eliza's words, they're so strangled and thin. "My faith is nothing to me now."

"Your faith is everything. To you, and to God."

Faith will hold you up, Eliza. Faith will turn your back to iron, stop your ears, shut your eyes if you let it. Faith will drown every true thing with its inescapable tide. Her mother and father are dead by now. They must be. Dead like Joseph, and she never saw them again after she left Harmony. She never read a word from her mother in a letter, never told her father he'd been right all along. It was faith that made all this.

Emma says, "I told you first."

"Why? Why did you bring me here, why did you give me this terrible news, I cannot bear it, Emma."

"I told you first because you loved him best. You loved him more than I ever did."

Now, at last, she looks up, slack-faced and suffering.

"I was his wife," Emma says. "His true wife, his only real wife. I will insist upon that, as I always have, until the day I die. I was his wife out of necessity, and because I took a sacred vow. But I would have had it differently if I could have arranged it. I loved another. It doesn't matter who. And Joseph loved another. He loved dozens of others. He loved them all, in his way—and each more dearly than he ever loved me."

Eliza shakes her head again. Emma doesn't know whether it's the same denial as before, or a fresh one, but it hardly matters. She understands the truth. Emma sees clearly now, into another world like the one Eliza sees, but this is not a cloud-land of fancy, a poet's delicate heaven. She sees the past. All these years she has longed to understand her own history, and now it opens its robes before her, it strips away all the layers of time. It's naked and stark, and in its way, not without an aberrant beauty.

"I was Joseph's wife by law," Emma says, "but you were his wife by love. And so you deserve to know."

The beauty is all in simplicity, in lightness, the way her spirit unburdens itself of the old weights—envy and hate.

"I can't live without him." Eliza is calm now with despair.

"You will learn to do it. I lived without him for seventeen years."

How easily those words come. They don't catch in her throat. There's no pain in speaking.

Curious, isn't it? Strange.

X

If the Salt Has Lost Its Savor

1838

And stranger still, the things you remember. The moments that were so insignificant while you lived them, perhaps you didn't even notice at the time the way the light moved over the grass. The pieces of light and blue-green shadow like patches of a quilt, geometric, sharply cut, all their corners stitched together so the whole ethereal mass shifted as one—light, shadow, the dapples of bright and dark under the catalpa trees, the wind in a tangle of branches. She remembered the way the leaves sounded in the wind. And down the long streets of Far West, from somewhere in the perfect grid of that town, a distant sound of women singing. Joseph had removed his waistcoat. He stooped in the mobile shade to lift Alexander Hale, their new baby, from the blanket where he lay. He tucked Alexander against his chest. The patchwork of light and dark slid over his arms, shading and obscuring his eyes, which were turned down to the baby's face. There was a green scent in the air, a June scent, vigorous with sap. The smell reminded her, for no reason she could name, of the caterpillars she used to find as a girl in her mother's garden. The tickle when they crawled along her extended finger, their blind bodies reaching from side to side, searching for a leaf.

The moments you never notice while you live them. But years later they come back to you. They torment you with their endless repetitions—a subtle disquiet, a dull remonstration as if there is something important in the memory, something you must see and understand. The past is a box to be unlocked or staved open with an axe. The past is a great treasure buried under the earth. If you can find it, maybe you will understand the here and now.

When Emma and Eliza arrived in Far West near the end of autumn, they found much more than a mere settlement. The refugees from

Zion had gone on doggedly with their work. They had made a town, and then a small city equal to Kirtland in size and commerce. Five thousand souls, a tidy map of dirt roads, still soft from their clearing. Nearly a hundred and fifty shops and businesses already. The place was thriving—a true haven for the Latter-day Saints, who knew by then to keep to themselves and avoid the Gentile towns in Caldwell County. Far West kept so much to itself that Emma had been shocked by its size and vigor, for in Kirtland they had scarcely heard of the new settlement. When they arrived, even Brigham had reined in his team to stare in awe before driving on.

Joseph hadn't been far behind. Perhaps he was bound for Far West from the moment he'd left Kirtland. He arrived in the city of the Saints victorious, thin and hardened from his trials in the wilderness. But he was upright, too, and steady—a striking figure on a sorrel horse, cheeks flushed, skin golden from the autumn sun, the tie at his neck blood-red. He'd been a blaze of color against the flat gray of the coming winter. Far West had turned out to cheer for him. The people had thronged the streets, shouting his name, calling him Prophet, and he'd looked down into the crowd and found Emma with his eyes, though she was one of thousands. He had smiled at her, and the cries of the crowd had been like a flock of birds rising into flight.

But it wasn't that day, when Joseph had ridden into Far West, which she still remembered. When she walked backward through her heart, her steps took her to that June day under the catalpas, the light and shadow moving.

Alexander had fussed in Joseph's arms. "He's hungry," Emma had said, and then, "Bring him to me."

She had allowed her spinning wheel to slow, and Joseph had passed the baby to her—such a small thing, light as a chick and downy, but he was healthy—all the midwives in Far West agreed. Alexander fussed more when Joseph passed him to his mother. The baby liked his father best. Or perhaps Alexander sensed, in some small and primitive way, the preference Joseph had for him. Emma had fallen pregnant only a few short weeks after the Prophet had come to Far West, and the whole town had kept up with news of the baby. When he was born, it seemed everyone in the village had lingered at their bedroom windows, listening to his cries. He was the luck of the city, the church's good omen. The

Prophet had brought forth new life in this place—and a son, at that. God looked down with favor.

She loosened the buttons of her bodice and bared a breast. Joseph usually turned away when she did this, tactful, perhaps ostentatious in his courtesy. Not this time. Alexander took his lunch, and Joseph watched with an affection so open and yearning as to be almost sorrowful. The way his face had fallen into stillness. In that moment she understood— she understands now, lifting the lid of this long-buried box—that Joseph also felt the gulf of distance between them. It's some comfort to her, now that Joseph is no more and she is alone and the hearth is cold, the ashes gray and pale. She knows, finally, that there was one passing moment when Joseph had loved her. The smell of green, the shadows moving.

She remembered looking away from Joseph. She couldn't bear it, the love in his face, and how foreign love felt between them. She looked instead at her son. Alexander Hale was a thing Emma couldn't quite explain. She had made him with Joseph—she must have done so; it was impossible that the baby had come about by any other means—but the act that had produced him seemed a blunt impossibility. She tried to recall the moment, the night, some memory of undressing with purpose, sliding under the quilts to find Joseph also bare beside her. She couldn't picture it. It was easier to imagine him in the arms of another woman—in the arms of those girls, Nancy Marinda and Fannie Alger. He fit there better than he fit with her.

"Brother Joseph—Prophet—surely you can see that this is a sign from God." It was Sampson Avard who spoke. The physician's English accent was unmistakable.

Emma had hidden from the men gathered in her parlor. She sat on the top step of the dark staircase, listening, holding so still her back ached. She had put the children to bed in their little room with the dormer window. Thank God, they'd fallen asleep readily enough.

Eliza had gone to the meetinghouse to help organize aid to the families who had recently arrived from Kirtland. Six hundred wagons had rolled in under the protection of the governor's militia—and under the watchful eyes of the Danites, one of Joseph's latest creations, more vigilante posse than the fraternal order of public servants they claimed to be. But the Mormons had been given dispensation to assemble at Far

West, providing they kept to themselves and carried on with their plans to push on westward, into Indian country, leaving Missouri behind for good. Eliza had taken it upon herself to find housing for the refugees, and to lead the women in planning for their future trek across the plains into the Rocky Mountains. She was often busy at the meetinghouse, and Emma was left alone, as now, in the dense shadows of the upper story.

She knew it was wrong to listen in on any meeting to which she hadn't been invited. And this was practically a sin, for a woman to eavesdrop on a meeting of the apostles and the other leaders of the church. Yet she couldn't tear herself away. Something small but commanding held her in place, a diminutive angel of common sense whispering up from the depths of her heart, *Stay and listen. Stay and know.*

Avard said, "The better part of the Kirtland congregation has been preserved for you. And God brought them all this way, through a hostile land that thirsts for our blood. Yet not one of our people was harmed by any Gentile."

"Like the three youths in the Book of Daniel," Joseph said, "thrown into the fiery furnace, but they emerged, and not a hair on their heads was burned, nor was the least smell of smoke upon their robes."

"Just so," Avard said. "I see it as a signal from On High. God means for us to understand that we are protected."

Sidney Rigdon broke in. "Brother Sampson, you must be wary. The Lord has sent us a Prophet for a reason. It's Joseph who will read the signs and tell us what they mean—if indeed they are signs at all."

"Brother Sampson isn't wrong," Joseph said. "God does intend a message in this arrival from Kirtland. Our numbers are increased—and our power."

"It's finally time, then, to strike back against the Gentiles. To avenge Zion." This was John Corrill, whom Joseph had recently appointed Church Historian.

"We ought not to seek vengeance," Sidney said.

"Bah! To Hell with your pacifist claptrap." Of course Brigham Young was there. "Listen to me, Rigdon: you fret over dissenters within the church. Don't deny it; we've all heard you weeping and wailing, we've seen you wringing your hands. If we put the Gentiles in their place, then we'll keep our own church members in their place, as well."

"Brigham is right." John Lee—a staring, quiet man. Emma had never trusted him. "Unless you want another Oliver Cowdery to arise."

"I can't deny," Sidney said slowly, "that I have concerns. I think it unlikely the church will survive another loss like the one Brother Oliver effected. But to make war on the Gentiles will put Far West at risk. And our outlying settlements—what of them? Adam-ondi-Ahman, Haun's Mill . . . ? They are vulnerable to attack, so far beyond the boundaries of our city."

A few men murmured assent.

"Cowards, the lot of you," Brigham growled.

Avard said, "We needn't make war. But we are sheltered now under God's shield. Whatever we do will be defended—"

The rest of Avard's words were lost in a din of rising voices. Emma struggled to pick Joseph from the tumult, but it was all one great rumble, a clatter like a rockslide, like solid ground giving way beneath your feet.

Then a gasp. The men drawing breath together; a stir as they stepped away from one another, as they fell back into their chairs. Emma knew that reaction. Only Joseph could cause it—the moment when he lurched to his feet, when his face turned so pale, he seemed almost luminous, lit from within by a sacred fire. The Prophet was about to call down a revelation. In the momentary silence—no more than a few ragged heartbeats—she felt sick with apprehension.

Joseph spoke: "Know ye not, brethren, that it will soon be your privilege to take your respective companies and go out to scout the borders of the settlements, and take to yourselves the spoils and the goods of the ungodly? For it is written, the riches of the Gentiles shall be consecrated to my people; and thus, you will waste away the Gentiles by robbing and plundering them of their property. And in this way, we will build up the kingdom of God, and roll forth the little stone that Daniel saw cut out of the mountain without hands and roll until it filled the whole earth."

She pressed a hand to her mouth, fearing she might cry out. How could he say something so dangerous?

The revelation continued. "If any of us should be recognized, who can harm us? For we will stand by each other and defend one another in all things. I would swear a lie to clear any of you; and if this wouldn't do, I would put your accusers under the sand as Moses did the Egyptian. And in this way we will consecrate much unto the Lord."

The men in the parlor murmured and shifted. Emma couldn't guess whether they favored Joseph's commandment or whether it had rankled them—this license from Heaven to lie and steal. The Ten Commandments were clear. No honest God, and no true Prophet, would condone such naked mendacity. Yet she could sense a current of glee flowing up from the parlor, climbing the stairs. A few of Joseph's men surely rejoiced at his words. No doubt Brigham and John Lee were among them.

Someone said, "I can't abide such talk. Brother Joseph, how can this be of the Lord?"

A sharp crack made Emma jump—Joseph's hand coming down hard on the arm of his chair. "If one of this Danite society reveals any of these things," Joseph barked, "I will put him where the dogs cannot bite him."

When the Danites left the parlor and returned to their homes, Joseph found her waiting in their bedroom. She had already lit the lamp. She stood beside the window, arms folded tightly, scowling out at the evening sky.

"A good meeting," he said cheerily, sliding out of his blue linen coat, loosening his ascot tie.

She rounded on him. "Good? How can you say such a thing? Don't you realize what danger you've put us in? Every woman and child in this city, Joseph—your own children. You've dropped us right in our enemies' laps."

He stood still, the coat sagging from his hand to pool on the floor. He held Emma to her place with those sharp eyes that saw everything, everything except his own folly.

"You were listening," he said. "You had no right."

"God help us all, someone must listen to your words, for it's certain you will not."

"I haven't put Far West in the Enemy's way. You're fretting over nothing."

"You told your men—your armed militia—to go out and raid the Gentiles' farms."

"I didn't say so. Not in those words."

"You told them to rob and plunder, Joseph!"

He moved toward her with such sudden fury that Emma cringed. Her back struck the wall.

He said, "We're owed retribution—justice for Zion. Do you think I've forgotten my people who were abused and starved, driven from their homes? Do you think I've forgotten our men who were killed?"

She clutched her body tighter. "If we're owed justice, you must seek it in the courts."

"The courts of Missouri?" His mouth twisted on something bitter. He would have spat if he hadn't been under her roof.

"Your men will take this . . . revelation, or whatever it pleases you to call it, as license. An invitation to aggress upon our neighbors."

"Good." Joseph threw up his hands. He grinned, and his eyes were wild, his teeth bared like those of a cornered beast. "Let the Danites fall on our enemies. Missouri did us wrong and the Gentiles tried to destroy us in Kirtland. Should I lie back and allow it?"

"The Gentiles will succeed in destroying us if you give them reason to hate us. We have peace now only because they beat us soundly once before. They no longer see us as a threat. They think us a harmless absurdity, and their derision keeps us safe. Don't remind them of the past. Don't give them cause to fear us again."

He threw his coat over the foot of the bed, turning his back to Emma. "God will protect us. You heard Dr. Avard, since you were sneaking about and listening in—since you were intruding on places where no woman has any right to be. The faithful of Kirtland came to Far West, and they arrived unharmed. God has stretched His hand above us. Neither the slings nor the arrows of our enemies can touch us now."

"I heard Sidney Rigdon, too. He spoke wisely. He counseled you not to seek vengeance."

Joseph seemed to settle back on his heels. Some of his towering anger fell away, replaced by an almost childlike bewilderment. He said, "Sidney wants to grow the Latter-day Saints. As a church, I mean. He wants to increase our numbers, the numbers of apostles and priests."

"I see nothing wrong with this. It's a worthy endeavor—one that won't put the innocent at risk. So long as we do it out there, on the plains, away from Missouri."

"I'm weary of this endless organization, these ranks and orders, the ordainments, the rites."

"Weary?"

"Why did God call me as Prophet if He only meant to leave me here, making lists of apostles and seventies? I'm languishing, Emma."

She huffed a short, hard laugh. She couldn't help herself. "I never heard you moan about this in Kirtland. All those months you spent alone in your store, playing shopkeeper so you wouldn't have to face the responsibilities of a prophet—"

Now, at last, he turned to face her. His eyes were hot with fury. "Don't. Don't start this."

"And now you say you're languishing."

"God is calling me to a greater work."

"The work of plundering your neighbors?"

"The Gentiles of Missouri may live near our town, but they are not our neighbors."

Julia had wakened, thanks to his shouting. Emma could hear her whimpering in the children's room. She said impatiently, "You ought to listen more to Sidney Rigdon and a good deal less to Brigham Young."

"Sidney wants to make the impossible—a thing that can never be, as long as Man is soiled by human nature. He thinks he can build a kingdom without sin."

She strode past him, toward her children. "Whereas you merely want a kingdom."

Joseph caught her arm, spun her around to face him. Emma tore herself out of his grip with such violence that she almost fell. She could still feel the pressure of his hand—how it had circled her arm, the bigness of it, the slenderness of her body. She had never thought herself a small woman before.

"Don't speak to me that way," he hissed. "Don't ever speak to me that way again."

"You're mad," she said flatly. "Either you're mad or you're a fraud. Or both."

His face fell. He drifted back, stepping away from her, lifting his hands in a gesture that was almost pleading. "Emma, you can't think it of me—not you, not my wife."

"I may be your wife," she said over the crying of her children. "I may be your wife in God's eyes, but I don't know you, Joseph Smith. I don't know who you are anymore."

He turned very slowly toward the window. His face was pale against the dark pane of glass—pale and sober. "No," he answered softly. "You don't know me, Emma dear. I think you never did."

She didn't know him, and never had.

She didn't love him, and never had, and yet she loved him more completely than Eliza, more than any other woman could have done, more than forty-eight other women, all claiming to be his wives.

It was because she knew him so intimately that she couldn't extract this thing from her heart, the sharp, painful hindrance which for lack of a better word we must call love. Joseph was many things. Stand over his bier and say it loudly enough for all the mourners to hear. He was everything men have accused him of being. A tyrant, a fraud, and strange and compelling. He was dangerous, reckless, and you couldn't help but be drawn to him. Perhaps after all that's the nature of the divine, though it seems impossible now that her husband could have had any part in divinity—flawed as he was, terrible as he could be.

Yet if Joseph wasn't sacrosanct, then what in this world is? He could enchant the very soul up from the center of your being. He knew how to see your heart, how to speak to it, how to make you feel and feel.

The nature of divinity is mystery. It's a thing that can never be understood. The closer you come, the faster it recedes. And if you see one facet of that dark gem as clearly as you see yourself in a glass, its other faces hide themselves in shadow.

By that summer, 1838, she already carried another of Joseph's children in her belly. Another act like the others had put it there—an embrace she couldn't recall, a moment of weakness and passion that seemed as if it should have happened to some other woman. Perhaps it had.

The month of July dawned torrid and slow, each new day dragging forward into a thick, oppressive heat. A dense haze gathered over Shoal Creek, the waterway that ran through the city, and over the low, dark line of cottonwoods some miles to the east, where the Grand River cut through a dazed and sluggish prairie. By the Fourth, the sky above Far West hung low and white, pulsing with a persistent glare. But there was no real sign of rain, so the celebration went on as planned.

Together with Eliza and her friends from the women's charity, Emma spread cloths over tables made from old crates. The tables were clustered in a miserly shade below the pawpaw trees. Women and girls came out from the nearest homes carrying loaves of bread, pies, baskets full of cheeses and preserves. They streamed into the lot that would soon hold the foundation for a new temple.

Far West had organized a grand parade—not only in honor of the Declaration of Independence, but to observe the dedication of the temple's foundation stone, which Joseph would place that day in the eastern corner, in the exact spot where a white stake had been driven.

She had asked Joseph to invite the Gentiles from nearby settlements to take part in the celebration. "Let them see that we're ordinary people," she'd said. "Let us show that we're cheerful and neighborly, and our only concerns are for our church and temple." Joseph had agreed readily. It should have worried her, how quickly he'd given in. She ought to have known Joseph and his men would see a different sort of opportunity in the day.

"Bring those nut cakes over here," she called to a group of girls with heavy platters in their hands. "The shade is best in this spot. We may hope it will keep the icing from melting—the cakes look so pretty as they are—but who can say, with this devilish heat?"

Eliza bustled up to the tables carrying stacks of plates.

"Here," Emma said, "place them on this corner, beside the cakes."

"Everything looks so delightful. Do you suppose it will make a difference? Will these Gentiles love us more if we welcome them into our town?"

"I'm far more concerned about Joseph's Danites. Will they love the Gentiles more if they see them as neighbors?"

After the tables had been laid, Emma and Eliza walked to the front of the temple lot to observe the Liberty Pole—a ten-foot-high cottonwood trunk that had been stripped of its bark and sunk into the soil of the road. A small stage, no more than three feet high, had been cobbled together at the pole's base. Someone had hung a felt hat with a broad brim from the top of the pole, with red corn poppies braided around the band. The Liberty Pole towered above the grounds. Scraps of cloth had been sewn together to create long streamers, which someone had tacked up below the hat. The streamers stirred lazily on a breeze that did nothing to relieve the heat.

"I suppose," Emma said, "you were accustomed to real silk ribbons for your Maypoles during your city days. Our patchwork ribbons must seem rather drab by comparison."

Eliza sparkled with amusement. "This isn't a Maypole, but a Liberty Pole. Different rules must govern the ribbons thereupon. If I were to make any complaint at all, I would grumble over that hat. Though I suppose an ordinary farmer's gambler is the most Phrygian article a town like Far West may produce. At least the poppies are red."

They laughed together, which seemed a miracle in that miserable heat.

An hour past noon, the men of Far West vanished to assemble their parade, and a pack of wary, wide-eyed Gentiles arrived at the temple lot. There were perhaps seventy all together, more men than women. Emma had hoped for a larger feminine contingency; men were usually on edge and all too ready to bite, and none more than Missouri settlers. Each man carried a pistol at his belt or had slung a shotgun over a shoulder. Emma smiled despite the display of arms and went out to greet the newcomers with a hand outstretched to shake.

"Welcome. Welcome to Far West, our good neighbors. My name is Emma Smith. We're so pleased you've joined us for our festivities."

One of the men, broad and small-eyed like Brigham Young, stared at her hand for a long moment before he finally took it, briefly, then pulled back as if her touch had burned him. He said, "We only came over to see what you Mormonites are like. See whether there's any truth in the stories about you all."

It cost Emma every scrap of her will to keep her chin up and her smile fixed in place. "I'm confident you will find us a perfectly pleasant lot. Now please"—gesturing to the tables under the trees—"help yourselves to refreshments. The parade and dedication ceremony will begin soon."

The Missourians kept to themselves, by and large, moving together in one tight, nervous formation like a school of fish darting from the shallows. Emma watched them closely as the afternoon unfolded. Among the smiling women of Far West and their gamboling children, the Gentiles slowly relaxed. The few women they'd brought even returned the Saints' greetings. Emma heard one young Gentile with golden braids exclaim over the fine quality of a berry pie and ask the woman who'd served it how the crust had been made.

By the time the music and the procession had begun, the Gentiles seemed as comfortable among the Mormons as they were ever likely to be. They shoaled together near Emma, watching as the parade emerged a few streets away and moved with great pomp toward the temple site.

First came the youths—boys ranging in age from twelve to eighteen, all dressed in their Sunday best with smart caps and boots black as jet. They carried flags on poles that had once been the handles of garden hoes. Most sported the American flag with its twenty-six jaunty stars against the dark-blue field, but a few carried banners of cornflower blue, stitched with the seal of Missouri in yellow thread. The Gentiles seemed to approve of that display. They murmured and nodded; one man even raised an appreciative hurrah.

After the boys, the priests and apostles strutted in their ranks, column after column of sober men in fine frock coats, straight-backed and clear-eyed despite the punishing heat. Joseph walked alone, the last in that vast display of holy power, set apart from the rest. His dignity and import were undiminished by his limp. There was a stirring among the Gentiles when they saw him, for there was no mistaking the presence of a prophet. Joseph seemed to color the very air around him. He thickened the stuff of reality.

The Danites rode at his back, at least eight hundred men armed and mounted. Emma felt dizzy at the sight. Never had she imagined Joseph had recruited so many men to his militia. The Danites laughed, spurring their horses to make them dance. They lifted fists into the air, shouting "Victory!" and "Joseph Smith or the sword!" The Gentiles drew more tightly together. She could feel a current of fear pass through them. She could all but hear their thoughts. *Have these Mormons brought us here to be slaughtered? Have we been deceived?*

It's I who was deceived, Emma told herself. *Joseph spat on my attempt to make peace with our neighbors. He has taken my offering of goodwill and twisted it to his own purpose, seized a chance to terrorize the settlers. We will never know peace again.*

"There's nothing to fear," she said. But if the Gentiles heard, they gave no sign.

Sidney Rigdon mounted the stage beside the Liberty Pole. The brass band fell silent; the watchers settled expectantly.

"Friends and fellow citizens." Sidney's voice carried easily above the crowd. "I am called upon to address you this day under circumstances novel to myself, and I presume as much so to the most of you—for however frequently we may have met with our fellow citizens in times past, in the places of our nativity, to mingle our feelings with theirs and unite in grateful acknowledgment to our Divine Benefactor on the anniversary of our national existence. But never before have we been assembled by reason of our holy religion, for which cause alone a very large majority of us is here this day."

Sidney continued at great length, extolling the many blessings of American liberty, dwelling on the lot of the Mormons—who had left their original homes to follow the dictates of their faith, facing trials wherever they had settled. He went on to speak of the affection all Latter-day Saints held for their religion, and their delightful anticipation at building a new temple on the very spot where they now stood.

Despite the uneasiness the Danites had inspired, the Gentiles seemed to warm again to Sidney's oration. It was a marginal thaw, to say the least, but it heartened Emma. The Missourians were not unreasonable people. They could be won over, turned from enemies to friends, if only Mormons and Gentiles could see eye to eye.

The speech wore on so long that the crowd grew restless. Children whined and tugged at their mothers' skirts. The boys from the parade began to kick each other's boots and clatter their flagpoles together in mock battle. Emma suppressed a sigh, and Eliza, swaying a little beside her, hid a yawn behind a hand.

Joseph, who had been standing beside the white stake, caught Sidney's eye and signaled with a nod.

At once, Sidney pulled himself up straighter on the platform. He loomed above the crowd. The tone of his speech shifted on the instant. "Our God has promised us a reward of eternal inheritance. Though we wade through great tribulation, we are in nothing discouraged, for we know that promise is faithful. The promise is sure, and the reward is certain. It is because of God's assurance that we have suffered the spoiling of our goods. Our cheeks have been given to the smiters, and our heads to those who would pluck us bald. We have not only turned our cheek when smitten, but we have done it again and again—until we are weary of being smitten, and tired of being trampled upon."

The settlers muttered. Eliza was suddenly alert. She stared at Emma, cheeks draining of color. Emma could only shake her head in helpless disbelief.

"We have proved the world with kindness," Sidney said. "We have suffered this abuse without cause, and endured without resentment until this day, and still the persecution and violence does not cease. But from this day and this hour, we will suffer it no more."

Eliza pulled Emma close. "God have mercy, we must stop this. What is Sidney thinking? What is Joseph thinking?"

Sidney spoke more loudly still. "We take God and all the holy angels to witness this day. We warn all men in the name of Jesus Christ to afflict us no more forever. For from this very hour, we shall bear it no more, our rights shall no more be trampled on with impunity. The man or set of men who attempts it does so at the expense of their lives."

Emma gasped. She spun to face the Gentiles, but they had already forgotten her. They had closed in a tight fist, women at the center, every man with his hand upon a gun.

"Go," she said to Eliza. "To Joseph. Tell him to stop this. He must stop before it's too late!"

Eliza darted off, shoving through the crowd. But Sidney spoke on, and the Danites on their horses had begun to laugh and cheer his words. The men grinned; there were shouts of "Amen!" from the Mormons, and "Devils, the lot of them!"

"And the mob that comes on us to disturb us—it shall be between us and them a war of extermination, for we will follow them till the last drop of their blood is spilled, or else they will have to exterminate us, for we will carry the seat of war to their own houses, and their own families, and one party or the other shall be destroyed."

Emma took the nearest Missourian by the sleeve of his coat. "Please, I knew nothing of this. You must believe me. I would never condone such threats. Our women and children are innocent—as innocent as your own."

The man shook her off. "You lured us here to be insulted and threatened."

"Go now," she said. "I beg you. If you leave at once, the men will let you pass. Only don't draw your weapons."

"We will never be the aggressors," Sidney boomed. "We will infringe on the rights of no people but shall stand for our own until death. We claim our own rights and are willing that all others shall enjoy theirs."

This sop was too little, and offered too late. Some of the Missouri men had already raised their pistols. A red roar filled Emma's head, almost loud enough to drown out that hateful sermon. The Gentile women were clawing at their men, pleading with them to holster their guns. The Mormons had finally begun to notice their visitors' distress. The crowd had pulled away, reeling back from the Gentiles, opening the way for their retreat. The Missourians glanced at one another as Sidney went on, making a silent consultation among themselves: retreat, or open fire on the Mormons?

"We therefore take all men to record. We proclaim our liberty on this day, as did our fathers. And we pledge this day to one another, our fortunes, our lives, and our sacred honors, to be delivered from the persecutions which we have had to endure for the last nine years, or nearly that. Neither will we indulge any man, or set of men, to cheat us of our rights. We this day proclaim ourselves free with a purpose and a determination that can never be broken. No, never! No, never! No, never!"

The Gentiles broke, hurrying through a gap in the crowd to the open street beyond. As they fled, the Danites chanted, "Never! Never! Never!"

"How could you be so reckless? How could you be so stupid, Joseph, so damnably naïve?"

There was a glass dish in her hand, a little hobnail pitcher from her dressing stand. The studs in the glass bit into her palm, for she gripped it so tightly she might have shattered the thing. She wanted to throw it—at Joseph, at the floor or the wall where it would burst with all the sharp rage and noise inside of her.

"Put that down," he shouted. "You're out of control, Emma!"

"I? I am out of control?" Thank God Eliza had taken the children to Jerusha's house. Emma couldn't have stopped herself from screaming. She never liked to shout where the children could hear, but her throat was raw already. "*I'm* out of control, and yet you told Sidney to—"

"Those were all his words, not mine."

"What sort of fool do you take me for? Every word breathed within this church is yours. You have made us what we are—you, and no one else. And now you've made us all corpses!"

He took a cautious step toward her. She raised the pitcher above her head; he backed away again.

"The Gentiles will keep to their places now," Joseph said. "They won't try us—not now they've seen our numbers and our strength. Word will spread to the rest of the county, then across the state."

"Oh, yes. Word will spread. You watch and see how it spreads. Like a brushfire."

"In Jesus's name, take hold of yourself." He sounded merely annoyed with her now, as if her fear and rage were over something trivial—a spider dangling in a corner, a mouse in the pantry.

"I would tell *you* to take hold of yourself, but it's far too late for that. It's too late for us all. You've signed the death warrant of every man, woman, and child in this city, Joseph Smith."

He came to her again, hands outstretched as if she were some untamed, dangerous animal. She liked it, the wariness in his eyes, the way his fingers trembled when he reached for her. She would have danced back, away from his touch, but the stifling heat held her in place, a charge of tension all around. Something was pressing against the walls of the house, kicking and striking and lashing at them.

He took the pitcher from her hand. She surrendered it easily, and hated herself for giving in. Joseph returned the pitcher to the dressing table with meticulous care. Then he took Emma gently by the shoulders. He held her lightly, smiling down, almost as if he loved her.

"Emma, dear. You must trust me. You know I speak with the Lord's voice. Don't you trust in God?"

She breathed deeply. The tremor left her limbs. She looked up into those eyes that could see everything, except what he didn't wish to see. Then she slapped him. So hard he staggered sideways. Her palm burned from the strike.

Joseph pressed a hand against his cheek. He stared at her, wiped clean of all expression. She would have preferred it if he had flared up in hate. But he was cold now, detached.

Emma fell at once to her knees. "Forgive me! I was wrong. Forgive me, Joseph, please." She didn't know then—she doesn't know now—why such fear and self-loathing took her. Perhaps she believed in that moment that Joseph truly was the anointed of God. Perhaps she read some omen in the day—that wasted day. She felt herself—felt the whole church, which was her world—staggering on the edge of a precipice and knew that everything would fall.

He turned without a word. He made for their bedroom door. Before he reached it, the pressure finally broke. The air shattered in a flash of white light, in a shuddering roar that shook the house and beat her to the floor. Seconds later, she realized she had screamed again—this time in terror, certain God had sent down one of His vast and final punishments, and the Last Days had come. There was a high, piercing whine in her ears, but it dissipated, and then she could hear the pounding of rain on the roof—a torrential rain, enough to flood the world. She had thrown up her arms to shield her face. When she lowered them, Joseph was gone.

In the morning, after the storm passed, the Mormons came out of their homes to survey the damage. Rain had sheeted down all night, stripping leaves from trees, flattening the crops in fields and gardens, turning livestock pens and roads to mud. Shoal Creek had surged beyond its banks. The wells were bitter, clouded by grit.

In the ruined street at the edge of the temple lot, the Liberty Pole lay splintered and blackened, its bright streamers stained by mud and burned by the fires of Heaven. She stood over it, clutching Eliza's hand.

"Farewell to our liberties in Missouri," Eliza said.

Emma shivered in the morning chill.

What crouched, terrible days of waiting followed. And worse was yet to come. Emma could feel that certainty as sharply as she felt the child fluttering in her belly.

You wouldn't believe her if she told you how much time passed. From July to the end of October—almost four months in all. The child grew as if nothing in the world were wrong, as if his parents' marriage were still as whole as it had ever been. In all that time, the Mormons recovered from the storm as best they could, the summer wore on, the fields flushed with green. The church forgot how the Gentiles had clutched at their guns, though Emma never forgot. That storm had been an omen. If Joseph could read the signs of God—if any boy could look up to find scrolls among the stars—then why couldn't Emma do the same? In four months' time she never stopped hearing the thunder. She never forgot the sight of their liberties burned in the mud.

Joseph spoke to her but little, and only when he had no other choice. Most nights, he slept on the sofa in the parlor, which suited Emma well. At least Eliza was some comfort. She never left Emma's side during the day, a constant bastion of sympathetic silence, a hand on her shoulder when the tears came and Emma hung her head, bowing to shame or fear. If some message needed carrying to Joseph, Eliza went to him. When Emma could no longer stand the sight of her husband, nor the feel of him brooding behind his office door, Eliza took her strolling outdoors. Their arms were linked together. She always had a smile and a kiss for Emma's cheek.

Once Emma said to her, mildly, "Why are you still here?"

"Whatever do you mean?"

"Why do you continue to live with us, terrible as we've become? I know it can't be comfortable to remain with Joseph and me. We're furious with one another, and I don't know if we shall ever mend. And why did you come all this way from Kirtland? Why any of this, Eliza?"

She laughed lightly. "Because," she said, "you are the sister of my heart. Sisters can't be parted so easily."

It was Eliza who held her up that day at the end of October, when a rider came in from the north on a horse wet with lather, crying out for the Danites, for Joseph, for God. The Mormon settlement of Adam-ondi-Ahman, some twenty miles away, had fallen under siege by the county militia.

"God preserve us," Emma said faintly. "This. This is the blow I knew would fall, that day when the storm came." At last she could see the cliff's edge, and over its sharp, stony lip, the fall that waited, the endless plunging into a black pit forever.

"Wait and see," Eliza said. "Our people have weathered sieges before."

"Find Joseph. He's up in his office, if I know him. And I do know him still, Eliza, better than anyone. Go and fetch him. He must hear the news. He must see that rider's face for himself and hear the terror in his voice. Joseph must face what he has done, or we'll have no hope of peace, not now, not ever again."

And what had Joseph done? What had he made that day outside

the temple lot—what fate had he molded for his people like clay in a clenched fist?

Lilburn Boggs. Governor, by that time, of all Missouri. Boggs had never forgotten the conflict between Zion and Independence. After Joseph's display on the Fourth of July, after Sidney Rigdon's open threats, the Gentiles had petitioned the governor for protection. Four months, or near enough—that was how long it took for Lilburn Boggs to approach the courts for aid and hear their final ruling: the Mormons' rights as citizens of America and the state of Missouri must not be infringed. Boggs wouldn't be deterred, however, not even by the law. He took matters into his own hands. Such was the power he held as governor of Missouri. He issued an executive order to skirt the judge's ruling.

The Mormons are to be treated as enemies and must be exterminated or driven from the state if necessary, for the public peace. Their outrages are beyond all description.

What could Joseph do under the shadow of extermination? He placed John Lee at the head of the Danites, and the militia rode north to try to break the siege on Adam-ondi-Ahman and free our people, save them from the wolves. The rest of us knelt in the meetinghouse, or at the cornerstone in the empty temple lot. We prayed.

Joseph was quiet that night after he received the news, after the Danite force had gone. He sat alone in the parlor. The fire crackled and dimmed beside him. In an agony of knowing, Emma paced the hall between parlor and kitchen. She felt the drag of gravity, a rush of blackness around her. She knew the depth of the pit. She paced, and asked herself whether Joseph would welcome her if she went to him now and sank to her knees, laid her head in his lap, and wept—for what? Not his forgiveness. For his understanding. For some acknowledgment of what must surely follow.

Eliza took her by the hand, led her up the stairs to her room. She helped Emma undress, then tucked her into bed.

"I know you're afraid," Eliza said, smiling gently, like a mother to a child. "I am afraid, too, now and then, when I think too long on our predicament. You will drive yourself mad with worry unless you occupy yourself."

"How? How can any of us think of anything but Adam-ondi-Ahman? Some of them may be shot already, they may be dead—"

"Hush. Strong women work. They do not weep and carry on. In the morning, you and I shall make plans for the future."

Bitterly, Emma said, "What future?"

"Any at all. That's how we keep going. We will organize the women of this town toward good work. And we will not let go of our hopes for tomorrow."

The women of Far West spun wool into yarn. They knitted warm stockings and gloves and hats for the Danites, for winter was peering around the corner with its white-frosted eyes, and God alone could say how long the siege would last. They collected old coats from the priests and apostles. They smoked meat and dried apples, baked hard bread that would last for months in a saddle bag. They coated wheels of cheese with wax and dried eggs to powder. They broke the metal from rakes and garden forks so the blacksmiths could make bullets and blades. The women tore their children's baby dresses into strips and rolled them for bandages. They ground herbs and roots, medicine for the field—coneflower, willow bark, valerian, oregano to wash wounds and keep infection at bay. They cared for one another's children so everyone could lend a hand. Side by side, the way sisters do, they toiled and organized. They planned. And when one woman stopped suddenly, covering her face with work-hardened hands, a dozen sisters flocked to her side, soothing her tears, bracing her spirit, leading her back to the cause.

For eleven days, the women gathered at the heart of Far West, preparing for war, while the companies of Danites who'd stayed to defend the city patrolled its borders. These were gray days, and heavy. The brittle air, the smell of burning, the sun rolling low across the sky. The nights were long and subdued. When the children were safely in bed, Emma and Eliza sank into their chairs beside the parlor fire, too weary for words. Their red hands curled in their laps. But Eliza had been right. The work was a welcome distraction. Emma felt . . . not in control, certainly not that. God Himself wasn't in control now. But she felt a little stronger than she had that day when the rider had come from the settlement. She wasn't without a small, fragile hope.

On the twelfth day, she sat on the floor of her parlor with some dozen women and girls, rolling bandages and packing them into leather bags to be carried to the settlement. Even little Julia helped. The girl had taken to relief work with a focus few seven-year-olds could match.

The front door swung open so suddenly that the women started; some cried out, afraid Governor Boggs and his militia had descended on Far West. But the next moment they saw Joseph on the threshold. He was grinning.

Julia leaped to her feet. "What is it, Papa?"

"I bring good news," he said. "Riders have just come from Adam-ondi-Ahman. John Lee and Sampson Avard have met with success. They've negotiated with General Doniphan of the Missouri militia. The siege on Adam-ondi-Ahman is lifted. Our people have been permitted to leave unharmed; they're making their way to Far West now, under protection of the Danites. They'll live here with us."

The women wept in gratitude. Laughter filled the parlor.

Emma rose to her feet. "You bring the most welcome news I've ever heard, Joseph." It had been so many months since she had spoken to him in kindness—so long since he had smiled at Emma. She almost felt like a girl of twenty-one again, walking with him up the hunter's path, watching him caper in the snow.

He lifted Julia and spun her around, then held her on his hip. "From what I've heard, this General Doniphan is a fine, upstanding man. He respects the law of the land, and doesn't countenance these rash actions by Lilburn Boggs, nor does he approve of militias menacing citizens."

Emma said, "Whoever could have predicted we would find an ally among the Gentiles?"

The women began to clear away the scraps from their work. Joseph set Julia on her feet; she scampered off to bring the news to her brothers.

Then he took Emma's hands. How had they ever quarreled? There was only peace between them, a warmth so glad and wholesome, all the bitterness that had plagued them through the autumn seemed impossible now. The women made their farewells, and soon enough, Emma and Joseph were alone.

"I pray this will be an end to it," she said. "The violence, the hatred. I pray that God will soften our neighbors' hearts and cause them to look on us with sympathy. We're no threat to the Gentiles. Surely, they will understand that now. This General Doniphan can speak on our behalf. He can make them see the truth."

"John Lee and Sampson Avard have proven themselves as leaders," he said. "They've impressed me. I intend to reward them both. Such fine fellows deserve a reward, don't you think?"

"Special appointments in the church, perhaps."

"I'd thought to make them commanders of the Danites."

"Perhaps it's time we said farewell to the Danites," she said carefully. "They nearly cost lives at Adam-ondi-Ahman."

"They saved lives. If not for the Danites' presence, the Gentiles would have felt free to do whatever they pleased. No, Emma—we must keep a strong militia of our own. But now we know we've a friend in Doniphan. He'll be our voice when the state won't listen to us directly. Governor Boggs won't ignore a general."

"And if you turn over command of the Danites to other men . . . Will they lead as wisely as you would have done?" She hadn't much confidence in the wisdom of Joseph's leadership—not where the militia was concerned—but flattery was often the only way to make him listen. He was no different from most men in that regard. "Sampson Avard is hungry for recognition. He's a good enough doctor, I'll grant you that, but he clamors for attention during the meetings. There isn't a drop of humility in him."

He tapped her lightly on the nose, a gesture so affectionate it made her blush. "If that's so, then Sampson will have all the recognition he desires when I name him commander. It's a high honor, after all."

"We must pray he'll be satisfied with the honor. We must pray he won't develop any cravings for glory in battle."

"And John," Joseph said good-naturedly, "what's your complaint against him?"

Emma stared pensively into the fire. "John has never pleased me."

He chuckled. "Shall I try to explain that to him? 'I've made Sampson a commander of the Danites, but not you, good fellow; Emma doesn't find you pleasing.'"

"Don't tease, Joseph. I'm trying to put my finger on what I don't like about that man. He stares. At me—at all the women. And his eyes are cold. Heartless."

"John is serious; I'll give you that much. But there's no wickedness in him. He has heart aplenty, Emma. He just doesn't like to show it. Most men are the same."

"He always agrees with Brigham."

Joseph bellowed with laughter. "I count that a mark in his favor."

"Brigham is hot-headed and spoiling for a fight."

"What, right now?"

"At every moment."

"Brigham kept peace ably when he brought you and the children out of Kirtland." Joseph grew somber. "I owe him much for that—perhaps even more than I owe to Sampson and John. Emma, I know we've had our difficult times. But God brought us together for a reason. Trust in the Lord, even if you still can't bring yourself to trust me."

She threw up her hands. "Do as you please. Maybe I'm only fretting because we've lived under this great strain for so long."

"That's it," he said. "Your spirits will lift, by and by."

Then he kissed her tenderly—on the lips, a thing he hadn't done for so long, it made her face burn. This wasn't the heat of a girlish infatuation. It was a flush of shock, almost outrage. She thought of Don Carlos at the edge of his field, back in Kirtland, in a violet dusk—insects humming in the tall grass, tears drying on her cheeks, the easy silence between them after he'd said, *If I had a wife, I would leave this church for good.*

But she was the wife of another man. She was the elect lady, bound to the Prophet, for better and worse. Emma prayed she'd seen the worst already, and only better days lay ahead.

She threw herself into the work of housing the refugees from Adam-ondi-Ahman. The weather had already turned and the ground was too hard for digging foundations, so Far West was obliged to make room for the castoffs among the homes and barns that already stood.

Emma led the women in surveying available space. She kept a careful tally of spare rooms and attics, hunters' cots, empty hay lofts. Disused wagons could be broken apart, their wood used to build new rooms in the barns and goat sheds at the edges of the town. These were primitive accommodations, but with luck, they'd be sturdy enough to last until spring.

On a gray day, while Emma directed her volunteers in measuring the loft of Heber Kimball's barn, young Sarah Ann Whitney idled at the haymow door, swinging it open and closed so the weak November light fanned and narrowed across the dim space.

Suddenly the girl stopped. Emma looked around and saw Sarah Ann peering out through the door with curious intensity. "What is it, Sarah Ann?"

"There's a fuss down at the house—riders. They look like Danites to me."

Emma hurried to the door, pushed it open wider. A handful of Danites milled outside the Kimball home. Their horses were lathered from a long, hard ride, and even at a distance, she could tell the men were agitated.

Vilate Kimball slid between Emma and the girl. "They're speaking with my husband," she said. "Heber looks upset. Has there been some trouble?"

From farther in the loft, one of the other women said, "Surely the Gentiles aren't marching on us again. What of the other settlements? Haun's Mill and DeWitt—"

"Hush," Emma said, not unkindly. "There's no sense in frightening ourselves. Let's go down together and learn what we may."

By the time the women had descended from the loft and stepped out into the yard, the Danites were riding away, and Heber had already fetched his rifle from the house.

"Heber," Vilate cried, "what is it?"

He took his wife under one arm, regarding the rest of the volunteers soberly. "Ladies, I'm sorry to be the one to give such dreadful news."

"Has there been another attack?" Eliza said. "Another siege?"

He smiled grimly. "There has been an attack, surely enough. But this time, those devils are the ones who've been whipped and beaten. John Lee and Sampson Avard have led an assault on the town of Gallatin. They've destroyed it utterly. Drove out all the Gentiles, burned their storehouses and homes, trampled the ashes into dust."

Emma pressed her notebook tightly against her stomach. The women clutched one another, murmuring in fear.

"They'll come right back at us!" Vilate was weeping now. "They'll do to us what they did to Zion!"

"This is dreadful news," Eliza said. "The Gentiles won't take this insult lying down."

"Joseph is behind this," Emma muttered to Eliza. "I'd bet on that. Will that man never learn? Go and find him. I must keep the others from losing their wits. Tell him he must call a town meeting this very hour, so we may sort out what's to be done. For we'll be forced to act, one way or another."

By early afternoon, the meetinghouse had filled. The congregation lined the walls and packed the aisles between the pews. Someone had raised the sashes on all the windows, for there were so many bodies packed inside that the meetinghouse had grown too warm. Mormons lingered outside the open windows and around the doors, straining to hear over the noise of the crowd.

Joseph addressed them all from behind the altar. "I know many of you are startled by this news. None of us has forgotten how Zion suffered—none shall ever forget! The enemy tried to humble us again at Adam-ondi-Ahman, but we prevailed."

Emma clenched her fists to keep herself from shouting. *We were driven out of Adam-ondi-Ahman. This is your own pride, Joseph Smith, not some divine retribution—and pride comes before a fall.*

He shook his fist. "God has strengthened the hand of the righteous, just as He told me He would do. I promised you once, brethren, that Zion would not go unavenged."

Cheers answered, but Emma heard just as many Saints muttering. Then, from somewhere close behind her, the commotion of a man rising to his feet from a crowded bench.

"This is folly, Joseph, and you know it."

There was no need for Emma to look around. She knew Don Carlos's voice; she could feel it thrumming in her blood. She willed herself to greater stillness, kept her eyes fixed on the pinewood altar.

Softly, Joseph said, "My brother. It pains my heart, that you of all men would speak so openly against me."

"Someone must. We've only just dodged a battle at Adam-ondi-Ahman. We should have counted ourselves lucky to leave it at that. Yet here you are, pressing our luck, only a few days later. And now you've pressed our luck so hard, I fear you've broken it for good."

"Hear, hear," someone called.

"Be not afraid." Joseph lifted his voice. "Know ye not that we are God's people? The Last Days are upon us, brethren! We know that neighbor shall turn against neighbor and army against army before Christ returns. But we know, too, that the Lord preserves the faithful. Bear up in the face of your fears! Hold fast against the enemy, for the glorious return is at hand! Are ye not Latter-day Saints? What is another day's struggle, or another year's, when we know that a millennium of perfect peace waits just ahead?"

"We're already hard-pressed to shelter the refugees," Don Carlos said. "What shall we do if the Gentiles retaliate by driving everyone out of DeWitt or Haun's Mill? We can't house them all. Some of our people will be left out in the snow."

Shouts from outside the meetinghouse grew so loud that the crowd inside fell quiet. The Saints nearest the windows craned their necks to see.

Someone called, "There are Danites in the road. Dozens of them— scores. They have wagons piled high. And stock! They're driving stock along the roads. Horses, cattle, hogs."

Don Carlos shouted, "Joseph, what is this?"

"A consecration unto the Lord. God promised us victory, an avengement for Zion. Once I gave ye Saints a revelation, but now I see that few among you had ears to hear. Once God said unto thee: 'The destroyer I have sent forth to lay waste to mine enemies. Not many years hence they shall not be left to mar my heritage.' The Destroyer has come. The Angel has ridden forth to do God's bidding. Everything of value in Gallatin belongs to us now, by God's decree. The Lord did not forget what was due the wretched, even if ye have forgotten."

Early the next morning, half concealed behind a cold gray mist, she stood with Don Carlos at the edge of the temple lot, watching as a long train of wagons left Far West forever. The Danites' plundering was more than some of Joseph's followers could bear. Emma counted the wagons as they rumbled past. She stopped counting at ninety-three, and still they came, a river of defectors.

Don Carlos sighed. "At least we'll find plenty of room for the refugees now. All these houses emptied."

"It's the rift at Kirtland all over again. I could spit. I could curse Joseph's name, if I were the cursing kind."

"I could wish you were among them." Don Carlos nodded at the wagons. He and Emma didn't look at one another and stood no closer than they dared. "You and your children. I would see you out of harm's way if it were my choice to make."

"You could have gone anywhere after Kirtland was destroyed. Why did you follow Joseph to Far West?"

He was silent for a long moment. The wagons rumbled on the road. At length, he said, "I went where my heart directed."

"You're a good brother to me."

She heard him breathe in once, sharply.

Emma said, "I would also wish myself away from Far West. My children, certainly. But where might I go? How can I provide for my children without Joseph's help? No good will come of this. We may pray for wisdom and temperance. We may pray that we can salvage some sort of peace. I see little hope for anything else."

Don Carlos turned to her suddenly. "Go with them. Please, Emma. There's still time. Any one of these families would make room for you and the children in their wagon. You're well loved by all of them, even if Joseph is not."

"I can't. Not in my present condition. I'm six months with child, and Alexander is still so small. I can't risk him or the new baby to winter on the road. And these people will meet violence along the way, wherever they're going, however long it takes them to get there. I don't like it any more than you, but my only real choice is to remain here and hope."

"Hope?" He laughed sourly. "What hope can we find now?"

She would have taken his hand to comfort him if she could have survived his touch. "We must pray General Doniphan will intercede on our behalf. At least we have one powerful friend among the Gentiles."

"Do you know what I will pray for?" Don Carlos smiled. There was neither amusement nor peace in his expression. "I pray that these wagons will keep coming and coming. I pray that everyone will leave— everyone. I pray that good sense will finally take the place of witless faith. I would see this church broken apart for good, and scattered so widely it's forgotten for all time. Not even a memory should remain."

"Surely not all your memories have been hard ones."

She could feel the desperate intensity of his eyes, but she wouldn't turn to look at him, not again.

"What if my wish comes true, Emma? What if the church breaks apart, and everyone leaves Joseph? Will you leave him, too, or will you stay by his side, even then?"

She had no chance to answer. A rifle cracked from somewhere close by; Emma and Don Carlos both spun in panic, searching for the shooter. Oxen and horses threw up their heads. Women in carts pushed their children down into the beds.

It was no Gentile invasion. Brigham Young came stalking down the road with several of the Danites on foot behind him. The muzzle of his rifle exhaled a blue line of smoke. "The last man has run away from Far West that's going to run! The next one of you who leaves this town shall be pursued and brought back, dead or alive!"

"That devil," Don Carlos muttered.

"I move a resolution," Brigham shouted, "that if anyone attempts to leave this county or even packs his things for that purpose, then any man who sees it shall, without saying anything to any other person, kill him and haul him aside into the brush. All the burial he shall have will be in a buzzard's guts! Nothing will be left of him but his bones!"

"Lord preserve us," Emma said. "Will no one stop him?"

Don Carlos nodded across the road, though Emma could see little through the column of wagons except the faint suggestion of cabins and chicken coops, gray in the mist. "Joseph," he said, "coming out of the meetinghouse."

Joseph emerged from between two halted wagons. He approached Brigham and his Danite friends with his hands outstretched, a placating gesture. Brigham shook his fist, raised his rifle above his head, hunched his shoulders and finally turned away. He vanished in the fog between the cabins. The Danites followed.

The wagons rolled on. Joseph stood with his arms folded, a lone figure in the mist, watching the dissenters fall away.

Did Joseph see the danger then, or was it only much later that he came to understand his folly? Even now, she can't decide. In the days after the exodus from Far West, while the remainder of the town prepared for another siege, he was light of spirit. He gave every appearance of confidence, and even slept soundly at Emma's side, murmuring and smiling in his dreams, while she lay awake almost until the rooster's crow, fearing for her children, doubting even God Himself could preserve them from what was to come.

On a Sunday, on the Sabbath, she and Eliza led the children warily through the white-frosted streets toward the meetinghouse. But the hall was empty.

"Everyone must have stayed home," Eliza said, "to prepare for . . . for the coming winter." Neither of them liked to speak of the Gentiles where the children could hear.

"It's a sin to work on the Sabbath," Julia said.

Emma sighed. "God will make an exception when our needs are pressing."

"No, He won't, Mother. A sin is a sin."

Eliza murmured, "Some needs are so great, they might provide absolution."

A chorus of cheers and good-natured taunts rose up from the rear of the meetinghouse.

Emma and Eliza glanced at one another.

"Is that Papa?" Julia asked. "I thought I heard Papa's voice."

They hurried around the corner of the meetinghouse. In the rear yard they came upon a circle of men—Danites, every one—stripped to their shirtsleeves, tussling like boys. They were jeering at two who grappled in the center of their ring: Joseph and Lyman Wight. Lyman swiped at Joseph's shoulder, but he danced back, then charged in again. Despite the old limp, Joseph was quick on his feet. His great size gave him the advantage. He struck quick as a rattlesnake, seizing Lyman by the back of his neck, and soon had the other man's head locked under his arm.

"I surrender!" Lyman shouted.

Joseph released him. Laughing, Lyman pulled his breeches straight and did his best to tame his hair.

"Mother of mercy," Emma said quietly. "If they must break the Sabbath, at least they could help with the preparations. We need every hand that can be spared."

"Who can throw the Prophet," Joseph shouted.

The Danites chanted their answer: "No one! No one!"

The rear door of the meetinghouse banged open. Young Joseph squealed and hid behind Emma's skirt. But it was only Sidney Rigdon, dressed for meeting in his black pulpit coat and wide-brimmed hat. He came down the steps into the yard. "What is the meaning of this," Sidney cried. He shoved through the Danites, into the ring. "You are breaking the Sabbath, and I'll not suffer it!"

"I told them to wrestle," Joseph said. "They've been sitting about looking mournful and cold. I told them, 'Get up, run, jump, do anything but mope around. Warm yourselves up; inactivity will not do for soldiers.' You know we must be on our guard, Brother Sidney."

"You are not even in your coat," Sidney said, "and this a Sunday!"

The Danites groaned. They waved at Sidney as if the old preacher were a bothersome gnat.

Sidney was undeterred. "What example do you set for your people? And where is your congregation, Joseph? This laxity of spirit will not—"

Joseph lurched toward him suddenly, arms ready in a wrestler's stance. The Danites howled with anticipation. "Brother Sidney, you had better get out of here and let these boys alone. They're amusing themselves according to my orders. You're an old man. You go and get ready for meeting if it pleases you."

"What meeting shall we have? The whole congregation is shirking the Sabbath!"

One of the Danites called, "The whole congregation is cowering in fear. But we don't fear!" The men cheered.

"I call this sacrilege," Sidney began.

He never finished. Joseph's long arm darted; he knocked the hat from Sidney's head. Joseph struck at Sidney again, pinning both shoulders under one arm. He gripped the old man's pulpit coat at the collar. With a sound like a wild animal tearing into a carcass, the fine dark silk parted. Sidney cried out as the buttons burst down his chest.

Eliza covered Julia's eyes with her hand.

"Go on, boys," Joseph said to his clamoring Danites. "Have your fun. And never let it be said that Joseph Smith got you into any trouble that he didn't get you out of."

XI

The Refiner's Fire

1838–1839

You remember where you were and what you were doing when the worst news comes. There are certain breeds of monster who rear their heads to howl, and you know there can be no more looking away. You remember every detail of that moment when your devils of fear come to life.

She was spinning by the fire. The wool was sliding easily through her hands, and the heat of the fire on her back raised beads of sweat that ran down the straightness of her spine. Eliza was in the kitchen, cutting onions for the next day's soup and singing—not a song from Emma's hymnal, but one she'd learned in the world beyond Far West. The song reminded Emma that there was another world indeed, that somewhere past the edge of darkness, bright things still existed. *I know a bank where the wild thyme blows, where oxlips and the nodding violet grows.*

The wool drafted like an easy breath. She paused in her spinning, pulled a nep from the fleece and tossed it into the fire. It smoldered, filling the parlor with the rank smell of singe. The door opened, and Joseph staggered in. He was carrying a child in his arms, a boy with dark hair and white face. Emma remembered the stricken father in the Kirtland meetinghouse, the dead child with stiff arm and blue skin. She thought, *It's all happening again. It never stopped—none of it. Nothing ever ends.* Then the boy turned his head and looked at her with vacant, hopeless eyes.

She stood so quickly that the stool tipped over behind her. "For heaven's sake, what has happened?"

"I don't know," Joseph said. "None of us has learned yet, but they're at the meetinghouse with Brigham and Sidney and—"

"Who is at the meetinghouse?"

"Three from Haun's Mill. One man, shot in the leg, and two women who helped him get here. This boy was with them."

He laid the boy on the parlor sofa. His trousers and shirt were stained with something dark, rust brown. Mud, Emma thought. Then she realized it wasn't.

"I must go back," Joseph said. "Something terrible has happened, but we can't get anything from the poor wretches yet. None of them seems able to speak a word, except to tell us they've come from Haun's Mill. This boy seems uninjured, but he won't speak. See what you can do for him, Emma. Maybe you can learn what has happened. Come and find me the moment you know."

She knelt beside the sofa and Eliza was there, too, pressing her hand against the boy's forehead. The child stared up at the ceiling. He never blinked, never moved, except for the shallow rise and fall of his chest.

"What has happened?" Emma asked gently. "Can't you speak to us, son? We'll never hurt you."

"Mother?"

Emma turned. Julia and Young Joseph were standing beside the hearth, hand in hand, dressed in their white nightgowns.

"Go up to bed," Eliza told them.

Instead, the children crept forward. They came to stand between Emma and Eliza, looking down at the stricken child who lay on the sofa as if on a bier.

Julia took the boy's hand. "You're safe now. My mother and Aunt Eliza are good."

He turned his face toward the sound of her voice. He met Young Joseph's eye, and slowly the vacant expression left him, replaced by a sharp and terrible knowing. The boy and Young Joseph stared at one another for a heartbeat. Then his eyes closed, his face contorted with some inward agony, and sobs began to shake his thin body. Young Joseph put his arms around the boy's neck. Julia sank to her knees, resting her cheek on his stomach.

"Broth," Emma said to Eliza. "And bread and water. We must feed this poor little scrap and give him something clean to wear. Then, when he feels strong enough, we'll hear what he has to say."

By and by, they coaxed the boy to sit up and drink a bowl of broth. Then Eliza carried him into the kitchen, where she stripped off his clothes and washed him in the old copper tub while Emma found one of

Julia's nightgowns for the boy to wear. He was bigger than Julia, some ten or eleven years old, but she thought the long linen shirt would fit him well enough. When the boy was cleaned and dressed, they returned him to the parlor sofa. Emma sent Young Joseph and Julia upstairs. The boy no longer stared with blank devastation. He had collected his wits, and no good mother would allow her children to hear whatever tale the waif was about to tell.

The three of them sat on the sofa, watching the flames shiver in the hearth—Emma and Eliza to either side, the boy between them, very white and still with his hands folded in his lap.

"My name is Willard Smith." His voice was high and small. It seemed as if the popping of cinders in the fireplace could drown him out. He spoke with careful precision, as if he had rehearsed the words, and all the while he stared into the fire. "I come from Haun's Mill. I was sent here to tell the Prophet because I'm one of the only men who wasn't shot dead."

Emma looked at Eliza. The color had drained from her face. She was watching the boy, her mouth working soundlessly, trying to summon up a question, a word of comfort.

"You had better tell us," Emma said faintly, "everything you know."

"I'm supposed to tell the Prophet."

"I'm his wife. So it's the next best thing, to tell me. Come, now. No one will be cross if you tell me first."

Willard's hands twisted together in his lap. He frowned at the flames. Then he drew a deep breath, exhaled slowly. "Two days ago, I guess it was, a pack of Gentiles came out of the woods a little before sunset. We guessed there was about two hundred and fifty of them. And we had all known that they might be coming, like they did at Adam-ondi-Ahman, but they didn't just surround us and mock us or try to make us hide in our houses. They came right out of the forest shooting. They never gave us a chance to hide."

"Two hundred and fifty," Eliza whispered.

"All the women and children ran for cover," Willard said. "Over the millrace and out into the cornfields, and hid wherever they could, among the trees or inside the sheaves that had already been cut. But they fired on us all the time, even while we were running."

"They fired on women and children," Emma said. "Are you sure?"

He nodded. "They were laughing, like they were shooting ducks on a lake. Or clay pots."

As if they shot at already-dead things, she thought. "Did you hide in the field?"

"Not at first," Willard said. "The men all decided to make a stand. I mean, we decided before, when we heard about Adam-ondi-Ahman. We thought we would hold the blacksmith's shop because there were chinks in the walls and we could put our guns through and pick off any Gentiles who fired on us without getting shot too much ourselves."

"And did you?" Eliza asked. "Did the men go into the shop?"

"Yes. All of them, and most of the boys as well, though I wasn't close when the first shots were fired, and I couldn't get to the shop in time. But my father was in there. My little brothers, too."

He stopped. Tears ran down his cheeks, though he didn't sob or wail. He only went on watching the fire as before, and the tears kept coming, bright in the firelight, falling on the nightshirt, leaving dark circles in the cloth.

Again, Emma looked to Eliza and found her with eyes closed, her face tipped up toward the ceiling as if bracing for a terrible blow. There was more coming. Emma could sense it, too.

"Go on," she said reluctantly. "You're a very brave boy, to tell this story. And you must tell me everything, though it makes you sad to think of it."

"I guess the powder must have got wet," Willard said, "because the men in the shop didn't shoot much at all, not like they planned to. And the Gentiles rode up and put their guns in through the chinks and . . ."

The boy stopped again. Emma hadn't the heart to force the details from his memory. She could picture it well enough—all the men of Haun's Mill like cattle in a killing chute. Like pigs in a slaughtering pen. The Gentiles dropping Mormons one after another, the smithy a charnel house, the floor dark with blood.

"Where were you," Eliza asked, "that you could see all this?"

"I hid in a woodpile at first. But they spotted me and fired on me, and I had to run again, over the millpond to the fields. I don't know why I wasn't shot, but they tried. There were bullets flying all around me, and hitting the ground and the trees where I tried to hide."

With that chilling calm, the boy recounted how he found an old grandfather bleeding, begging for a drink of water, and when Willard brought him water from the pond, he saw that the old man's hands had been hacked to pieces by a corn cutter. How he found six little girls cowering behind a house and he made them run, one after another, over the narrow footbridge of the millrace while Gentile bullets struck the water around them, and when they all were over safely, the girls scattered like prairie chickens into the brush.

"I hid behind a big elm tree on the other side of the pond," Willard said. "After they thought all the men were dead, they got down off their horses and went into the shop and then I could hear shooting again. They wanted to finish the job, be sure no man would live to tell the tale. And then they went through the houses one by one, and even our tents, and took whatever they could find. Our clothes, our food, everything. They took all the horses they could catch, and they were singing and laughing, and finally they left, and everything was so quiet, I thought I was the only one left alive in the world."

She took the boy's hand. He didn't clutch at her, but neither did he pull away.

"When I was sure no one was coming back, I went back over the pond and into the shop. I had to see if anyone was still alive inside. I . . . I saw my father, first thing. He was dead right in front of the door. But I heard someone moving and found my little brother Alma under the bellows. He was trying to crawl to the door, but he was shot bad, with blood all down his leg, and he didn't seem to see me. And . . . and on the ground beside him was my other brother, Sardius."

"Was he hurt, too?" Eliza asked.

"He was dead," the boy said faintly. "Alma was the only one left alive in the shop. I picked him up and carried him out over my shoulder, and my mother came out of the woods and cried, 'Oh, they've killed my boy Alma.' I told her, 'No, he isn't dead I think, but you can't go into the shop, for Father and Sardius are killed, both of them, and I don't want you to see what I just seen.' And then she made a noise—an awful noise—like I'd killed her myself just with those words."

"It wasn't your doing," Emma said, and cursed herself for having nothing more to give the boy than platitude.

"What happened next?" Eliza asked gently.

"All the women and children came back into the village, for there wasn't anywhere else to go, and we made beds as best we could to tend those who'd been shot but hadn't died. Alma was bad. Part of his hip had been shot away. But Mother made me go and dig elm roots for a poultice, and after a day, Alma got a little stronger. He told us what happened in the shop."

Emma didn't think she could bear it. But if that child had survived such horrors, then she must be strong enough to hear his tale.

"Alma was hid under the bellows while all the shooting went on," Willard said. "He saw our brother Sardius fall—not because he was shot, but because all the dead men toppled over onto him. And when the Gentiles came in, they found Sardius trying to crawl out from under the weight. Somebody pulled him free. Alma thought they would let him go, seeing that he was just a little boy, only seven years old. But one of the Gentiles put a gun to his head.

"Another said, 'Don't shoot; he's just a boy.' But the man who held the gun said, 'Nits will breed lice.' And then—"

Eliza broke in. "You don't have to say any more. Not about that, you poor thing."

Emma realized there was still a smell of burned wool hanging in the parlor. She remembered pulling that nep, tossing it on the fire, just before Joseph came through the door with Willard in his arms. She could have choked on the smell now, the lingering evidence of a world that had existed once but could never be real again—a time before she'd heard the boy's story, before she'd seen in her mind's eye the close walls of the smithy, the red glare of sunset between the chinks in the wall. The muzzles of the rifles jutting through, a roar of gunfire, the heat of a father's blood striking the face of a child.

From the threshold, with her arms braced in the doorway, she shouted at Joseph; she screamed. "You cannot play God any longer. This has all gone too far. For years now, from the start."

Cornered in his office, he backed against the shelves. He was surrounded by his papers, the books of his revelations and commandments, the sheaves and bound notes, the letters which Brigham Young had risked his life to carry out of Kirtland. Paper and ink—that was all. Words any mortal hand might have written. He shrank before Emma's fury, hunching in the corner while the walls pressed in.

"By God, Joseph, they've murdered our people. They have murdered little children!"

He covered his face with his hands, but she knew he could still see it, too—the cracks in the walls of the blacksmith's shop, flaring red, and black steel thrusting in.

"I never thought it would come to this. I never dreamed this was possible."

"You must do something. Something real, Joseph. No more revelations."

"If Sampson and John hadn't led the Danites to Gallatin—"

She slapped the frame of the door. "Enough! You lay the blame at any feet except your own. But this is your doing. This is a monster of your making."

"I've only done as God directed."

"Have you? Will you swear to that on your final day, when you stand before the Judge of All?"

He drew himself up, came toward her, two quick strides across the room. "Don't mock me. You of all people—don't ever mock me."

"I'm not mocking. I'm in earnest. When you look within your own heart, you know the truth. You know it at your core."

"I know no other way to be. I am what God has made me, for His own purpose."

"Fifteen good men are dead, and children have died because of your church, because of your Danites and your revelations. And I still can't say whether this is some game to you, or whether you believe."

"Emma, I can't lose you. I can't lose your faith. If you cast me aside, the world will cast me off, too."

"Then fall aside, and let your people live."

He raised a fist—not to strike her. He flailed at the air before him. His face was a mask of anguish, red from weeping. He struck at nothing, and shuddered.

She thought of Jacob on the bank of a river, wrestling an angel no one else could see. She said, "Ride for Jefferson City at dawn. Take some of your Danites for protection. But go to Lilburn Boggs and fall on your face before him."

"Never, Emma. How can you suggest it?"

"Fall on your face and beg for mercy. Beg for his aid."

"Boggs wants us dead!" He was shouting now, his desperation loud enough to shake the house. "He has called for our extermination, as if we're mice or fleas!"

"As if we are nits breeding lice. Why will you not listen to me, Joseph?"

He drew calm down upon himself, an icy stillness. He donned that mood as suddenly and easily as he put on his jacket in the morning. "It's the man who's the head of the family, not the woman. It isn't your place to tell me what I should and shouldn't do."

"God made me your wife for a reason. He must know the reason, for I can't see it. But He gave me to you, Joseph—so if you will not listen to me, then you cross the will of the Lord."

"Get out. Get away from me, you hateful woman."

She pushed harder against the doorframe. She made herself immovable. "I will not leave. You will face what you've done, what your sin of pride has wrought. And you'll do what is right by your people—now, at last, to make amends for all the wrongs you never righted before. They murdered a child! That boy was hardly older than your daughter."

He collapsed upon himself, sagging under the weight of his guilt, and sobbed into his hands. "Oh, God! Have mercy on me. Have mercy on all Your people."

"It's Lilburn Boggs whose mercy you need."

"He'll never grant it. He'll murder me, too, if I go to him. And once I'm dead, he'll fall on our people. It'll be worse than Haun's Mill. Our blood will never stop flowing."

"Then write to him. Send word by letter. Tell him you're ready to sue for peace, if only he'll keep the militia in check."

"He wants us gone from Missouri."

"Then we shall go. No patch of land is worth the price we've paid. And Boggs will extract more from us still. We'll return to Kirtland—"

"No, not there. Our enemies came for us there, too. And all the faithful have left Ohio; they've come to Far West. Nothing remains for us in Kirtland. Nothing."

Emma threw up her hands in disgust. "Find some other place, then. What does it matter? Send your fittest men out to look for a new settlement, someplace far from Missouri, as far from any Gentiles as we may get. A wilderness no sane man would want. But find a new home for your church, Joseph, and placate Lilburn Boggs, or else you'll consign us all to death."

It must be said in Joseph's defense that he did as Emma told him. He put Brigham Young at the head of a small scouting party—the most fearless men in Far West—and charged them to find a new home for the church before the turn of the year. Then he sent word to the governor, pleading for clemency and time to relocate beyond Missouri's borders. But though many had fallen away after Gallatin's plunder, the Mormons still numbered more than seven thousand strong. It would take time for Brigham to find a suitable location. The going would be difficult in winter. And Boggs wasn't inclined toward patience, nor mercy. He replied to Joseph that the militias had their orders and would do as they thought best. The time was long past, he said, when the Prophet might have sued for peace.

When word came that Boggs wouldn't relent, not even until spring, Emma and Eliza fell weeping into one another's arms. How do you spare your children from that stark, cold terror, the knowledge that their deaths wait around every bend? How can you keep your little ones safe in a world that howls for their blood?

Far West could do nothing but cringe in the snow and wait for Brigham's return. And week after week, the Gentiles came down like hail on the Mormons. The smallest outposts and villages were struck first. DeWitt was burned, its inhabitants driven into the cold. Then the Mormons who'd remained in Clay County were cast out by their neighbors, who feared the militias would come for them next, burning every home they saw, whether its inhabitants were Mormon or not. Even in Livingston County and Daviess, neighbor turned against neighbor, and Mormons were turned out to walk all the long way to Far West. They prayed with every step that they wouldn't meet militias on the road. Christmas brought no joy—only refugees, bruised and weary, wretched as Mary had been on her desperate flight to Egypt.

"This won't cease," Emma said quietly. "Not until Lilburn Boggs has what he wants."

"Hush," Eliza said, smoothing the hair from Julia's brow. The girl was already asleep, as were her brothers in the bed beside her. It was a wonder any child could rest so peacefully when all the world had gone mad.

Eliza blew out the candle. Only then did Emma pull back the curtain in the children's bedroom. They kept the windows covered now whenever a light was burning. Better not to draw the eyes of any scouts out there on the open plain—the governor's men. The night was clear. Moonlight brushed the mounded snow and lit the flat uniform simplicity of the prairie in winter, pale blue to the horizon. Nothing stirred in the world outside, yet she could feel dark creatures circling, the Gentiles coming closer all the time.

Eliza took her by the hand and led her from the room. She closed the door softly.

"You know what Boggs wants," Emma said.

"Joseph's life."

Emma sighed. She leaned back against the wall, too weary to stand up straight. "They won't cease to hunt us until they have my husband. I know it's true. And yet I can't help but wish Joseph were in the governor's hands."

"Emma! You cannot say such a thing. You mustn't even think it."

Her mouth twisted. "It's late in the day for that. I've thought of nothing else since we learned of Haun's Mill."

"You don't wish Joseph dead. I know you better than that."

"I wish our people safe and delivered from this evil. If I thought I could convince Joseph to turn himself over to justice, I'd do it without hesitation."

"Then you would condemn him to hang. Or worse."

"And I would save countless others in the process." She covered her eyes for a moment, blocking out Eliza's drawn, determined face, the sight of the home she shared with Joseph, the moonlight through the window—everything. "It's a Devil's bargain. But I would strike the deal if I still had the power to move my husband's heart. I can't stop thinking of it—that story Willard told us. The boy killed in the blacksmith's shop. I'd do anything to see that it never happens again, to any other child."

Eliza pulled her away from the wall, wrapping an arm around her shoulder. "You mustn't give in to despair. We must all have faith now. God will—"

A strange cry sounded from somewhere outside. Eliza fell silent. The sound was high and weak, wavering—yet unmistakably feminine.

"Who was that?" Eliza whispered.

"I don't know. It sounded as if it came from the road."

They went downstairs together, clinging to the bannister, groping for every step in the dark. They shuffled across the parlor to the window and peered out warily.

A thin figure stood amid the snow, alone in the moonlight. At first glance, Emma thought it was a ghost—a lost soul cast up from its grave, or from the well pit at Haun's Mill where the villagers had buried their dead, too afraid of the Gentiles to spend time digging proper graves. The figure in the moonlight was gaunt and pale. The next moment, Emma saw that the ghost had left footprints in the snow. The weeping stranger came forward, one slow step after another, pausing now and then to wring its hands or tear at its long, tangled hair. Its face was cast up to the indifferent moon. A wind stirred and the stranger's ragged skirt lifted, flapping behind like the wings of some bedraggled, half-dead bird.

"It's a girl," Emma said. "Whose is she? Where did she come from?"

Eliza made for the door. "She needs our help."

Together they ran out into the road, calling rather timidly. The girl stopped when she heard their voices, but she didn't look at them. She remained as she was, staring up at the sky.

"Could she be blind?" Eliza asked quietly.

Emma moved a little closer to the girl, who flinched back at once, wrapping her arms around her thin, battered body.

"Be easy," Emma said. "Be easy, child. I won't hurt you."

The girl was perhaps sixteen years old. She had been badly used. Her unbound hair was a mass of knots and tangles. A patch above her temple had been torn clean away. Bruises like dark stains spread across her cheekbones, her wrists. The marks of some man's fingers still circled her throat. She wore a gray wool dress that had been torn almost to pieces. Bare skin showed through the rents; there was no shift beneath. Yet there was a sturdy pair of leather boots on her feet—a man's boots, much too large.

"Mother of mercy," Emma whispered. "What has happened to you?"

"What is your name?" Eliza asked.

The battered girl made no answer. She stared past Emma and Eliza both, into some long, terrible distance.

"We must get her inside," Emma said. "Gently, now. She's frightened."

Emma was stiff with cold by the time the girl finally allowed her to touch her shoulder. She guided her off the road, up the path to the front door. Eliza hurried ahead to light a lamp and stoke the fire. The girl paid no more heed to the warmth of the parlor than she had to the frigid night outside. She only stared, swaying from side to side.

"Tell me your name, darling," Emma said.

The girl didn't respond.

"Perhaps she is deaf and mute," Eliza suggested.

"No. Something dreadful has happened. I don't recognize her. She must be from one of the outer settlements."

"Could she be a Gentile? Have the Danites struck another town?"

"Whoever she is, it's plain to see she needs our help. Go and fetch a good flannel nightgown from my chest. Bring a few pairs of stockings to warm her feet. A comb, too. I'll set to work untangling her hair. It isn't much, but it might make her feel a little better, poor pitiful creature."

When Eliza returned, Emma tried to remove the girl's torn dress. She whirled and struck at Emma's hands so fiercely, she jumped back with a startled cry.

"We won't hurt you," Eliza said. She held up the flannel nightdress. "Look, my dear; we've brought you something clean and warm to wear."

Emma tried the buttons again. This time, the girl allowed her to remove the tattered dress—but she wept while Emma did it, sobbing with a dull, hopeless surrender that sickened Emma to her core. The old dress fell away. Bruises and lacerations covered her body, confirming the worst of Emma's fears. There was no mistaking the injuries to the girl's thighs and groin, the bite-marks on her breasts.

Eliza pressed a hand to her mouth, but she couldn't stifle a moan of pity.

"God in Heaven." Emma's vision blurred. "Why would You allow such a thing, why, You who claim to be merciful?"

The girl made a small sound, a hopeless whimper. Emma blinked away the worst of her tears. When she could see clearly again, she found that the girl was looking at her directly, staring into her eyes. It was like looking into a sepulcher, haunted and hollow.

Now she could see bruises around the girl's mouth. Her lips were torn in half a dozen places, caked with blood. The girl opened her mouth for just a moment, drawing a deep, shuddering breath.

"God's sake," Eliza whispered, "look at her teeth. They're broken."

"They hit her," Emma said. "The men who did this to her. Men—I call them beasts. Or devils, not fit to be counted men at all."

Days later, though, after Emma and Eliza had nursed that poor, ragged child back to health, she began to speak. She told them everything.

Her name was Louisa Johnson. She had lived with her family in a small cabin in a clearing just up Shoal Creek—not so far away, ten miles off, perhaps a little more. There had been no one else for miles around. The Johnsons had heard of the tragedy at Haun's Mill, of course, but her parents had thought they'd be safe deep in the forest, far from any other Mormons.

But the Missouri men had hunted them out. The Gentiles had killed every member of Louisa's family, even her two little brothers, even the baby. Killed them all, except for her.

They had used her for sport for days. She didn't know how many— how many days, how many men. When they'd tired of using her, they tied her to a tree, tight against the trunk so she couldn't move. She stayed that way for days, in the cold, alone in the forest, pleading with God so that He would let her die, so that He would send a wolf to take her, or let her fall asleep and never wake again, not until she was in Heaven at the side of Jesus Christ. She hadn't wanted to live, and yet her body had made her do it. The pain of her hunger had been so great that she had chewed the tree bark for food. That was how her teeth had broken.

"How did you get away?" Eliza asked, holding the girl's hand.

Louisa lay back on the parlor sofa. She stared up at the ceiling, and now at last her face opened with wonder. She looked as she must have done before the men had found her, when she'd still been a girl with bright dreams and an innocent heart. She said, "An angel came to me in the forest. He untied me from the tree and told me to come here, to Far West, and seek the Prophet."

Emma and Eliza withdrew to the kitchen. Eliza sank into a ladder-back chair, pale and shaking.

"An angel, my foot," Emma said. "Those boots we found her in—a man's boots. Some Gentile dog thought better of his sins and came back to set her free. Put his own boots on her feet so she'd have some hope of making it to Far West in one piece."

"Of course," Eliza said dully. "But why did the Gentiles turn her loose? Was it from remorse, or was that girl sent to us as a warning?"

The next afternoon, Emma marched to the meetinghouse with Eliza and the Johnson girl trailing behind. The sun was high, the sky clear; there was a light like cold fire on all the world, a glare of mist. Light and cold alike brought tears to her eyes. It was only the weather that did it. Every emotion in her breast had been burned away, save for rage, and that was hot enough to scald.

"Slow down, Emma," Eliza called. "Louisa isn't strong enough to keep up."

The meetinghouse was crowded. The better part of Joseph's priests and apostles had assembled there, along with some hundred or more of the Danites. The men were intent on their own business; they didn't look around when Emma opened the door. No doubt they thought she was just another man come to take part in their meeting, until she swept up the aisle toward Joseph. Brigham Young and his scouts had returned from their mission—that very hour, it seemed, for Brigham still wore his traveling cloak and his long hair was dusted with snow. He had unrolled a map on the altar table and was poring over it with Joseph, pointing out features, making marks with a piece of charcoal.

"Joseph," Emma said.

The men all turned in the pews. Joseph raised his head from the map almost sheepishly. He smiled at the sight of her—a tentative, foolish expression.

Emma heard Eliza lead the girl over the threshold. A murmur followed—the men of the church taking in the sight of the poor waif, her bruises and her swollen lips. Emma held out her hand, and Louisa came to stand beside her—placed herself under Emma's arm, in the shelter of her towering anger.

"Look at this girl," Emma said. "All of you, look. You can see for yourself the state she's in. Would you care to guess what has happened to her?"

Louisa hung her head. She began to weep. "Emma," Eliza said quietly, "have mercy."

"Shall I tell you what was done to this girl, and all in the name of this church? Must I lay it out for you—all you men, who refuse to see how women suffer?"

She recounted Louisa's story. The men held themselves in perfect stillness. None of them would look at Emma or the girl. If they thought they could hide from the truth by refusing to see, they were mistaken, for they couldn't escape Emma's words. Louisa wept at her side, covering her battered face with her hands. Emma knew she was cruel, to parade the girl's suffering so openly. But if this display couldn't touch Joseph's heart and turn him from his folly, then nothing would.

Brigham straightened above his map. "We're working, Mrs. Smith. This is important business—men's work. We'll thank you to come back another time."

"Another time? What other time? After your wives and daughters have been raped? After she was freed, this girl was sent here to find you, Joseph Smith. She was sent with a message. Let him who has eyes read the message plainly. I assure you, no woman in Far West has missed the intent of this warning."

Eliza swept her cloak around Louisa's shoulders and hurried the girl away, back down the aisle, out of the meetinghouse. Emma remained, her eyes locked with the Prophet's.

"Go," Brigham barked. "You're no use here."

"I'm Joseph's wife, not yours, Brigham Young."

"Thank God for that."

Some of the apostles chuckled. Emma did not look around. She held Joseph with all her steely resolve. "This charade has gone far enough. You will sue for peace with the Gentiles—one way or another, any way you can, no matter what the cost to you personally. You will do this, or I will organize the women of this church against you."

Gently, Joseph said, "Emma—"

Brigham cut him off. "What offense is this! A woman telling any man what he will and will not do is bad enough. For you to speak this way to the Prophet of God! If you were my wife, I'd put you in your place. I'd give you a taste of my hand."

"I would taste it, all right," Emma said. "Come and learn for yourself how hard I can bite."

"Please." Joseph stepped between them. "We have trouble enough. No good will come from fighting."

One of the men shouted from the pews, "Why ought we to listen to a woman berate us?" The priests murmured in agreement.

She spun to face the meetinghouse. "Do you think I jest? Try me, if you're man enough. I have a daughter. I won't see her used as that girl was used. Are you so eager for the same fate to befall your daughters and wives? Your sisters, your mothers?" She rounded on her husband again. "Think of Julia if you'll think of no one else. That tender soul who calls you Papa, who trusts you to protect her, to always do what's right. How do you suppose the Gentiles will use her, when next they come to Far West?"

Joseph let out a long, weary breath. "You're right, Emma. There's real danger here, even for the most innocent."

"You can stop this. Go to Boggs. Surrender to the law."

The meetinghouse erupted. "Never!" "They'll kill him—kill our Prophet!" "What kind of wife sends her husband to be slaughtered?"

Brigham's voice boomed above the rest. "She wants Joseph dead; you all heard her say it."

Joseph quieted Brigham with a hand on his shoulder. The priests fell silent, too, waiting to hear what their Prophet would say.

"Joseph will come to no harm," Emma said, "not if God protects him." She held her husband's eye. Silently, she dared him to deny it.

He swallowed. His eyes slid shut, briefly. The light from the meetinghouse window fell on him, a cold winter light, and hard.

"Emma speaks the truth," he said. "We can't allow . . . what happened to that girl . . . It must never happen again. Brigham, Sampson, John Lee—go and find General Doniphan. Find him and beg like a dog for peace. I'll ride by myself to the Liberty Jail, and trust in God to preserve me."

She ought to have left Far West, left the church and Joseph Smith on the same day he went with a handful of his men to the jailhouse at Liberty. She ought to have taken the children and Eliza, and the girl Louisa Johnson, who had no one else to care for her. She could have convinced Don Carlos to leave.

She stood at her bedroom window. Evening light stretched long and blue, out to the faint suggestion of the river beyond the fields. A low drag of carmine red hung at the southern horizon. She watched the empty road where, minutes before, Joseph and his men had ridden. They had been quiet and sober. They knew they might not return. And Emma knew she could leave that night, yet she remained.

Was it guilt that kept her there? If Joseph was killed at Liberty, they would call her to account—all the men who'd heard her speak in the meetinghouse. They had heard her insist the Prophet must go. Or did she stay because she had spoken at last, had told Joseph Smith, This is what you will do, and he had done it?

If she'd thought the Prophet's surrender would spare Far West from the militia, that hope had been in vain. Only two days after he'd gone, the youths who kept watch from the corners of the farthest fields beat their copper kettles to give warning, then went to ground in the trenches they'd dug below the hazel hedges or under piles of broken saplings. When the alarm sounded, the women of Far West picked up their children and fled—for the narrow band of cottonwoods along Shoal Creek, if they were lucky enough to reach them. For the root cellars and the haystacks in the barns, if they were unlucky.

Emma and Eliza had been leading the children back from a visit to the shops at the heart of town. The clattering of the kettles silenced their conversation. Emma shared a grim look with Eliza. She saw in Eliza's expression—drawn, resolute—the confirmation of her own thoughts. She had expected the alarm every minute. Somehow she had known, though she never realized until now, that the militia would come whether Joseph surrendered or not.

Eliza lifted Young Joseph in her arms.

"What's that sound, Aunt Eliza?" the boy asked.

"Nothing to trouble you, little man. Julia, come along. We must get home quickly, and you must keep up."

"We'll cut through the rear of the temple lot," Emma said. "It's a faster route."

"Children to the root cellar once we've made it home?"

"Yes. I'll bring blankets down, and a few baskets of food. We shall—"

"Look, Emma. Who are those men? Over there—running."

"Elders of the church. That's Phineas Barber, isn't it? And two of his brothers." Six men hurried past the temple, cloaks wrapped tightly around their bodies.

"They're headed out of town," Emma said, incredulous. She thrust Alexander into Eliza's other arm. "Get back home quickly. I'll come right after you."

"But Emma—"

"Go now! The sooner you're down in the cellar, the better."

Emma lifted her skirts and ran after the men. "Here, wait, you! Stop and speak with me."

Phineas glanced over his shoulder. He slowed, then halted while the other men hurried on. He shifted impatiently from foot to foot. His breath came in short white puffs. He was red-faced, impatient to be away.

"Just where are you going?" Emma demanded.

"Away from Far West."

"How could you? You'll leave women and children undefended? You know what happened at Haun's Mill."

Phineas held up his hands, a pleading gesture. "Mrs. Smith, we're under strict orders from the Prophet."

"To abandon the innocent?"

"Not all the men have been commanded to leave. Brother Joseph told us, the highest leaders remaining—saving himself and the counselors who went with him to Liberty."

"What did he tell you?"

"To flee Far West if the militia came."

"What a great convenience for you."

"We do it for the gospel's sake! So we may carry on the Prophet's teachings and the true word of Christ, even if . . . if Far West is . . . That is to say—"

She spat into the snow at his feet. "Cowards. God will judge you for this."

"No, Mrs. Smith; we do what the Prophet has commanded!"

"Go, then. Run for the safety of the trees. Much comfort may you find when you hear the screams rising from Far West, when you smell the burning!"

Phineas muttered a curse. He ran to catch up with the fleeing elders, who were halfway across the Kimballs' field by then, dark figures pressed into a flat, white world. A contingent of Danites rode past, raising their rifles. For a moment the thunder of hooves drowned out the sound of the copper kettles, the cries of fear from inside the city. Then the Danites were gone. The fleeing elders were far and small, struggling through the snow. She knew her own home was waiting, the dubious shelter of the root cellar. Her children were waiting for their mother to provide whatever protection she could. But she couldn't move, couldn't think. She seemed incapable of doing anything but standing in the cold, watching those men as they fled.

A sound came from the trees along Shoal Creek. Small, muted pops, muffled by distance. A lazy echo rebounded from the side of Kimball's barn. And one by one, the elders dropped in the snow. Someone was picking them off from the shelter of the trees, easy as hunting rabbits on a spring day. All six of the elders fell, one clean shot apiece.

Emma lifted her skirts and ran.

For nearly a week, Far West cowered under siege, encircled by six thousand jeering, grinning men of the Missouri state militia. When set against the red tragedy of Haun's Mill, they were lucky, for no one had yet been killed except those who'd tried to escape. General Clark, who commanded that pack of wolves, was waiting on news from Liberty regarding Joseph's fate.

Once Joseph faced a judge and was held to account for the Mormon outrages, Clark would consider the matter settled, and swore he would leave Far West in peace. But if Joseph escaped from jail or found some other means of dodging justice, the general promised to reduce Far West to ashes long before the Prophet could slink home to his people.

In the meantime, he licensed his men to do whatever they pleased, short of murder. Every animal was shot—the hogs, the cattle, the Danites' horses. Even the chickens' necks were wrung, whenever a man could catch one. The men barged into houses and smashed jars of preserves, threw loaves on the fire, ripped sacks of flour and barley and scattered them to the wind, to the rats and sparrows. There was nothing left to eat save parched feed corn in a single silo—My God, the women said, weeping. It's Zion come again.

And let us not speak too much of the other things that were done. Any woman they caught, and any girl, was likely to be tied to one of the heavy benches in the schoolhouse, or to the pews of the meeting hall. Poor Louisa Johnson fled in the night, running for the distant cottonwoods. Emma could only pray the girl had made it safely through

the siege line, into the arms of some friendly woman, some kind
benefactress—for a few families had escaped Far West before the noose
had tightened around them.

Brigham had assigned ten Danites to stand guard on the Prophet's
home, so Emma and Eliza—and, more importantly, the children—were
passed over by the roving mobs. There was easier prey within the city,
but Emma had no doubt that the moment tensions escalated, Joseph's
wife and daughter would be the only prizes the militia would want.
Brigham knew it, too. More often than not, he patrolled the cabin himself, barking commands to his fellow Danites, casting hard stares at any
Gentile who passed by.

Brigham proved himself a capable leader in those dark days. She
won't begrudge the man his due, even if she couldn't like him then, and
will not like him now. From the first hour of the occupation, he stepped
readily into the void Joseph had left. It was he who parleyed with
General Clark, and walked out fearlessly to do it, though he'd seen the
elders shot in the Kimballs' field. And Brigham organized the Danites,
directed their patrols; he took stock of the corn silo, rationing out mea-
sures of food to every family. There was no telling how long they must
make the parched corn last. She might have come to respect him then,
if not for the way his eyes narrowed—the advantage he found in every
circumstance, even this.

She invited Brigham into the house one afternoon and set before him
a bowl of corn porridge.

"You're feeding me?" He lifted a spoonful of porridge, let it run back
into the dish.

"A gesture of gratitude," she said. "I'll swallow some first, if you
think I might try to poison you."

He grunted, then tucked in with a ready appetite.

"We must speak," Emma said. "You and I. We've lived like this for
six days now, with no relief and no word from Liberty. Clark won't remain patient much longer, and his men may rebel against him at any
moment."

Brigham scraped his bowl. "That's always a risk in situations of this
kind." He spoke as if it were an everyday affair, for a state militia to terrorize an entire city. "What do you think I can do? I can't break the siege
with a wave of my hand. I'd have done it already if it were so simple."

"I know you can't rescue the whole of Far West. I'm no fool."

"What do you want, then? I've already kept your home under guard every hour of every day. The ten men I keep back for you are not protecting other women."

"I know, Brigham. You mustn't think I'm ungrateful. But the longer we go without word from Joseph, the more dangerous our situation becomes. I've seen what those Gentile monsters do to girls. I won't allow it to happen to my daughter."

He chuckled, mirthless and bleak. "You won't have much say in the matter, if they decide to do it."

"I will." She looked pointedly at the butchering knife stuck tip-down in the carving block. Brigham pressed his lips together.

"I'll do what I must," Emma said, "to spare my daughter that suffering. Believe it. I'm strong enough to protect her."

"I believe you are. After your display at the meetinghouse—shaming our Prophet into sacrificing himself like some damned sheep upon the altar—I'd believe anything of you."

"It doesn't have to come to that—mothers shedding the blood of their own children. Not if we make some other plan now."

"We? I'll decide the best course of action."

"And I will, as well. We must work together if we hope to make the best effect."

"The men of Far West already trust me. They do my bidding."

"And the women trust me. I'm the Prophet's wife, the mother of his children. They see my son Alexander as a talisman of God's favor. The people of Far West—even the men—will follow me as readily as they follow you. We must work together, you and I, if we hope to save lives when Clark's men finally slip their leashes and fall upon this city."

"Save lives—or the church."

Emma tossed her head. Let the church fall to pieces. Let Clark's men burn it, reduce it to ash, scatter the dust of it all to the wind. The church meant nothing to her now. It was the women she cared for—the mothers cowering in the root cellars, the girls lashed to benches and abused. It was the children, hiding and weeping in the dark. If she must save the church to secure Brigham's cooperation, then so be it. She would bring Brigham Young willingly to her side or make peace with the butcher knife.

She asked, "Can you get a message to General Clark?"

"Of course."

"Tell him I wish to go to Liberty and speak with Joseph myself. I'm his wife; the jailer will permit it."

"Clark may not permit it. He won't like to set you free. You're his prize, Sister Emma."

"I'll travel under his guard if it pleases him. His men may accompany me there and back. But we must have some word of Joseph's condition and expectation for a trial. Tell the general my going will benefit him as much as the Mormons. Surely Clark understands how tenuous is his hold over his men. My going may speed the trial, or at least satisfy the militia for a few more days. It may buy us time."

"Time—that's what we need. I need time to think of a suitable plan, look at it from every angle."

"Then go and tell the general I need to visit Liberty Jail." Emma pushed back her chair. The knife rattled in the butcher block. "And think quickly, Brigham. God alone can say how much time we have left. It may be too late already."

The carriage halted outside a forbidding, peak-roofed structure at the edge of the Liberty settlement. The jail was more chaotic heap than construction, a windowless assemblage of sandstone blocks and timber beams. Pale and silent, it crouched like some heavy-limbed beast amid a wasteland of white. Even the village of Liberty felt a hundred miles away, though Emma had only just passed through its mud-dark streets.

General Doniphan set the brake and hurried around the carriage to offer his hand.

"This place looks like a tomb," Emma said.

"It isn't exactly cheerful, I'll grant you that. I've been working with the judge here in this county to bring in more blankets—mattresses— warm clothing. Any small comforts we can provide."

"You've been a steadfast friend to our people, General. I thank you for it."

"I only seek to uphold the law, Mrs. Smith. Your men have not behaved honorably. The raiding of Gallatin was a grave misdeed, and I'm afraid those responsible must be held to account. But this retaliation against your people has been unlawful, too."

"We'll see to it that those who attacked Gallatin face justice. I'll take the matter in hand personally, if only we can lift this present siege and prevent more violence."

Doniphan led her toward the jailhouse. "You and I share that goal. But this state is . . . well, Missouri is Missouri. We're fighting against the current, I'm afraid. The governor himself told me to execute your husband and his men. You must forgive my speaking so frankly. I wouldn't do it, however. Every man must have his day in court, and the law must be applied equally to all. It would have been cold-blooded murder, to carry out the governor's orders, and I told him so. Joseph Smith and his followers are owed the protection of the Constitution—that's what I said to Boggs. He may not like it, but there's at least one man in Missouri who will uphold the law. When I heard you wished to visit your husband, I insisted that I should be the one to escort you. It's not that I feared you would be harmed, Mrs. Smith. I rather wanted to show General Clark and the rest of his men that the law still has its eye on the Mormons."

They paused outside the jailhouse door. There was no sound from within. Even the nearby village was silent. Emma could hear nothing but the moan of wind over the peaked roof and the scolding of a jay from somewhere far off, among the white haze of the river.

"I've no doubt," Doniphan said quietly, "that Boggs granted your request and permitted this visit because he hopes you'll talk Joseph into giving up his right to a trial."

Startled, she looked up at the young general. "Why would I talk Joseph out of a trial?"

"Some wives might become so fretful that they try to convince their men to plead guilt in exchange for lighter sentences. Or run. If you'd talked him into attempting an escape, then the guards would have excuse to fire on Joseph without being held to account."

"I would never be so foolish."

"Boggs doesn't know that. He's eager to be rid of your husband. Your people have caused more trouble in Missouri than they're worth—even I will admit that much. Take care that you don't guide Joseph toward any rash behavior. I don't like Boggs any better than you do. Let's not give that man even a crumb of what he's craving."

Doniphan pushed the door open. The stench of confinement rushed out—a reek of unwashed bodies, urine, and a thick, humid fug from the prisoners' labored breathing. The interior was dark, lit by a single small lamp. It burned fitfully at the far end of the building.

"General Alexander Doniphan," her guard announced, "escorting one Mrs. Joseph Smith."

There was a rustling among the shadows, a murmur of hoarse voices. Footsteps came toward her, and the silhouette of a man's body swallowed the spot of lamplight, then revealed it again when he reached the door. The guard squinted at Emma.

"You can see I have no weapons," she said.

"I vouch for this woman," Doniphan added. "She means no harm to anyone. She has only come to speak to her husband, and Governor Boggs has permitted it."

The guard grunted his assent and stepped aside. "End of the row. Cell on the left."

Emma pulled her shawl more tightly around her shoulders and stepped into the room. Her eyes adjusted as she moved slowly into the dim space. She could feel the ceiling before she saw it, not quite three hand-spans above her head. It would give Joseph only a bare inch or two of space. She felt as trapped as she'd been in the back of Brigham's dray. She couldn't have borne the days of captivity Joseph had already endured—that close, pressing darkness, the bitter cold.

At least the lamplight was stronger there in the rear of the jail. She could see Joseph clearly, kneeling at the door of his cell, reaching through the bars to touch her. His shirt and trousers were stained by mud and fouler things. His face was gaunt, his eyes staring, but they still held the old compelling fire. She rushed to him and clung to his hand.

"Emma, thank God! What welcome mercy, to find you here."

The floor of his cell was hard-packed earth, damp and reeking of the grave. In the shadows behind him, she could see more men shivering, hunched close together—all the faithful who'd gone willingly to prison at the Prophet's side. His brother Hyrum, Parley Pratt, Sidney Rigdon. There were more. Emma couldn't see all their faces, but she could feel their expectant silence, their hunger for news of Far West. There were no benches, no cots, not even mold-spattered mattresses on the ground. The men had only a heap of rotting straw for bed and blanket.

"Oh, Joseph." She pressed her cheek against his hand. "I hadn't any idea it would be like this. If I'd known, I never would have insisted—"

"Hush," he said tenderly. "Hush, my heart. I have no regrets. You were right. We must make peace, not war. And if we hope to make peace with the Gentiles, then a price must be paid."

"But not this! Not your life."

He chuckled. "My life? Goodness, Emma, it's not my time to die yet. God has told me so. He has plans for me still—and plans for His church."

"If only I could believe that."

He squeezed her hand. "You must believe. Now tell me how our people fare. We've thought of nothing else, save Far West."

"The town is held by Clark's militia," Emma said. "But . . . but no real harm has yet come." She couldn't tell the worst of it—the women and girls tied up and used, their food stores destroyed, the parched corn that would hold out another two weeks at most. She couldn't bring herself to add to their burden now.

"They've done their best to be rid of us already," Joseph said. "Poisoned our food."

"If you can call it food," Hyrum muttered from the straw. "That pig slop they feed us—stale bread and weak broth."

"We were all vomiting, and worse," Joseph said. "We were supposed to be dead by now, I've no doubt, but perhaps they didn't use enough poison."

Parley managed a dry little laugh.

"God help me, Joseph," Emma said, "I never meant to send you to this miserable state."

"It was right, that someone should be held to account."

"When will you stand trial?"

He sighed. "I don't know."

"Someone must be able to tell you. If we know there will soon be a trial, then Far West will be safe. I mean to say, we might avoid the . . . the dangers we most fear. Have you heard nothing about a trial yet, nothing at all?"

"Not a word. Doniphan has been our friend, as ever, trying to secure the cooperation of the courts. But they'll keep us here till we've all dropped dead from old age, if they have their way."

"Lilburn Boggs hopes you'll try an escape. So he can have an excuse to fire on you. You must be careful. You mustn't give them any reason to think you'll run or fight back. They'll kill you the moment they see their chance."

"None of us will play into the governor's hands. I give you my word on that, Emma."

She took messages from the other men to their families back home. From Joseph, she memorized a special blessing to strengthen the spirits of the whole congregation. Finally, he laid his hands on the crown of her head, just as he'd done that far-off day in Harmony, when with the voice of the Lord, he had named her elect.

"My children I bless through you, that they will be strong and protected, and righteous in the eyes of God all the days of their lives. And to you, Emma Smith, I call down every angel under the Lord's command, to guide and defend you. Amen."

She opened her eyes and there he was, pressed close against the bars of his cell, so close she could almost feel his warmth.

"I love you, Emma," he said quietly. "Whatever may happen, know that I love you. I always have, from the day I first saw you, from the day I knew you would be my wife."

It was the first time she could remember him saying it. He had never spoken those words so directly before, unveiled by revelation.

The days moved, relentless as winter—slow and dark, inevitable. Ten days had passed since General Clark and his six thousand men had ridden into Far West. With each day, the walls of Emma's home pressed in. The town itself seemed to lean as if to crush her with its weight. She felt the menacing closeness of the dray again, but it wasn't the dray. The very world had tightened like the jaws of a trap. Like a noose around her neck.

There was little she could do, save carry on. The children needed tending and feeding, there were stockings and sweaters to darn, wool to spin, food to be cooked—though she would have given anything to taste something other than parched corn. By night she dreamed of beef and onions and woke with her stomach rumbling, her mouth full of water. Then, in the feeble light of a December morning, with the house silent around her and the bed empty at her side, she remembered everything, and her thoughts turned to Joseph shivering in his cell.

One evening, as Emma and Eliza sat mending stockings beside the fire, the front door burst open and the women leaped up from their chairs. Cold wind rushed across the parlor, carrying a whirl of snowflakes. The light from the hearth dimmed as the flames bent and wavered. Brigham Young was a black brick of a man. His dark cloak concealed his body; the narrowness of his eyes concealed his thoughts.

Emma pressed a hand against her racing heart. "You frightened us!"

"No time for apologies." He closed the door, stamped the snow from his boots. "You're leaving Far West tonight, Emma."

"Tonight—how? Where shall we go?"

Brigham glanced around the parlor. "Are the children still awake?"

"Yes," Eliza said, "they're playing upstairs."

"Good. Let them go on playing, wear themselves out. I've been hard pressed to find another supply of valerian root, but I've managed to scare up a little. It might not be enough to keep them quiet till you're beyond the range of Clark's scouts."

"We can't simply pull up stakes and leave, quick as that," Eliza said. "We must know where you plan to take us. We must prepare for the journey. It may take us another day to make ready—"

Emma stepped forward, eager or desperate. "We'll go. Tonight. Whatever the cost, however long the journey."

"Good," he said. "You must be ready in two hours' time. I can't give you longer. A chance to spirit you out of Far West has come up suddenly. The opportunity may not come again."

He led them to the kitchen. Eliza lit a candle while he delved into a pocket of his cloak and brought out a folded paper. He opened it in the circle of light. It was a map, crudely drawn but simple enough to interpret. There was no mistaking the confluence of Shoal Creek and the Grand River—nor the site where Haun's Mill had stood.

"You'll go north." He tapped the map with a dirty finger. "To this place, one hundred and sixty miles, more or less—a spit on the Mississippi River, good land, unclaimed. It's the site I found for Joseph. He'd planned to relocate the whole church to that place. We would be there now, if these Gentile shits hadn't broken their word and fallen on us the moment they had Joseph in their hands."

"Language," Eliza murmured.

"I want you there," Brigham said to Emma, "so Joseph will go to you when he's freed. He must have no excuse to linger in Missouri. Boggs will have him shot like a pig if he stays one day longer in this state."

"Will he be released soon?" Emma said.

"I believe so, though I can't say for certain. I've been keeping correspondence with that Doniphan fellow. He says the trial can't be delayed much longer. There's no legal basis to put it off; it's all an act by our enemies. They're hoping Joseph will take sick and die behind bars if they delay long enough."

"I fear a trial as much as I fear the absence of one," Emma said. "No one in this state loves us. Not even Doniphan. He reveres the law and upholds it, but he hasn't any great liking for our people. A judge may condemn Joseph to death and give Boggs what he wants after all. How can we know this trial won't end in a hanging?"

"Don't say such things," Eliza said weakly. "You mustn't even think—"

Brigham folded the map into a compact square and handed it to Emma, along with a small packet of valerian. "I'm quite confident that Joseph will come out of this with his hide intact. I believe in the might and righteousness of God, even if you do not."

Eliza straightened. She was pale and shivering, but she faced Brigham with resolve. "We shall be ready in two hours' time."

"Not you," he said. "This will be a dangerous gamble—far riskier than the one we took at Kirtland. It'll be a true miracle if I can get Emma and the children out of Far West alive. Another woman is another burden—one I can't afford to carry."

"Eliza must come," Emma said. "I can't manage three children on my own; not in my condition."

Brigham scowled at her hard-set face, then down at her belly. He clicked his tongue and turned away, heading for the kitchen door. "Please yourselves. But if you get us caught and killed, remember with your dying breath that it was you who brought that fate, not I."

When he'd gone, Emma and Eliza stared at one another for a long moment. Beyond their circle of candlelight, the hungry darkness leaned in.

"We did it once," Emma said. "We can do it again."

"Of course." Eliza smiled, but it was thin and trembling. "Through God, all things are possible."

"I feel a coward, leaving now. I feel worse than a criminal. I think of what they did to Louisa, what they're doing to other girls . . . I ought to stay and help."

"What can you do, Emma? What can one woman do against an army of men?"

"Still, it isn't right, that I should leave when others must stay. And yet I will do it. I'll go, knowing I'm a despicable traitor. It's only a matter of time before they come for Julia."

Eliza took her hand.

"For my daughter's sake," Emma said, "I'll do anything, even if it damns my soul."

"I will be with you, every step of the journey."

"Then let's prepare, and quickly."

Emma poured their week's ration of parched corn into an old flour sack while Eliza fetched her sewing basket from the parlor. She set the kit on the table, began sorting through bobbins of thread.

"What in Heaven's name are you doing?" Emma said. "We won't be able to take our sewing with us. We'll need every bit of space in our bags for the children's clothes, and every ounce will matter."

"I don't intend to bring these threads. At least, I don't intend to pack them." Eliza lifted the heavy wool of her outer skirt, revealing the stiff white petticoat beneath. "Bring me those empty flour sacks from the pantry. Then go up and fetch Joseph's papers from his office. I'll sew them into my clothing—yours, as well. We will carry God's word out of Far West, one way or another. I won't let these devils have their way in all things."

They waited in the darkness behind the house, sheltered from the road. The night was muted and flat, the snow muffling the world to silence. The cold burned Emma's cheeks. The baby, Alexander, rode in a tight sling against her chest. Eliza carried Young Joseph in her arms. The boy was bundled in layers of wool, sleeping as peacefully as if he lay in his own bed. There hadn't been enough valerian root for Julia. Neither Emma nor Eliza would have been able to carry her, in any case, for each was burdened by a full leather pack—and they had sewn every revelation and manuscript they could find into their petticoats. Eliza had even donned a second petticoat, the better to carry Joseph's writings.

Emma's back already ached from her pregnancy. The pack and Alexander dragged at her. "I could wish for Brigham's dray again," she whispered. "I never thought I'd see the day when that cursed wagon would feel like a luxury."

Eliza only shook her head. She seemed to be listening—for what, Emma couldn't say. Brigham had told them they would know when the time was right to flee. They would hear a commotion and then they must go—set off toward the creek as quickly as they could. They weren't to stop until he met them in the woods. But what commotion? And how far would sound carry through a dense winter night?

Julia shuffled in the snow. "Mother, I'm frightened."

"I know, dear," Emma whispered. "But you mustn't speak. Everything depends on being silent. And remember, you must keep pace with Aunt Eliza and me. We'll go very fast—fast as jackrabbits."

"But where will we—"

"Hush," Eliza said. "Do you hear it?"

Emma strained to listen. The silence itself was all she heard—a long, vast nothingness so great it seemed a physical presence. A small, distant shout scarcely disturbed the quiet. A man cried out in anger or pain. Then, like water coming to a boil, the voices surged and swelled. Fighting at the heart of town.

"Mercy," Emma breathed. "Brigham has started a battle."

"The better to set us free." Eliza strode out into the winter night.

Emma and Julia hurried after.

"Men may be killed in that fighting," Emma murmured. "Women, too. I don't like it."

"Nor do I, but we must go." Eliza cut a swift glance toward Julia. "Remember why we do this, Emma, and press on."

The field they crossed was at least thirty acres wide. They were exposed against the pale breast of the snow, pinned like butterflies to a scrap of cork. Long before they reached the dim line of the cottonwoods, Emma's breath came in short, ragged gasps. Terror bloomed like some dark flower inside. It filled her chest, stole the air, stung her eyes with tears. The child in her womb twitched. They struggled through snow almost knee-deep; they floundered forward like oxen mired in mud. And all the while, the sounds of conflict blared through the night behind them: bellows of anger; women's screams; the stiff pop of gunfire; and above that terrible din, the brass horn of the Danites wailing and howling, calling men to battle.

Don't stop, don't turn to look back. Remember Lot's wife on the flight from Sodom. She pushed on and on. She clung to her baby in his sling, and to her daughter's hand. She kept her eyes fixed on Eliza's back, the slender darkness of her dress as she cleaved through a darker night toward freedom. Don't stop, don't stop to think about the eyes that watch you from the city, don't ask yourself how far their bullets may fly, how fast their horses may run. Don't stop until the branches of the cottonwoods reach up around you, a roof above your head, the shelter of their shadows.

"You did it."

Emma blinked. She couldn't see Brigham, but she could hear him close by, his familiar bulldog's growl rolling from the trees. "I wasn't entirely certain my plan would work."

"You gambled with our lives, then." Emma wiped her tears on a sleeve.

"And I won." He emerged from a void between the cottonwoods. He had wrapped himself in the black cloak again, so he seemed nothing more than a hard face peering out of the cold, the spirit of winter made flesh. "Come. The Danites have made a scene at the meetinghouse, calling for Joseph's release. It turned into a fight, just as I'd hoped, and pulled the attention of Clark's men. But they'll soon return to their posts. We can't be found lingering here when Clark sends his scouts out again."

They followed Brigham through the forest until the canopy gave way to a wide swath of sky. The clouds hung low, but the moon had risen somewhere behind, casting a sickly backlight. The clouds seemed to reach for Emma and her children with gray, greedy hands. She took Julia by the shoulder, pulling the girl against her heavy, wet skirt.

They'd reached the southern bank of Shoal Creek. The water ran some twenty feet wide and more than ten deep, but the surface had frozen, and the ice lay pale and shining in a weak flush of moonlight.

"Cross it," Brigham said.

"Are you mad?"

"It's thick enough to hold."

Eliza held Young Joseph tightly. She glanced down the open bank.

They could still hear the horns and shouts behind them. She said, "Come along, Emma. Let us have this over and done with. The sooner we're on the other side, the better."

"One at a time," Brigham said. "The ice is thick, but perhaps not thick enough to hold us all at once. Eliza, you go first."

She held Emma's stare for a long moment, face white with fear.

Emma nodded. "We can't go back—not now. Our only path is forward."

Eliza stepped out gingerly. Emma could hear her boots scraping over the ice. The sound mingled with the noise of battle, sending a terrible, hot pulse up her spine. Eliza moved slowly, sliding one foot forward, then the other. She shifted carefully with every step, struggling to balance the weight of her pack and the sleeping boy. Emma never knew she'd been holding her breath until Eliza reached the far bank and scrambled up the slope to solid ground.

"Now the girl," Brigham said.

Julia gripped Emma's skirt, shaking her head in mute terror. "Go on," Emma said. "Aunt Eliza is waiting."

"Come with me, Mother."

Emma breathed deeply and moved toward the ice, but Brigham said, "The girl only. I can't say whether the ice will hold you both. Go on, child. The Gentiles could ride by at any moment."

Eliza beckoned from the far shore, reaching out to Julia. The girl moved toward the ice and stopped with her toes at the milky blue edge.

"Slide your feet," Eliza said as loudly as she dared. "It's easy. You need only move an inch or so at a time."

Julia stepped out onto the frozen creek. She skidded at once, pinwheeling her arms, biting back a cry. Emma's heart seized in her chest. But Julia regained her balance and did as Eliza told her, sliding the soles of her boots carefully. She crept to the middle of the creek, each second passing as slowly as eternity.

"Make her go faster," Brigham muttered.

"I can't."

"The Danites won't be able to hold Clark's attention much longer. He may already have sent the better part of his men back to their posts."

"Do you think I don't know that?" Emma hissed. "Do you think we're taking this as one great holiday?"

Finally, Julia hauled herself up the opposite bank and buried her face in Eliza's skirt. The poor girl was weeping with fear, but at least she wept silently.

"Go," Brigham said.

The noise from Far West had diminished. Time had run too swiftly.

Every grim terror in her heart seemed to clamor just behind her, leaping and snapping like a pack of wolves. If she could only reach the other shore before Clark's sentries found her . . . and yet she was hot, suddenly flushed with a new consciousness of her children—Alexander's small vulnerable body curled against her breast; the new life inside her, dreaming of its future.

She wanted to run. She wanted to scream from the relentless pressure of fear. Instead, she moved more slowly than even Julia had done.

Step by precarious step, she moved across Shoal Creek. She was dizzy with panic, breathless, all her senses trained on the sound of the conflict dying down across the field. Each time she moved, she was just as apt to slide to the left or right as forward. The weight of her pack, of the baby, her belly—the weight of Joseph's doctrines sewn into her petticoats—every burden pulled her in a different direction. She felt the world spinning like the bright wheels of fortune that whirl at harvest fairs, a disorienting blur of color and sound.

"Hurry," Eliza whispered from the bank. "Oh, do hurry."

Midway across the creek, a hollow cracking split the night. She froze, staring at Eliza, too terrified and unbalanced to look anywhere else. Was it a gun—so near? Had Brigham been shot? Then she felt another reverberation—the hum of the ice underfoot. She glanced down. A dark line, thin as a hair, was snaking out from her boot. The ice was breaking under the weight of all she carried.

Emma sucked in a cold breath, hugging Alexander more tightly. She slid her feet faster, leaning over the swell of her belly, trying to outpace the split in the ice as it spread. She would have reached beneath her skirt and torn the petticoat away if she'd had a free hand to do it. She would have left Joseph's work behind, but it was her fetter now. *If you ever loved me*, she prayed to a distant God, *then save me now. Save my children. See me to the shore.*

Emma closed her eyes so she wouldn't see the ice cracking, but she could hear it still, the echo of its voice through the cottonwoods. She kept moving, shifting herself against the jostle and tug of gravity until finally someone took her by the shawl, just in the place where it was knotted at her throat, and hauled her to the bank. Emma sobbed with relief.

For a moment she thought it was an angel who held her. When she opened her eyes, she found Eliza.

"No worse for the wear," Eliza said with forced cheer. Julia threw herself at Emma, sniffling against her skirt. "Now, now," Eliza said, "let's not lose our heads."

In moments, Brigham was beside them. His face was dark with the effort of crossing the ice so quickly; his breath rose in rapid white plumes. "Quickly," he muttered. "We aren't safe yet."

He pushed past the women, into the cold blue density of the forest. Eliza took Julia by the hand. Without a word, they followed.

Why does it come back here, always, to the orchard behind the Mansion, the tall grass between the trees? This is where Governor Ford's men direct her, so this is where she goes. And she finds the governor at the far end of the orchard, among the slender young apples reaching to the sky. Ford stands as far as a man might hope to get from the sick tension stretched across Nauvoo. You can feel the beat of waiting anywhere you happen to be—a rhythm of fear and rage, the pace increasing the longer the militia remains, the longer Nauvoo must go without word of their Prophet. Ford is smoking his cigar again, moving aimlessly from one corner of the orchard to another, his head drooping in contemplation, blue smoke riding the air.

She stops under the branches of a tree. It's just old enough now to produce a few small, hard fruits; its supple arms are gemmed with growing apples, green as peridots and jasper. Joseph will never see his orchard bear fruit, but she will. She will watch the apples blush to red, the branches sag with bounty. Year after year, the yield will increase, and the boughs will twist and distort with the weight of fecundity. She will make these fruits into sweet, wholesome things—jellies and tarts, pies and cakes, even cider to lift the spirits. There will come a time, she feels, when her spirit will rise. God knows, she has waited long enough.

Ford turns at the corner of the orchard and starts his passage again, trampling a track in the grass. But he sees her, the black of her widow's weeds sharp against a blur of summer green. He stops, waiting for Emma to approach. The smoke eddies around him. She can smell it from where she stands. She won't go to him. This is her home, her orchard, her city, her people. Let the governor come to her.

When he comes, he is hesitant, looking down at his boots. She glances down, too. There's a fragment of white cloth caught in the grass. She steps on it, pressing it into the dust, and doesn't know whether she does it to hide the scrap from Ford, or whether she's trying to crush out whatever power the cloth still holds.

He stops a few paces away. This suits Emma. If Ford thinks she will buckle as some women would, if he thinks she will fall, then he doesn't know her well. But who does know her—who, of all those left living?

"I see you've dressed in black," he says carefully.

"And I see you for what you are: a coward who can't deal honestly with a woman."

"Mrs. Smith."

"You knew my husband was already dead—"

"I didn't know."

"—and yet you said nothing."

"I did not know, Mrs. Smith. Not till I set out for Carthage. Some of my men met me on the road, less than an hour from Nauvoo. They'd been riding here to bring me the news."

"That was why you returned so quickly. I knew it then; I understood the truth, even if you were too craven to tell me."

"I didn't know how you would react. How your people would react."

"Do you fear us so much? Women and children, old men? Are we so great a threat to your thousands in the militia, with all your guns and swords?"

"No one in Illinois has forgotten how your people laid waste to Missouri—towns plundered, livestock stolen, houses burned."

"And not one of us has forgotten how Missouri dealt with us. Speak the name of Haun's Mill, even to this day. It's a blow to our spirits."

Ford sighs. There is a shadow over him, a deep gray sorrow. "It was murder, Mrs. Smith—cold murder, a violation of every law. Your husband was not well loved, but that's no justification for murder."

When she knows she can speak without her voice breaking, she says, "Tell me how it was done."

He glances at her, pulls on his cigar, opens his mouth so a wall of smoke rises between them. It's a relief to him, Emma can see, to hide from her eyes, even for a moment. "I don't like to speak of such sad things. Not to a grieving widow."

"Look at me, Governor. Am I grieving, am I broken?"

He looks, when the smoke clears. Whatever he sees in Emma's face proves satisfaction enough.

Joseph, Hyrum, and nine of the faithful had been held in the upper story of the Carthage jail since their surrender. The Carthage Greys were set to guard the jailhouse—the local militia, who had been clamoring for months for the Prophet's death and the expulsion of the Mormons, since long before the burning of the press. And who had appointed the Greys—Joseph's most hateful enemies—as guards? Thomas Ford won't say. But she understands the truth. She sees it in the way his eyes slide away, in the way his smoke rises to hide her from his sight.

He says, "One of my men told me the Carthage Greys had made threats against your husband—against all the Mormons we held in that cell. I didn't believe the threats were imminent. I take full responsibility for that, Mrs. Smith. I ought to have listened more closely."

On Thursday, early in the morning, Cyrus Wheelock came to Carthage, claiming he'd brought counsel from Joseph's lawyer. Naturally, Ford says, he allowed Wheelock inside. Every man has a right to a trial.

"My husband had no lawyer," she tells him. "If he had ever consulted with a lawyer, he might have acted more wisely. God knows, I tried to convince him. I did all I could."

Wheelock brought no counsel, but he had hidden a pepperbox pistol in the lining of his coat. It was small enough that none of the Greys took notice, and he passed the gun to Joseph.

After Ford departed for Nauvoo, when the Greys could be certain he was well on his way and wouldn't hear the commotion, two hundred men of the militia smeared their faces with a black paste of gunpowder and stormed the jail. The Greys who stood guard fired their guns over the heads of their friends. Watching from the one small window of his cell, Joseph thought for a moment he was saved. The Danites had come, or so he believed, and by the strength of God they would overwhelm the militia and carry him to freedom. But it had been nothing more than a show, one last way to taunt the Mormon Prophet before they did him in. Just when Joseph thought himself saved, the Greys turned and joined the attackers. They overwhelmed the prison, they rushed up the stairs, bellowing for blood.

The Greys fired into the cell. Joseph's men threw themselves to the ground; they rolled under the cots and pressed themselves against the walls, they cowered in the corners. A bullet pierced the wooden door and struck Hyrum Smith in the face. As he fell, he cried out, *I am a dead man.* He was.

Joseph did his best to block the door so the Greys couldn't open it. But the enemy was hungry, and the taste of vengeance was in their mouths. They pushed the door partway open. Their guns thrust into the gap. Standing over the body of his brother, Joseph used a walking stick to beat their guns away. Still they came. He drew the pepperbox and reached into the hall; he fired every bullet, blind, frantic, but not one man fell.

The Greys threw their weight against the door until it gave way, and when it did, there was Joseph, lone and defenseless before them.

He ran for the window. What else could he do? That howling mob behind him, their faces black to hide their sins. The window was narrow, yet he pressed himself through, even while the bullets struck him in the back and ripped his coat and stained him red. Someone fired a musket from the outside. It found his chest, almost his heart. He raised his hands in a last desperate plea for help. He cried out to his God, but no one answered.

That is what will stay with her all the remaining days of her life. She knows it, even as she hears Ford speak those words. That Joseph called upon God as he fell. And falling, he knew only silence and emptiness. He knew nothing.

"I believe," Ford says, "he was already dead by the time he struck the earth. I'm sorry, Mrs. Smith. It can't be easy to hear such a story—not even for a woman as strong as you."

Her mouth is dry by then. Quietly, she says, "Thank you. For telling me. It's better to know than to wonder."

"I would have you know this, too: I won't allow this injustice to stand. Joseph Smith was not well loved by anyone outside your church, but he was a citizen. He deserved his rights. I will hold those responsible to account."

She nods and doesn't turn away from him. "And when will you be leaving Nauvoo? There is no work for you here, not anymore, now that Joseph has gone to face the Lord."

"I'll leave your people in peace as soon as I'm satisfied that there will be no more violence in Illinois, no more presses burned—"

"No more prisoners shot like shoats in a pen?"

"Just so, Mrs. Smith. I'm as eager to be away as you are to see me go. I would put this sad affair behind us all, the sooner the better. Can you give me some guarantee that Joseph's followers won't rise up?"

She breathes in, slowly, considering. "There is one man with whom we must still reckon. Brigham Young holds almost as many hearts as Joseph ever did."

"I know him. I've seen him. A troubling man."

"Give me time to speak with him, Governor. If any person can bring Brigham to reason, it might be me. But I can make no promises."

"Thank you, Mrs. Smith."

"You've dealt more fairly with our people than anyone else. I've seen enough sieges to last a lifetime. I don't love you, but I can't deny you've handled us with greater care than anyone who has handled us before."

His smile is apologetic. He says, "You look handsome in black. It suits you."

"Well it might," Emma says, leaving him, returning to her house. "God knows, I've worn it all my life."

XII

Water, Fire, Truth, and God

1839–1841

"A rider! Look lively, men! A rider is coming!"

Emma stood as quickly as her cold-stiffened muscles would allow. The damp wood of her cookfire hissed. She coughed—she hadn't stopped coughing since they'd come to that curve of the Mississippi some three weeks before—and waved her hands, trying to clear the smoke from her vicinity. All around the encampment, women called anxiously to their children and men ran for the clubs they'd fashioned from heavy tree limbs and river stones.

She heard the door of her small cabin open and fall shut again. A moment later, Eliza was there.

"A rider," Emma said.

"So I heard." Fear tinted Eliza's voice, though she tried to conceal it behind a dignified manner. Little wonder she was frightened. Emma had become so gripped by the terror of a pursuing mob that fear no longer seemed a transient state. It was constant now, so central to her being that, like the sound and feel of her heartbeat, it had long since receded from awareness.

"The children," Emma said.

"Napping in the cabin, all three. Bundled up as warm as I could make them."

The sentry's voice rang out again. "It's Brother Brigham! Brigham has come!"

Eliza laughed with pleasure—the first time Emma had heard the least sound of joy since their arrival.

"Thank God." Emma smiled at her own words. "I suppose that will be the last time you ever hear me praise the Lord for sending Brigham Young."

"You know Brigham is a blessing. We never would have survived without him. We would be in Far West still—likely in its graveyard, if the militia had had its way."

Brigham had certainly proved his utility in the escape from Far West. After they'd crossed the frozen creek, he'd led them through the night to a Baptist's remote farm. The Baptist man had owed Brigham some obscure yet important favor and had agreed to house the women and children in his barn for the night. Once Brigham had seen them safely burrowed into a great heap of straw, he'd bid them a terse farewell and returned to Far West.

The Baptist had wakened them just after dawn and helped them into a wagon. Posing as a poor family of Gentiles fleeing the conflict at Far West, they rode with the Baptist all the way to the Illinois border.

Then they'd been left to their own devices, but thanks to Emma's obvious condition, and the presence of the children, they won sympathy from drivers on the road. Day by day they moved north, taking shelter at night from farmers' wives and preachers in village churches. As long as they avoided talk of Mormons and militias, they found the people of Illinois charitable enough. Some donated food for their travels and warm clothing for the children, and finally they reached the spit of land on the Mississippi, the place Brigham had identified as the Saints' next stronghold.

Emma's first look at the site had turned her stomach with dread. It was bleak and cheerless and miles from the nearest village. A high hill rose above the curve of the river, which was the site's only saving grace. At least it would be easy to defend. Several small islands—sand bars crowned by willows—sheltered the bank from excessive winds. The broadleaf forest was stark and bare in winter. The woods ran down to a marshy expanse hard with ice. When the spring thaw came, the spit would be a quagmire. Very likely, Emma had thought, they would be plagued by mosquitoes and flies. But the undesirability of the land had also struck her as a queer sort of benefit. No one was likely to trouble the Saints in Illinois as long as they kept to themselves. The marsh would prove a great challenge, but no Gentiles would covet that land and try to drive them away.

Emma and Eliza took shelter in a rough cabin, one of several old, abandoned buildings dotted around the site. They weren't exactly warm, but they didn't freeze, and after a few days spent huddled on the bank of the Mississippi, more Mormons arrived, trickling into Brigham's isolated haven three and four at a time.

"There he is," Eliza cried, darting around the cookfire. "Brigham truly has returned!"

Eliza rushed out with the rest to greet Brigham Young, but Emma remained at her fire, turning her flour cakes slowly, watching from a distance as Brigham received his welcome. The ragged Mormons clamored around. A string of several grouse and even a few chickens hung from his saddle. He lifted the birds high for all to see. "A feast tonight! A feast for everyone! I bring good news!"

"What news?" the people cried. "Tell us, Brother Brigham!"

"Where is Emma Smith?"

Emma stepped around her fire, moving clear of the smoke.

"Emma." Brigham strode toward her, laughing, grinning. "You made it to the encampment after all. You've survived all this time."

"I'm afraid I have," she said. "I'm sorry to disappoint you."

He laughed again. "What a wit she has, eh, boys? It's no wonder she holds the Prophet's heart. Emma, my good lady, I bring you happy news. The siege on Far West is over—lifted by order of a Missouri judge. And Joseph has been acquitted. They've set him free."

She closed her eyes, let out a ragged breath—one it seemed she'd been holding all those weeks since she had scolded Joseph into prison. The people cheered. Someone took the string of birds from Brigham and began plucking them. Feathers drifted around the muddy clearing.

"Where is he now?" Emma asked when the clamor died away.

"Somewhere in Illinois," Brigham said. "I told him it was for the best if he hid for a time. He's a known man, and apt to fire up anger wherever he goes like a spark to gunpowder. We need time to strengthen ourselves in this new place before we draw the attention of any Gentiles. Joseph will find us by and by. I made certain he knows the location."

That afternoon, Emma and Eliza shared a roasted grouse with the children. No manna from Heaven ever tasted so good.

Emma licked the grease from her fingers and tossed a picked-clean bone into the fire. "I can't help but feel as if Brigham is misleading us about something."

"Misleading?" Eliza stared. "What in Heaven's name could he be lying about?"

"I don't know. I can't put my finger on it. Perhaps Joseph isn't truly free. Perhaps he's been—"

"I confess," Eliza broke in quietly, "his survival does seem almost a miracle too great for God Himself to grant."

"Brigham may be lying about what he told Joseph. Does he truly know that we're waiting for him here? Has he come to Illinois at all, or is he wandering Missouri, where any rogue may shoot him dead? That would please Brigham, I believe."

"Hush," Eliza said. "Don't frighten the children. There's nothing to these fears. You've no good cause to doubt Brigham."

"I simply don't trust that man—that's what it comes down to. I've never been able to like him, no matter how I've tried."

"Have you tried so very hard?" Eliza asked with a note of fond amusement. "You and Brigham are both too powerful in your own ways."

"Powerful?" Emma scoffed. "I?"

Eliza was sober now. "You have never understood your own strength, Emma. Your great intelligence, your quiet dignity—"

"I'm no leader of men, nor of churches."

"Not yet, perhaps." Eliza nudged a fragment of wood back into the fire with the toe of her boot. Her smile was cryptic. She said more briskly, "You ought to have more gratitude. Brigham has done us one good turn after another. He doesn't deserve your scorn. I believe he stands on the right side of God, even if he is rough around the edges."

"I believe Brigham Young is little better than a devil."

"For shame, Emma. Recall everything he has done for us. He has saved our lives twice now, and the lives of your children. And he has run every imaginable risk in service to Joseph and the church. Let these suspicions go, dear. Reach down into your soul and find forgiveness for a man who has only ever done you good, even if his manners are rough."

"You're right, of course," she said. "This misliking for Brigham is a failure in my character. He has done us good. I've no real cause to suspect him. I'm a wary creature by habit. I must try harder to like him for the sake of his good deeds. He's brave, at least. I'll give him that."

The days passed more cheerfully after Brigham's return. Refugees from Far West swelled from a trickle to a stream. Soon the woods rang with the sound of axes, the ground reverberated with the fall of tree after tree as the land was cleared to make room. Emma watched Brigham marshaling the Mormons with natural ease—directing them in the construction of new cabins, leading parties out to set trap lines or hunt with the few rifles the men still possessed. He was taking command of Joseph's church, as if the Mormons were his by right—as if Joseph Smith had never existed. Whatever gratitude she owed the man was far overshadowed by her suspicion of his motives and manners. She could only pray that God would grant her Eliza's perfect faith and allow her to trust Brigham without restriction.

At last, the blessed day came. Joseph called out from the crest of the hill, I have come, my good people, you faithful Saints. Even before her heart leaped with relief, Emma turned to see Brigham's face. He was stony, eyes blank with surprise. His mouth twisted as if he had tasted something bitter.

He told Joseph where we were situated, surely enough, Emma realized. *But he'd hoped the Gentiles would find him before he found us.*

When Joseph came striding down the hill—tall, splendid, and whole despite months of torment—Emma ran with the rest to greet him. It was Eliza who reached him first, for she'd been closest to the foot of the hill. She threw herself weeping at the Prophet, kissing his cheeks. Then she recalled herself and stepped aside, thrusting Emma into his arms.

He held her for a long while, rocking back and forth, breathing so raggedly against her neck she thought he might have been weeping.

After a long while, he released her and stepped back, surveying the encampment, the small new cabins clinging doggedly to bare ground. His eyes shone when he took in the bend of the river, its fringe of sandy islands. The water was perfectly blue under a clear sky, hopeful in the bright face of spring.

"The faithful have gathered again," Joseph said. "In this place, this blessed place—this land which God has blessed above all others."

"What shall we call the settlement?" Eliza asked.

Joseph beamed at his seedling of a village. "We shall call it Nauvoo. The Beautiful City."

Someone had laid thick planks of wood in the low places along the river trail. Emma moved slowly, placing each foot with exaggerated care. The yoke on her shoulders bore the weight of two full pails of river water, but she was obliged to steady the pails with her hands and couldn't thrust her arms out to correct her balance. Nor could she see over the nine-month swell of her belly. The planks were slick with mist—with the pervasive, heavy wetness that hung above Nauvoo—but at least her boots remained dry.

She crept from the river bottom, through its thickets of cattails and sweet flag thrusting blue buds toward the sun. Her back was in agony by the time she gained drier ground. The slope was littered with half-sawn planks and dropped tools. Nauvoo had been taking shape at a rapid pace, until a powerful fever struck the settlement, dropping four out of every five people into their beds. It was the foul air of the marsh that had spawned the illness; Emma felt sure of that. Winter had given way to spring, and the thaw had set ill humors free from under the ice. She could only pray the disease would weaken once summer advanced.

She paused at the edge of town, where two large houses had been stalled in their construction. She eased both pails onto a stack of planed timber, removed the yoke, and straightened as best she could, groaning at the heaviness of her belly, the ache in her hips where the bones had already begun to loosen in preparation for birth.

"Emma," a woman called from a nearby lot. "Land sakes, you shouldn't be carrying so much weight. Not in your condition."

Dully, she looked around. Ann Whitney was hurrying out of a nearby cabin, wiping her hands on her apron. Her daughter Sarah Ann—fourteen years old now—followed on her heels, carrying a shallow basin that had been covered by a cloth. Sarah Ann paused to toss the contents into a thick stand of brush. She left the basin in the grass, then ran to catch up with her mother.

Ann took one of Emma's pails. "Lord have mercy; you'll work yourself into early labor."

"We must have water, and who else can carry it?"

"I can. Or I can send one of my children—Sarah Ann, hurry up; take these pails to . . . Where is the water needed, Emma?"

"Our house. Joseph's and mine."

The day after Joseph had found his way to Nauvoo, the Saints had set about building a fine home for their Prophet—one so large they'd named it the Mansion. With so many eager hands to share in the work, it had

taken little more than two weeks to finish. Nauvoo had spread out from
Joseph's mansion like ripples on a pond, rapidly expanding until that
draining, lingering fever had stilled the axes and mallets. The homes
that had already been finished were given over to the sick. The Mansion
was no exception. Those whom the fever had spared returned to their
canvas tents and the few primitive cabins that still remained.

Ann Whitney put an arm around Emma's shoulders, nodding
sharply to her daughter. "Sarah Ann, carry these pails up to the Prophet's
house."

The girl ducked under the yoke, but Emma protested. "Sarah Ann
has only just recovered from the fever. She mustn't work too hard—not
yet."

"Mercy, Emma, it's you who mustn't work so hard. Look at yourself,
fit to burst from that baby. Go on, Sarah Ann, be quick."

When the girl had hurried away, Emma said, "I'll feel dreadful if
your daughter takes the fever again. She's such a good, helpful little
thing. And yet I'm glad not to carry that water any further. I'm so miser-
ably tired, Ann. I never felt this way with the other children."

"It's only strain wearing you thin. You've hardly stopped working
since the fever struck. You're the best nurse Nauvoo has. How much
longer till the baby comes?"

"Days now. Perhaps a week or two at most."

"Well, that settles it. You aren't to lift a finger again till well after
you're delivered."

"There are so many people to care for. I can't allow anyone to suffer."

"And what about yourself, suffering with all this work? No, I won't
hear another word. You go right back to your tent and rest. I'll send
Sarah Ann over this afternoon to fix a bite of bread and soup for your
little ones, but you're not to rise from your bed again until I say so."

"I'll do as you say," Emma promised, "if you'll allow me to see Eliza."
Ann sighed.

"I'll be brief. I promise."

"Then after, straight to your bed."

Eliza had taken the fever several days before. She was laid out now on
a pallet on the floor of the Whitneys' new home. Emma made her way
down the rows of makeshift beds where the Saints groaned, moving fee-
bly under their thin blankets. The air was stale, heavy with the stench of

illness. When she came to Eliza's pallet, she took a dipper of water from a nearby pail and knelt beside her friend.

Eliza struggled to sit up. Her voice was hoarse and small. "How good to see you, Emma."

She held the dipper to Eliza's lips.

"I'm feeling much better," Eliza said, when she'd had her water, "though you wouldn't know it by looking. I'll be up soon, helping nurse the others."

"You mustn't rush. Take all the time you need to recover."

Eliza groaned softly and fell back on her pallet. "I'm going mad, lying here, listening to everyone suffering all around me. The day I can stand to use the chamber pot without any help is the day I'll walk out that door and into fresh air." She frowned, suddenly concerned. "Is Joseph still well?"

"He hasn't taken the fever, if that's what you mean, but he's worn terribly thin. He's been trying to drive this infection back by laying hands on every head he can find."

"He has healed some of us," Eliza said. "We've heard the stories."

"A handful of foolish men have jumped up out of their beds when Joseph commanded them to. Either they'd already recovered, or they hadn't been so very sick to begin with. Or they ended up back in their cots the moment he left their sides."

"His blessings do help. They may not cure the body, but they fortify the spirit. When will he come and bless us in this house again?"

With great effort, Emma rose, gritting her teeth to keep from crying out at the hundred aches in her body. "I'll ask as soon as I see him. God willing, he'll come to bless you soon. If it makes you feel a little less miserable, then let him bless you until his voice gives out. I suppose a fortified spirit is worth something in this world."

Outside, Emma sucked greedily at the fresh air and lumbered toward her tent. The last crusts of dirty snow had receded. A carpet of new growth was springing up to replace the mud between houses. The world was green, the forest canopy lively with birdsong, but none of it could lift her spirit. Would this miserable ague ever relent? If it wouldn't, the Saints would have no choice but to abandon Nauvoo and search for yet another haven. No city could thrive in a pit of disease.

Two men stood guard outside the door to her tent—Lyman Wight and Porter Rockwell, both fervent members of the Danite militia. Rockwell had been a loyal Mormon since the church's earliest days, but only in recent months had Emma taken notice of him. As the tensions with Missouri had escalated, Porter had become an ever-greater spectacle, growing his hair as long as a woman's, wearing a full, untrimmed beard in defiance of church custom. Rumor held that Joseph had given Porter a particularly affecting blessing, calling on him to act as a personal guard, admonishing him never to cut his hair, or else his strength would fail, and Gentile bullets would find his heart. Porter certainly made for a strange sight in Nauvoo. His long hair was plaited into two thick ropes hanging over his shoulders. The tangle of his beard gave him a bestial air, underscored by the smallness and sharpness of his eyes.

He lifted his hat as Emma approached. "Good morning, Mrs. Smith."

She nodded politely, not quite meeting Porter's eye. Since Joseph had blessed him, the man had seemed almost too eager to serve the Prophet. The heat of his faith was like that of a campfire when you stand too near. Menacing.

"Joseph is inside, I assume," Emma said.

"Indeed, he is—resting for a spell. Then he means to go on blessing the sick."

She pushed into the dim tent and found her way to her cot. She lay back, sighing, every bone in her body shuddering. Joseph was in his own narrow bed. He shifted when he heard Emma. He had thrown an arm over his eyes as if to block the light, but there was little light to speak of in the tent.

"You aren't taking the sickness, are you?" she said.

Joseph smiled weakly. "I think not. I'm only weary. I've been blessing and healing for days now, but I couldn't stay on my feet another minute. I had to lie flat for a spell. Do you know, some poor weeping mothers came into this very tent and touched me with their kerchiefs. They wiped their cloths on my brow and hands."

"Whatever for?"

"They mean to put their kerchiefs on their children's heads. They hope to carry some of the Lord's power—a blessing in my absence, to heal their little ones."

Emma sat up, reached around her bulging stomach, and fumbled with the buttons of her boots. She freed her swollen feet from that miserable confinement and turned her ankles. The joints cracked. She said, "You've men standing guard on our tent now."

"Oh, yes. I intend to keep guards at all times from here out. I don't mean to fall into the law's hands again if I can avoid it. I was acquitted this time, but I still have enemies."

"But guards on our own home—such as it is—right here in Nauvoo? Surely that isn't necessary. What do you have to fear from any Mormon?"

He lowered his arm, staring up at the roof of their tent. "I don't know what I ought to fear. I've asked God to enlighten me, or else take the fear away, but He won't. The fear remains. It's cold—as if the cold of that jail cell never left me. It has settled into my very spirit."

Emma lay back once more. She, too, stared up into the shadows at the peak of the tent. The dimness pressed down upon her, heavy as her guilt. She wanted to tell Joseph she was sorry for the part she had played, convincing him to surrender. The words wouldn't come. Instead, she told him, "I suppose guards are well enough, in their place. But you must be careful of the impressions you give. You can't afford to be too militant, too grasping."

He turned to look at her. "Grasping?" There was amusement in his voice. At least he wasn't angry.

"We must keep quiet and keep to ourselves. We mustn't give Illinois any reason to fear us, as Missouri did."

"We've lost so many members of our church, Emma. Why should anyone fear us now? We're a fragmented people. Reduced."

"Perhaps that's the way the Lord wants it. He has winnowed us— separated the wheat from the chaff. Those who followed you from Fayette to Kirtland, and from Kirtland to Far West, and now here to Nauvoo—they are the truest in faith."

"No—God tells me He means for His church to be large, not small. We're meant to grow, to welcome more into our faith. We're meant to spread the restored gospel to every corner of the world. We must go out to the Gentiles and carry the word with us."

"Then if you must search for more members, do it far from home. Don't trouble the people of Illinois."

She could feel him thinking, turning over her words in careful examination. She was grateful he had listened.

At length, he said, "Perhaps, once enough men have recovered, I'll send another mission to Canada."

A sudden, stone-hard inspiration struck her. She said, "You ought to make a mission to England."

"England? What gave you such an idea?"

"Eliza still gets letters from her friends in Cincinnati, though I don't think she has received any since we came to Nauvoo. But her friends have told Eliza what they've read in the newspapers. Life is very hard for a great many people in England. The poorest families must work in dreadfully dangerous factories—men and women alike, even little children."

"Such desperate souls must hunger for comfort," Joseph said. "And depleted as we are, hardworking members would benefit the church as much as the church would benefit them. This is a worthy idea, Emma."

"And," she said, "you must send Brigham Young to lead the mission."

"Why Brigham?"

"If you could have seen him in your absence, Joseph—"

"I've heard the tale. Brigham led the church admirably while I was away."

"Too admirably. I don't deny that he was a bulwark, but the speed with which he took control . . ."

"He has a natural talent for leading men."

"Joseph, I will speak frankly." Now that the shadows lay between them, she felt courageous enough to talk without restraint. "Brigham has an even greater talent for leading men than you have. Over the years I've watched him watching you. Whenever the Lord sees fit to make you stumble, Brigham is right behind you. He walks steadily where you do not. Remember how he kept his head during Zion's Camp. And he has acted twice now to save your own family when you couldn't."

"I'm grateful. He's like a hero from the old myths."

"I'm sure you are grateful. But don't think for a moment that you're the only one who has noticed his heroism."

She could hear him breathing, slowly in, slowly out. He said, "You believe he may try to challenge me for leadership of this church."

"I see that it's possible. If he does, Joseph—when he does—Brigham will have no shortage of admirers ready to throw in their lot with him.

Your people love you, I don't deny that. But I fear a good many of them respect Brigham more."

Later, she would ask herself why she ever said such things to Joseph. Perhaps it was only her bone-deep mistrust of Brigham, seeded at the moment of their first meeting when he had intruded upon her in a vulnerable state. Perhaps she wanted to thwart his designs out of petty dislike. Later she would realize she could have stayed silent in that tent, on that weary day. She could have allowed Brigham to slip the reins right out of Joseph's hands before the Prophet was even aware his hands were empty. She might have been a shopkeeper's wife again—a life which she preferred a thousand times over to the life she led by then.

"Very well," he said. "I'll send Brigham to England. May God bless his work."

How swiftly a year flies. That was her first thought when she pushed for the final time and the baby slid from her body—that great, tearing relief, the feeling she knew so well by now.

Women and girls had crowded into the Mansion to help with the birth any way they could—dozens of women, all eager to see the Prophet's newest child come into the world. They sighed and cooed and wept sweet tears as the new baby drew its first breath and screamed to announce its coming.

How swiftly a year flies. The girl Sarah Ann held up baby Frederick— the first child Emma had birthed in Nauvoo, the one she'd carried in her womb on the flight from Far West. Frederick was a year old now, almost to the day, born just as the terrible fever had begun to abate, releasing Nauvoo from the Devil's grip.

"Look," Sarah Ann said to little Frederick, "you have a baby brother of your own now."

"It's a boy?" Emma clutched at the women around her, pulled herself up from the birthing stool, wavered on her feet. "I have another son?"

"Don't go walking about just yet," Ann said. "Pass the afterbirth first, and let me check to be sure it's whole. After that, you may dance a jig for all I care."

Eliza laughed. Tears shone at the corners of her eyes. "She will dance; you can count on it. Another healthy son! What a blessing, Emma."

The women cleaned away the mess and wrapped the baby in warm blankets while they waited for the last necessary phase of birth. The baby never stopped crying until they pressed that precious bundle into Emma's arms.

Never had she known such contentment. A slant of honey-yellow light came in through the nearest window, illuminating the new child's face—his fine features, his dark curly hair, so like Emma's own. She could tell already that this baby would have her nose, too, not Joseph's, thank goodness. He was perfect—fat and robust, pink as the wake-robin flowers in the forests of Harmony. Through the window, beyond the sphere of her bliss, Nauvoo had flourished into a large and prosperous town, almost a city in its own right. Brigham and his missionaries had sent new migrations of freshly baptized Saints from England every other month. The population of Nauvoo had steadily increased. Now the melodious accents of the English newcomers could be heard on every corner, in every alley of the town.

Five healthy children all her own, thank God. And thank God for Eliza Snow's continued sisterhood. Emma never could have managed alone. She'd taken in several girls, too, all of whom had been orphaned in the violence at Far West. She gave them room and board in Joseph's beautiful Mansion in exchange for their help with the children. With a newborn in the cradle and Frederick still so small, every hand in the Prophet's Mansion would be full.

She called two of the Far West girls to her side—a pair of sisters, nineteen and sixteen years old. Lizzie and Emily Partridge were rather shy and retiring, and sometimes cast sullen looks at Emma when they thought she couldn't see. But they had lost all their family in the destruction of Zion and Far West. If the Partridge sisters were sometimes less than perfect in manners or charity, Emma hadn't the heart to chastise them too severely.

At least the girls smiled now, leaning in to peer at the baby's face. "He's so terribly sweet, Mrs. Smith," Lizzie said.

"He is. And I want you and Emily to go out into Nauvoo and give the good news to everyone."

The sisters exchanged a grin. It was a great honor, to announce the birth of the Prophet's latest son.

Emily said, "What will you call him, Mrs. Smith?"

Emma gazed at the baby. He had settled into contented sleep, his bow of a mouth working, one tiny fist curled beside his face. She had already given Joseph three strong boys, each of whom resembled their father more with the passing days. This boy, dark and fine-featured, belonged to Emma alone. Joseph may have sired him, but there was no hint of the father in this child.

She knew his name in that moment. "His name is Don Carlos," she said. "Tell every soul in Nauvoo."

The end of the year 1840 was approaching; autumn was coming in. A tint of gold among the drying leaves; the deer, when you saw them, sporting antlers in velvet. The heat of the summer dissipating at long last. In the evening, the sunset lingered and the breeze from the river was cool. Twilight was rich with the odor of wet wood and the unfamiliar, lemonish bite of the flowers the English women had brought across the sea, seeds sewn into the pockets of their dresses. Bee balm, catmint, geranium. She could have enjoyed the evening despite the racket the children had been making as they'd run from room to room, shrieking while the orphan girls chased them. It was a night filled with joy and the comforts of a gentle season. Why, then, did her stomach tighten on some unknown tension? Her head ached, not only from the children's noise. There was a pressure all around like the onset of thunder, but when she stepped outside to cut a basketful of greens for the supper table, she saw that the sky was perfectly clear—red and violet, even along the horizon.

She stooped in the mustard patch, gathering the stalks together, and slashed with her knife. The fresh green scent rose up all around her, colored by spice. She heard footsteps on the garden path and called out, "I'm almost ready. Is the water boiling yet?" for she expected to find Eliza there. But when she straightened with a fat bunch of mustard leaves in her hands, she found Joseph at the edge of the patch. He held their youngest in his arms, little Don Carlos, who looked at Emma with a worried expression. Beyond the garden, Porter Rockwell paced from the kitchen door to the fence and back again, his wary eye fixed on Joseph.

"Oh," Emma said in surprise. "Is Carlos well?"

"He seems well enough," Joseph said. "Only . . . troubled somehow. Restless. Like his father, I suppose. There's something in the air tonight. Can you feel it, too?"

Emma dropped the greens into her basket. "It's like thunder coming. What does it mean?"

"I wish I knew. It has made me feel rather sick since I got up this morning. I've tried to ignore it and go on with my day. I've prayed that God might tell me what He intends. I've begun to feel as fussy as this little fellow here. I thought we might take a stroll together—Carlos and his papa. It might improve our moods."

Joseph squinted through the dusk. A man was hurrying toward the Mansion from the southern end of town. There was no mistaking the urgency in his stride. "Who could that be?" he said.

But Emma had recognized the man at a single glance. An intoxicating warmth flared in her chest, coupled with guilt, as always. She said, "It's Don Carlos."

Joseph's mouth tightened. He handed the baby to Emma and went to the garden gate. His back and shoulders were rigid. He hadn't entirely forgiven Don Carlos for beating him, despite the fact that Don Carlos had followed him all the way to Nauvoo. Joseph had frowned when Emma had told him she'd named their youngest son in honor of his brother. But he held the gate open for Don Carlos, ushering him into the garden.

"Good evening," Don Carlos said quietly. He smiled rather sadly at the baby in her arms. "Hello, little man."

"Say hello to your uncle, Carlos."

The baby regarded his namesake soberly.

Joseph said, "What brings you here tonight? You look unsettled."

"I'm afraid I've good reason to be. I spent most of the day in the town of Carthage, arranging next year's affairs for my farm. I heard a dreadful rumor there, and I've wondered all the way home whether I ought to tell you. Maybe it's wiser to leave it be. People love to talk. There could be nothing to this story, nothing at all, and I—"

"Out with it," Emma said, more sharply than she intended. She couldn't stand it any longer—the great weight hanging over their heads, poised to fall.

"Word has made its way," Don Carlos said, "from Missouri to Carthage. Lilburn Boggs, the governor, you know—"

"I'm not apt to forget him in a hurry," Joseph said.

"He's still chafing over Gallatin. He feels justice wasn't done properly, and the matter is still unsettled."

Joseph's mouth fell open. "Not done properly? My men and I suffered in that hell of a jail for months."

"Perhaps there's no truth to the story," Don Carlos said.

Emma laid a hand on his shoulder, though it pained her to do it. It pained him, too, from the look in his eyes. "Tell us," she said. "Everything you know, everything you've heard."

"They say Boggs means to secure a warrant for your arrest. He wants to put you on trial again under a new judge—one who's apt to find you guilty."

"He can't do it!" Joseph was all but shouting now.

Emma had never seen him so angry. Instinctively, she turned her shoulder to Joseph, shielding the baby from his rage. The kitchen door opened. Eliza came out onto the stoop, drawn by the raised voice.

He roared, "I've already been acquitted, to say nothing of the time I served in prison while waiting for my trial. There are laws against such things. A man can't be tried endlessly till his accuser finds a judge who agrees to call him guilty!"

Don Carlos said, "Boggs means to find new charges to bring against you—some other reason for a trial."

Joseph left them abruptly. He stalked along the garden path. "Then let Boggs do his worst. He'll find I've worse yet to do myself."

Emma called after him: "Joseph, you mustn't lose your head. We'll find a lawyer to guide us."

He kicked a stone with such force that it flew through the dim evening, arcing over the garden fence, into the tall grass beyond. He followed it, springing over the rails. A moment later, he was lost amid the trees at the edge of their lot, swallowed by the dusk.

The baby whimpered in Emma's arms. Eliza came rushing into the garden, pale with worry.

"I'm sorry," Don Carlos said. "I was afraid this news would upset your peace."

"It's better to know what's in store than to find an unpleasant surprise. I had hoped we were finished with Missouri. This past year has been so quiet, so happy, with the city growing and the new members coming from England. I ought to have known. I ought to have realized peace couldn't be had as easily as that."

Eliza said, "I believe we'll never be finished with Missouri, nor its governor."

"Nor its militia," Emma replied. "The truth is, Joseph went entirely too far."

Eliza glanced toward the woodland, where Joseph had disappeared. Then she looked at Emma with frank disappointment. "The way you speak sometimes, Emma Smith. How can Joseph go too far if he does God's will?"

Emma brushed the baby's hair with her lips. She couldn't meet her friend's eye. Nor could she look at Don Carlos. He of all people saw her heart clearly. He understood.

"Well?" Eliza had never been so pert before.

"Sometimes," Emma answered carefully, "I find it difficult to maintain perfect faith."

Eliza fell silent. Her incredulity was a palpable thing, thick as the humidity that rose from the marsh in summer. Don Carlos, realizing he had no right to hear such a conversation, walked away to the garden gate. He lingered there, a gray silhouette.

Emma groped for something to say—any plausible thing that wouldn't break Eliza's heart, yet still could be called true. "There are times when I'm plagued by doubt, when God sees fit to test me with questions I can't answer, riddles I can't solve."

"Emma, how could you?"

"You have a poet's soul. It's easier for you to believe without proof."

"Everything we have suffered—the journeys we've made. And the terrible things that were done to our people. Have these meant nothing to you?"

"Are these things a sturdy enough peg on which to hang one's faith?" Emma had spoken as gently as she could, but Eliza recoiled as if she'd been slapped.

"You're questioning my good sense."

"No, Eliza—"

"You think me a fool."

"Never."

"Do you know what I think? I think Joseph has led us through count-less dark passages. He has suffered much for the sake of spreading God's word and saving souls in the Last Days. And I believe the Prophet de-serves a wife whose faith is as strong and pure as his own."

Before Emma could answer, Eliza lifted her skirts and all but ran down the garden path. Don Carlos opened the gate for her. She brushed past without a word. Moments later she vanished around the corner of the house.

Don Carlos returned to Emma and picked up her basket of greens. "A fellow like me ought to learn to keep his mouth shut. I've brought you nothing but grief tonight."

A pale bar of light moved through the dusk as the moon came up over the river. She watched the faint moonlight spreading across the garden because she couldn't look at Don Carlos, not then.

"I don't understand why Eliza should be upset," she said. "But I was unwise to speak so frankly. No one in this church can understand what's in my heart. Nor can they understand what isn't in my heart—the faith I lack. Anyone who felt as I do now—Oliver Cowdery, the Whitmers, even Martin Harris—they've all been free to leave. But I . . ."

"We're bound to Joseph by something stronger than faith," Don Car-los said. "It's an iron chain. It can't be broken."

She nodded. She kissed her baby's forehead, because she couldn't kiss Don Carlos. She said, "You understand."

The things we cannot break: our names, our families, the histories that make us real and knit our substance together. The words we speak, which bind us—why do words have power? Once you make a declara-tion, of knowledge, of faith, it becomes the very stuff of your body. To unsay words you've spoken brings the same hot, hollow agony as spill-ing your own blood. If you say you believe, then you must believe, you will believe. The words themselves, once spoken, are shackles around your limbs. This is the secret that lies buried in the old words, the books on Mother Smith's shelf, the shadowed workings she brought from her ancestral land and breathed into the spirits of her children.

You cannot break a word. You cannot break a vow to God unless you long for hellfire. You can't cease to be a woman who has carried the children of a certain man within her body and given those children life. You are bound to him forever. It doesn't matter if you love him. You can't walk away from your children, not ever. Easier by far to tear out your own tongue.

Judge her, if you must, for remaining at Joseph's side, even though she didn't believe. Think her a coward and a fool. Any scorn you have for Emma, she has heaped upon herself already, and done it a thousand times more. Mock her, despise her, pity her, condemn her. She has heard it all, and heard it in her own voice.

If she knew how to break the iron chain, she would have snapped it years ago. But there is power in the word, and the word is binding.

There came a day, late in the month of September, when Joseph didn't come in to supper. Emma and Eliza fed the children and the Far West girls in strained silence. They waited for the sound of the door opening, the sound of his boot on the threshold. But all the doors remained closed, and Joseph's chair was empty.

When the children were in bed and the washing-up was finished, and still Joseph hadn't returned, Emma walked through a cool, gentle night to the meetinghouse. She hoped she would find him there. Perhaps he had called some conference of his priests and apostles. She would have welcomed finding the men in a drunken revelry, as she'd found them after the Kirtland dedication. But the meetinghouse was silent, all its windows dark.

The next morning, she went to Don Carlos with her fears. He assembled the Prophet's most faithful counselors; they filled the meetinghouse for hours. They rumbled and shouted and shook their heads over the rumor Don Carlos had heard in Carthage, the news that Missouri was coming for their Prophet again.

Emma sat in the front pew of the meetinghouse, eyes downcast, listening as the men chased each other's words in endless circles. Don Carlos was steadfast to her left; Porter Rockwell, hunched and muttering, to her right.

"He slipped away without telling me," Porter said. "If I'd known he planned to leave Nauvoo I would have been there beside him. I would have protected him from God's enemies, whatever the cost."

She listened to their arguments for two hours at least. Then the door to the meeting hall crashed open. Emma turned amid a rustle and murmur of surprise.

Joseph was there on the threshold, heaving for breath as if he'd been running. One eye was blackened. The sleeve of his coat had been torn away. He stared over the heads of his followers to the altar at the far end of the room. Then he limped down the aisle. Whispers swelled to cheers. Joseph paid no heed. He mounted the dais and stood behind the altar, displaying his sorry state before his people with grim determination.

Silence spread across the hall. They waited for the Prophet to speak.

"I went to Carthage," he said without preamble. "When I learned that Lilburn Boggs meant to arrest me and try me—against all laws of the land—my wife, Emma, advised me to seek out a lawyer who would defend me in a court of law, so that was what I did. I rode to Carthage alone, but I was taken on the road."

"By whom?" John Lee cried. "Tell us, Joseph—is Missouri to blame?"

"I was taken indeed by a sheriff who carried a warrant signed by Governor Boggs." The men groaned. Some pounded their fists on the backs of the pews. It sounded like the drums of an army. "This posse of lawbreakers carried me off toward the Missouri border. They would have taken me over it, but I managed to induce one man to carry a message to Doniphan, who was ever our friend. They kept me overnight in a jail cell on the border while the sheriff waited to learn what he could do with me. When dawn came, there also came a letter from Doniphan, with a writ of habeas corpus."

"What does it mean?" Porter asked.

"It meant I couldn't be held without trial. Not unless that Missouri sheriff could prove lawful grounds for my confinement. He could prove no such thing, and he knew it. I was sent on my way."

The men cheered again.

"As I was released from that stinking prison," Joseph said, "it was given unto me to know that God will bless this place. He has commanded that a temple should be built to Him here—a shining temple on the high hill, a beacon to the hearts of all men, and a sign to our enemies that we stand steadfast! The Latter-day Saints will be driven forth no more from any land! Like our temple, we shall be immovable, too mighty for God's enemies to afflict!"

The men cried out in triumph. But Joseph's jaw was set, his face white with outrage where it wasn't bruised to black.

"We won't bear this insult meekly," Joseph thundered. "I say unto thee, with the voice of God, that Lilburn Boggs has damned himself to a violent death."

"Joseph!" Emma lurched to her feet, but half of the assembled men did the same, beating the air with their fists. They howled like hungry dogs.

His voice cracked like a whip above the crowd. "Boggs won't last a year before the Destroying Angel finds him. His death is written and sealed into God's book. Hear me well, ye Saints—hear the revelation of God. Lilburn Boggs will meet a bloody end. Thus saith the Lord. Amen!"

She fell back into her pew. Porter Rockwell had gone still beside her, eyes fixed on Joseph. Don Carlos took her hand. She hadn't the presence of mind to pull away. She scarcely felt his touch. What Joseph had set in motion couldn't be stopped. She felt that certainty like a blade against her throat.

All the children were asleep, the girls from Far West. Everyone slept, save for Emma. She had jolted awake because of an absence beside her, the place where her husband should have been. She put her hand on the mattress. It was cold, as if he'd never come to bed at all.

She slipped out from under the quilts and paused beside a burned-down fire, the embers pale and small among the ashes. What hour was it now? Well past midnight. The embers crackled faintly. There was a sighing of wind around the eaves, but otherwise silence, until she heard the parlor door open and close again, softly.

She went to the window and looked down on a flat, dark world. The sky was half-clouded. Only a few stars shone here and there, and they were weak, but she could make out Joseph, unmistakable even in the deepest night—his height, his permanent limp. He was dressed all in black. She recalled another September, a lifetime ago, driving with Joseph to the foot of a hill. Fear had held her to her place back then, but now it was fear that made her follow. She was mother to five children, guardian to half a dozen orphaned girls. She couldn't sit idly by, allowing one man to endanger them all. She hadn't broken the chain; perhaps she never would. But she had learned how to drag her fetter handily enough.

She wrapped a dressing robe around her flannel nightgown, then tied her warmest shawl around her shoulders. She donned her boots so hastily, she had time to fasten only three or four buttons on each. Then she was down the stairs and out the door, staring through the darkness, searching for any sign of her husband.

She didn't see Joseph, but rather a flicker of movement—black against black on the road that led to the crest of the hill. The previous morning, the church had gathered there to lay the cornerstones of the new temple. Emma followed him as swiftly as she dared. She wouldn't allow herself to come too close. If he heard her footsteps and found her on the road, he would only send her away.

He climbed the hill in perfect darkness. There was no shovel braced on his shoulder now, but he did carry something under his arm—a dense pale brick, some solid thing. Emma maintained her distance until he'd gained the crest of the hill. She watched him walk out into the cleared lot where the temple would rise above the city of the Saints.

Emma waited at the verge of the road. The night was cold, but the creatures of summer still went on doggedly living, the crickets singing in the grass, the frogs. They made a melancholy chorus. Listening to that song, she felt an unbridgeable distance between herself and creation. The things that bound her to Joseph also held her apart from the world.

He walked out into the field. He fell on his knees beside the nearest cornerstone and began to dig with his hands, scrabbling in the loosened soil like some small, desperate animal. Only then did Emma go to him. He didn't seem surprised to find her there. He'd removed his jacket, pushed up the sleeves of his shirt. His hands and forearms were black with soil. He had burrowed into the ground beside the cornerstone, into the secretive earth.

The thing Joseph had carried lay now on the grass beside him. It was a stack of papers, carefully bound along one edge with scarlet twine. The twine had frayed in places. The papers were warped by damp and age, spotted now with mildew. But Emma recognized the pages—the original manuscript of the Book of Mormon.

"Joseph," she whispered, "what are you doing?"

He paused, sitting back on his heels. He panted for his breath, and wiped his brow with his wrist, grinding dirt into his skin.

"Burying it," he said. "I've had enough trouble with this book."

Then he went on digging. Stone scraped his knuckles and made them bleed. The soil ran like sand through his fingers.

XIII

The Restoration of All Things

1841–1842

Some in Nauvoo called it the Blessing of Jacob. That was its first name, the first murmur Emma heard in the streets as she walked from shop to shop and back home again, with the orphan girls trailing behind, chatting among themselves in their bright young voices. The Blessing of Jacob, one man would say to another, and turn to watch them as they passed, Joseph's wife and the lovely, biddable girls of his household.

Soon some began to call it celestial marriage. Some called it spiritual wifery. Those who were honest called it adultery, and a shame—although few men by that time could claim any honesty. They tempered their understanding of probity by the Prophet's approval and disapproval.

Joseph himself called it the Restoration of All Things. The Last Days were at hand. If the Gospel had been made anew by the coming of the Prophet, then why shouldn't the original laws be restored upon the earth, the laws that had governed Jacob and Abraham? In Exodus it is written: if a man entice a maid that is not betrothed, and lie with her, he shall surely endow her to be his wife. And if that man has a wife already? God is silent on that point.

She can't tell you now the precise date, nor even the year when the doctrine of spiritual wifery emerged. A disappointment, surely, for there is nothing the world longs to know about the Mormons more than this— the greatest peculiarity of our peculiar people. The doctrine has marked us for time and eternity. It defines us in your eyes, if not in our own. Strange, then, that Emma can't tell you—none of us can—when and how it started.

It came up like a new spring under the ground, a patch of mud where there had been only weeds the day before, or a flush of deeper green in a slight depression. Little by little, it seeps to the surface—an inch of water standing in a bootprint, an inch that will not drain. And one day you look out the window of your parlor and there's a puddle in the corner of your garden, then a pond, for everyone to see. You can do nothing about it, so you rearrange the vegetable beds. You tell yourself at least the frogs make a pleasant sound in the evening.

First it was a pain in Joseph's heart, for he found himself drawn to women who were not his wife, and he knew this to be a sin. Shouldn't a prophet be stronger than sin? But Joseph had learned the lesson of his life and learned it all too well. He had written his book. The book had won hearts and minds. He had made a church out of nothing, from a raw idea. He had taken hold of the world around him, shaped it into the form that pleased him best. His church had gone on, growing. New Mormons came from the eastern states, from England, from Canada, from other places besides—more every week, almost every day. If God had wanted Joseph to stop, wouldn't He have stopped him?

Whosoever looketh on a woman to lust after her hath committed adultery with her already in his heart.

But a man can't commit adultery with a woman who is his wife.

When she can bear to think on the subject at all, she believes it began with Fannie Alger.

That girl hadn't been infatuated with the Prophet—not at first—but Joseph had been preoccupied with her, tormented by her presence—or by his inability to ignore her presence. The sinful way his eye had strayed again and again to her youthful body, her blushing cheek. Emma had seen clearly that day when she'd looked through the window of Joseph's store. And sometimes she will think about the way Nancy Marinda came down the stairs in the Johnson home, pausing for Joseph to see. She'll remember the string of beads around the girl's satin neck. She never removed them.

Did Joseph begin whispering to his most trusted apostles then, in Fayette? Did he wait to reveal this secret doctrine until the Mormons had come to Kirtland? She recalled the old charges of bigamy. But it hardly matters now. By the time Nauvoo was established and thriving, knowledge of the Blessing of Jacob was spreading faster than the infections that rose each spring from the marsh. Booklets were published by the town press under names no one in Nauvoo had heard before—secret names to hide the identities of the real authors.

For a woman to continue performing the rituals of the marriage bed without any love for her husband is fornication in the wife; it is a sin. But a divorced man is not known in the whole canon of scriptures. In ancient times under the law of God, the permission of a plurality of wives had a direct tendency to prevent the possibility of fornication in the wife. But the man marries the woman, and the woman is given in marriage. The husband is not the property of the wife in any sense of the word. There is no positive law of God against a man's marrying Leah and Rachel both. To God only are men accountable in this matter, and not to their wives.

Did every man in Nauvoo uphold this new doctrine? Of course not. There were some who spurned it and saw it for what it was—the grasping of a man intoxicated by power, or a man unmade by fear. William Law, who ran the newspaper, the *Nauvoo Expositor*, scoffed at the Blessing of Jacob and told Joseph flatly that he would never take a second wife, wouldn't even consider it. His wife, Jane, was all the woman any honest man could ask for. Don Carlos had brawled with two fellows who'd taken him aside in the newly built Masonic Hall to tell him about the wondrous new teaching, the latest revelation handed down from God. Don Carlos had blackened one man's eye. He had shaken his fist in the face of the other, and said, "Any man who will preach and practice spiritual wifery will go to Hell. Be sure of that. Even if it is my brother Joseph."

It started as a pain in Joseph's heart. It became a fist he could tighten, a way to test the loyalty of his men, a way to bring some closer than others and flatter them, that they were privy to celestial secrets. It became a liquor to him—sweet at first, this power to shape the earthly realm, this power to declare a thing was the will of God and be believed without question. But even the sweetest wine goes sour with the years. Like wine, power intoxicates. An intoxicated man leaves all his sense behind.

Little by little, the doctrines changed. The shape of not only this earthly realm, but even the shape of Heaven changed, all in service to Joseph's desires. He had no power to tear his eyes away from the women of Nauvoo. But he had the power to recast sin as salvation. He told the church: God Himself was once as we are now. Every man who grows sufficiently in spirit can become a god at the end of his life, with worlds of his own to govern—worlds to populate with spirit children.

A man needs countless spirit children if he hopes to populate entire worlds. If a man may get a handful of children from just a single wife, how many more children can he make with two wives? With three? With a dozen?

Perhaps it was only greed and lust that drove him to this act. Or perhaps the very substance of spiritual wifery was fear. For by that time, the early summer of 1841, Joseph had seen the inside of a jail cell more often than he liked, and he knew Lilburn Boggs was hunting him. All of Missouri would cheer to see him strung up by his neck and kicking.

In her more generous moments, she thinks fear must be the reason for the change that came over Joseph that year. The booklets first, then discussions at the weekly debating clubs. Then sermons about Leah and Rachel given from the pulpit on Sunday, in a crowded meetinghouse, the women of the congregation lowering their faces to hide their troubled eyes. Joseph knew by then that his power couldn't continue forever. There are limits to what even a prophet may do. You may handle and shape the world around you, and mold reality to your whim. But every time you set your hand to the substance of the world, it bends and folds and weakens. All too soon, it will take a shape even you can't recognize. And then the world you've made is ripe for another man to pick up and hold.

It was early in the month of July—a hot evening, the air still thick with the breath of the river. Emma walked alone to the southern end of town, to Hyrum and Jerusha's house where Julia had spent the day with her aunt and cousins in a sewing bee. Emma passed the small, humble house Don Carlos had built. Don Carlos was outside—she could sense him, a suggestion of movement at the periphery of her vision, a flash of golden light. She knew he would call out to her, and she would be obliged to stop and speak with him. She wanted to speak with him. She was desperate for it, every moment of every day—and she feared to do it, the way she feared hellfire.

"Emma."

His voice stopped her in her tracks. The sound of him, the awful yearning of years, the way his longing hollowed out that word, her name. He didn't call her "Sister." She was only Emma to him on that hot, close evening—an Emma no one had seen so clearly before, not even Joseph, not even herself.

Don Carlos shuffled his feet at the edge of his yard. "Please," he said. "I would talk with you."

He bade her sit on the step at his front door. The sandstone block was warm from the sun, rough beneath her hand. She pressed her fingers into it, almost dug into the stone. The slight pain kept her face neutral and calm. She thought Don Carlos would sit, too, but he remained on his feet. He paced with an awkward gait—stiff, as if he wore something restrictive and unfamiliar. He limped a little as he moved. One knee wouldn't quite bend.

"I must tell you," he said. He looked out at the road, at his bean plants swaying on their poles, up to the roofline of his house—looked at anything but her. "I must tell you, Emma, I've decided to marry."

The most curious thing was that the news didn't strike her as a blow. There was a gentle unfolding of sorrow, a breath released slowly. Grief came in. She held it and wouldn't let it go. *Of course*, she thought. *A man of his age wants a wife, a family.*

He said, "I've asked Agnes Coolbrith to marry me, and she has agreed."

"Agnes is a good woman. I know she'll make you happy."

Now at last he looked at her. He stepped close, so he seemed to fill all the world, like the summer's humidity, a thing she could never escape. "I would have it otherwise. You know I would, if there were any way. I've waited and hoped, but my hope has been in vain. He's too strong for us, Emma. He holds all the world in his hands."

"Not all the world. It only seems that way, because Nauvoo is so isolated, but this isn't the world."

"It may as well be. Neither of us is strong enough to break what holds us here. What does the rest of the world matter when you live your life in a cage?"

Tears came to her eyes. She couldn't look at him any longer.

"I was at the Masonic Hall this morning," Don Carlos said. "In the upper floor. We've been holding our rites there until the temple is finished."

She nodded. She couldn't speak.

He cleared his throat. Hesitantly, as if he spoke of something dangerous, he said, "There are rites a man must undertake. Before he is married."

"The endowments," Emma said. "I know. Joseph discussed them
with me years ago, when he was writing them for Kirtland."

"No." The word came out strangled, almost a whisper. "I went to the
temple often enough in Kirtland; I ought to know. The rites are different
now. He has changed them. By God, I don't know what these changes
mean."

Startled, she looked up at him, blinking back the tears.

Don Carlos pulled at the collar of his shirt, loosening one button,
then another. Emma flushed. How giddy and ridiculous she felt, going
pink like some virgin girl. She thought perhaps she ought to get up and
hurry away, but she was fixed in place, her fingers biting into the stone.
Then she realized Don Carlos hadn't exposed his skin. He wore something under his shirt—a garment made of white linen.

"What is it?" she said.

"A special piece of clothing. All in one, like a union suit for the
winter—but it's summer, and it's monstrously hot." He touched his
neck, then his wrist, then pointed to his feet. "It goes from here, to here,
to here. Covers the whole body, another layer under the clothes. We're to
wear it at all times, we men who've been endowed in the temple. Except
when we're bathing or . . . well, you can imagine what else."

"But why?"

"For protection. Spiritual protection—that's what I was told. But
truly, because Joseph said to do it, and who will tell him no? What man
will refuse him when everyone else in this world obeys?"

He lifted his boot and placed it on the step beside her. She had just
enough time to realize it was the leg on which he'd been limping, and
then he was pulling up the cuff of his trousers and the white garment underneath. Emma swallowed hard. She couldn't look away from the bare
flesh, the paleness of his skin where the sun had never touched him. It
was white as marble, and the hairs of his leg were a curious olive-bronze,
like wheat in August. The hairs bent like a wheatfield in the wind; they
wrapped around the curve of his muscle, his strong, honest calf. The
cuff rose higher, to the place where he had tied a bandage tightly over a
wound, just above his kneecap. Red seeped through.

"You're hurt," Emma said.

"I'm marked. For life. Cut deeply enough to scar. It's part of the rites now. A washing, an anointing—"

"That was done in Kirtland."

"Yes, but cutting wasn't. I was made to swear my loyalty to the church. I was made to promise I would reveal nothing about the ceremony to anyone who hadn't undergone it himself. And to seal my vow, they told me I must consent to have my guts spilled and my tongue torn out if I break my word."

"Don Carlos!"

"It's true. They drew a knife across the white garment, just at my navel. They cut the fabric to show me how they would deal with me if I told. Then they took the knife to my knee—real blood spilled, to seal my promise. To bind me to Joseph and his church."

She pressed a hand to her stomach. The heat, the heaviness of the air, the slow breath rising from the river. She felt weak, fragmented, small. "Don't tell me any more. What if it's true? What if you've damned yourself by speaking?"

He let the cuff of his trousers fall. "I'm not afraid."

"But you are. If you weren't afraid, you wouldn't be marrying Agnes Coolbrith. That's why we've never left. We can't leave, because what if it's all true? What if this is God's restored church, and the Last Days have come? How will we be damned, if we cut ourselves off from Christ?"

Don Carlos moved toward her, just close enough that he could touch her face. His fingers brushed her cheek, only for a moment. If anyone had seen from the road or from the window of some neighboring house, they might have taken it for brotherly affection.

In August, when the summer's heat peaked and the land seemed to crouch and tremble under the sun, Brigham Young returned from England. Nauvoo gathered at the river front—all who were well enough to leave their beds—cheering and waving kerchiefs as the church's steamboat pulled to its pier. Brigham stood at the rail, one hand raised in solemn salute, waiting for Joseph to detach himself from the crowd and walk down the pier to meet him.

"England's climate must have agreed with Brother Brigham," Eliza observed. "He's stouter than ever before."

"England's climate, or England's food," Emma said. The air was thick, and doubly so along the shore. It made her feel sluggish and heavy, shortening her temper, which had never been especially long to begin with. Sweat trickled down her back. Beneath her corset she felt like an overused dish rag, grimy, wet, and limp. "This air is abysmal. It's making me ungenerous."

Eliza smiled, tucking her embroidered kerchief in her sleeve. "Not that you've been so terribly generous with Brigham in pleasanter seasons."

"There are more pressing concerns than his tender feelings. The ague, Eliza—I can't believe it's back so soon."

"Back? By my reckoning, it never went away."

They had lived three springtimes in Nauvoo. Each year the foul humors drifted up from the marsh to infect a certain number of residents—fewer each time, thank goodness for small mercies. This year, the men of the city had managed to drain the boggiest parts of the riverbank. Emma had hoped that draining the marsh would curb the worst of the annual fever. Instead, the disease had held on, persisting for weeks after it should have subsided. All around her, the congregation bore signs of recent illness: sallow skin, hollow eyes, bodies weak from weariness, lips cracked and pale.

"Ann Whitney isn't here," Emma said. "I suppose she has taken the illness again."

"She takes it every year, but never so badly that she can't recover."

Eliza spoke as she often did now—not in a hostile tone, but with a detachment Emma sometimes found overly polite, almost arrogant. They were still friends and Eliza still lived under Emma's roof. But an uneasy distance had persisted between them since that night almost a year ago, when Eliza had run weeping from the garden—when she'd told Emma that Joseph deserved a better wife. Perhaps that coolness had always frosted the edges of her personality, but Emma hadn't noticed until now.

Joseph made his way up the pier to welcome Brigham home with a hearty embrace. When he laid his hands on Brigham's head to bestow a blessing, the crowd murmured into silence. Emma could just hear the intonations of Joseph's voice, rising and falling in that bold, commanding music, the way he always prayed. But she couldn't discern his words from her place on the shore.

When the blessing was finished and the crowd began to clap and sing again, Emma said, "There are so many faces missing from this gathering. I pray God lifts the illness soon."

"If it has been an especially long trial, at least the ague hasn't claimed so many lives this year."

Joseph led Brigham to the shore. The men who had thus far submitted to the temple endowment—some forty all told—gathered to offer their prayers over the returned missionary. Don Carlos wasn't among them, nor had Emma seen Agnes, his new bride. She sent up a quick prayer to Heaven that neither had taken ill. She tried to amend that prayer with a hope that they were enjoying the blissful early days of their marriage, when every word and touch was lingering and sweet. She wanted to wish Don Carlos all the happiness she lacked, but her spirit withered. Whatever seeds of generosity she might have planted fell on stony soil. The best Emma could do was to tell herself, *It's only the heat that makes you grudging.*

The crowd shifted and parted. Joseph and Brigham walked up the slope toward the Masonic Hall, where a feast had been laid for the whole town. Emma and Eliza fell into step far behind the men. They moved slowly in the muggy air.

"Tell me," Eliza said, all her accustomed coolness melting in an instant. She was warm and frank again, the way she'd been in Kirtland and Far West. "What do you think of this Blessing of Jacob? I've heard so much about it, but—"

"What a strange subject to raise now." Emma dabbed her neck and brow with her kerchief.

"I hope you don't think me improper. I seldom have a chance to speak with you unless the orphans are near, and it's no fit subject for girls of their age. But of course, the debating clubs are fairly abuzz with talk about the Blessing. I've been longing to know what you think of it."

"I think you're overly fond of gossip, Eliza Snow. You always have been."

Eliza nudged her with an elbow. "Come now. It's not gossip if the whole town is talking about it."

"That's the very definition of the word."

Eliza laughed so merrily that Emma felt as if she'd said something foolish.

"How does it strike you?" Eliza persisted like the ague. "Some believe Joseph couldn't possibly have given such a commandment. Others are ready to swear they learned of it directly from the Prophet himself."

"It can't be true. Men taking more than one wife—and God smiling down on it? How scandalous, even to think of it."

Wistfully, Eliza said, "I don't know if it's scandalous, exactly."

"Of course it's a scandal! Or it would be, if there were any truth to it. An upright woman wouldn't take so much glee in listening to these shameful stories."

"I don't take glee. I have a curious mind." Eliza looked around uneasily. The women nearest them had begun to sing; Eliza slowed until they were almost alone at the tail end of the crowd. "What if there is some form of truth to this story?"

"Form of truth? What on earth are you talking about?"

"What if the Blessing of Jacob isn't a rumor? What if this is a real commandment from God?"

Emma barked a short, hard laugh. "Do you believe in a God who rewards lust? Do you believe in a God who approves of women comporting themselves like . . . like common whores?"

Eliza's cheeks reddened at the coarse language.

"I'm sorry," she said. "It's only this heat."

After a moment, Eliza said, "If it were a true commandment from God, that men should take many wives, then I suppose no woman who married an already-married man could be called . . . what you said. A woman of loose morals."

"I can't believe you're even entertaining such thoughts. What has come over you?"

"It is only a venture of the mind."

"A venture?"

"An experiment with thought. I am a poetess, after all. It's my calling to imagine and to ask, 'what if.'"

"You should be careful with those ventures. Stray too far along an experimental path, and you may find Satan waiting at its end."

"If I don't stray far enough along the path, I may not see some critical facet of our nature. That is what fascinates me, Emma dear—what I try to capture with my poetry: the hidden dells and valleys of the human heart. And this business of the rumored Blessing—well, it brings out some of the most intriguing behavior. You know how people can be."

"Lustful," Emma said.

"Gregarious. Lonely. Longing for connection, and for bliss."

The baby had begun to cry. "Best go and see to her," Brigham said to his wife.

Mary Ann Young rose from the table, laying her napkin carefully beside her plate before she left the dining room. Emma couldn't help but notice that Mary Ann had scarcely touched her supper, though she had cooked as fine a feast as anyone in Nauvoo had seen—roasted lamb and potatoes flavored with herbs, shelled beans in cream, stewed onions, a summer salad of purslane and Indian-cress blossoms with a bright, peppery bite. Had she taken ill? Emma peered more closely at Mary Ann's face as she left the room. There was no flush on her skin, no sweat—none of the typical signs of the marsh ague.

"I'll come along and help you," Emma said. "It has been too long since I've seen your little darlings. Excuse me, Joseph, Brother Brigham."

She followed Mary Ann from the room, into an umber corridor paneled with dark wood. After the festivity at the Masonic Hall, Brigham had insisted Joseph and Emma should join him for supper—a private celebration of his homecoming. Brigham had been so wildly successful in his mission to England, Joseph couldn't have turned him down if he'd wanted to.

Emma could imagine a thousand ways she would rather spend the evening than in Brigham's company—especially now that he was inflated by triumph. She had consoled herself with thoughts of Mary Ann—who, as a highly skilled herbalist and a woman of great culture and education, could always be counted on for fascinating conversation. But Mary Ann had been subdued all evening. She had spoken little, and even then, her gaze had remained fixed on the floor.

She followed Mary Ann into the children's room. No lamp burned, but a fat moon rode low in the sky and its silvery light fell upon the children's faces where they slept in their narrow beds. The two eldest, Joseph and Brigham Jr., were fine strong boys of seven and five years. They lay sprawled across their bed, blankets askew, but their breathing was regular and deep. There was no sign of the illness on them, either. The little three-year-old girl, named after her mother, clutched a rag doll to her chest and snored lightly, her soft golden curls fanned around her face. Alice, the baby—just over a year old—had pulled herself up inside the crib. Her crying hadn't wakened the other children, thank goodness. When she saw her mother and heard Mary Ann whisper her name, the baby settled at once, allowing herself to be lifted from the crib without any fuss.

"You have the sweetest children," Emma said. "They all look quite well."

"Oh, yes." Mary Ann swayed the baby from side to side. "The boys are so healthy they've about run me ragged. It's a blessing they're sleeping now. I thought they'd never stop climbing all over the Prophet."

"Joseph has always enjoyed games and riddles. I think little children can sense the fun in him and love him for it."

A pause. Mary Ann bounced the baby on her hip, half turned away as if she were trying to hide her face.

Emma said, "You were so quiet at supper, I thought perhaps you were preoccupied. I worried that one of your children had taken the sickness."

"Not these little scraps."

"Are you sure you're well? This is the most I've heard you speak since we arrived."

The baby had sagged back into sleep. Mary Ann returned her to the crib, tucking a little patchwork blanket around her. She straightened with a sigh. "I'm troubled in my spirit. I've heard such scandalous talk, and I don't know what to make of it."

"You refer to the Blessing of Jacob, I suppose," Emma said wryly, "the doctrine of spiritual wifery."

"You've heard of it, too?"

"Lately I feel as if I shall never hear of anything else. Eliza nattered at me all through the day's celebration—celestial marriage this, Blessing of Jacob that, and what it might mean and how it might be carried out and who might or might not have taken it up already."

Mary Ann's face fell. She was a plain woman, round and unrefined, a startling contrast to her brilliant mind. Her nose was entirely too long and thin, her brows forever arched, fixed in an expression of bewilderment or pained disapproval. Her looks weren't improved by the misgiving that came over her now. "It's true, then? Have the men of our city taken other wives?"

"Land sakes, no, it isn't true." She recalled herself and lowered her voice. She didn't want to wake the baby again. "It's only rumor. You know people lose their wits when they fall under the spell of gossip. It's a shocking story, and that's why they spread it—for the thrill it gives them. But it's sinful to gossip, and worse to think up such scandalous tales. They'll come to regret their wrongdoing soon enough, all these tongue-waggers and clatterans."

"Then the Prophet has said nothing to you about such . . . practices?"

"Not a word. Set your mind at ease. And for Heaven's sake, let's give no more credence to the story. The gossips of Nauvoo will lose interest someday and move on to a fresher tale."

They left the children's room. Side by side, they moved down the dark hall. A line of golden lamplight showed at the bottom of the dining room door. Emma could hear Joseph's voice coming through the crack in the door, too.

Something about the sound of him raised a prickle along her spine. This wasn't the way he usually spoke—not to a friend like Brigham—so quiet as to be almost secretive. The low urgency of his tone filled her with caution. She caught Mary Ann by the arm, slowing her without speaking. When Mary Ann looked at her in surprise, she held a finger to her lips.

Together they stole forward until they were almost pressed against the door—until they could hear their husbands' words.

"I tell you," Joseph said, "no man will attain the fullness of exaltation in this world or the next unless he does this thing. If a man is to become like God, and reign over his own worlds, he must populate those worlds with spirits. How else is it to be done?"

"Is there no other way, no alternative?" Brigham spoke with a strange vigor, a lilt to his voice Emma had never heard before.

"No other way. This is the holy order of the family. This is how large and righteous families are made. God Himself is no stranger to it. He taught the order to Jacob, who married Leah and Rachel, and also took their handmaids as wives. This was the origin of Israel."

Mary Ann gripped Emma's hand.

Joseph said, "You see, with the Last Days close at hand—practically upon us already—every ancient law and custom must be revived. Even this. Perhaps this above all others, for God means to make of us a great people, a vast church practicing the true, righteous ways. A church large enough to fill the world. Abraham was promised that he should be the father of nations. God offers us the same blessing, but we must have the courage to accept it."

"Think of the difficulties it'll raise. How the women will quarrel!"

The sly, laughing cant to Brigham's voice soured Emma's stomach. He was making a show of protest, playing at reluctance, all so he could later claim he hadn't done this thing for lust—his intentions had always been pure. Such bitterness rose in her throat that she almost spat on the floor. Did Brigham think he could deceive the Almighty? She had seen him grin at young women in the streets of Nauvoo, and in Far West. He was chafing for an excuse to set free the darker devils of his heart.

She remembered Eliza's admonishment to reach into her soul, to find acceptance and forgiveness for Brigham Young. She had earnestly tried to do as her friend had asked. Had she been a fool all this time, to extend goodwill toward that man?

Brigham said, "I tell you I'd rather die than take another wife. One is enough trouble. You ask too much, Joseph." Lightly, almost teasing. "If you command me to do this thing, I'll do it, but I'll envy the corpse in its coffin at every funeral I see."

"You needn't do it if it disagrees with your soul," Joseph said. "You may stick to your one wife and live as any unremarkable man does. But God takes note of those who are bold in faith. Those who follow the commandment shall be exalted in the world to come. They shall reign over worlds; they shall be Creators themselves, with all their wives at their sides. Those who have no stomach for the doctrine will have no wives at all in the next world—no, not even the one wife they clung to in this life. She'll be taken away and given to a worthier man, and he shall serve as ministering angel to his betters."

Mary Ann shuddered. Emma realized the poor woman was holding back a sob. She wrapped her arms around her, pulling her close in the darkness.

"As you say," Brigham said. "Yet still it's a hard thing to contemplate."

"These are the Last Days. If Christ is to come and dwell with us again, then all ancient customs must be restored."

Emma pressed her cheek against Mary Ann's temple, whispering in her ear. "Don't make a sound. We mustn't let them know we've heard. We mustn't let them see us this way."

Mary Ann breathed raggedly; her whole body heaved with the effort of quiet. "The rumors are true. Preserve us, Lord, in your wisdom and righteousness. Shelter us from sin."

She was silent on the carriage ride home.

"Did the devil steal your tongue?" Joseph asked, his grin a blue shadow.

Emma answered as if through some other woman's mouth. "I'm only tired. It has been a weary day."

She ought to confront him about it, that thing she and Mary Ann had overheard, that terrible thing, the unthinkable, the unforgivable. But how did one say to the Prophet of God—or even to an ordinary husband—You have lied to me, you have wounded me, you have made me look a fool. Nor did she understand how to order the great black rush of feelings in her gut, the words that whisked so frantically across her mind she could hear only fragments of her own thoughts.

Joseph whistled as he drove. Whistling, while Emma could scarcely swallow her own spit because her throat was so tight. *He'll be angry if he knows I listened. He'll deny I heard what I know I heard, what even Mary Ann heard. He'll deny it all, the way he denied Fannie Alger.* She hated him in that moment—the way he sat so easily on the carriage seat, almost lounging with the reins sliding through his fingers, not a care in the world. *While I,* Emma thought, *While I have been made a fool before the entire city. Women will pity me. Men will laugh behind my back. And that show Brigham made of being revolted by the idea. As if he hasn't thought of it already, the brute.*

She didn't sleep that night. She paced the parlor, watching shadows glide across the room. A band of moonlight came in at the window and lay harsh along the floor. She wept as silently as she could manage, for she didn't want to wake Joseph or the children or Eliza—especially not Eliza. She knelt to pray and asked herself why she did it. When her knees began to ache, she sat straight-backed on the sofa, staring out the window into an indifferent night. She watched the moon's reflection on the

Mississippi, a band of white in a black, black world. Then she stared at
the wall beside the window and saw nothing. By sunrise, she was sick
to her stomach, and hoped for a moment that it was the ague, that God
would take her up to His bosom and spare her this humiliation. But even
as she prayed for a merciful death, Emma knew she wasn't ill. She was
only exhausted by grief and mortification. Stray too far along a path and
you'll find the Devil waiting.

When morning came, Joseph went to the Masonic Hall to plot and
plan with Brigham. Emma left the children to Eliza and climbed up to
her bedroom. She locked the door. She fell into bed, too stricken to weep,
but she could smell Joseph on the sheets—a dry scent of ink, the familiar
bite of his body sweat. She knew his smell better than her own. She got
up and found a kerchief perfumed with lavender, went back to bed with
the kerchief draped across her face. That shut him out. Later, when she
sat up against the headboard and pulled the kerchief away, the light at
the window was low and golden, and she knew it was late afternoon. She
had slept, then, though she hadn't dreamed. That was one small mercy.
Sleep had brought a little clarity. She knew she must speak to Joseph and
tell him, calmly, with great dignity and composure, that she had learned
of his plans, his sinful ideas, and she spurned them. And knowing that
she must confront him—that she would confront him—was a form of
mercy, too.

She heard Joseph come in through the parlor door, the children running to greet him, the girls from Far West calling from the kitchen,
Good evening, Prophet, supper will be ready soon. Emma left the
room. If she was quick, she could catch Joseph before the orphans got
to him. She would tell him, We must talk, you and I, and we must do it
now, alone, where only God may hear.

But by the time she reached the staircase, with her hand upon the
rail, the parlor door opened again. Someone else had arrived. "Brother
Joseph, thank God I find you here." It was a woman. She was weeping,
choking on her words. "You must come quickly, please. You're all the
hope he has now."

"Agnes," Joseph said.

Emma froze.

"It's Don Carlos," Agnes said. "He's taken the fever. Had it for two
days. I thought he would get better, strong as he is, but he's weaker

now than ever. Please, Joseph, come and bless him. My prayers haven't helped."

Emma found herself at the bottom of the stairs before she realized she had moved. Vaguely, from a distant corner of her mind—the only place where she was still composed—she scolded herself. What if she had tripped on her skirts and fallen? She might have broken her neck, running down that way.

"Emma." Joseph was surprised to see her.

She didn't look at him. All her attention fastened on Agnes. The woman was red-faced, her dress stained under the arms with sweat and along the front with fouler things. Her hair had pulled out of its bun and stood out around her face, a halo of stiff tendrils, brambles in a thicket. Agnes was a beautiful woman, even in distress—fine-featured, slender, delicate like a china cup. You wanted to cradle her in your palms and turn her to catch the light.

"Please, Prophet—Mrs. Smith. Please come. I fear Don Carlos may not survive if you don't help him."

The children, gathered around their father, had fallen silent. They stared up at Agnes with wide, stricken eyes. Emma said, "Julia, where is Aunt Eliza?"

"Seeing to Little Carlos," Julia said.

"You run along and help." Emma shouted toward the kitchen, "Emily, Lizzie, where are you?"

The Partridge sisters appeared at once, wiping their hands on their aprons. No doubt they'd been pressed against the door, listening.

"Joseph and I are going with Agnes. We don't know when we'll return. See that the children eat their supper and put them to bed if we're late."

They walked briskly to Don Carlos's house. Agnes talked all the way. Words seemed to help; they gave her fears a kind of order, a logic she couldn't find in God's cruel whims. Don Carlos had been tired, four days ago. No interest in eating. Seemed to recover after that, went out to work in the field but kept coming back to the house because he was thirsty. And next day he was shaking when he woke, complaining of the cold but with sweat on his brow. He was flushed, glassy-eyed. Couldn't get comfortable, like a baby with the colic.

"I thought it would pass by this morning." Agnes held her skirts up too high so she could walk unimpeded. Her little boots flashed in the sinking sun; even her feet were small and fine. "This year the sickness has hung about for a day or two and then vanished—when it has stricken strong young men, at any rate. But he was so fitful last night. His breathing was labored."

Emma said, "Have you brought a doctor? Sampson Avard, or—"

"None. I meant to bring one today if he wasn't better, but he was so very much worse that I feared to leave his side at all—and anyhow, yesterday the whole town was down at the docks for the celebration."

They reached the house. There was a fresh new flower bed along the front of it, edged in chips of limestone, already set with roses and lilies. A garden for the new bride. Don Carlos must have dug it himself.

They followed Agnes into the house. One curtain was pulled aside on the parlor window. A long, failing stretch of light illuminated a book left open on a small table. The light rested on one side of a blue sofa, where Agnes and Don Carlos must have sat together, in the thrilling small moments after a man and woman are married. Then Agnes opened the door to their bedroom. A thick, repellent odor came out like a hand to slap her. Emma hesitated on the threshold. The room was dim, unlit except by a covered window and the rapidly fading sunset. She could see the footboard of a bed, a bedpost stark against the brown darkness. The rumple of a linen sheet. There was a strange rasping sound. It seemed to come from everywhere at once, from inside Emma's head.

Agnes cried out and ran into the room. Only then did Emma understand what she was hearing. She had come in time to watch Don Carlos draw his final breaths.

Joseph shouldered past her. She was numb, still as an uncomprehending animal, half in the room, half not. Don Carlos's head was turned to the side as if he longed for the window, the world beyond. His hair, his golden hair, was matted and dark with sweat. His eyes were open, but they didn't see—or they saw into another realm. He was mostly gone already, and gone too far for Emma to pull him back. Joseph laid his hands on his brother's head. He began to pray. Be healed, Don Carlos; I command thee in Jesus's name.

Emma forced herself to step into that room, but she didn't go to Don Carlos, not at first. She tore back the curtains and pushed up the sash and fresh air came in, the scent of the lilies, the low, thick spice of the river on a hot day. A smell of wheat drying in the sun, of soil between the rows. The curtain stirred. It lifted on a merciful breeze.

Only then did she go to Don Carlos's side. Agnes was clinging to one of his hands, pleading, praying, pressing her forehead against his knuckles. Emma took his other hand. Strange, how she didn't tremble.

"Leave him be," she said quietly to Joseph. "Don't touch him. There's nothing you can do for him now." There was nothing Joseph ever could have done, not for Don Carlos. She said, "He loves the fields, the world outside. Let him breathe in that good air before he goes to be with God."

Don Carlos inhaled again. A painful sound, a long rattle. She kissed his hand. She said, "I'm here."

And then he didn't breathe. Such a holy and terrible stillness filled the room, even Agnes stopped her weeping. Joseph halted in the middle of his prayer. The words he wouldn't say hung like spirits above the bed, jostling, waiting. He made as if to close his brother's eyes, but Emma moved first. His eyelids were damp under her fingers. His cheek was rough with stubble, with dirt from his fields. She allowed her hand to linger there. It didn't matter to her now, who saw.

Joseph wept, pressing his fist against his mouth, trying to hold back grief and regret, but he could restrain nothing now. There were some things beyond his command—many things, if truth be told. He'd never known until that moment.

"What shall I do without him," Agnes said, quiet with despair. She pulled down the sheet that had covered Don Carlos's body as if to look at him one last time, all of him, whole and solid, still present in this shifting world. Don Carlos wore only the garment he had put on after his temple endowment—white linen, all of one piece. Emma's eyes went to the place where the priests in the Masonic Hall had slashed the belly with their knives. One long cut from side to side, a reminder of what God or man would do to him if he told.

The world constricted around her. Black walls falling in, a high whine in her ears, a sick sensation of being pulled backward into a long dark unseen place. Her vision narrowed. All she could see was a pale circle, the small white accusation of Don Carlos's sacred garment and a slash through the linen.

"Emma," Joseph said, far away, muffled, "where are you going?" That was the first she knew that she had risen and was moving, walking out of the room, then running, past the parlor, to the door, out, outside, but where could she go, how could she hide from God? The flat yard, the smell of the lilies, too sweet. The road was empty. A last flush of crimson hung in the sky, just behind the elms that bristled on the flank of the hill. From the top of the hill, she could feel the temple rising, an imminent upward creep of white stone.

She fell to her knees in the short grass. She turned, half-crawling toward the hill and the temple. *Forgive me*, she prayed. *Forgive me and do not rebuke me again.*

God had seen her every sin—her unchaste longing for Don Carlos, and the knowledge he had given her of secret rites, knowledge no woman should have held.

You have the man I loved now, Emma said to God. *Be satisfied, I beg of you. I will trust in Thy word, I will obey Thine every command. Only do not chastise me again, Lord. My soul can bear no more.*

By now you've long since asked yourself what held her to this church, this fearful pattern of God, a hunched and hungry creature of Heaven with watchful, slitted eyes. You've wondered why she never left, why outrage piled on outrage and pain upon pain, and still Emma remained.

Do you think she hasn't asked herself the same question? More times than she could count, until it became a litany, then a background hum like the drone of cicadas in a summer field.

She did find an answer, by and by. It was a heavy black knowing in the marrow of her bones, in the pit of her spirit where fear never stopped chittering, her knowledge that God's wrath always came. He would chastise her again. He would whip her back to the path, this God whom she'd been taught to believe was loving and merciful, but whose love and mercy she never knew.

The blow came, as she'd known it would. And by the time she and Joseph had returned, trembling and silent to their home, the Destroying Angel had already passed unbarred through their door.

Eliza came to meet them with the baby in her arms—little Carlos. He was red-faced, listless with the fever. Emma fell to the parlor floor. Fell and couldn't rise again, though Eliza wept and the baby's breath rattled, though Joseph slapped her across the face to bring her back to her senses. He begged her, with tears in his eyes, to stand.

Dull, surrendered, she stared up at the ceiling. She prayed to her ravenous God: *I am poured out like water. All my bones are out of joint.*

When they buried their son five days later, Emma sat motionless beside the grave. The smell of turned soil was all around her. It was the way Don Carlos had smelled—not the child, but the man who'd held her heart. The smell of furrows in the field, mud on his hands. This love could only ever end in suffering. She had lusted after a man who wasn't her husband, and the wages of sin is this: Your child under the earth, your child consigned to dust. Your heart like dust, poured out and blown away.

She pressed her Book of Mormon to her heart. It was small comfort, but it was a thing in her hands to which she could hold, so she tightened her grip and prayed.

O God, my Father, my angry and brutal Father. I will follow Your every commandment. I will not doubt Your Prophet again. I will be perfect in my faith, as perfect as Eliza wishes me to be.

She still had children living. Four precious knives pressed against her throat. She couldn't lose another. She wouldn't give God the chance.

When she looked up from her grief, she noticed first that autumn had already passed. The leaves had flown from the trees. The branches of the elm forest were bare, and she could see the wall of the temple through them, blocks of sandstone low and white, like ghosts reclining on the hill—ghosts stretched out to reenact their own demise. And second, she noticed that the Restoration had transitioned smoothly from rumor to fact. It was everywhere, talk of the Blessing of Jacob. The talk was breathless, not with scandal but with excitement, for the Mormons were doing God's will, making way for Christ Himself to come.

I'm too late to stop it, she told herself. She'd come home from the shops with a basket full of items—barley, hair pins, molasses in a tin. She'd been going about all this time, shopping, greeting people on the street, doing God knew what else—sewing, spinning, kissing her children's foreheads—but had never known it. She had moved like a wraith through a foreign world. The city had reordered itself to Joseph's liking. They were building the kingdom of God, the ancient ways were being restored, and Emma had revived herself from grief too late to stop it, if she could have dared to stop it at all.

Eliza came into the kitchen to help put the shopping away. "Poor dear," she said when she emerged from the pantry. "You've been in mourning so long."

"I'm better today." But even to herself, she sounded faint and fragile.

"You need work, Emma—some task to occupy your hands."

"I work plenty. I work enough for two women."

"You do, in the home. But it's larger work I speak of. Something for the community—something that will make a difference to those who are suffering. Nothing heals our own wounds like tending to another's."

"I can't tend anyone just now. I've only enough strength to hold myself together, and to care for the children."

"You will find a new wellspring of strength once you're looking outward again. Winter is around the corner, and many families have suffered. We know all too well how terrible the fever has been this year. I've been thinking . . . What if we were to start a mercy organization?"

Emma blinked. Her thoughts were like puddle water, cloudy and still. "Mercy?"

"An aid society. We could meet once a week to hear about the less fortunate souls of Nauvoo and decide together how best to help them. During the remainder of the week, each member will work to ease her neighbors' burdens."

"The only work I want to do just now," Emma said wryly, "is to fortify the morals of our women. If Joseph says this Restoration is a commandment from God, then so be it. But we can at least ensure that any woman who participates is doing so for righteous reasons, not for lust."

Eliza's cheeks colored. She took up the iron poker and prodded the kitchen fire so vigorously, the sparks rose in a red column. "I think that's a fine idea. If you will lead the organization, and be our mistress in all things, I will be your strong right hand."

Emma smiled, surprised she could still do it. "As ever."

"As ever." Eliza took her by the shoulders. "It's good to see you among the living again. This is where you belong. I know you'll find this new venture invigorating. We have missed you—all the women of the church. We have missed your strength of spirit. And now we shall follow that same strength as an army follows a banner, toward good works."

That was how the Female Relief Society began. And if truth be known, the Society was a balm to Emma's broken heart, almost from the first day. As she compiled her lists of Nauvoo's women and all the skills they possessed—the herbalists, the midwives, the seamstresses and singers, the child-minders, the bakers, those who could comfort the dying—she realized she had long since grown weary of sadness. The pain of losing Don Carlos and the son she had named for him hadn't abated. But now that she worked to soothe a hundred pains in other hearts, at least she felt as if those two deaths hadn't been in vain. Through the channel of her grief, a passage deep and endless as the sea, she could make compassion flow. She rose each morning with new purpose. Eliza had been right: the wounds would never stop aching, but they were healing enough that she knew she could survive.

The spring of 1842 was gray and wind-blown, but the terrible marsh-borne fever hardly touched the city that year—the combined result of draining the bog and Mary Ann Young's brilliant and dogged herbalism—so despite lashing rains and overcast skies, opinion in Nauvoo held that the season was blessedly mild. A sense of boundless optimism prevailed. The temple rose swiftly on the hill. More missionaries departed for England every month—and for other nations, too. New Mormons arrived, waving and calling out greetings from the deck of the church-owned steamboat that carried newcomers up the Mississippi. They spoke in the accents of England and Ireland, Scotland and Denmark. The city itself was spreading; the hill had long been cleared, the forest replaced by houses and streets. The Mormons numbered well over three thousand. The church was regaining the size it had boasted in Far West. If now and then some women wept, what was their small and common pain set against a flourishing church?

If the gentle promise of that spring had continued—if nothing worse had troubled Emma than an occasional broken heart among her friends—she might have accepted the Blessing of Jacob, with time. The Mormons' ways were peculiar, even to themselves, but they had minded their own in Nauvoo some four years running. An occasional whisper implied that Missouri still hunted for the Prophet, but the outside world seemed to be losing interest. The dangers they'd faced in Missouri felt far behind them now. Peace and security came as such a relief that Emma prayed earnestly for a humble heart that could accept the Restoration in fullness. Nauvoo was a haven where her children could grow and thrive, untroubled by persecution. So long as God maintained that peace, she would do her level best to accept His strange new doctrines.

But no peace could last forever. Not in a world of Joseph's making.

On a windy Saturday, mid-May, she was leading a delegation of the FRS from door to door, collecting old clothing that the women would recut and tailor into new garments for those who had recently arrived in America.

The troop of FRS women had just accepted a large donation of old canvas trousers from Jane Law. Her husband, William, ran one of two printing presses in the town.

"I like William Law most wholeheartedly," Emma muttered to Eliza, "but land sakes, these trousers are so stained with ink, I don't know how we'll ever make anything halfway decent from them."

Phebe Carter hoisted the heavy bag of donated clothes into the back of their pony-cart. The women marched on, leaning into the teeth of the wind. A scattering of rain gusted across the road, stinging the side of Emma's face. She hitched her long black shawl up to cover her head.

"I'm grateful the fever has been mild this year," Phebe said, "but I'm almost tempted to grumble about the weather. If we must give up our balmy springs in order to keep the fever at bay, then what use is springtime at all? It's as miserable as winter out here in the streets."

They came to a crossroad that led up a shallow slope to the Masonic Hall. At least a dozen men were gathered outside, pacing and punching the air.

"What do you suppose has gotten into the men?" Eliza said.

"Who knows what gets into men," Phebe muttered, "in any sort of circumstance."

They watched the men mill and argue until one shoved another. Someone threw a punch; a man skidded in the mud and went down.

"Good heavens," Emma said. "That's no fit way to behave."

Vilate shook her head. "Something has upset them. Do you suppose there's danger?"

"Eliza, run up and find out what has happened," Emma said. "But don't get too close. It wouldn't do to catch a fist by mistake."

Eliza hurried up the street. Emma watched her speak to one of the men outside the hall. Moments later, she was returning at a rapid clip, walking as briskly as she dared in the slick conditions.

"There's danger, all right," Eliza said. "News has come from Missouri. That governor of theirs, Lilburn Boggs, has been shot."

"Killed?" Phebe said.

"I'm afraid not. Boggs was shot in the head, but he has survived. The men are waiting for Joseph and Brigham to arrive and tell them what it means, and what Nauvoo must do next."

"Why must we do anything?" Emma's pulse thrummed along her limbs, a dreadful, urgent rhythm. "Who shot the governor?"

Eliza shook her head rather vaguely.

"Tell me, Eliza. Who shot Boggs?"

Still Eliza refused to speak, but Emma reeled back as if she had admitted the truth. She knew, with a sick shiver, exactly who had done it—who had made Joseph's prophecy come true. Emma had been too mired in grief, and too busy with the FRS, to notice Porter Rockwell's absence. She noticed it now. How many weeks had flown by since she'd seen her husband's guard lurking outside their home—how many months? She forced herself to count backward, through the long dark seasons of her depression. Porter had vanished the previous summer, days before she'd lost Don Carlos.

Her hands fell limp to her sides. The wind licked at her body and caught her shawl, pulling it high into the air. Like some bleak banner, the shawl unfurled in the sky. It hung over Nauvoo, black as mourning, black as death.

Weeks and months crept by in the wake of the news from Missouri. Old fears of Far West and Zion were resurrected to shamble once more among the streets of Nauvoo. Everywhere you went, you could feel a tension of waiting. Accusations of blame and cowardice flew like arrows, accusations that the Prophet had reached too far. Newspapers in the Gentile cities found renewed interest in the Mormons, reviving their articles about the strange sect. Clippings poured into Nauvoo—speculation about Joseph's involvement in the failed assassination, and a new flurry of scandalous fictions on the marriage customs of the Mormons.

One afternoon, Mary Ann Young brought a clipping from the *American Bulletin*, a paper out of St. Louis, to a meeting of the FRS. Mary Ann said nothing as she entered the meeting well after it had started. All the women in Emma's parlor turned to look at her, and saw at once the paleness of her face, the way her hands trembled. She held up the clipping as if she wished the whole Society to read it at once. But she never spoke a word, poor soul.

The women passed the article around. In groups of three and four they read, peering over one another's shoulders. The parlor was quiet, the air heavy with something that might have been shock, or perhaps the absence of it.

They all remembered Martha Brotherton—a bright, self-possessed girl of eighteen who had come with her family from England that spring. Martha and one of her brothers had vanished from Nauvoo later that season without a word of explanation. Now they all knew why.

The *American Bulletin* was the first to publish Martha's confession—an affidavit sworn before a Justice of the Peace in St. Louis. But soon other papers printed the story, too—in Illinois, in Missouri, in Pennsylvania and New York. Along the Atlantic Coast and north into Canada; even across the sea, in London, in Edinburgh. The story spread across the Christian world.

Martha had been in Nauvoo only three weeks when Vilate's husband, Heber Kimball, led her to a meeting room above one of the town stores. There she found Joseph waiting—and Brigham Young. Joseph left the room. He locked the door, so Martha couldn't evade Brigham's questions, nor his eyes, nor any other part of him. Brigham made the girl swear her silence. How could she refuse, with no way out except a window two stories above the street? He demanded to know what feelings Martha had for him. Did she not have an affection for Brigham, and could she not accept him as her husband if it were lawful and right?

The girl was quick-witted and calm. Martha kept her head, but wrote in her confession, *What, thought I, are these men, that I thought almost perfection itself—deceivers!* She revealed none of her true thoughts to Brigham, for she was alone with the brute. If she hoped to escape with her honor intact, she must keep him happy. She answered that if it were lawful, perhaps she might accept him as her husband. But it was not lawful; there was nothing to be done.

"Well," said he, "Brother Joseph has had a revelation from God that it is law-ful and right for a man to have two wives; for as it was in the days of Abraham, so it shall be in these last days, and whoever is the first that is willing to take up the cross will receive the greatest blessings."

He promised to take Martha to the celestial kingdom, to rule as a goddess after she died. He said, If you will have me in this world, I will have you in the world that is to come, and Brother Joseph will marry us today, right here in this room, and you can go home to your parents. They will know nothing of it.

She pleaded her age. She was too young to marry without her parents' permission. Brigham said it didn't matter. She would be old enough to make up her own mind by the time her parents found out. He told her not to worry, not to think. It was he who would do the thinking. It was he who knew what was right before God, and if after all God found some sin, Brigham would take the blame. Her soul would be free from hell-fire. He kissed her. She had no choice but to allow it. Then he left, and Joseph locked the door again, and Martha was alone, trapped in that room above the store with her anger and bewilderment, her rising panic. Alone with the thought, *Deceivers.*

After some time—God knows how long—Brigham and Joseph re-turned. "I know this is lawful and right," Joseph said. "Look here, sis; don't you believe in me?" Then he said, Go on and do it. There's no need to fret. Do as Brigham wants. He's the best man in the world, except me.

The Prophet said to the girl, the eighteen-year-old girl separated from her parents, locked in a secluded room: I have the keys to the kingdom. Whatever I bind on earth is bound in Heaven, and whatever I loose on earth is loosed in Heaven. Brigham will take care of you. If he doesn't, come to me. I will set him straight. And if he casts you off, come to me, Martha, and I will take you as my wife, so you will not be disgraced.

The poor girl swore on her own death that she would tell no one, not even her parents, what the Prophet and his favorite had done and said to her that day. She wouldn't tell, if only they would give her time to think. A few days—that was all she needed for reflection and prayer. An oath on her own life satisfied Joseph. "That's the principle we go on," said the Prophet. An oath on your own blood. They unlocked the door and finally, finally let the poor child go.

She returned at once to her home and wrote down every word she could remember. Then, two days later—after the Sabbath, when no one would remark on her absence—she fled with her brother from Nauvoo.

"I had wondered," Eliza said quietly, "where Martha had gone."

Emma pressed her hands to her stomach. "Celestial marriage as an ordainment from God may be one thing. This is something else altogether. Locking women in rooms—young girls! Coercing them into accepting a . . . a proposal such as this! God in His mercy may see fit to forgive Joseph, but I never shall."

The women glanced at one another in disbelief. Never had Emma spoken a word against the Prophet where anyone but Eliza might hear.

"And as for Brigham Young. You told me once, Eliza, that I must reach into my soul and find respect for that man, in remembrance of all he has done for us. I took your counsel then, but now I see I was a fool to do it. Brigham is a scoundrel. I've always known. I will insist upon that fact until my dying day."

Mary Ann Young turned her face toward the wall.

"How can this be a holy process?" Vilate said. "That poor child, isolated, locked up! If Heber knew what Brigham intended when he led Martha to that room, then I'll make him regret the day!"

"I must speak to Joseph," Emma said, knowing already he would deny it. He would say Martha was a liar, even though the whole Society knew her to be an honest, upstanding young woman.

All that miserable summer, Nauvoo was like a beast backed into a corner, cringing and snapping while the Mormons waited to learn what Lilburn Boggs would do. And the pamphlets and articles and exposés poured into the city, a relentless tide of rumor.

Some of the tales the Gentiles printed were inventions of depraved minds—accounts of worship conducted in the nude, concluding with group congress, described in the most shocking terms. But other stories held enough truth that Emma couldn't dismiss them so easily. When she questioned the FRS about the latest publications, too many women shifted in their chairs and refused to meet her eye.

"But it's false," she proclaimed one afternoon before her assembly. "The Blessing of Jacob is a spiritual calling. There is nothing of lust in it, no reason for shame. Those few women who've been called into such marriages go as handmaids before the Lord, for a sacred purpose. These allegations in the papers, these stories of lustful doings—they're falsehoods. They can't be true. Look here; this one asserts that Joseph is already married to at least a dozen women! What nonsense. I would know if my husband had another wife. And this article has the audacity to list names! Sarah Pratt, you're named here. It says you're one of Joseph's spiritual wives."

Sarah rose trembling from her chair. Her hands were clasped, fingers twisting like snakes—that shocking moment when you pick up a leg of firewood to find snakes writhing in a knot beneath.

"It . . . isn't entirely untrue, Sister Emma."

She stared at Sarah. There was a strange rustle in the parlor, a collective breath drawn in. Every woman turned to gawp at Sarah Pratt.

"I wouldn't have told you at all if I could have avoided it," Sarah said. "There's no reason to break your heart—you've always been such a friend to me. But you deserve to know. You're the best of us, the very kindest and bravest, most righteous woman in all Nauvoo."

"Out with it," Emma said.

"A few weeks back, the Prophet did approach me while Orson was still in Europe, gathering books for the university Joseph told him to build. Joseph told me God had called me to become his spiritual wife."

Emma could do nothing but stare. She couldn't even breathe. *Here, in front of everyone, before the eyes of every woman who once respected me.*

"He said God had already promised me to him," Sarah went on, "and there was no sense resisting. But I didn't do it, Emma. I wouldn't, not even for the Prophet. I told him I was already a married woman, and he a married man, and God would never require me to break a holy vow. I told him I was Orson's wife. I love Orson—you must believe me, Emma. I would never stray from my marriage!"

"I believe you," she said faintly.

She dismissed the FRS and sank into a chair, alone in her parlor. She believed every word of what Sarah Pratt had said. Of course Joseph would do such a thing. He had always believed he held the world in his palm, that men and women and God were his to command. And who had ever told him differently?

The articles, the pamphlets, the books purporting to know all the secret, shocking ways of the Mormons—they fell on Nauvoo like a barrage of hail. They beat upon the walls of the church; they shook the city to its foundation. And when rumor rose to so high a pitch that it seemed a constant wail, the whole congregation gathered in the meetinghouse. Every man and woman witnessed a vote among the apostles and the seventies to uphold the Prophet as a righteous man.

Only one stood in opposition: Orson Pratt. The apostles turned to him in scorn. A hiss rose from the congregation. Pale, silent as the grave, Orson walked out of the meetinghouse with Sarah clinging to his hand, begging him to wait, to speak to the Prophet privately—Joseph would explain, then all would be well.

That night, no one could find Orson Pratt. Sarah came weeping to the Mansion and fell to her knees in the parlor, clutching Emma's skirt in her fist. "Help me find him, Sister, please. He's in a terrible way."

Joseph sent a faction of Danites into the summer night, shouting for Orson, setting their dogs to sniff out his trail. They did find him. He was returned to the city in one piece, and thereafter professed his eagerness to get back to work at the growing university. He would take up teaching mathematics, he said. What a pleasant distraction the university would be; he would welcome his first students in the fall.

Weeks later, Emma learned where the Danites had located Orson. He'd been sitting on the riverbank some three miles outside Nauvoo, watching the moon come up across the blue Mississippi. The moon was a sickle in the sky. Orson's hat was gone, and behind him, stretching above the flat dark water was an ancient oak with gnarled limbs. Orson had already tied his noose to the tree.

"You've brought me here, now speak."

Brigham is treading from one end of the parlor to another. It seems he has expanded with rage, become larger than he was before, his shoulders a beam of wood, a battering ram.

Affront blows out before him like a wind off the river, with intent to tear your house apart, plank by plank. It's more than he can stand, this news that the Gentiles have done away with the Prophet as easily as you kick off your boots, as casually as you would take any other man's life. But now, now this woman has called him like a spaniel. And worse, he has come. He wears no coat, only a linen shirt open at the collar as if he dressed in a hurry, as if the news had caught him while he'd slept, and perhaps he resents that, too, the fact that he wasn't first to know.

Emma is self-possessed beside her hearth. "Ford will leave us in peace, and leave this very day, if you swear to take no vengeance."

"No vengeance," he roars. "They've martyred our Prophet—your own husband! You loiter there, calm as a June day, telling me to take no vengeance?"

She had expected him to thunder, and he has obliged. You don't fear a thing you've seen coming.

"Let Ford go, Brigham. The sooner the Gentiles have left our city, the sooner we may put our affairs in order and go on with our lives."

He stops and stares at her. His eyes had always seemed narrow before, so slitted with calculation that for years she'd never known their color. They are wide now, and cold with disbelief. "Perhaps you can carry on as if plain murder never happened, Emma. I cannot."

"You must think of others now, not yourself. This city is home to more than ten thousand: powerless women and children who depend on the church's wisdom for protection. Act rashly, and we'll have Far West all over again. We'll have another Haun's Mill, but worse by far. If you can't temper yourself for the sake of defenseless children, then at least do it for your own wives. How many do you have now?"

"There's one woman I'm grateful not to have." Disgusted, he turns away. "Joseph never knew how to keep you in line. We all would have been better for it if he had."

"The men who were imprisoned with Joseph and Hyrum are making their way back to Nauvoo. They're bringing the bodies home for burial. It would please me if Ford has left before the funeral, so we may mourn without interference."

"It would please you?" He snorts, kicks at the parlor rug. A bull pawing the ground, making up its mind to charge. "What do I care whether you're pleased?"

"Joseph is gone, but the church remains. Someone must lead."

He bellows with laughter. There's no amusement in his eyes. He slings his head back as if entreating Heaven for patience. "You? You think to lead?"

"Not I," Emma says coolly. "My son Joseph—"

"Is twelve years old. I suppose you think to keep Young Joseph under your wing, is that it? You'll whisper in his ear, prod him this way and that, so you may alter the church to your liking. You grasping harpy."

"It isn't my choice, but Joseph's. Before he went to Carthage, he blessed our son and named him successor."

"And who witnessed this blessing, other than yourself?"

"My other children." It's the honest answer. She knows Brigham won't accept it. She is undeterred; God is on her side. The better portion of the congregation—all whose hearts are free from sin—will come to her side, too.

"You expect the Quorum of Apostles, you expect the seventies to uphold this? The witness of little children who are under their mother's sway?"

"I'm more than a mother—more than any other woman. You've read Joseph's revelations. You know God named me the elect lady."

He shakes a finger in her face. He expects her to shrink from it. "I don't give a shit what God said to you. You're nothing to me. You've always been nothing."

She doesn't flinch, and it's he who reels back away to pace the parlor once more.

"It is my church now," he says. "Make peace with the fact. It is a fact; it will remain a fact. You can do nothing to change it."

"You aren't the Prophet of God."

"No." He casts a hard look at her. Then he grins. "I'm no prophet. I've never claimed to be. I don't need prophecy to lead men. I have something better. Joseph endowed me President of Apostles; he gifted to me the keys of the kingdom. Did you know that, Emma? Of course you didn't. Women aren't privy to the business of God. It happened this April last. Every ordinance of the holy priesthood is mine, in Joseph's absence. And every one of the Apostles witnessed it, heard every word Joseph said. Ask any of them—Orson Hyde, Amasa Lyman—they'll all attest. Joseph said: 'Now if they kill me, you've got all the keys, and all the ordinances. You can confer them upon others, and the hosts of Satan won't be able to tear down the kingdom as fast as you can build it up.' Question the witnesses if you don't believe me."

She smiles at him archly. "You have what you've wanted all these years—what you waited so patiently to gain. A ready-made kingdom, complete with people tamed to your yoke. A seat of power emptied of its rightful owner. It's still warm for you, and now you'll sit upon your throne."

"Why shouldn't I take what I've waited for? I was patient enough. I risked my life, again and again, to preserve what Joseph was building—to preserve you, for his sake. If it had been left to me, I would have seen you tied to a bench in the Far West schoolhouse and left for the Gentiles to claim."

She tilts her head, unconcerned—which only increases his fury. "Joseph was grateful to you for your sacrifices."

"I was always loyal to him, but his head was in the clouds. It was all fantasy with him—those capricious revelations, the commandments that came so conveniently, whenever he needed to bend someone to his will."

Her cheeks burn. She curses herself for allowing Brigham to see her surprise. It's too great a shock to hide. All these years, she'd thought herself the only one who had doubted.

She says, "Our people expect to be led by revelation."

"Then our people are fools who see what they wish to see instead of what's before their damned noses."

"You never believed in Joseph's power."

He watches her face for a long moment. "Did you believe? No, don't answer, Elect Lady. A virtuous woman never lies. I *did* believe in Joseph's power, but it wasn't the same power others saw."

She nods; she understands. "He made a world of his own. With or without divine revelation, he created what he envisioned, and his followers made it true."

"They still believe it's true—and so it is true, by their reckoning. The church holds, but it won't hold for long without a good leader. These are my people now. They believe I hold the keys to the kingdom, and if they believe it, then I do." He moves back, lifting the weight of his scorn from Emma. "I'd thought you'd be only too glad to leave this church to me. I'd thought you would take the chance to finally put this all behind you, get your children away, someplace where they may grow up in peace. Now that you're a widow, there's no reason for you to stay. Why do you care, Emma? Why would you see this church continue, knowing what you know?"

Beyond the parlor window, the streets of Nauvoo lie still. News of Joseph's death is running through the city on devil's legs, but the sunlight on the river is bright and bounding, as if this is the same world it ever was, the world she has known from the age of twenty-one. She knows the answer to Brigham's question. She's under no obligation to answer.

This is all I've had, all God gave to me—this church, this community, strange though they may be. And if Joseph shaped the congregation to his will, I can shape it to mine. I can make of it, in the fullness of time, something righteous and true.

When Brigham sees that he'll have no answer, he makes for the door.

"Wait," Emma says. "I didn't lie—you know I didn't—when I said the people expect to be led by revelation."

He waves a hand in curt dismissal. "They'll grow used to a new way."

"Not many will. If you wish to be king over ten thousand, you must give your people what they expect—or a taste of it, now and then."

"Prophecy? What, from your stripling son?"

"Let us lead the church jointly, you and I."

His mouth falls open. He barks a laugh, but he doesn't go, only waits for her to say something more.

"You hold the power of the ordainments, as you say. You've witnesses who will back you. But I hold the esteem of the church's women. All of them, Brigham."

"What do I care for women's esteem?"

She tips her head to one side. "You saw what disruption women may cause in the affair of Martha Brotherton."

She can see him clenching his jaw, the muscles bulging. Those eyes narrow again.

"We're half the population of this city," she says. "I can turn any woman against you in a trice. Your wives included. And once I turn the women, you know some of the men will follow. If you wish to retain your kingdom entire, let us work together as allies. I won't call us friends, but we may become effective partners."

The great tower of his anger subsides a little, softening. His eyes slide away.

She says, "I have but one condition: the Blessing of Jacob is finished. There will be one wife for each man, one husband for each woman."

Brigham folds his arms. "No."

"Why not?"

"Because this way of living suits me. Simple as that."

She had expected his response. She says, "Then you shall not have the women. Our church will be split in two, your power reduced, and after a time, your followers will grow dissatisfied. They'll long for the closeness to God that Joseph gave them. They'll come seeking prophecy. You won't give them prophecy, Brigham, but I shall."

"I'll keep the Danites in check and let Governor Ford go without retribution, if you will hold the women to me and guarantee their loyalty."

"I'll hold the women to Joseph's church if you will renounce the practice of spiritual wifery. It's what Joseph wanted, in his final days. He told you that much. He knew this mad experiment was over; he intended his church to be moral and righteous again."

"You must make up your mind quickly, Emma. You know my terms."

"And you know mine. Let Ford leave in peace, so Nauvoo may mourn. Joseph's body will be here soon. The funeral must be observed, the Prophet and his brother must be buried. After that, you and I may resume our quarrel and hash out the terms between us."

"The Danites will stay in Nauvoo, but I'll have your cooperation where the women are concerned."

Thinly, she smiles. "We shall see."

"Joseph told me the hosts of Satan would try to unmake his church. Never would he have guessed his own first wife was in Satan's hand."

"You know where to find the door, Brother Brigham."

"I'll have my answer in three days' time." His hand is on the door. He cracks it open, bright light pours in. "Secure the women to my cause, or I'll take your husband's legacy from you, and from your children. I'll cut you off entirely."

"God be with you," Emma says, and then he is gone. Only the sound of the door slamming remains, a rebounding echo in the parlor.

XIV

The Saint of the Black Veil

1843

On a winter's night, early in the year, the music reached up to the sky, flute and fiddle and William Law's shrill brass trumpet, and tin buckets beaten with thimbles nipped from women's sewing baskets, even the smooth-polished ram's horns the newcomers brought from Ireland and Wales, shepherd's flutes, sweet and hollow. Up into the sky, where the last snowflakes had whirled away and the stars showed now like diamonds against black velvet, a flash of diamond-whiteness through gaps in the cloud. The Mansion was full of revelers. They came and went, laughing, dancing, clapping their hands. They filled the yard outside and trampled the snow flat; they spilled into the street, waving torches around a ring of jigging men.

Deliverance had come. Brother Joseph was safe, and all of Nauvoo celebrated. Since May, the church had expected Missouri to try again for the Prophet's life. By extradition, by kidnapping, by a bullet in his back while he rode from town to town—one way or another, Missouri was determined to have him. But finally, word had arrived from General Doniphan: Joseph Smith had been cleared of all charges. He would not stand trial as an accessory to the attempted assassination of Lilburn Boggs. There was insufficient evidence to place the blame at Joseph's feet, and any man who sought to avenge himself on the Mormon prophet would be made to answer in court.

When Hyrum brought the news, such a weight lifted from Emma's heart that she toppled into her parlor chair, knees suddenly weak. She hadn't realized until that moment just how much she had feared for Joseph. Guilt over his first incarceration still returned to haunt her now and then. His new teachings on the nature of marriage vexed her sorely, despite her determination to accept God's restored law, but Joseph was still the father of her children. She couldn't wish him harm, even though the space between them had grown cold of late. When she recovered her wits, she called for a celebration. The whole city was to be invited. The Mansion would resound with music and laughter from sunup until well after dark.

The dancing, games, and speeches had lasted all day. Joseph seemed never to tire, shaking every man's hand who had come to offer his best wishes, kissing every woman and child on the cheek. He glowed from within—that strange, pale radiance that was all his own. The years collapsed and thinned; she was a girl again in Pennsylvania, in a gray wood, on a day that was snowy and sharp-edged, distinct like today. And she felt that now at last she could love Joseph, truly love him without reservation. If his hand lingered too long in the hand of another woman, or if that woman blushed and lowered her eyes when Joseph smiled at her, Emma did her best not to notice. She remembered Don Carlos and the small grave out back. She reminded herself that God's will would be done.

Emma helped the Partridge sisters stack empty dishes in the dining room. The mahogany clock in the corner tolled out the hour, scarcely audible over the music.

"It's eight o'clock," Emma said. "Have the boys gone up to bed?"

"Frederick is asleep, but not Alexander, nor Young Joseph," Lizzie said. "I saw them last out front, with the dancers in the street."

"Bother; I must go out and find them. They've probably dug themselves into a snow fort by now."

Emma returned to the party. Musicians still played in the torchlight, but the crowd had begun to thin. As she stepped into the yard, she could see groups of women walking together toward their homes. Their wide winter bonnets and fur capes looked strangely angular in the light of the torches. The night was bracing and cold, a welcome contrast to the heat of the teeming Mansion.

Young Joseph and Alexander were galloping around the yard, riding sawed-off broomsticks for horses. They dodged among groups of guests and circled the musicians; they charged at their father, who roared like a bear and reached for them with clawed hands.

"Come, boys," Emma said, "it's long past time you were upstairs, washing your faces."

"But Mother," Young Joseph said, "we aren't tired. Anyhow, I'm ten. I'm a grown man. I should be able to stay up as late as I please."

"Don't make a bad example for your brother. Take him up to your bedroom and see that he cleans his teeth, like a proper grown man should do."

The next moment, a woman screamed from the edge of the dancing ring, out in the trampled street. The music faltered. The circle of torches wavered; men jostled and shouted; another shriek split the night. Someone cried, "A Missourian!"

Joseph pushed the boys toward Emma and bolted into the crowd. The yard erupted into chaos; women ran for the newly planted orchard behind the house. Men charged toward the knot of commotion. Shouts of "A Missourian!" and "Missouri has come for the Prophet!" rang in the brittle air.

"Into the house," Emma told her boys, "at once."

This time there was no need to scold. The boys ran for the door with their broomsticks clutched in their hands.

The crowd surged to the edge of the yard, then seemed to crumple and fall back. By the flare of torchlight, she could see Joseph grappling with another man. His feet slipped on the hardpacked snow; his opponent wrenched his arm behind his back, but in another moment, Joseph twisted away, dodged, swung back and locked the other's head under his arm.

"Mercy," the man cried. "Mercy, Brother Joseph, don't you know me?"

Joseph released him. The stranger stood upright, pulling his tattered coat straight. The torchlight revealed his face, chapped red from long exposure. For a moment, Emma was too stunned to recognize him, though the crowd began to murmur with wonder. Then she blinked— the thick beard, dusted with snow; the long braids hanging over his shoulders.

"It's Porter," Joseph cried.

"Heard the goings-on," Porter said, "and came here first thing to learn what all the fuss was about. Someone asked me where I'd come from, so I said Missouri, which was the truth."

Joseph pounded his guard on his shoulder. "Now that the business with Lilburn Boggs is behind us, I hope you're back for good." He tugged one of Porter's braids. "Never cut your hair, and God will make you invincible. Like Samson in the days of old. You're the Lord's champion, and mine."

Emma let out a weary sigh. Now that she knew Joseph was in no immediate danger, she could bear no more of that long day. The celebration had been a great success. She was satisfied, and worn down, and ready for her bed. She saw to it that the boys were comforted, assuring them no Missourian had come to snatch them in the night. When she'd heard their prayers and tucked them into their beds, she helped the Far West women with the tidying-up and chivvied Julia out of her velvet dress and into a flannel nightgown. By then, only a handful of guests remained in the parlor, listening as Porter recounted his adventures. William Law and his wife, Jane, were especially transfixed by the tale. William meant to print Porter's adventures in the paper. It would make for fine reading; Emma had to admit that much, even if she suspected Porter was guilty of the attempted assassination.

"I hope you'll pardon me if I don't sit and listen," Emma said. "It has been such a long day."

"Long but joyous," Eliza answered.

"Don't mind us," Joseph said. "You've put on such a marvelous party, Emma. A man was never made to feel so loved."

For a moment she stood in his affection as one stands in a ray of light. It warmed her; it drove back all her persistent thoughts of the Restoration, all suspicion of the women of Nauvoo. She was Joseph's wife. She knew it in that moment, with assurance as unshakable as the bones of the earth.

What sound woke her—one hour later, or two? Something jolted her from sleep. A whisper in the hall, two sets of footsteps moving together when there should have been one. She sat up in her bed, in a square of cold pale starlight. She listened through the darkness and didn't know what she was listening for.

She rose from her bed, moving at the command of some fearful instinct. Why did she see again a red flash, Nancy Marinda's dress, the girl's pointed boots pausing on the stair?

Emma crept to her door and pressed one ear against it, but heard only the faintest rustle, the brush of a hand over smooth fabric, or the lifting of a petticoat. She threw her bedroom door open. God knows why. Some bitter angel told her to do it, and when she did, she saw.

Eliza and Joseph broke away from one another. They stared at Emma, both with desperate, pale faces. She had found them in an embrace. There was no doubting it. They'd been kissing one another. On the mouth, as husband and wife do.

The wings of her pain stretched wide. The sound that ripped from her throat was the cry of an animal caught in a trap. *You, of all women. You who were a sister to me.* The next moment Eliza was falling, bouncing down the stairs, and Emma screamed again, with fear this time. She hadn't meant to push Eliza. Or she had meant it but hadn't known she would really do it until the deed was done. Time dilated around her. Every angle and jolt of Eliza's body as she fell seemed to pause and hang in the substance of reality. Emma knew as she watched that she would never be free from this image, Eliza pushed, Eliza falling.

Joseph was shouting. Holding her back by her arms and shouting, "Mary Elizabeth, Emily, come quick!" And then the children, crowding at the head of the stairs, weeping, calling down to their aunt Eliza. "Go to bed," Emma said to them—screamed at them.

Eliza stirred. Thank God, her neck wasn't broken. She rolled onto her side, tried to push herself up from the floor.

"Don't move," Joseph said.

Horrified, he thrust Emma away. Her back struck the wall hard enough to knock the wind from her chest. Then the girls were there, the Far West girls, kneeling beside Eliza, pressing their hands to her skull to feel for fractures.

"What have you done?" Joseph roared up at Emma.

She tried to answer and couldn't. There was nothing in her lungs, nothing inside. She willed herself to breathe and the air rushed in, the rage rushed in—it filled her, consumed all sense and prudence, all thought of God and His new laws.

"What have I done?" she screamed at Joseph. "What have you done? What have you made of me, what have you made of every woman in this city?"

"You know very well the Restoration—"

She pointed down the stairs. "You had no right to her! My only true friend, who I have loved and trusted above all others. You had no right!"

Nor had Eliza the right to deceive Emma. If she had ever been a friend, she would have come to Emma and told her. She would have explained that Joseph had asked, that God had called—

She ran down the stairs. The Far West girls shrieked in panic, pulling Eliza to her feet.

"Get out," Emma cried. "Get out of my house, Eliza Snow, you deceiver!"

Mary Elizabeth tried to hold her back. "Please, Sister—"

Emma slapped the young widow so hard she reeled back, clutching her face.

She advanced on Eliza again. "Get out. Never show your face before me. Hang your head in shame and clear yourself from my path, you liar, you adulterer. Get out!"

Eliza stood her ground, though she trembled with shock. "Emma," she said thickly, "you must control yourself. Let me explain."

"There's nothing to explain. My eyes were closed all these years, but I see clearly now. Leave, you Jezebel. Never return." She could hear Joseph struggling with the children, forcing them back into their rooms.

Eliza pulled all her great dignity around her like a mantle—that cold armor. "This is my home, too. You've no right to turn me out."

"Your home? No harlot has a place under my roof." She reached out and took the first object that came to hand—a broom handle one of the boys had left leaning against the newel post.

She swung, catching Eliza on the arm. Eliza cowered, retreating a few steps toward the door.

"Do something, Joseph," Emily Partridge screamed. "She'll kill Eliza!"

Emma thrashed Eliza again and again, striking her on the back, the stomach, the legs, anywhere she could. Eliza cried out piteously with every blow, but drew herself up and tried to speak, tried to reason away the unreasonable.

"Stop!" Joseph shouted.

He was almost on her now. She threw the parlor door open and saw that a few people still lingered in the street—the last of the revelers, heading home. They must have left the Mansion just as Emma had risen from her bed—in the very moment when Joseph and Eliza had kissed. William and Jane Law stared from the gate. No doubt they'd heard the cries from inside.

"Get this foul creature out of my home," Emma screamed into the night. "This adulteress!" She shoved, and Eliza staggered backward over the threshold, fell onto the hardpacked snow.

Jane Law ran forward to help.

Joseph thrust Emma away and knelt beside Eliza. Sallow light fell out through the open door, illuminating them both. Joseph and Eliza were isolated against the darkness, the frail woman and her lover, touching her with tenderness. Never had Joseph touched Emma that way, as if she were a thing to be treasured, as if she were a woman worthy of love.

Eliza struggled again to rise. She was weeping now in a high, keening voice, a cry of such searing loss Emma stilled herself and listened. Joseph cupped her face in his hands. He kissed her brow, which made a taste so foul and bitter rise to Emma's throat that she choked on it.

"We must get her to her feet," Jane Law murmured. "She needs Patty Sessions, and quickly. William, come and help."

Patty Sessions. Why would Eliza need the midwife?

Joseph cast his eyes—those eloquent, expressive eyes—back over his shoulder. He fixed Emma with a look of such contempt that she felt her soul wither. When the men raised Eliza to her feet, she could see the dark stain spreading through her skirt, the patch of red on the ice where she had fallen.

She called on Jane Law two days later. Joseph hadn't returned to her bed, nor given her a single word, kind or unkind. She thought perhaps he would never speak to her again, and she knew his anger was righteous.

"Poor soul," Jane said when she found Emma trembling on her doorstep. "Come in and let me care for you."

The Laws installed her on the sofa in their little parlor. She wasn't permitted to move or speak until she'd taken two cups of tea—Irish comfort, William said, from the bonny old homeland.

She set down her empty cup. The tea had braced her somewhat. All her thoughts came into sharp focus, so sharp she was afraid to handle them.

"We aren't to drink any tea," she muttered, "nor coffee. Joseph's revelation . . . spirited drinks . . ."

William winked at her. "It's a bit late for that, don't you think?"

Jane rubbed Emma's back in small circles.

"Is Eliza well?" It took every ounce of her will to ask the question.

"The midwife told me Eliza will recover," Jane said. "She expects no lasting complications. But her heart is broken, the poor thing, as one might expect."

Emma covered her face with her hands. She couldn't bear for the world to see her, not anyone, not even these good friends. "I never meant to harm her. And I never knew . . . about the baby. Not until I saw the blood."

"No one knew. I don't believe Eliza had even told Joseph."

Jane spoke so simply. This fact, this reality, that a man may have other wives, as many wives as he cared to take. The Restoration was already a thing beyond Emma's power to change. And it was just as far beyond her power to accept the Restoration. She knew that now. She had told herself she could embrace the Blessing of Jacob with time. She'd even realized, in her few quiet moments, that Joseph must have already married other women, for if God had commanded it of all the righteous, then surely the Prophet himself would obey.

But she had built walls of fantasy to shield her heart. She had told herself Joseph's wives would be women she didn't know. Nauvoo was a large city—ten thousand people and growing by the day. If she didn't know the other wives, then she could still tell herself that Joseph's spiritual marriages were chaste, merely symbolic. Those women would serve as handmaids in the world to come, but they wouldn't take her husband's heart now, in the earthly realm. God wouldn't be so cruel as to let him love another woman while Emma, who had been his faithful helpmeet through all these long bleak years, received nothing but his scorn.

What a fool you are, she told herself. *What a callow sop you've always been. When has God given you anything but cruelty?*

She began to weep—great, tearing sobs that sickened her and made her choke for breath.

Jane's hand went on, drawing slow circles on her back, and William sat in sober pity, staring into the fire.

"I killed an innocent." Emma could hardly speak for the self-loathing that wrenched at her. "I killed one of Joseph's children. The sin of murder is upon my soul."

"No, Emma—no." Jane took her face in her hands, forcing her to look up. There was so much compassion in Jane's eyes that Emma couldn't bear it. She only wept harder. "What happened was a tragedy, yes, but also an accident. God sees your heart. He will understand."

Emma shied away. God had always seen her heart. That was why the lash had fallen upon her again and again. The children she had lost, and Don Carlos—all rebukes for her sins. Her soul was too flawed for Eliza's perfect faith. Whenever she thought she had tamped down jealousy or spite, they came rearing up again like the serpent of Eden. And now she had beaten her dearest friend, her sister. She had called Eliza such dreadful things. She had broken Eliza's heart.

William cleared his throat. "I would give you advice as a friend, Emma, if you choose to hear it."

She pulled a kerchief from her sleeve and dabbed at her eyes. She nodded.

"You needn't remain with Joseph. You've evidence enough that he has used you badly and strayed from your marriage. Jane and I are witnesses to . . . what befell Eliza Snow. We could speak to a judge in favor of your divorce, if any judge requires testimony."

"William," Jane said sharply. To Emma she said, "It's true that a judge would grant you a divorce easily enough, the situation being plain. But I don't know whether it's the wisest course, Emma. For you it may be, but what about the rest of us?"

"The rest? I don't understand."

William sighed. "Jane and I have talked this subject over many a time. We've seen how sorrowful you've been, Emma, since the Restoration was announced. You mustn't think we've been gossiping. We're your friends. We've worried over you."

"William and I agree," Jane said, "that if you were to leave Joseph, it would break the church apart. Imagine how it would seem to every other Saint in this city: the Prophet's wife losing faith in him so entirely that she can't even remain in her marriage. The church itself would shatter."

William muttered at the fire, "Jane and I only disagree on whether this would be a good thing or a bad thing."

"It would be terrible," Jane insisted. "You know how the Gentile world despises us. We've made ourselves so strange. None of us has

much hope to find community elsewhere. Try to live outside Nauvoo—
try finding work to support a family—and see how far you get. The
Gentiles will run you out of town with their guns aimed at your back,
crying, 'Mormon! Mormon!' There are too many people who rely on
this church. We must hold it together at all costs. And if we don't, we
know who will suffer worst: the women and children."

"Bah," William grunted.

"You won't think William a heretic, I hope. It's the nature of a news-
paperman, to question everything and blurt out any wild idea that comes
his way. But I keep him in line."

Emma tried to smile. "You've been harboring contraband tea all this
time."

"I'm not the only one," William said, "I can promise you that. Not
when you consider how many have come from the Isles of late. Expect an
Irishman to give up his tea? Or an Englishman, come to that? Not even
God Himself could make us do it."

Suddenly the stillness of the Law home struck her with significance.
She had grown so used to living with Eliza and the Far West girls. There
was no murmur of female voices, no woman singing down some distant hall. She said, "You haven't accepted the doctrine yourselves—the
Blessing of Jacob."

"No," William said at once. "I never shall. Joseph may bluster at me
all he pleases. He may threaten me with damnation; he may send his
worst bullies my way—Brigham, Porter, I care not. My Jane is the only
woman for me. I took a vow to keep her as my wife, to cleave only to her,
and by God, I meant it."

"You've given me much to think on." Emma drew a long breath.
"Eliza—"

"Joseph has already set her up with a little cabin on the hill," Jane
said gently. "You won't need to worry about facing her again. Not until
you're ready."

"I must go home now. My children are waiting."

"Come again any time you'd like a taste of the contraband," William
said. "Or if you need us as witnesses before a judge. We stand ready. We
always shall."

Jane kissed her cheek and bid her farewell, but it was William who followed her out the door. "See here," he said quietly, holding her arm like a brother. "You're stronger than you think."

She laughed and heard all the bitterness in that sound. "Mr. Law, I don't think myself especially strong at all."

"Don't you?" He was genuinely surprised. "I've never known a woman as resolute as you, Emma Smith. In fact, I've never known a man with your steel spine. The things you've suffered—yet you've borne it all with grace."

She turned her face away. "Not all of it, I'm afraid."

"What you haven't borne with grace, you've borne with righteous fury. Like a lioness roaring. One day you'll know for yourself what a force you are in this world. I see it in you already; I ever have. A time will come when you shall see it, too."

The sin was upon her soul, the death of an innocent—and all the sins that had gone before, the secret lusts, the resentments she had nursed until they'd grown fat and indolent, until they couldn't be moved from her spirit. The doubts, most of all. The times when she had questioned Joseph, in her heart if not aloud. The box split open by the blow of an axe, the sand running through her fingers, the desire she'd had to lift the linen and see the golden plates, to know rather than believe.

The weeks and months that followed flashed before her, a rapid succession of night following day, dark following light. She would rise from bed with a hardened will to accept the Blessing of Jacob and do whatever God commanded—how else was she to remove the stain of murder from her soul? But the dark would close around her in an hour or two, and she would know to her very bones that she couldn't bear it another day, another moment, this humiliation which Joseph called the will of God.

From one hour to the next, Emma swung between desperate obedience and choking rage. She yearned for her husband to come to her again and yet she hated him, the look on his face when he stood at the pulpit, his arrogant self-assurance, his beguiling smile. A hundred times, she made up her mind to bring her case before a judge and plead for a divorce. Let the church break apart, let the whole congregation scatter to the winds. But as soon as she felt the matter settled in her soul, the city would ripple with some new rumor of an omen, fresh evidence of God's precise and patient wrath.

Six men watched the stars fall above the still-rising walls of the temple, and saw the moon bow down in the place where the spire would one day be. Every child in the school at the northern edge of town burst out in tongues when their teacher asked them to recite their reading. A stick of wood burned for six days in Orson Pratt's hearth, but never was consumed.

One incident in particular struck a deep, resonant chord of dread in her spirit. Call it a miracle or call it a horror; there is seldom any difference.

Sidney Rigdon's daughter Elizabeth took the fever that spring—it still came up from the mud each year, slithering wet like a salamander through the town. The poor young lady suffered terribly with the illness. Not even Mary Ann's tinctures could protect her. Dr. Avard did his best, bleeding Elizabeth to drain away the humors of the marsh, purging her, prescribing baths of cold river water that left her stiff and blue. Elizabeth Rigdon fell into a sleep from which she couldn't be roused—and then, two days later, her breathing stopped, her heart ceased, and Avard took Sidney by the shoulder and told him to be brave. There was nothing more anyone could do. Elizabeth had gone to Heaven.

Sidney wept, begging Elizabeth to return, for her mother's sake if not for his, but she had gone up to the angels, and no power in earthly hands could call her back again.

Then her sister Nancy, having heard the dreadful news, came weeping into the room. At the sound of Nancy's cries, Elizabeth sat upright in her bed. The pallor of death was still upon her, but she opened her eyes. She spoke.

"Nancy Rigdon, you have been called by God to become a wife of the Prophet. Yet you have delayed. It is in your heart to deny this work, and if you do, the Lord says it will be the damnation of your soul!"

Her message from Heaven thus delivered, Elizabeth fell back again. But she didn't die—not a second time. Sidney and Nancy joined in prayer, hands clasped over her bed. Nancy vowed that she would do as the Lord directed. And little by little, the color returned to Elizabeth's cheeks. Her breath grew steady and deep. By the close of the week, she was up and singing, sewing a dress for Nancy's wedding day.

Against such terrible witness, what could Emma do? If God would raise a woman from death to push another into spiritual wifery, then He would do far worse to anyone who stood athwart His plans. She told herself that if she chose new wives for her husband, then she wouldn't resent the arrangement. She would have no cause to hate them, for it would be she, not Joseph, who had brought them into the family.

She made her selection. She called the Partridge sisters into the parlor and bade them sit in the hardest, meanest chairs.

"You've heard, by now, the doctrine of celestial marriage," Emma said. Emily and Lizzie shared a long, silent look. Lizzie nodded.

"God has given me to know that you—both of you—are to wed Joseph as his spiritual wives. It's only natural. You've lived under our roof all these years. You've kept this house as if it were your own, helped raise our children. I know you both to be good, honest girls, hardworking, obedient. It would please me"—mouth going dry, eyes blinking—"if you would accept this calling and agree to bind yourselves to our family for time and eternity, and become the Prophet's wives in truth and in practice in the hereafter. You understand my meaning, do you not?"

The girls looked at one another again. Lizzie's thin brows drew together in an obstinate frown.

Emily shook her head, silencing her sister. To Emma, she said, "We'll do what you ask of us, of course. It's an honor to be called a wife of the Prophet."

Emma left them in the parlor. She walked up the stairs to Joseph's study and entered without knocking. He looked up from his journal, narrow-eyed, the way he'd looked at her every day since that business with Eliza—if he looked at her at all.

"If you must have more wives than one. If I am no longer sufficient. Then I give you Emily and Lizzie Partridge. As Sarah gave her handmaid Hagar to Abraham."

He dropped his quill on the desk. His expression softened—not to affection, never that, but to bewildered surprise. The moment hung between them far too long. Then he seemed to understand that some acknowledgment was necessary. He rose from his chair and came to her. He took her hand, a thing he hadn't done for months. Emma shuddered at the touch.

He said, "I thank the Lord for teaching you the righteousness of His law. He will make you content with this arrangement, Emma; I know He will. The doctrine is a blessing to women as much as it is to men."

That night, Brigham came to the Mansion to perform the marriage ceremony and seal the Partridge sisters to Joseph in this world and in the kingdom yet to come. Emma took each girl by the hand, leading them to Joseph. Emily was nervous, almost giddy with apprehension. She smiled and fidgeted and couldn't resign herself to the gravity of the moment. Lizzie scowled at Emma, and jerked her hand away almost as soon as Emma had touched her.

After the deed was done, Joseph bought a gift for Emma—a fine new carriage with shining sides and high wheels, a jaunty fringe around its top. She hated the carriage, though Joseph had meant the gift kindly. She wanted no material wealth in exchange for the sanctity of her marriage bed.

Emma tried—God knows how she tried—to look on these new wives with tenderness. Or with patience, at least, if she couldn't summon an ounce of affection. Nothing had changed, she told herself, not truly. Lizzie and Emily had been familiar faces in her home since Nauvoo was founded. There were times when she'd considered those girls almost as dear as daughters. But now she knew Joseph looked on them the way any man may look upon his wife. They were nineteen and twenty-three, fresh and pretty. What man wouldn't prefer their youth, their beauty? Few of Emma's thirty-nine years had been kind to her. Every pain, every denial, every silent hour of suffering had scored itself into her face— deep lines, a hard expression she couldn't seem to change. And motherhood had robbed her body of feminine appeal. Her breasts hung flat and low. The abdomen that had swelled so many times with new life bulged and sagged now, even in her stays. There were times when she took a quiet pride in her matronly figure. Like the battle scars of a warrior, these were the visible marks of her triumph, the children she loved beyond all reason, beyond even God's ability to comprehend. But when one of the Prophet's youthful new brides glided past—round and firm as some delicious fruit—she forgot all her pleasure in what she had accomplished. She saw the years reflected in her aging body. And she hated herself for becoming this drab, forbidding thing.

Emma lashed out at the Partridge girls far too often, criticizing every misstep, no matter how slight. She spoke to them bitterly when she could bring herself to speak. If one stumbled and dropped a dish in the kitchen or allowed a kettle to boil over—if another was slow to rise in the morning or lingered too long in the garden—Emma would strike the girl on the back of her hand, or on the back of her head. Sometimes she would insult one or the other with mocking names.

Lizzie grew more sullen with every day. She would move slowly, casting hard eyes over her shoulder at Emma, and when Emma told her to step lively, she would creep along more sluggishly still. Emily, who had once been so cheerful and bright, cringed and squeaked and scurried away whenever she crossed Emma's path. She'd become a mouse of a girl, a timid, infuriating thing. The Partridge sisters would run from the room when Joseph came into it, for they feared what Emma might do if she saw him kiss another wife's cheek, or take her hand, or smile at her. They remembered Eliza's fate.

It was little wonder their strained arrangement held together only a few weeks. Then it fell like a castle built of cards.

"You know," Lizzie Partridge said one day after Emma had scolded her for the tenth time since sunrise. "We were wives of the Prophet already."

Whatever words Emma had planned to say next withered on her tongue.

"It's true," Lizzie said airily. "We've been Joseph's wives—oh, for months and months before you told us we ought to marry him."

Her sister took her by the arm and hissed, "Don't, Lizzie. You know how she gets."

"I'm not afraid of her. You oughtn't fear her either, Emily. What is she? A dried-up old nothing, that's all—a harridan who can't control her temper."

"You lie," Emma whispered.

"Oh, do I? Ask Emily; she'll tell you."

Emily hung her head. "It's true, Mrs. Smith. The Prophet taught us the doctrine some time ago, and we prayed on it, and agreed to be his wives. So when you told us to marry him, we went along and played as if we'd never done it before. We thought it was the only way to keep peace."

The next moment Emma was running up the stairs. Some high, terrible scream filled the Mansion. She thought she had hurt one of the Partridge sisters, but then she knew it was her own voice.

She could feel it tearing at her throat, the rage and disbelief, the knowledge that she could bear no more of this humiliation. She hurled herself into her room, slammed the door, locked it with her key. She threw the key across the room. It skittered under the bed.

Joseph had come out of his study. "In God's name, what has happened now? Can't a man have peace under his own roof?"

She could hear Lizzie Partridge shouting downstairs. "Peace, with Emma beating us and insulting us every minute of the day?"

He tapped on her door. Then he pounded. "Open at once. We're going to hash this out, all of us, here and now, and I'll hear no more of this foolishness. I'll have no more of this disrespect."

Emma leaned against the door. She could hear his boots in the hall, returning to his study. She straightened and closed her eyes, tried to find some fragment of calm so she could think, so she would know what to do next. William Law. He had said he would stand as witness . . .

Then Joseph was returning. There was a faint jingle of keys on a ring. Emma reeled back from the door.

When he opened her lock and entered, he found her sitting placidly on the bed. She held the sharp end of her sewing scissors to her throat.

"Mercy, Emma!" Joseph lurched toward her.

She jerked the scissors up higher, making ready to bring them down in a quick slash.

She would welcome it, the feel of this all rushing out of her, the hot rage, the thick sorrow that had filled her all these years. She would go then to a place beyond his reach, where no one would look at her with pity again.

Joseph stretched out a hand. "Don't do this, Emma. You must think of our children."

"And why must you not think of the mother of our children?" She spoke with such perfect calm that he trembled. "You've humiliated me. You've drawn me into your devilish pageantry, made me dance to your tune. Well, now you shall dance to mine, or my blood will be on your hands."

"Put down the scissors, Emma."

"Don't come near me, or I'll cut."

He backed off a few steps. He swallowed; she could taste his fear.

"You will renounce the practice of spiritual wifery. You will declare to every man and woman in this church, in this city, that it's a false doctrine, or that God no longer requires it—whichever you prefer. But it will cease, Joseph. One way or another, this sin will cease."

"It's no sin." His voice was little more than a whisper. There were tears standing in his eyes. "Please listen. I do what God has called me to do. I can't alter His will."

"You have altered His will and His word a hundred times before to suit your fancies. There may be others in Nauvoo who believe this has come from the Lord, but I know better."

The tears broke and spilled down his cheeks. "I am led by God toward righteousness, that I may not sin. That no other man may sin."

"By laying with women who aren't their wives?"

"By laying with women who are their wives."

"A neat trick, Joseph. A clever turn. Do you think God will be convinced that your soul is spotless when you stand before Him and answer for your life?"

"Put it down, Emma, please. We can talk about this. We can arrange everything to your liking—"

"Here is how it will be arranged. Here is what I would like. Give up every one of your false wives. Every one. Turn them out from under your roof. Swear before the entire congregation that you have but one wife, the one you married under the law and before the eyes of your Lord. Proclaim me the only wife of Joseph Smith and swear that you will never take another."

He drew himself up, though he shook with the effort. "And if I won't?"

She lowered the scissors to her lap. She smiled. "If you won't do this thing, Joseph, then I will indulge my own lusts. For that is all this doctrine has ever been, and well do you know it."

Hyrum came to see her that night. She hadn't left her room. She had told Joseph she would never leave until all his Jezebels were gone from the house. She would remain locked away without a bite to eat until the refuse had been swept out. If he brought her food, she promised she would throw it out the window. So he brought his brother instead.

Hyrum came into Emma's room grinning, slapping his thigh as if she had played some grand joke on all of Nauvoo. She received him in perfect silence.

"I asked Joseph to let me come and speak with you," Hyrum said. "I told him I could convince you the Blessing is free from sin. Do you know what he said to me? 'You don't know Emma as well as I do.'"

She arched a brow. "Joseph was correct."

He took something from the pocket of his coat, a folded sheet of paper. "Listen, now, and listen well. I've convinced Joseph to write down the commandment, so that I may read it to you. You've been with this church from its infancy, and even before. You know the power of revelation. You know the true word when you hear it. It's called the New and Everlasting Covenant. Pay special heed: everlasting. This can't be changed—not by you, not by Joseph, not by anyone but God."

She sat in silence while Hyrum read the revelation. It was long and wearisome, a rambling justification of all Joseph's sins, an excuse for every humiliation Emma had borne. She schooled herself to patience, waiting for Hyrum to exhaust himself, for Joseph's words to stagger to their finish.

The revelation addressed her by name. It commanded her to cleave to Joseph and none other, to forgive all his trespasses against her. She couldn't hold back a wry smile. Thankfully, Hyrum kept his eyes on the page.

"'I command my handmaid Emma Smith to abide my servant Joseph. But if she will not abide this commandment, she shall be destroyed, saith the Lord, for I am the Lord thy God, and will destroy her if she abide not in the law.'" Hyrum cleared his throat. He folded the paper again and returned it to his pocket. "There you have it, Emma, plain as day. You must turn from this wickedness and amend your ways and make up your mind to accept the New and Everlasting Covenant. Joseph fears for your soul. He doesn't wish to see you destroyed."

"The Lord said that if I forgive Joseph, I, too, shall be forgiven."

"Yes, that's so."

"And the Lord will bless me and make my heart rejoice."

Hyrum nodded. He came toward her, eyes shining, certain of his triumph.

"How will the Lord make my heart rejoice, do you suppose? Will he give me another new carriage like the one Joseph bought me as a reward for permitting his whoredoms?"

The smile fell from Hyrum's face.

"And how have I trespassed against my husband or my God, Hyrum? Tell me that. I've held myself clear of temptation. Don't think, because I'm no longer young and beautiful, that my life has been without temptation. Yet I resisted. I upheld my sacred vows." She rose from her bed and swept toward him. "While Joseph has bent and sullied God's word to suit his own sins. He has perverted the Gospel. He has turned the holy word into a rag with which to scrub away this shadow from his soul."

"You cannot speak so."

"Stop me if you can. Joseph thinks he will tilt holy commandments this way and that until he sees himself on their surface, the way he wishes to be seen: Spotless. Perfect. But he will always look through that glass darkly. He's a man, Hyrum—like you, like any other. And Satan may enfold any man in sin."

Hyrum staggered back.

"Now get out, you fool, you misguided devil. Jerusha—your only true and lawful wife—may never have had the strength to call you what you are. But I have. And I won't suffer you to stand a moment longer in my presence. Get out and take that insult of a revelation with you."

Joseph tried again that night to convince her to hang her head, be meek and silent like Jerusha, like a thousand other women in Nauvoo. But Emma wasn't just a woman. She understood that now. William Law had called her a lioness.

When Joseph brought another copy of the New and Everlasting Covenant, imploring her to sit with it, to read it in privacy, to pray over those words for guidance and truth, she whisked the paper from his hand. She went at once to her little hearth where she'd already laid the evening fire and tossed the revelation into the flames. The page curled and blackened, subsiding into ash.

One day, years from now, when all of this is over, she will learn the extent of Joseph's sin. Her shame-faced sons will bring a list of the Prophet's wives—an inventory as complete as they can make it. This will be when Emma is an old woman, when her sons are men grown with wives and children of their own.

The list will take her by surprise—not its length, for by 1844 she understood that Joseph had indulged every passing fancy and fleeting desire that had drifted across his path. What will startle Emma is the lump that will rise to her throat while she reads—the way she will recall, as vividly as if they stand before her, the faces of all those women. They will be more real to her by that time than Joseph's memory. And the hurt will surprise her, too—a deep, hollow agony at the sight of so many names, so many whom she had thought her friends.

Fannie Alger, a name that won't surprise her, and Lucinda Harris, a name that will. Emma had known Lucinda and her husband well—that is to say, her true husband, not Joseph, whom Emma had never known as well as she'd thought. Tall, stately Prescinda Buell, whose beauty she had always envied as much as she had admired it. Nancy Marinda Johnson, but not when she'd been a girl, thank God. Joseph only wedded Nancy Marinda after she'd already married the apostle Orson Hyde. After Orson learned the truth, he put Nancy Marinda away. Emma will trace the name with an age-gnarled finger. She will wonder whether Nancy Marinda kept the string of pearl beads all those many years.

Mary Elizabeth Lightner is the first name on the list that will cause her real pain. The young widow, sweet-tempered and golden-haired, had lived so many years in the Mansion and had cared for Emma's daughter as if Julia had been her own. Mary Elizabeth had seen Joseph for the first time in 1831, as a girl of thirteen. She had feared him then, for the Prophet could read your thoughts—that was what her friends had said—and his eyes had been so terribly blue. Joseph had laid his hands on the child's head and sealed her unto him. And three years later, he told her time had come to consummate their marriage. She wouldn't do it, for she knew the Prophet was wedded already to Emma. She married another man instead, but her husband was killed at Far West. The Lord made way for Joseph to claim her. He had her at last in Nauvoo. He took her to a room in the Masonic Hall where Brigham Young was waiting. He said, You were mine before you came to this earth. All the devils in Hell will never keep you from me. Mary Elizabeth asked, What will Emma think of this? And Joseph had answered evasively: Emma thinks the world of you.

Patty Sessions, the old midwife of Nauvoo—wedded most probably to keep her quiet, for someone must deliver all of Joseph's children without wagging her tongue. Patty's daughter Sylvia, though, was married for her beauty.

The list is long. Forty-eight names in all. Some of them you know already, and some you haven't heard.

Lucy Walker, one of the orphan girls whom Emma took under her wing. I have a message for you, Joseph said one day to Lucy—a day when Emma had driven to Carthage to order furniture for the Mansion. He said, I've been commanded to take another wife, and you are the woman. I have no flattering words to offer; it's the will of God. You have until tomorrow to decide. If you reject this message, the gate will be closed against you forever. This, Lucy told Emma's sons, aroused every drop of Scotch in her veins. She looked the Prophet fearlessly in his eye. She said, If God will give you revelations, then surely, He will give them to me. I won't do this thing unless God tells me it must be done. Joseph beamed at the girl, blessed her for her faith. And that night, while she tossed in her bed, her room was lit as if it were day, as if at a heavenly presence. When she ran out of her room, heart singing with wonder, she found Joseph waiting. He took her by the hand and said, Thank God, you have the testimony. I, too, have prayed. They were sealed together in celestial marriage that very night, while Lucy still wore her nightgown.

Forty-eight names. Some you know. Eliza, the poetess beloved by all of Nauvoo, wronged and abused by Emma Smith; her fame only grew in the months that followed. She bore the loss of the Prophet's child with cultivated dignity. She filled the newspapers and book shops of the town with her poems. Her songs became the songs of every woman— lonely, isolated in a city of thousands, longing endlessly for love. Emily and Lizzie Partridge. Maria and Sarah Lawrence, sisters, another pair of handmaids taking charity under Emma's roof.

The sharpest pain comes from the youngest brides on the list. Sarah Ann Whitney, daughter of Emma's old friend Ann, who was seventeen when her parents gave her to the Prophet. And Vilate's little girl Helen, only fourteen years old. Joseph's own daughter was but twelve when that marriage took place.

The Saints called these women blessed, but never to their faces, for the New and Everlasting Covenant was kept secret, lest the Prophet and his loyal men be hunted like animals again. They called these women blessed but hid the truth behind a veil. Children were born, and claimed by other men—husbands of convenience, some of whom knew the truth, some of whom believed their wives faithful and chaste, and the Prophet a wholesome man.

They called them Mothers in Israel. They were honored in whispers, and in the cryptic lines of Eliza's songs, but there is little comfort in honor, and behind the veil there is no hand to hold, no comfort for a lonely heart.

From the stillness of the parlor, she can hear the clock in the dining room, measuring out the hours. She can hear the other women in their rooms down the hall, weeping into pillows, praying on their knees. There is wailing in the streets of Nauvoo—grief unrestrained, now that Ford and his men have gone—cries that we are lost, all is lost, the kingdom of God is broken. There are Danites shouting for vengeance, Brigham Young barking at them to hold, to let the militia leave in peace. Outside the noise is like a flock of black birds beating the air. But in the parlor, nothing. A space around her—not a void where Joseph once had been, but something smooth and quiet. She listens to the time passing, an even rhythm, the cycle of the clock's hands. She remembers a field in New York, a blue evening, the wild peas tangling around her boots. The sweetness of the hayfield, and the white trunks of birches against a lingering sunset, the trees like letters scratched into gold. Don Carlos as a boy, sitting on a stump, swinging his legs with a heel of bread in his hands.

A light tap at the front door. Porter Rockwell opens it, leaning inside, hat pressed against his heart. He meets Emma's eye. She nods, and he steps back. He admits Eliza Snow into the parlor.

She is dressed in black, as suits a widow. The years have been kinder to her than they ever were to Emma. Her face is desolate now, but once the grief has lifted some—as it will, as it always does—Eliza will be beautiful again. She meets Emma's eye and doesn't flinch—nor does Emma. They are both calm now, resigned to what can't be denied, and they stand face to face so that they may see each other plainly.

"Thank you for coming," Emma says.

"Brother Heber walked with me from my home. He told me the apostles have washed Joseph's body, and Hyrum's, at the Masonic Hall."

"Yes. They will bring them here in their coffins, and all who wish to mourn will be invited in."

"I would have liked to have done it," Eliza says, "helped prepare him for . . . for burial."

"I know. I would have seen to it that you'd had a hand in the work, if it had been left to me. But Brigham had them taken to the hall the moment the wagon arrived. The best I could do was to give you time, however long you need, to grieve privately, before the rest of the congregation comes."

Eliza nods. Emma can see her throat working as she swallows— once, twice, fighting down tears. Her eyes lower to Emma's stomach, low on her belly where a hand rests. Emma pulls her hand away, hiding it behind her back. The pregnancy isn't evident, not yet, not with her stays and black crepe on. She is only four months along. But it was Eliza who undressed her and put her to bed. No doubt she saw the truth then.

She had thought her life one great ache of longing. But now, in Eliza's lowered face, Emma sees the years differently. She has children with Joseph's face, his remarkable eyes, children who have grown and thrived. They throw their arms around her neck when she kisses their brows. And now she will have one more, a last gift by which to remember the man—all of him, the terrible and the wonderful, the sublime, the infuriating, the ordinary. And Eliza will have nothing.

How Eliza must hate her. How she still loathes herself for the part she played in her friend's grief. If this life were hers to live again, Emma would have offered her own knee as the midwife's stool. She would have wrapped that child in velvet and silk and loved it as one of her own—not for Joseph's sake, but for Eliza's.

"When will the apostles come?" Eliza lifts her gaze from Emma's body. It costs her great effort to do it. Emma can see her shaking.

"Soon now. I asked you here early because I wished to speak to you in confidence."

"Very well; I will listen."

"Now that Joseph is gone, this church is in danger of falling to pieces."

"That is what you've prayed for, is it not?"

"No. Jane Law told me once that too many people rely on the church to let it go so easily. I believe she's right. This church is their shield, their only community—these women you and I have called our sisters and friends. I want to keep this community intact as a legacy for Joseph—for

I did love him in my way, though mine never took the shape of the love you bore him."

Eliza stares into the empty hearth, waiting for Emma to say more.

"There is some difficulty with Brigham."

Weary, Eliza says, "When have you not had some difficulty with Brigham?"

"Joseph blessed our son and named him successor. But he also conferred the keys of ordainment on Brigham. There were witnesses to the conference."

Silence while Eliza considers. She breathes in, looks at Emma squarely. "So, there will be a schism. You and your son on one side, Brigham on the other."

"I mean to lead the church in a righteous new direction until Young Joseph comes of age. I would ask you to stand at my side as president of the Female Relief Society, as champion of our women. They've always admired you. They'll rally to you if you ask them."

"I see."

She turns to the hearth again, the black empty mouth of it. Suddenly Emma can smell the mineral bitterness of the ashes.

Eliza says, "And what is this righteous new direction you speak of?"

"You know that just before he was taken, Joseph declared the Blessing of Jacob finished."

"No."

"Word ran through the town, and no one has listened to gossip more keenly than you. It was Joseph's will that the Restoration should be abandoned. You know this."

"I heard talk of it. I've no doubt Joseph spoke the words you put into his mouth. But I don't believe he meant it—nor do I believe God wills that the Blessing be unmade. This is your will, and you are not the Lord."

There is a strange quivering deep in her chest, a pain she has never felt before. She is losing Eliza for good this time—no chance left to mend what has broken.

Eliza says, "Brigham will uphold the New and Everlasting Covenant?"

Emma nods.

"Then I shall follow him."

"Eliza, please. Consider what you're doing."

She lifts her chin, that old familiar haughtiness. She seems about to speak—a denial, Emma feels certain—but then she turns aside, lowering her face again.

"I will think on it," Eliza says. "I give you my word on that. I will think and pray and then I will do exactly as the Lord wills. I will do His bidding, Emma. Not yours."

She can ask for nothing more. And she can already see it, the great strength that will flourish between them, Emma and Eliza united by a common goal—leading the women of this world toward salvation. The day is heavy and somber, but Emma could almost smile, almost. She will have Eliza back. What other blessing does she need?

When the apostles come with the velvet-covered coffins, Emma takes Eliza's hand. The men have built oak stands to support the coffins; the parlor smells of freshly sawn wood and the herbs of embalming, the wax from the death masks, recently made. Heber Kimball waits for Emma's signal. She doesn't nod until she feels Eliza brace for the blow.

Only then does she allow the men to lift the coffin lids. The sight of him strikes her as would a vision of an angel, if she'd ever had a vision of her own—white, stark, with a cold that goes right through her. He is still and peaceful as he never was in life, never, all the years she knew him. Waxen white, so none of this seems quite real, though she knows it's the most authentic, the most factual thing that has come from Joseph's life.

Eliza cries out. Her hand tightens around Emma's, and Emma holds her, too, lacing their fingers together.

"Oh, Joseph," Eliza weeps. "Joseph, they have killed you at last."

The men withdraw. The widows must have their time to mourn. Side by side, they stand over their husband's body. They look on him as they had done before, while he had still lived—with great love and great despair.

XV

Hear the Wolves Howl

1844

"Why will you not speak?" Brigham stalked across the small room, turned, paced back again. He could go no more than four or five strides before he met a wall. "Open your damnable mouth, you harridan!"

Emma sat up straight on the hard milking stool, which was all the accommodation Brigham and Joseph had provided. She kept her arms folded and her mouth shut. She watched Brigham pace, watched Joseph watching her—leaning from his ladderback chair, those shocking blue eyes fixed on her with an intensity she had never seen before. The room above the redbrick store felt close from Brigham's fuming, his hot breath. The window was shut, the curtain drawn, so no one would hear in the streets below if Emma shouted for help. But she wasn't one to shout, not over something like this, and she had long since learned that the only aid she would find was that which she made for herself.

"No, she won't speak." Joseph's voice was little more than a rasp. "She'll keep her counsel, this wife of mine."

He was still sallow from the illness that had taken him that morning. He'd come down to his breakfast and had his usual cup of coffee. But he'd had no more than a few bites of buttered toast, had drunk no more than half the cup, when he'd lurched up from the table and stumbled toward the kitchen door. He hadn't made it outside in time. The vomiting had been like nothing Emma had seen, not even when her children had been ill.

Joseph had retched so violently that his jaw had dislocated, and among the bile Emma had seen bright, fresh blood.

"She won't speak a word," he said, "because she knows she'll damn herself. She knows what she has done."

Emma had sent Mary Elizabeth running for the doctor, for Patty Sessions, for Mary Ann Young—anyone who could help. She had feared the worst, appendicitis, but when Dr. Avard arrived, he'd put her concerns to rest on that point if on no other.

"You poisoned the Prophet." Brigham stopped pacing in front of her. He towered, a monolith of hate. "We've more enemies than we can count, Gentiles howling for your blood, Joseph. And yet the worst threat of all has come from within. From your own hearth and home."

Dr. Avard had pronounced the illness nothing worse than an ulceration of the stomach, brought on by anxiety. Wryly, Emma had thought, *Whatever could be weighing so heavily on his mind?*

"If she won't confess to poisoning me, then she won't confess," Joseph said, turning away in disgust.

She felt a pang of relief. For hours, Joseph and Brigham had kept her locked in that room above the store, questioning, accusing, tormenting her with promises of Hell. It was, perhaps, the same room where they had locked Martha Brotherton away.

"You're too soft on her, Joseph. You always have been."

Brigham raised his fist. Emma looked at it calmly. She wasn't afraid. Brigham was certainly capable of beating her—it was in his nature— but it wasn't Joseph's style, not even at the steepest pitch of his anger. Brigham wanted her to fear him. He needed her to confess she had poisoned the Prophet. Perhaps Joseph needed that confession, too— some reason to put her aside so he could be rid of her for good, so his edict of celestial marriage could spread without hindrance. Emma still held the hearts of the women; the FRS was hers. A good number of the women had heeded her counsel. Lately, the men's proposals of spiritual wifery were rejected at least as often as they were accepted. The tide of favor was turning against the Blessing of Jacob—at least where the women were concerned. Joseph's most loyal men glared at Emma in the streets. Darkly, they muttered her name. She smiled through it all, hardmouthed and cold.

Brigham spun away, pacing again, his fist still raised and shaking in the air. "Damn it, Joseph, if you'd brought her to heel years ago, we wouldn't be in this mess now. The women of this city are half ready to rise up in rebellion! And here she has poisoned you. Your own wife, whom God commanded to be meek and submissive, poisoned you!"

Joseph looked down at Emma without the least warmth or sympathy. She, the mother of his children.

"Speak," he said, "you child of Hell."

She folded her arms and kept her mouth closed.

She tries now to find the day, the exact moment when the church took its body in its own hands and tore itself apart—flesh ripping red, bone breaking, the gore of shame spilling out for the world to see. Perhaps it was that day when Brigham and Joseph accused Emma of poisoning. Perhaps Joseph saw, in the blood he vomited onto the floor, an omen of what was to come. Something changed in him that day. He became ravenous, ravening, where before he had been merely hungry.

If it wasn't the day of the so-called poisoning, then it was an evening that followed—a week after, maybe more. They were just finishing supper. Julia was clearing the table in that quick, cheerful way she had, the sprightliness she affected whenever the air between Joseph and Emma was strained. The entire household had eaten without a word. Not even little Frederick had made a sound.

"Take your brothers upstairs," Emma said to Young Joseph, "and help them make ready for bed."

The Far West girls and the junior wives all went to the kitchen to help wash up. Emma paused in the hall, just beyond the threshold of the dining room. Joseph hadn't risen from the table. He remained with his hands splayed on the wood, palms down, as if he held the table in place, as if by force of his will he kept the world steady around him.

She was about to speak. Joseph, what has come over you? Or, Joseph, I never poisoned you; you know it's true. But a shout rose from outside— Porter Rockwell yelping an alarm, and then the sound of a scuffle at the door. An instant later, the parlor door was thrown open and someone was calling for Joseph. Calling in an Irish brogue.

Emma and Joseph reached the parlor at the same moment. William Law was trying unsuccessfully to wrench his arm from Porter's grip.

"Leave him," Emma said.

Porter obeyed her at once and slunk back outside. Later, she would find his quick obedience surprising, and gratifying.

"This is the limit, Smith," William said. "The very limit, you mark my words."

"A good evening to you, too, Brother William," Joseph said.

"I've come to have words with you, and if words won't suffice, I've two fists to spare."

"Whatever has gotten into you, man?"

"I would hesitate," William said, "to speak of these things before your wife—your good, saintly wife. But I know already that Emma sees and understands what sort of debauchery you get up to."

She moved toward him. "Please, William, don't upset yourself. You'd better explain."

"Oh, I shall. Do you know who came into the newspaper office this very evening to sign an affidavit—an affidavit they wished printed for all the city to read? Three women, Joseph Smith. Three women so ashamed and mortified by what they'd been subjected to that they wore veils! They didn't wish their identities known, except by me. They asked me to witness their signatures on a statement attesting that although they are all three married, the Prophet and his brother Hyrum endeavored to seduce them!"

"Now, see here," Joseph said.

William thundered on. "These women said you and your brother made the most wicked proposals and pressed them to become your wives! They wished me to publish the account and redact their names, for they felt they couldn't face their neighbors. But they agreed to make their identities known to me. When they lifted their veils—" William's face had gone quite red. He clenched a fist, gritted his teeth, struggled to marshal his words. "When they lifted their veils, whom did I see among them but my own wife, Jane!"

Joseph grunted as if William had relayed some obscene joke. He turned away in dismissal.

"Don't think to brush this off," William said. "You know who I am. You know the power of the press. I give you one choice—one straight and narrow path to make this right and atone for your sins. If you've reformed this church once, you can do it again. Announce an end to this debauchery for good and all."

"It isn't my decision to make," Joseph said coolly. "This is God's commandment."

"Do you think I'm such a fool?"

"The Blessing of Jacob is an ancient law."

William laughed bitterly. "Ancient, these many long years since we founded Nauvoo."

"The Old Testament—"

"Says quite clearly: 'Thou shalt not lie.' And I will not lie when I print this story of your theft of other men's wives. I'll print it in Nauvoo, and I'll send the article to every other city, to every corner of the world. Every Christian soul will bear testament against you. They'll call you a liar and a fraud, a seducer, a ruiner of women. I'll do it, unless you call an end to this madness. Go before the church's High Counsel, fall on your knees, confess your sins, and beg every man and woman in Nauvoo for forgiveness."

Joseph pitched toward him suddenly. The Irishman didn't back down.

"I'll be damned if I do," he snarled. "If I admitted to the charges you would heap upon me, it would prove the overthrow of my church!"

William turned his grim little smile up at Joseph. "Is that not inevitable already?"

"Then we can all go to Hell together," Joseph shouted, "and convert it into Heaven by casting the Devil out!"

He threw up his hands in wild surrender; he circled the parlor, laughing.

That was what struck the deepest chill into Emma's heart—the sound of his laughter, high and frantic, as if he could already feel the flames licking at his heels.

He cried, "Hell is by no means the place the fools of this world suppose it to be. Oh, no, on the contrary! It's quite an agreeable place!"

Emma caught sight of Young Joseph on the stairs. The boy clung to the bannister, white-knuckled, staring down on the scene. She pointed up the stairs, and at once Young Joseph fled.

"If you think so highly of Hell," William said, "you can enjoy it then. But for me, I will serve the Lord. You have my terms, Smith. I give you until this time three days hence to make your confession to the High Counsel, put off all your *wives*, and declare to the church that the Blessing of Jacob is no more. After that, the affidavit will be printed." He settled his hat on his head. "That's my final word."

Emma followed William into the yard. "I had no idea about Jane."

He took her hand. He was trembling faintly. "You mustn't blame yourself. I said what needed saying, and if your husband doesn't repent as a proper Christian ought, then I'll do what needs doing, too. You must brace yourself for what will come next. I'm afraid men of his sort don't often do the right thing. A man like him would rather destroy himself than be humbled."

"I know," she said. "I know it well."

She looked back at the house. The parlor window was a square of yellow lamplight; Joseph's shadow moved across the pane.

Another figure stirred near the corner of the house. Porter Rockwell, hackling like a dog keen to bite.

"You must take care," Emma said quietly. "Go nowhere without friends around you. Porter is dangerous. So is Brigham, and all Danites. They won't love you, William, even if you have your way."

"I'll be cautious—I promise you that. But don't fret too much on my account. God didn't make me an Irishman for nothing."

He tipped his hat and walked away, almost cheerful now. But there was a smell of woodsmoke on the air, and down along the river wharves she could see the refuse fires burning, red as the blood that had fallen on her kitchen floor.

Emma didn't see Joseph the following day. None of the women in the Mansion could tell her where he'd gone, nor where he'd slept the night before, whether on the parlor sofa or in one of their beds. The children wept in their rooms, and there was a curious, muffled quality to the house. When she lit a fire to cook the morning porridge, the chimney refused to draw.

By evening, Joseph still hadn't returned. She feared he might have fled Nauvoo, and yet she didn't believe he really had gone. She could feel him somehow. His hand was still upon the church; his hand was scoring the substance of the world.

After the children had their supper, she took a light shawl from the hook in her bedroom and walked through the blue-gray dusk to the Young home. Mary Ann was in her garden, cutting bunches of herbs. The scent of dry earth and crushed stems hung around her. A pall of sadness hung around her, too, the same subdued nature she had worn since that night when Joseph had taught the Blessing of Jacob to Brigham at his table.

"Good evening," Emma said. "I hope I'm not disturbing you."

"Not as such. You ought to make your business fast, though. Brigham is inside. You know he doesn't love you, but he loves you even less today. I've heard him curse your name a hundred times since sunup."

"I only came to learn if Joseph is here. There was a scene last night. I don't know whether Joseph stayed at home, for I never saw him in the morning, and I've heard no word of him all day."

"The Prophet was here late last night," Mary Ann said. "That's all I can tell you. I wasn't permitted to stay and hear him speak. Brigham sent me away—me, and the other women. But Joseph looked upset, almost beside himself with worry. I'd feared you were unwell, or one of the children, but I reasoned Joseph would have fetched me with my herbs if there'd been some sickness. Now you must go, Emma—"

The kitchen door was flung open. Brigham came barreling into the yard.

Mary Ann dropped her herbs into her basket. "Go," she whispered, and hurried away, taking a path that would lead her clear of her husband to the front door.

Brigham trampled some of Mary Ann's plants underfoot in his haste to get to Emma. She waited for him with her hands clasped easily together.

"You," he said. "The very last creature I could wish to see."

"I understand Joseph was here last night."

"Well, he couldn't stay under his own roof—not with all your accusations."

Emma lifted her chin. "Joseph told you about William Law, I suppose."

"He was beside himself. I've never seen a man in such a state, and to think it was you who reduced him to it—you and your friend William, scheming between you."

"I had nothing to do with William's proposal."

Brigham huffed. "Proposal? Is that what you call it? Shakedown is a better word. And Joseph was set to do it, Emma! He was convinced already to abandon God's great work, to drop the Restoration in the mud in the very midst of the Latter Days."

She blinked. "Joseph agreed to renounce spiritual wifery?" She had reason to hope, then.

"Do you think I'd allow him to do something so foolish? He said he meant to go to the High Counsel and repent, call the whole thing a folly, or if I wouldn't accept folly, then call it a test of Heaven. The way God tested Abraham with Isaac."

"Of course—the test of Isaac. It's the perfect way to end it all while saving face. It will hold the church together, and William Law will be satisfied, and the women who've been wronged may not feel so ashamed."

"I told him to shit on that idea."

She stepped back, buffeted by his foul language and the coldness of his eyes.

"Listen, Emma, and listen well. I'll only say this once. We have what we want now, we men of the church. It's an idiot's fancy to think you can pry it away. Not even the Prophet will take it from us now."

She met his hard eyes. "Then I will part with Joseph. And when I leave, all his masks will be shattered. The disguise will fall away. The whole church will know he is no prophet, and never has been. Without a prophet to guide them, the people won't follow—not any leader, not even you."

"Do you think that's so? Try it and find out. I'm the hero who brought the Prophet's family to Far West, and then brought them out again when the wolves began to howl. I'm the one who founded Nauvoo, who traveled all the way to England to spread the word of the Latter Days. Seven thousand men and women have crossed the Atlantic at my command. Three quarters of this church revere me at least as much as they revere the Prophet. I told Joseph as much. He saw it plainly, by the time our conversation was through. If he renounces the Blessing of Jacob, he will lose my loyalty. And if he loses me, he'll lose everything else. Like the snap of a twig, it will be broken, easy as that."

She tried to draw a steady breath, but it rattled in her throat. Brigham was right.

"Let me give you a word of advice," he said. "Return to the path of righteousness. Uphold your husband in all things. Resign the women of the Relief Society to the Blessing of Jacob, and counsel them to accept what they can't prevent. Because I assure you, Emma, no one will prevent me. I've waited too long, labored too many years in service to this church. No one will unmake what Joseph and I have made. Not even the Prophet himself."

She struggled to find some reply.

"The only thing I've never understood," Brigham said, "is why Joseph has always loved you so damnably much. For it's a certainty I could never love a woman like you."

She was struck mute for a moment. Finally, she managed, "Love?"

He spat into the herb bed. "I told Joseph you were a damned woman already. I advised him to let you go, if you wanted to part with him. Or to put you in a cabin on the edge of town, like the little cage he built for Eliza, where you couldn't influence this town any longer. Do you know what he said to me? 'How strange, that you should hate her so, for Emma thinks the world of you.'"

She frowned. She couldn't imagine why Joseph would say it. Why he would even think it was so.

"He told me," Brigham said, "'As for damnation, I tell you this. I will have Emma in the hereafter if I have to walk into Hell to claim her.'"

THE NAUVOO EXPOSITOR
JUNE 7, 1844

It is with the greatest solicitude for the salvation of the Human Family, and of our own souls, that we have this day assembled. Feign would we have slumbered, and "like the Dove that covers and conceals the arrow that is preying upon its vitals," for the sake of avoiding the furious and turbulent storm of persecution which will gather, soon to burst upon our heads, have covered and concealed that which, for a season, has been brooding among the ruins of our peace.

Emma strode the corridors of the Mansion, calling for Joseph. She threw open doors to the other women's rooms but found only the girls—eyes red from weeping, or staring and dazed, with the freshy printed pages of the *Expositor* bunched in their fists. "What will come of this, Sister Emma?" the women pleaded. "What will happen to us now?"

She pounded on the door of the Masonic Hall, demanding they send Joseph out. "We haven't seen him, Sister," the apostles said, and she knew by their bewilderment that they told the truth. She shouted up to the room above the redbrick store. But the curtain was open and even from the street she could tell the room was empty.

At noon she climbed the hill to the temple, where a smell of wet mortar hung in the air. The men clinging to the great wooden scaffolds put down their mallets and trowels and watched as Emma searched the grounds, thrusting her arms into hazel thickets to part the leaves, staring helplessly up into the oak branches as if her husband might have climbed to the canopy. She found no sign of him, nothing but birds singing in the dappled green—singing as if the last days hadn't come.

If she could only locate him before this madness spread too far. She would sit with him and Brigham, and with William Law, and forge a truce among them. For now that she had read William's declaration for herself, she could feel the old fears rising. The Gentiles would turn their attention to Nauvoo. Zion, Far West—their ghosts rose up to stand around her in a tight ring. She could smell the gunpowder drifting from their shrouds.

We all verily believe, and many of us know of a surety, that the religion of the Latter-day Saints, as originally taught by Joseph Smith, which is contained in the Old and New Testaments, Book of Covenants, and Book of Mormon, is verily true; and that the pure principles set forth in those books, are the immutable and eternal principles of Heaven, and speaks a language which, when spoken in truth and virtue, sinks deep into the heart of every honest man.

By the time she returned to the Mansion, she had already counted four Danite patrols in the streets. The riders' eyes darted. Their hands rested on the handles of their guns. Whenever a man would shout from some alley "Heresy!" or "Fallen prophet!" the Danites turned their heads, moving as one body.

Porter nodded to Emma from her own garden gate. There was a shadow from the brim of his hat, a black line where his eyes should have been.

"Have you seen Joseph?"

Porter shook his head. "Best get inside, Sister Emma. I don't like the feel of the city today. Something troublesome's brewing."

Julia and Young Joseph ran to meet her in the parlor.

"Mother," Julia said, clinging to her arm, "what has happened? The girls are all crying and won't say a word, and we've seen patrols from the windows upstairs."

"Nothing to concern you," she said, but even she could hear the tremor in her voice.

Julia began to weep.

"It won't be like last time," Young Joseph said, "will it, Mother?" His fists clenched. She could see how manfully the poor child struggled to control his tears. "It won't be like in Missouri, will it?"

"Of course not." She kissed his hair. "But if you hear me call for you, you must come at once, and go wherever I send you."

"To hide?" Young Joseph asked.

She hesitated. She looked at their innocent faces, Young Joseph with his forced bravery, Julia blinking back tears. Her heart fell into her stomach; her heart, like wax, melted to nothing. They had been so young, yet every dreadful moment they had suffered in Far West was printed forever in their minds. Every crack of gunfire, every lick of the flames. And now they would live that terror all over again—and worse, far worse, unless she could find Joseph. Unless she could stop this madness.

We believe that all men, professing to be the ministers of God, should keep steadily in view, the honor and glory of God, the salvation of souls, and the amelioration of man's condition: and among their cardinal virtues ought to be found those of faith, hope, virtue and charity; but with Joseph Smith, and many other official characters in the Church, they are words without any meanings attached—worn as ornaments; exotics nurtured for display.

She never knew what drew her to the back of the house, to the grove of fruit trees scarcely grown beyond saplings. Perhaps she only wanted a moment's peace to collect her thoughts. Perhaps she wanted privacy so she could pray. But when she looked down the length of the orchard, there was Joseph, with the sun bright on his golden hair and his white sleeves. He was luminous and still, sitting under one of the young apple trees. His back was turned to Nauvoo.

Slowly, she made her way toward him. His old bedroll from Zion's

Camp was spread along the ground. A ring of scorched stones marked the place where a little cook-fire had burned. He looked up at her. Neither of them spoke. They only stared at one another across the distance between them.

After some time—minutes, it might have been, or hours or eternities, for all Emma could tell—she moved closer. Not near enough to touch, or for him to touch her, but closer, so they could speak. She sank down and her dark skirt pooled around her. Low, close to the earth, she could smell the grass, a green sweetness, and the honey perfume of wildflowers dotted between the trees. From somewhere close by came the droning of a bee, and then, far across the orchard, the repetitious call of a yellow warbler, a lazy sound in the summer heat.

"I like it here," he said quietly, "among the trees. It reminds me of when I was a boy, back in Vermont. I would go out into the forest where there were only trees and birds and leaves moving in the wind. And shadows on the forest floor. I would go there to think my own thoughts. To imagine."

She could picture him, a boy just like their sons, but golden instead of dark. Wiry and sweet-tempered, big for his age, bright of eye and mind. A boy like the one Don Carlos had been, picking grubs from the garden, dropping them in a can. She wanted to speak. She wanted to tell him, William Law has printed the affidavits. Every soul in the city is reading his article now, reading and talking. I've read it myself, Joseph, and I can find no fault with anything William has said.

But she hadn't seen Joseph this way for so many months—not happy, but at peace. And anyhow, her throat had gone too tight for words.

She reached out. The new green heads of grass seeds brushed the back of her hand. Joseph reached, too, and took her hand in his.

She said, "You knew one day this would all go too far. How could you not know it?"

We appeal to humanity and ask, what shall we do? Shall we lie supinely and suffer ourselves to be metamorphosed into beasts by the Syren tongue? We answer that our country and our God require that we should rectify the tree. We have called upon him to repent, and as soon as he shewed fruits meet for repentance, we stood ready to seize him by the hand of fellowship,

*and throw around him the mantle of protection; for it is the salvation of
souls we desire, and not our own aggrandizement.*

The shouts in the alleys of Nauvoo turned to chants of "Fallen prophet"
and "Sin! Sin!" And soon there were packs of men roving, calling for
Joseph's ouster, for him to be whipped in the public square as pen-
ance. Calling for Hyrum and Brigham Young and every member of
the church's leadership who had outraged a woman to be locked in the
stocks or fined until he was penniless or hauled to Carthage for a trial
before Gentile judges.

And yet other mobs formed—loyalists, those who had tasted Jacob's
fruit and found it too sweet to relinquish. The men fought. They beat
each other with fists, with the handles of their tools. Thank God no one
was fool enough to draw his gun—not against a fellow Mormon.

The Danites charged through the city, claiming they only sought to
restore order, but little by little the packs of dissenters were broken up
and driven back. The friends of William Law retreated to their homes.

By sunset, the Danites had assembled a swarm of some two hundred
men. They marched on William's office and pulled him from the building. They beat him, but he escaped with his life and fled.

*It is absurd for men to assert that all is well, while wicked and corrupt
men are seeking our destruction, by a perversion of sacred things; for all is
not well, while whoredoms and all manner of abominations are practiced
under the cloak of religion. Lo! the wolf is in the fold, arrayed in sheep's
clothing, and is spreading death and devastation among the saints: and
we say to the watchmen standing upon the walls, cry aloud and spare not,
for the day of the Lord is at hand—a day cruel both with wrath and fierce
anger, to lay the land desolate.*

When night came—a full, heavy darkness—there was a pounding on the
Mansion door.

Emma looked down from her window. She could see the crown
of Porter Rockwell's hat, and beside him, a woman. Her arms were

wrapped tightly around her body. She shifted from one foot to another, dancing with fear.

Emma rushed down the stairs, threw open the door.

"The *Expositor* is burning," Eliza said. Her eyes were wild with terror. "Where is Joseph? Is he safe?"

Emma pushed past Porter and Eliza, out into the night. A damp chill had come up off the river. She gripped the pales of the garden fence, staring over the city to where a sickly red flower bloomed. Never had she dreamed a fire could be so large.

Someone seized her by the shoulders and spun her around. Her hands tore painfully away from the palings. Eliza was there, staring into her face, shouting at her, only inches away. "Tell me! Where is Joseph?"

She led Eliza to the orchard, but the overcast sky gave them no light, and there was no small cook-fire glowing out there among the trees. Joseph was gone. She could smell the stench of the *Expositor*'s destruction hanging among the branches.

Those whom no power or influence could seduce, except that which is wielded by some individual feigning to be a God, must realize the remarks of an able writer, when he says, "if woman's feelings are turned to ministers of sorrow, where shall she look for consolation?" Her lot is to be wooed and want; her heart is like some fortress that has been captured, sacked, abandoned, and left desolate.

"Oh God, what shall I do?" Eliza threw herself at Emma.

Fear crashed in her mind, but Eliza wasn't attacking her. She wrapped her arms around Emma and clung there, sobbing, pleading with God to spare Joseph's life.

Emma stroked Eliza's back, though she still quivered with the shock of the moment. "Now, now," she managed, "Joseph will be well, wherever he has gone. The Danites will protect him."

"I can't go back, Emma. I can't return to my home. It's so lonesome there, you can't imagine. The silence, and the forest all around me . . . I've no one there, never anyone to talk to unless Joseph comes to visit. And if I go back, all I will think of is the city burning. God help me, it feels like Far West come again."

"What's this?" she said. "Can this be the same woman who was so fearless when we left Kirtland in the back of a wagon, hidden among the potatoes? The same woman who was first to cross the ice when we fled from Far West?"

"I was never brave," Eliza said. "I only went where love compelled me."

"There's nothing more courageous than that." She pulled back, holding Eliza at arm's length. "You'll stay here in the Mansion with me and the children for as long as you please. We'll sit together in the parlor and wait for Joseph to come. And we'll pray together for his safety."

They did pray, while the rioters roared in the streets and men ran to the temple for shelter. They prayed until well past midnight, when Nauvoo quieted and the Danites rode back to their homes, clutching victory in bared teeth. They prayed until Eliza sagged down across the sofa. In minutes she was breathing deeply, surrendered to sleep. Emma covered her with the little lap quilt Julia had made.

Another knock came at the Mansion's door, not loud enough to wake Eliza. Emma opened the door by a finger's breadth, peering out cautiously. Porter Rockwell again. She lifted her lamp, and its paltry light brought Porter's face from the darkness with astonishing clarity—the tangle of his beard, the urgency of his eyes.

"News of Joseph?" she whispered.

"No, Sister, but I thought it best that you should know. Lyman Wight was up in Carthage when all this mess began. He only just rode back to town. I fear there's grim news."

She drew a deep breath. She told herself she was ready to hear it, but who is ever prepared?

"The Gentiles got their hands on the *Expositor*," Porter said. "They've read Law's screed. And somehow—maybe a spy in Nauvoo, for all I can say—they've learned already what the Danites did. Destroying the press, I mean."

She opened the door wider. "What does this mean for us?"

"The Gentiles are mighty unhappy about it. Declared it an attack on the Constitution itself—freedom of the press, and the like. Lyman said the sheriff of Carthage tried to cool things off, but they had a bit of a riot there, too. Now the governor has agreed to raise up the militia and bring them down on Nauvoo to settle the affair once and for all—

make Joseph stand trial and answer for the destruction of the press. The governor is expected to be here sometime tomorrow."

So it would be Far West again, just as she and Eliza had feared. When Porter had gone, resuming his endless circuit of the Mansion, she set her lamp on the pier table beside the door. She walked out into the quiet yard, to the edge of her garden, staring at the river. It was a vast expanse of perfect blackness, so wide it may as well have been an ocean—just as hostile, every bit as difficult to cross. Emma would be pinned there when the Gentiles came—she and her children, trapped against the banks of the Mississippi, along with the rest of Nauvoo. It wasn't fear that struck her then, so much as bleak resignation. It came to her as a memory: the burning cold in her chest, the weight of a pack on her shoulders and the weight of a child in her belly. From the toe of her boot, along the flat pale face of the ice, a dark line appeared, spreading its filaments like a spider's web.

At least the fire at the *Expositor* office had burned itself out. It hadn't spread to any other businesses. It had spared the homes along the street, too. She could smell wet ash like springtime mud. She stared at the place where the press had been, a void in the shadows of the city.

And as she looked, the slow thread of a new emotion wrapped around her and tightened. It cut into the body of her dread, pushing back her fear just far enough that she could think, and plan. Emma straightened. Something had coaxed a spark of hope to light inside her breast. What had it been?

A pinprick of gold on the river. Like a star fallen, floating on the water. No, not on the water—on one of the small islands beyond the wharves, the sand bars where the willows grew.

She hurried back into the house and changed into her darkest dress. She fetched a good, sturdy shawl and returned to the parlor, moving carefully so she wouldn't wake Eliza. She extinguished her lamp and pressed herself against the pane of a window, watching Porter Rockwell make his round. When he'd passed, Emma slipped out the Mansion's door and ran down the garden path to the road.

She made her way alone to the waterfront. Nauvoo was quiet, the Danites resting in their homes for the battle yet to come. The city crouched and trembled, waiting for the governor's blow to fall. No one noticed Emma, for she was dark as a whisper, hidden from human eyes, as on a September night long ago. When she reached the wharves, the planks of the pier rang hollow underfoot, drums calling men to war.

She found a small rowboat and eased herself down into its rocking belly. Her hands shook, but she managed to lock the oars in place. She untied the mooring, pushed herself away from the dock. The boat drifted out into the featureless black. Emma began to row.

Her back burned with the effort by the time she felt the sand bar scraping along the hull. She pulled harder at the oars, gritting her teeth against the pain, and the little skiff beached itself on the island. When she stepped out, her boots splashed in shallow water. She waded up onto the sand.

The light of Joseph's campfire drew her deep into a tangle of willows—a feral, grasping forest. She found him huddled far back from his fire, hidden in a thicket, in fear of her approach. He had pressed himself like a hunted animal against the damp ground.

"Joseph. Come to me."

Shuddering, he rose and stumbled to the fire. His shirt was torn, his trousers stained with mud. His coat was gone. He stood above the small flames, shame-faced, waiting for her to speak.

"You love me," she said. "Our love has never been something I could understand, but I know you love me, and I have loved you."

He moved closer. He took her hand. Emma closed her eyes for a moment, feeling the nearness of her husband, beside her now, united with her as they had never been before, not once.

She said, "You can't run from this—this thing you've created, this monster you have made. There are ten thousand people in that city. And when the governor arrives with all his men, you know what they'll do to us. You've seen it play out already, at Zion, at Haun's Mill."

He was silent, but Emma could feel his surrender in the warmth of his hand.

"Come back with me, Joseph. You must."

He said, "They'll kill me if I go back. The governor, his militia. Maybe William Law and his friends. I'll be finished, Emma, for good."

The small fire crackled. A few sparks rose up to Heaven, or as close as they could get before they disappeared. "If you save ten thousand lives," she said, "it may wash the stain from your soul—this guilt, the mark of all you've done these past mad years. Save the city—save your people—and you may yet be redeemed."

In the first pale flush of dawn, they returned to the Mansion together, walking hand in hand. Eliza came out into the garden to meet them. She stared at Joseph's face, wordless, parched for his presence. The children followed her out the door. Joseph held them all together, wrapping those small precious bodies in his arms, pressing his cheek against each beloved face, one after another.

Eliza said, "Heber Kimball was only just here with the news. The Illinois militia has nearly arrived. They are perhaps five miles away."

"Then there isn't much time," he said.

He led them all into the parlor. Young Joseph brought a chair and set it before the fire. One by one, Joseph instructed his children to sit. He laid his hands upon their heads and blessed them solemnly, with grief tempering his words: Young Joseph to carry on the church after his father's death; Julia for every happiness she would desire over the course of a long and honorable life—and for a husband, just one, to love her and gladden her heart.

Frederick and Alexander to delight and comfort their mother, to be steadfast in faith as they grew. He laid a hand on Emma's belly. Whatever blessing he conferred upon that baby, she never heard, for Joseph willed it silently into the child's spirit.

He stood next before Eliza and touched her face—held her face in his hands as if she were his greatest treasure. He would take the memory of her with him into the waiting dark. Eliza would be the lamp to light the Prophet's way on a new path, one he had no power to shape. Emma watched their silent exchange, a love that needed no words for expression—not even Eliza's words.

A murmur rose from the streets outside. Then a shout, a clamor. The militia had come to Nauvoo. Joseph turned toward the sound. His face was pale and still.

Emma took him by the arm. "Bless me, too. I would have your blessing before . . . before you take your leave."

"I haven't much time left," he said quietly. "I must be alone to pray, now while I still can. Write down the blessing you desire, Emma, my dear one—my dearest of all. This mess will be finished soon enough, and I'll come back after my trial. Then I'll sign whatever blessing you've written with my own hand, so you'll know the Lord will grant it."

She went up to his study and sat alone at his desk. The small things of his life lay all around, mute witnesses to the man. The year's journal where he'd recorded his doings faithfully each day, the magnificent and the mundane. On the shelf beside his desk, all the journals for all the years that had gone before. Those pages described a momentous history, and no history at all—a tale the Prophet had told himself, a tale he'd asked them all to believe. There were manuscripts half-penned, books never finished. A copy of Emma's hymnal, a book of Eliza's poems. And symbols carved into wood with the tip of a whittling knife. There was a stone at the corner of his desk—an ordinary stone, smooth and round, small enough to fit in the palm of your hand.

She opened a drawer and took out a sheet of foolscap paper. She brushed it with her fingers. It made a quiet hiss, a breath long held and finally released. She wondered what she ought to write for her blessing. What did she want God to make of her now? She thought, *At least Joseph expects that he'll come back from Carthage.* Emma wished she could feel as certain.

After she'd written a few lines, she heard a commotion in the street below. Hurriedly, she returned the paper to the drawer and stood, peering down into the road. Her heart pushed outward; it filled her throat. Horses—men—men in uniforms. The governor had come with the militia at his back. She wiped her tears away. It was time for Joseph to surrender.

She went out into the orchard herself. She would allow no one else to do it. This was her task alone—a thing only a man's wife could do.

She found Joseph where she knew he would be, sitting on the earth between the trees, the branches arching over his head like the great soaring vaults of Heaven. She went to him slowly. *Let this moment draw out*, she prayed. *Let me have him for a little while longer.* Something moved—a pale thing, small, flitting away on a breeze. What was it? The warblers called, the wildflowers nodded and gave up their gentle scent. Another white thing flew from the Prophet's hands.

When she stood beside him, Emma saw that he had taken her sewing scissors. A sheet of white linen lay across his lap. No—not a sheet, but an article of clothing, pure linen, all of one piece and slashed across the middle. It was the twin of the endowment garment she'd seen on Don Carlos's body. Joseph was cutting it into fragments, disassembling it, scattering it into the orchard. He lifted the scissors, snipped at the linen. He held a white scrap up between his fingers. The wind took it and carried it away.

It's all over now, and finished—as over as it can be.

The faithful of Nauvoo streamed into the parlor all the long, weary day before, weeping, wringing their hands over the bodies of the Prophet and his brother. They called out for God's vengeance or mercy, they fell to their knees or stood in silence, looking down at the unmistakable grayness of death. They kept coming long past sunset, into the night, and the girls lit the lamps until the parlor glowed like midday. When the last woman had cried over Joseph, Brigham Young came with a handful of Danites to bear the bodies away. He buried the coffins at the gravesite, but not the bodies of the Prophet or his brother. Instead, Brigham had filled the boxes with bags of sand, for he was certain the Gentiles would desecrate the corpses to mock Joseph, even in death. The bodies lay now in a quiet place no one would know—no one save Emma and her family, and Brigham. And Eliza, of course. Her, too.

She sits now with her back against an apple tree. The sun on her shoulders is the gentlest thing she has felt for years. The baby has been moving inside her all day, turning, stretching its limbs, eager for a life that will soon be its own. She can hear the bees in the cups of the flowers. And the wind, intermittent, bending the grass.

She can hear footsteps approaching, too, the hush of grass against a woman's skirt. She opens her eyes. Eliza is coming through the orchard, straight-backed and calm. She, too, is preparing herself, like the child, to enter a new life.

"I'm sorry to disturb your peace," Eliza says.

"You don't disturb me. You never will."

Emma climbs to her feet. She is slow with weariness, but when has she ever been granted more than a moment's rest? She'll be busier still in the days to come. She has a church to lead now, a city of people who will look to her for guidance—or half a city. That will depend on Brigham Young.

Eliza takes a folded, sealed note from the pocket of her dress. She passes it to Emma. "From Brigham."

Emma takes the note, slides it into the pocket of her skirt. "I asked you," she says, "to think about what I proposed. To consider joining me at the head of this church."

"And I thought, as I promised I would do."

Eliza raises her face, looks at her with perfect calm. For a moment Emma can feel the future gathering around them, a bright ring of possibility. She will stand at the center of it, with this good woman at her side. There is little joy to be had just now, but there is happiness in this—a sisterhood restored, everything forgiven between them. They will go on working together. They can be friends now, unimpeded.

"My answer is no," Eliza says.

She breathes in sharply. She hadn't expected this—not the denial, and not the pain it brings.

"You asked me to consider," Eliza says. "I ask the same of you. Consider what you ask me to sacrifice, what you would take from me. If the Restoration is made false, then I will not be Joseph's wife in the world to come. If celestial marriage is undone, then I was never his wife at all."

Now it's Emma who lowers her face. She can't claim surprise. "I understand."

This is the moment when Eliza should turn and walk away, go to Brigham Young and tell him she'll work for his designs. But she hesitates, swallows. Her hand moves toward her pocket and darts away again, clenching. Whatever is concealed in that pocket, Eliza is considering keeping it for herself. But finally she reaches in and she removes something flat and round and silver.

"Heber Kimball found this on Joseph's person while . . . while the apostles were washing his body. He asked me to give it to you."

Emma takes the medallion. She turns it in her hand, so the sunlight runs along its edge like honey, a line of fire.

"What is it?" Eliza asks.

She closes her hand around the talisman. "Only something Joseph's mother gave to him, long ago."

Eliza holds her eyes, but there's nothing left between them, no words left to say. She nods, satisfied with this new reality, and walks away, into the heart of Nauvoo.

When she is alone again, Emma climbs the stairs to the Prophet's study. She stands for a moment at the threshold. The space is empty of him, and yet it never can be. She can feel him everywhere, his words printed on the pages—and unwritten, hanging in the air. She sits at the desk once more and feels the weight of it, all the authority of leadership bearing down upon her, on that place, that small, unassuming room.

With a knife, she breaks the seal on Brigham's note. His hand is neat but hard-angled. Even the way he writes is a demand. *I will know your answer. We have discussed what must be discussed, and now that the funeral is over, we must move forward, or I will move on without you. Will you uphold the Restoration, or will you—*

She casts the note aside. No need to read more. She has other business to tend to, a path to lay into the future. She opens the drawer of Joseph's desk, takes out the paper that holds her blessing.

The word is a binding power, and there is power in the word. She knows it now, this mystery Joseph learned, drawing circles in the ashes of his mother's hearth. She reads the words she has written, a timid scrawl: *Make of me a worthy woman. Make me brave and true.*

Strengthen me, O God most powerful.

Emma dips her pen and signs her own name to the blessing.

Brigham's letter is waiting with all its rash demands, its impatient greed. The church is waiting. Its fate hangs like a thread from her hand. She takes another sheet from Joseph's desk, smooths it under her palm. The paper is cool, dry, ready for her answer, ready for her will. From here, she can see the world stretching out before her. Past, future, all the way to a flat horizon, vivid and clear. She dips the pen again. She puts her strength upon the page.

Emma thinks the world of you.

Acknowledgments

My personal thanks to the following individuals who have been so supportive of this book and of my career: my agent, Carolyn Forde; my editor at William Morrow, Tessa Woodward (and the whole WM crew); my sister, Georgia Schelgel; my mom, Cheryl Grant, who read the first version of this book; my dear friend Tim Batson, who has been cheering this book along for eight long years; and my husband, Paul Harnden, for believing in me from the start.

About the author

About the book

Insights,
Interviews
& More...

Meet Libbie Grant

Photo courtesy of the author

LIZZIE GRANT has been passionate about American history—especially the early days of the Mormon Church—from a young age. She was raised in the Latter-day Saint faith and has deep roots in Mormon culture, though she is no longer a practicing member. Under her pen name, Olivia Hawker, she is a *Washington Post* bestselling author and a finalist for the Washington State Book Award and the WILLA Literary Award for Historical Fiction. She lives in the San Juan Islands with her husband, Pau. ⌒

Author's Note

On August 8, 1844, the Quorum of the Twelve Apostles voted that Brigham Young should succeed Joseph Smith Jr. as leader of the Church of Jesus Christ of Latter-day Saints. Emma refused to leave Nauvoo—and refused to cede her son's claim on church leadership, regardless of the Quorum's vote. Two years of chaos followed Joseph's death, but finally, in the summer of 1846, Brigham began leading his loyal members west to a land that was, at the time, part of the Mexican wilderness, and, therefore, beyond the reach of the laws of the United States. In 1850, it would become Utah Territory, though the Mormons called it Deseret.

Emma remained in Nauvoo with those members of the church who'd broken with Brigham over his refusal to give up polygamy. They held together in a loose, unaffiliated way, until, in 1860, Joseph Smith III—by then twenty-eight years old—claimed he'd received a revelation that he was to lead the church his father had founded. The new church was called the Reorganized Church of Jesus Christ of Latter-day Saints. Today, it's called the Community of Christ.

During the turbulent years after Joseph's death, Emma met a non-Mormon man, Lewis Bidamon, who soon proposed marriage. A Methodist minister led the ceremony. They remained living at the Mansion, which Emma operated as a roadside inn—just as her mother had done. Her marriage to ▶

3

Lewis was not without its troubles, but by all accounts, it was happier than her marriage to Joseph had been. They remained together until Emma died in 1879.

Although this is a work of fiction, I have nevertheless done my best to stick to documented fact as far as I was able. Most of the alterations I've made have been small and relatively insignificant. Still, I feel it's best to list them here, so curious readers can have a foundation for exploring the true history behind this novel. Here are the most serious deviations I've made, more or less in chronological order:

Emma was the first member baptized into the new church, but Oliver Cowdery performed the rite.

The final translation of the Book of Mormon was completed in Fayette. Joseph moved to Fayette because Peter Whitmer coaxed him into finishing the translation there. Joseph first met Sidney Rigdon when the latter came to Fayette, curious about the emerging religion and the "Golden Bible." Joseph's blessing on Sidney was given at Fayette, not at Kirtland.

Emma gave birth to her twins on April 30, 1831, and they were born prematurely. In the novel, I depicted her giving birth in early March at full term. I made this change purely for pacing reasons. She did, however, adopt the twins of a recently deceased woman only a few days after her own babies died.

With real regret, I had to leave out the formation and collapse of the Kirtland Safety Society—a fascinating side trip through LDS history. Its inclusion would have made the novel far too long. The dissolution of Kirtland's communistic practices had more to do with the collapse of the KSS than with Zion's Camp— and Joseph's series of arrests and trials in 1837 was more a consequence of financial fraud committed via the KSS than any other cause. Novelists must be forgiven these occasional alterations; we do, after all, write fiction, not biography or history.

There is no evidence that Emma had anything but sisterly feelings for Don Carlos, though they did have a close relationship from the start. I used the device of romantic interest to heighten Emma's distress when Don Carlos and her baby of the same name both died within hours of each other. William Smith was actually the brother who started the debating club that criticized Joseph, and it was William who called Joseph a false prophet and William who fought him because of his authoritarianism. I gave these roles to Don Carlos to heighten the drama of Emma's secret attraction to him. While I'm on the subject of Don Carlos: he was married to Agnes Coolbrith for several years before his death. After, Agnes became one of Joseph's plural wives.

Oliver Cowdery quarreled with Joseph over his affair with Fannie Alger and ▶

Author's Note (continued)

left the church over it, as depicted here—but these events occurred in 1838, not 1837. This was another alteration I made for the sake of pacing. Cowdery took many key figures of the church with him when he defected, including Martin Harris and several members of the Whitmer family.

In Far West, Joseph attempted to create municipal laws that violated the Constitutional separation of church and state, which chafed many members of the church, Cowdery among them. Based on contemporaneous writings by and about the individuals involved, it seems Cowdery was mainly outraged by Joseph's infidelity, while the Whitmers, Harris, and most of the other defectors were more offended by his violation of American rights. The end result was the same, however: an exodus of important figures from the Saints' community. This was the first serious schism the church ever faced.

After their defection, Oliver and his band of dissenters actually returned, attempting to rejoin the church—a testament to Joseph's hypnotic influence over his followers. He refused to allow them any peace among the Latter-day Saints. Fawn Brodie writes that he "did not rest until he had seen Oliver Cowdery and John and David Whitmer cut off from the church. Their expulsion left him with no rivals of any stature. Of the eleven witnesses to the Book of Mormon, only Joseph's father and brothers were left in the church."

I changed the birth order of two of Emma's sons, Alexander Hale Smith and Frederick Granger Williams Smith, merely to heighten dramatic tension within the story. Frederick was actually born in 1836.

The lead-up to the Extermination Order was more complex than depicted here; it involved several confrontations between the Mormons and the Missouri settlers, but I had to conserve time and pages.

The Mormon War of October and November 1838 was also broader than I depicted, and involved more settlements (both Mormon and Gentile) than Adam-ondi-Ahman and Gallatin. I compressed this piece of history not only for the sake of pacing, but also because Emma would likely have had little access to the details of these confrontations. The raids on non-Mormon settlements around Caldwell and Daviess Counties were largely carried out by the Danites, who operated under such secrecy that many residents of Far West didn't believe they existed at all, or thought them only for pomp and ceremony, as at the Fourth of July parade. It wasn't until Nauvoo was established that the Danites were widely acknowledged as an active paramilitary force.

I should also note that it was Sidney Rigdon who threatened to shoot defectors at Far West, not Brigham Young— though Brigham made plenty of other threats against defectors and apostates. ▶

Author's Note *(continued)*

The Haun's Mill Massacre—an event still remembered with somber horror by the LDS—actually occurred on October 30 1838, in the midst of the other raids of the Mormon War. I set it apart from the rest to underscore its especial awfulness.

When Nauvoo was founded, there was already a tiny village on the site called Commerce. The first Mormons bought out the settlers, who moved away.

The Partridge sisters were among the earliest acknowledged plural wives of Joseph Smith. Their real names were Emily and Eliza—for obvious reasons, I changed Eliza to Lizzie. Although Emma took in many girls who'd been orphaned by the conflicts at Far West, the Partridge sisters didn't move into her home until May of 1840, when their father died. Joseph didn't marry them until early in 1843.

Joseph faced several attempted captures and extraditions to Missouri for various charges between 1840 and 1843. For simplicity's sake, I condensed them into one incident. He did issue a prophecy that Lilburn Boggs would die within a year, but that happened in May 1841, not September 1840 as depicted here.

Joseph did indeed bury the original manuscript of the Book of Mormon under a cornerstone, but not the cornerstone of the temple. Rather, he buried it under Nauvoo House, which was to become the town's first hotel. The building of the temple and the hotel were announced on the same day, however, and possibly in the same revelation—and both buildings were clearly regarded as sacred places by the Mormons, though they certainly were not equal in importance. Joseph did say of the buried manuscript, "I've had enough trouble from this book." But he made this declaration before many witnesses, at the public dedication of Nauvoo House—not in the dark of night.

Like many other Christians of his time and place, Joseph had a strong association with Freemasonry. Echoes of Freemasonry can still be found all throughout the religion. Nauvoo's Masonic Lodge was dedicated in 1842, not 1841. I shifted the date so I could use Don Carlos as the lens through which Emma viewed the inclusion of Masonic rites and the evolution of the church's temple rituals. It was also more convenient for me to discuss the two earth-shaking changes to the LDS theology—the emergence of Joseph's idea that man can become as God, and the threatening slant to the temple's endowment vows—in a single chapter.

Readers with some knowledge or experience of the religion will note Joseph's use of coffee, which is in opposition to a social guideline known as the Word of Wisdom. The Word of Wisdom first appeared in 1833, but it was "to be sent by greeting; not by ▶

Author's Note *(continued)*

commandment or constraint." Early Saints viewed it as a suggestion—perhaps a strong one, but no requirement. Later, after Brigham's ascendancy, the Word of Wisdom became a constraint, and all faithful Saints were expected to adhere. But during Joseph's time, members complied to varying degrees. Joseph himself was known to be very fond of coffee.

Eliza Snow's early history with the church was markedly different from how I depicted it. She did come to Kirtland, but her entire family had already converted to Mormonism, and her brother Lorenzo even rose to the presidency of the church in 1893. She was a celebrated poet, however, and enjoyed an especially close and confidential relationship with Emma, living in the Smith home for most of her life after her arrival in Kirtland, up until her plural marriage to Joseph was discovered. Emma did beat Eliza after finding her in an embrace with Joseph, and even knocked her down the stairs, resulting in a miscarriage. Eliza never had children; some historians have speculated whether the injuries Emma inflicted upon her robbed Eliza of her fertility. This sad event happened in the spring of 1844, not in 1843.

Speaking of Eliza, the cry of "Oh Joseph, Joseph, they have killed you at last" is attributed to Emma. I gave the line to Eliza instead, to underscore the love she felt for Joseph at a time when Emma's feelings toward him had long since ceased to be warm or even congenial.

With real regret, I was forced to leave out a few fascinating points of early Mormon history, simply to keep this novel to a manageable length. I'm sure fans of the history were disappointed to find no mention of John C. Bennett in this novel—an infamous figure in Nauvoo society with whom Joseph had dramatic beef. Also sadly left out was Joseph's campaign for president of the United States (on a surprisingly progressive platform, considering the era).

Having grown up in the Church of Jesus Christ of Latter-day Saints— and having been a devout Saint into early adulthood—I'm familiar with outsiders' curiosity about the temple endowment ceremonies and the garments most endowed Saints wear under their everyday clothes. Much mythologizing and giggling surrounds temple garments, perhaps because they're often referred to by outsiders as "underwear." But the garments are no different from any other article of clothing a person of another religion might wear as a symbol of religious commitment. LDS temple garments are analogous to a Jewish man's yarmulke or a nun's habit and wimple.

It's not forbidden for Saints to talk about their garments, though many decline to do so, simply because non-Mormons often resort to ridicule. I must disappoint the reader by ▶

Author's Note (*continued*)

disclosing that modern-day temple
garments are remarkably unremarkable.
They're simple white-cotton articles
resembling secular boxer shorts
and undershirts, embroidered with
sacred symbols in a few places that
correspond with some of the parts
of the body anointed or sworn upon
during temple rites.

When first introduced in 1842,
the garments were worn only by
men, and resembled a "union suit,"
or long underwear, and bore the same
markings they bear today. Traditionally,
the garments were (and are) viewed
as protection against bodily harm—
though few contemporary Saints
believe the garments offer *literal*
protection. They're symbolic, worn
closest to the skin to remind the
wearer of spiritual commitments and
the protection God will offer if His
commandments are obeyed.

Joseph certainly removed his
garments before he allowed himself to
be transported to the Carthage jail. The
fact that he died without his garments
on remains a point of discussion—
and sometimes debate—among church
members and historians. We know
from the testimony of Heber C. Kimball
that shortly before the Illinois militia
arrived in Nauvoo, Joseph commanded
his Twelve Apostles to "lay aside their
garments and take them to pieces."
The exact reason for this command is
unknown, but most historians assume—
and this novelist concurs—that it was

an attempt to prevent his enemies from obtaining and defiling sacred objects.

I'm sure my depiction of Joseph cutting up his temple garments will strike some readers—particularly Saints—as shocking or even blasphemous. Yet it's a documented fact that Joseph himself commanded the cutting up of garments, at least for church leadership. I must presume he did for himself exactly what he told his Apostles to do.

My sources are as follows: *No Man Knows My History: The Life of Joseph Smith* by Fawn Brodie; *Mormon Enigma: Emma Hale Smith* by Linda King Newell and Valeen Tippetts Avery; *Joseph Smith: Rough Stone Rolling* by Richard Lyman Bushman; *History of Joseph Smith by His Mother* by Lucy Mack Smith; *The Refiner's Fire: The Making of Mormon Cosmology, 1644–1844* by John L. Brooke; *An Insider's View of Mormon Origins* by Grant Palmer; *Early Mormonism and the Magic World View* by D. Michael Quinn; *The 1838 Mormon War in Missouri* by Stephen C. LeSueur; *Fire and Sword: A History of the Latter-Day Saints in Northern Missouri, 1836–39* by Leland H. Gentry and Todd M. Compton; *In Sacred Loneliness: The Plural Wives of Joseph Smith* by Todd M. Compton; *Brigham Young: Pioneer Prophet* by John G. Turner; *American Crucifixion: The Murder of Joseph Smith and the Fate of the Mormon Church* by Alex Beam; "Emma Smith Lore Reconsidered" by Linda Newell King (from *Dialogue: A Journal of* ▶

About the book

Author's Note *(continued)*

Mormon Thought, Fall 1984); "Joseph Smith and Kabbalah: The Occult Connection" by William J. Hamblin (from *Dialogue: A Journal of Mormon Thought*, Fall 1994). Special thanks to *Last Podcast on the Left* for their excellent series on Mormon history and its ties to old European religions and occult practices.

—Libbie Grant
August 2021

Reading Group Guide

1. Early in the novel, Emma asks herself whether it was love, fear of God, or simply having no other choice that kept her married to Joseph. Which of these factors do you think contributed most strongly to her decision to remain in her marriage, even as Joseph's actions created more danger for Emma and their children? Or do you think some other factor was a stronger influence in holding the marriage together?

2. The rural areas of the northeastern states during the nineteenth-century are sometimes called the Burned-Over District by historians and anthropologists because of their fiery zeal during the Second Great Awakening. How did the broader culture of the Burned-Over District contribute to the creation and popularity of the Mormon faith? Do you believe such a religion could have flourished in any other setting?

3. When Emma had the chance to look beneath the shroud and see the golden plates for herself, why do you suppose she didn't do it? What do you believe was under the cloth? The people who were granted sight of the golden plates saw them in a spiritual sense—as miraculous visions. Would such an intense ▶

personal experience be enough to make you believe? Why or why not?

4. When do you believe the church started to slip from Joseph's control? Which people or which events do you think were most responsible for changing the church into "a creature unto itself"?

5. A religion that arises from the merger of other religions or cultural practices is called a syncretism. Do you believe Mormonism is a syncretism? If so, which religions and cultural traditions can you identify in some of the practices and beliefs described in *The Prophet's Wife*?

6. "Then sin, and live. Sin to keep your son and daughter alive if you haven't enough sense to save your own hide." Brigham Young is portrayed as a coarse man who serves his own ambitions. Yet he is often more sensible than the other characters. What is your opinion of Brigham, as he's portrayed in this novel? Did any of his actions change the way you thought about the other characters or the situations they were in?

7. At the end of the chapter where Brigham rescues Emma and Eliza from Kirtland, just as the characters cross the Missouri River,

the narrative voice shifts subtly. It begins to slip in and out of present and past tense. The perspective also becomes less stable, occasionally shifting into second person (addressing the reader directly, as in "Be as careful as you like; there are snares laid for the unwary, and trenches cast about you.") What do you suppose the author was trying to convey with this crumbling stability of the narrative voice?

8. Most Americans consider faith to be a virtue, but throughout this novel, the value of faith is repeatedly questioned, and faith is even blamed for some of the most unfortunate circumstances the characters face, as when Emma muses, "Faith will drown every true thing with its inescapable tide." Did you expect a different depiction of faith when you first decided to read a novel about the founding of a uniquely American religion? Were you surprised by the role faith played in this story? Do you see any parallels between the nineteenth-century Mormon community, as depicted in *The Prophet's Wife*, and certain faith-centered factions of American culture today?

9. What do you believe is the turning point for Emma, when she finally finds the strength to push back against Joseph? ▶

10. In Emma's final scene with Governor Ford, he tells her she looks handsome in black. She answers, "Well I might. . . . God knows, I've worn it all my life." What do you suppose she meant by this remark?

11. At what point in their relationship do you believe Joseph and Eliza Snow married? What clues in the story made you suspect that they were married by that time?

12. What event—or set of events—do you think most influenced Emma to remain in Nauvoo and fight for control of the church, rather than leaving the city after Joseph's death? What convinced her that she had the strength and authority to act independently of the men whom Joseph had appointed to lead the church? ∾

Discover great authors, exclusive offers, and more at hc.com.